THE
PLAYBOY

USA TODAY BESTSELLING AUTHOR
MARNI MANN

For my ladies who love heroes who ...
Crave you.
Need you.
Devour you.
Worship you.
And would do absolutely anything to have you ...
Macon is for you.

PLAYLIST

"Movement"—Hozier
"Fistfight"—The Ballroom Thieves
"All on My Mind"—Anderson East
"Lost"—Dermot Kennedy
"Behind Bars"—Jelly Roll, Brantley Gilbert, Struggle Jennings
"13bullets (pt. 1)"—Stop Light Observations
"Heaven"—Jelly Roll
"Save Yourself"—KALEO
"We Ride (Acoustic)"—Bryan Martin

Click here to check out the Spotify playlist

PROLOGUE

Seven Years Ago

Macon

"Six beers deep before noon. Now, that's a style I can get behind," Cooper, my middle brother, said as he stood in the doorway to my room.

He was wearing a black suit and light-blue tie. His golden-brown hair was styled and gelled and looked so put together that I almost had to shield my eyes.

He walked in and slid the chair away from my desk. Rather than turning it around to face me, he straddled the wooden seat and sat backward.

I could smell his cologne and cleanliness all the way across the room from my bed.

"I suppose I can stop being such an ass and offer you one." I grabbed a beer from the twelve-pack on the nightstand. "Here."

"I'm good. I'm headed to work in a few. Uncle Walter would lose his shit if he smelled beer on my breath."

Uncle Walter, my father's brother, was the founder of Spade Hotels—a high-end, super-exclusive luxury hotel brand with locations all over the world. Until my father had retired, he'd been partners with Walter. My uncle eventually bought him out, but that didn't stop the next generation from working for the family business. My oldest brother, Brady, had an executive role. Now that Cooper had graduated from the University of Southern California, he was employed there too, and he'd be moving into his own place in a few weeks.

I was the baby of the family.

Once summer was over, I'd be starting my junior year at the University of Colorado, and like my older brothers, I'd follow in their footsteps upon graduation and join the brand within the next two years.

"Suit yourself," I replied. "That just leaves more for me."

Instead of putting the beer back in the pack, I twisted off the cap and took a sip of drink number seven.

Cooper rested his arms across the top of the chair. "You want to talk about it?"

"Talk about what?" I flung the metal cap across the room, aiming for the small trash can by the desk, hearing it clink to the bottom when I made the shot.

"The reason you're drinking, in bed, and it's not even"—he looked at his watch—"eleven in the morning."

"No, I don't want to talk about it."

"Come on, Macon. What the fuck is going on with you? You're grumpier than normal. You took off all day yesterday, didn't answer your phone, and you didn't get home until, what, two this morning? And now, I find you like this."

I stared at the trash can that held all seven metal beer caps.

But inside, it also held something else.

2

A picture.

One that had traveled with me to school the last two years.

One that I'd brought home for the summer and planned to pack up and take to Boulder when I headed there for the fall semester.

Would have—but not anymore.

My parents' housekeeper would be coming in sometime this week, and she'd empty my trash can, dumping the picture into the bin that would be pushed out to the curb.

I couldn't wait for that day.

I never wanted to see that fucking picture again.

I took a long drink, wiping the leftover liquid off my lips. "What do you mean, *like this*? Drunk?" I sighed. "I'm far from that."

"You're making this difficult when it doesn't have to be."

I lifted my phone, scrolling through Instagram, done with this conversation.

Until I heard, "Is this about Marley?"

My hands shook from the sound of her name.

My stomach ached.

My heart beat a rhythm that was far too fast.

I glanced up at my brother. I didn't like the expression on his face.

Shit, I wanted to wipe it away and never see it again.

"So, that's what this is about," he said. "Yeah, now, it all makes sense." He lifted his chair and moved it closer until he was about a foot away from my bed, resting his feet on the end of my mattress. "You guys break up?"

There it was.

The statement that had been pounding through my chest since I'd left Marley's house two nights ago.

There was no reason to hide the truth.

It wasn't a secret.

It just hurt—to think about, to say out loud.

To come to terms with.

I took another drink. "Two fucking years of my life ... gone."

He clasped my shoulder, shaking it. "What happened?"

"Nothing happened. That's what is so fucked up about this. She just couldn't deal with everything—the long distance, the unknown at the end of the night whenever I went out with my buddies even though I assured her every single fucking time that I wasn't hitting on anyone and there wasn't a chick in my bed." My head dropped, hanging low toward my chest. "The idea that something *could* happen became too much. I wouldn't cheat on her, Coop. You know I wouldn't. I loved that girl ..." My voice faded, my hand gripping the bottle so hard that I was waiting for it to smash. "But her jealousy took over and created scenarios that didn't exist."

I tapped the screen of my phone, the background a picture of us when she'd visited last semester and I took her skiing. I tossed it. I couldn't stand the sight of it.

Marley and I had begun dating my senior year of high school. Not the best timing, considering I was heading off to Colorado for college and she was going to Florida, but we made it work. We visited each other as often as we could. We talked all the time. Texted nonstop. We spent every summer together.

Until now.

She was going to London tomorrow to start her semester abroad, and for the last week, she'd been telling me we needed to talk.

All we did when we were away from each other was talk.

We were finally together again; a conversation was the last thing I wanted.

I was talked the fuck out.

But Marley forced a discussion, and her emotions spiraled

as she explained how she'd been feeling the past two semesters and told me she couldn't do it anymore.

She was giving up.

Two years in ... and she'd quit.

Us.

Cooper tapped his foot against my shin. "You know, if Brady were here, he'd say, *I told you so.*"

I rolled my eyes. "That asshole told me from day one not to get tied down before I went off to school. I should have listened to him." I adjusted the pillow behind my back and sat up straighter. "In fact, now, I'm going to do exactly what he's done all these years." I pulled at my shirt, getting a strong whiff of beer and day-old clothes. "Fuck feelings. Fuck being tied down. Fuck any kind of relationship. I want no commitments. No emotions. I want—"

"To be a playboy."

"Yeah," I replied, "that."

Because there was no way I was ever going through this again. No way would I ever allow myself to feel this way.

To hurt this badly.

To want something—and someone—I couldn't have.

I would never give my heart to another woman.

Ever again.

Cooper chuckled, like he actually found my reply funny. "I'm not Brady. That's not even close to what I'm going to say." He adjusted his cuff links, his arms returning to the top of the chair. "Instead, I'm going to give you the best piece of advice anyone will ever give you."

"Sure you are."

His brows rose. "You don't believe me?"

"You're only two years older than I am, Cooper. What the hell do you know about life and women at this point?"

"More than you."

5

I downed the rest of beer number seven, added the empty to the pack, and took out number eight, missing the trash can when I tossed the cap in its direction.

Maybe I was starting to feel buzzed.

"I can't wait to hear this," I groaned.

"There are women who will come into your life who are there just to have fun. Like some of the dudes you go to college with—they're a blast when it comes to partying, but after you graduate, you won't see or hear from them again." He paused, like he was letting that sink in. "Then, there are women who will come into your line of vision, and the moment you see them, they'll blow your fucking mind. You'll do anything to be near them. Talk to them. Hear their voice." He closed his eyes and shook his head. "Smell their skin." When he opened his eyelids again, he added, "Those are the women who will completely change your life."

Like Marley?

Fuck that.

I hissed out all the air I'd been holding in. "I don't believe it. That shit doesn't exist—at least not anymore."

"All right, we'll see about that. But when a woman has the power to make your grumpy ass smile—and I'm talking really smile, where it starts in your stomach and goes up your chest and you feel it deep in your bones—you'll know she's the one."

I chugged half of my beer, not bothering to wipe my lips. "Bullshit."

He smiled in a way I hadn't seen before. "Just you wait and see, brother."

ONE

Macon

"How do I bring all of you to the best strip club on Kauai and not one of you"—I circled the air around the Daltons (Dominick, Jenner, and Ford—a group of three brothers), along with their cousin Camden and their best friend, Declan Shaw—"motherfuckers get a lap dance?" I shouted across the party bus that we'd rented for the night.

I already knew the answer to my question.

They were wifey'd up and didn't want a woman on top of them who wasn't their girl. Lawyers from LA, they were now part of our family, professionally and personally. Although my introduction to them went all the way back to high school when I'd played soccer with Camden. That wild kid had been my best bud ever since. But Walter had known the Dalton family for much longer and had been using their law firm since he and my father had built their first hotel.

Now, the Spade and Dalton families were merging. Jenner was marrying Jo—Walter's daughter, my cousin.

And this weekend, their whole crew, along with my brothers, had flown to Hawaii—where I'd been living for the last month—to celebrate Jenner's bachelor party. Since our hotel was still under construction, I'd been staying in a suite at our biggest competitor—a resort a few miles from where we were building. Some of the guys were crashing with me; some were in the suite next door to mine. Not because of the money—this group's combined income was in the billions—but because we all wanted to be together.

It felt like college all over again.

"You want to know why?" Declan asked from the seat across from mine. "Because Hannah would have me by the balls if she caught wind that a woman was straddling me, naked. She doesn't care if I go, she would care, however, if I got a lap dance." He ran his hand over the side of his beard. "I enjoy my balls far too much to lose them—or her."

There were two stripper poles between us, strobe lights flashing throughout the bus, music blasting to the point where it was difficult to hear one another.

But Camden, who sat next to me, had heard his future brother-in-law and laughed at Declan's response, regarding Camden's twin sister. "Hannah would do far worse than just have you by the balls if she found out you got a lap dance."

"So would Oaklyn, you fool," Declan shot back.

"Which is why I did no more than just look," Camden replied. "Something Oaklyn has no issues with."

Camden had been with his girl for a decent amount of time —a relationship I'd seen coming for years even though he denied it. Hell, I'd even helped move that duo along since the idiot had been too dense to realize how much he wanted her.

Declan had fought settling down with Hannah—he couldn't seem to sort his feelings—when we all knew that bastard was in deep.

Each of the Dalton brothers had had interesting buildups to their relationships as well.

And then there were my brothers and me—single as fuck and the only three fellas of the group who had partaken in a lap dance.

I looked at Camden. "You're telling me Oaklyn is cool with what went down tonight?"

"She's realistic about the expectations of a bachelor party," Camden said. "So, yeah, she's okay with it. Does she love it?" He chuckled. "I doubt it. Would any woman *love* it?"

"She won't ask all the questions and want to know every detail that happened tonight, and that won't lead to any heated discussions or cold shoulders or no fucking in your immediate future?"

"The *no fucking* part? *Daaamn*," Cooper said from my other side. He grabbed his crotch. "My dick hurts, just thinking about that."

Camden took a drink from his red Solo cup, filled with vodka and soda, like mine. "I'm positive the questions will come. As for the fighting"—he whistled out a breath—"I hope the fuck not. I'd told her what was going to go down tonight, and I stayed true to my word."

But I could still hear the dread.

"Here's what I can tell you," Declan replied. "Strip clubs are always a touchy subject whether you do the right thing or not. You just have to approach the conversation at the right time. Like after I get home and make her breakfast in bed. I don't talk about it now or while I'm away—absence will ultimately lead to a fight because she's missing me."

"Isn't that the truth?" Camden agreed.

"And whether they scream or give you the cold shoulder or hold out on sex, they're definitely going to bury you with words," I confirmed.

Declan's and Camden's girlfriends were best friends. Hannah was a litigator. If anyone knew their way around an argument, it was her.

Camden's head hung down. "You're right about that. And when our women are pissed"—he guzzled the rest of his drink— "*whoooa*."

"That kind of anger turns me on, and it's why I fell in love with Hannah," Declan said, now rubbing his hands together. "But when it's aimed toward me? Fuck."

Jesus, I was glad I didn't have to deal with any of that bullshit.

The must-have conversations that you knew would lead to fights. The ignoring, the cold shoulders, the days that would pass where you didn't get laid.

Fuck all of that.

Since I'd made the playboy pact seven years ago, I was living the life I wanted.

Everything—and I meant, everything—was fucking perfect.

I took a sip, nodding toward the rest of the group—all in different stages of conversation, their expressions and gestures telling me the liquor had kicked in. "It's good to have you all out here."

Although I wasn't talking to anyone in particular, Camden replied, "Why? Don't tell me you've been lonely."

Cooper and Brady laughed.

"My baby brother? Lonely?" Brady rolled up his sleeves, revealing his newest Patek Philippe—a watch that probably cost more than my Porsche. "Come on. Everyone in this bus knows that for someone like Macon, that's impossible."

"Brady's right," I said to Camden. "I don't know what lonely means." I grabbed his shoulder, squeezing it. "I told you about my latest conquest, didn't I?"

"The real estate agent?"

I blinked, trying to piece together who Camden was talking about. "Who?"

"The agent you were telling me about the last time you were in LA. I can't remember her name ..."

"Real estate agent, real estate agent," I repeated, releasing his shoulder. "Nope, doesn't ring any bells."

"Seriously? We had a long conversation about her ..." His voice faded as he looked at me, slowly shaking his head. "There's been so many that you can't even keep them all straight." He pounded my fist. "Untamed—that's what you are, my man."

I shrugged. "It's a big island. Over five hundred square miles. You know how many women that is?" I laughed.

"By the time you move back to Los Angeles, I have no doubt that you'll know exactly how many women that is." He clinked his cup against mine, although I assumed his was empty by this point. "I've missed your ass. It's time to come home."

"But I barely just got here."

Sure, there were moments when I wanted to be in LA, but there was something about Kauai that I was really digging. The weather was gorgeous. The beach was relaxing enough. The water was refreshing when I needed something cool.

And the women? *Fuck.* The women were incredible.

"I guess that's true," Camden said, "but it feels like you've been gone forever."

"I've got several more months to go."

Construction wasn't slow by any means. It was just detailed, and it took someone meticulous to make sure everything was going the way Walter wanted. That was only half my job. The other half was dealing with our tenants. Spade Hotels wasn't in the restaurant business, so every eatery within our establishments worked on a lease. Those tenants would fly into

Hawaii periodically to check the progress and to meet with me about their terms.

First up was the Westons—a group of four brothers and a sister who owned the most successful, highest-rated steak house chain in the country. When you ate at Charred, you thought about your meal for weeks after. It wasn't just dinner; it was an unforgettable experience. Not only were they building one in our Kauai hotel, but they were also constructing a club, so our guests could eat dinner and then go dancing for the night.

"When you get back to California, will you be grounded for a while or taking off right away to build the next hotel?" Declan asked.

"I'll be home for a bit," I replied. "We need to reconfigure some of our older properties. Increase efficiency and their processes. Cut costs without skimping on labor or service or amenities. Walter hasn't updated those hotels in years. It's time I dig in and get dirty." I smiled at Camden. "Which means you'll be seeing plenty of me."

"Looking forward to it, buddy."

I stared at the ceiling—which was a mirror that reflected the flashing strobe lights—as though it were a woman with the most beautiful set of tits. "*Ahhh*, the third wheel. My favorite role."

Camden rolled his eyes. "If you just settled down, you wouldn't have to be. Oaklyn would befriend anyone you got into a relationship with. Think of all the double dates we could go on, the places we could travel." He nudged my arm. "We'd have a lot of fun."

"Or you could just come out a couple of nights a week without her, and we'd have even more fun."

That was how our friendship had rolled before Oaklyn shackled him.

She was great—I wasn't knocking her as a person. But, man, things had been different when he was single.

I'd had my best friend's time and attention whenever I wanted it.

"Suck a dick," Camden groaned. "You know, I actually like hanging out with my girlfriend, but I realize that's a concept you don't understand."

"You're right. I don't."

The party bus came to a stop. As we stepped onto the sidewalk in front of the club, Camden's arm shot across the top of my shoulders.

"The thing is," he began, "I look forward to having dinner with her. Opening a bottle of wine. Going to bed together. Bingeing a show or two before she falls asleep on my chest."

At twenty-seven, I was three years older than Camden, but, shit, he sounded like he was well over the hill.

"What are you, fifty?" I chugged the rest of my vodka and tossed the cup in a nearby trash can. "That's marriage talk, my man."

"I am going to marry her, you dipshit."

"And I'm happy for you, but don't expect that for me." I nodded toward the club now that the rest of the guys had exited the bus. "I don't know about any of you, but I need a shot."

Their agreement was loud and simultaneous, like they were still on the bus, fighting for airtime over the music, and they followed me inside the club. I'd been to several others on the island. This was my favorite.

The two-story structure had a back wall made entirely of glass, so you could see the beach and ocean from anywhere you stood inside. Within the interior, there were stages set up at different levels—some occupied with dancers the club employed, some with patrons. And then there were the birdcages that hung from the ceiling, where women covered only in feathers danced on perches.

I liked the vibe.

The nakedness.

The smell of sex in the air.

The way that, no matter where I looked, there were women in my view, whether they were on a stage or dancing on the floor or on a perch or serving me alcohol—like the waitresses were doing now.

I'd reserved a private section in the VIP area, giving us several couches to sit on, a coffee table that had full bottle service—vodka, tequila, scotch, and all the mixers and garnishes my buddies would need.

We'd been assigned two waitresses, and they were hard at work, making us drinks.

I waited until everyone had one before I ordered, "Tequila shots," from the server closest to me. "One for each of us."

She began to fill the small glasses, handing them out.

Once she was done, I raised mine in the air. "Who wants to do the honors?" I asked the group. Although I wasn't afraid to make the toast—Jenner was marrying into my family after all—I assumed a Dalton would want to do it.

"I've got this," Dominick said, a wide, cheerful smile on the oldest brother's face. "Jenner, Jenner, Jenner," he started.

My ears were focused on Dominick's voice, but something made me glance to my side. It was a feeling in the pit of my stomach that guided my gaze across the banister that over-looked the dance floor below. But the feeling didn't take me all the way down to where the general population was grinding on each other. It took me across to a stage that was mid-level, large enough for one dancer, and on top of it was a woman.

Not just any woman.

Or dancer.

This was the most gorgeous woman I'd ever seen in my life.

The sexy, tight black dress wasn't like the costumes the club required their employees to wear, so I knew she was a patron. Her hair was as dark as midnight, and it fell in waves down her bare back, almost reaching her waist, where her hips rounded toward a perfect, heart-shaped ass. As she moved to the beat, I took in the rest of her body. The arch of her neck, the softness of her collarbone. Tits that were the most sensual size. A figure that blended just right with curves and a narrow waist, a flat navel, thighs that had just the right amount of thickness, and calves like a runner.

Each scan of her body revealed something new, something achingly beautiful, something that taunted me from all the way over here.

But it wasn't that ass that was making my dick hard or her tits that I wanted to bury my lips in; it was her face I couldn't get enough of. She had eyes that were icy blue, a color so unique they reminded me of a husky's stare, and they were so intense I could see them all the way over here. Lips that were plump, a tiny and sloped nose, skin that was creamy and sun-kissed. Features that seemded simple as I traced them with my eyes, but the combination was fucking breathtaking.

Who is this woman?

And how quickly can I get to that stage?

As the music sped up, so did her moves.

Her hips.

Her arms as they lifted over her head, swinging as though she were trying to shimmy through the tightest opening.

As she gyrated the air, my imagination took over. It filled in the spots that were covered by her dress, like I was getting the chance to peek underneath the fabric. In my head, I could see the hardness and pink hue of her nipples, the sweat that dripped between her tits, and the delicateness of her pussy.

But that wasn't enough.

Neither was just looking at her.

I needed to be close.

I wanted to inhale her scents.

I had to know how her skin would feel against my lips.

How her taste would change the flavor on my tongue.

I had—

My thoughts were cut off, my mind going blank as my eyes connected with hers.

My heart pounded.

My hands clenched.

My legs shook, like they were fucking dying to stand me up and rush me over to her.

Her lips were slightly parted. Not like she was going to mouth something to me. More like her thoughts were so overwhelming that breathing through her nose didn't bring in enough air.

Her eyelids narrowed, a hunger causing that frozen blue to pull at me.

Tug at me.

Show me an expression that was feral.

Enticing.

Electrifying.

And then she turned, and it was over.

It had lasted only a second.

But in that span, it'd felt like an hour.

Come back.

She swiveled her body as though her feet were balancing on a top, her hips rocking, like she was straddling me. A position I desperately wanted her in.

I couldn't wait a minute more to hear her voice, to have her smile at me.

To have her holding my hand as I escorted her down the ladder she had climbed to get on the stage and walk out of the club with me.

Just as that idea began to take shape, my ears were

suddenly filled with, "Cheers," and for the second time in less than a minute, my thoughts came to a screeching halt.

I dragged my attention toward the group, where everyone echoed, "Cheers."

Jenner's toast.

His bachelor party.

The whole fucking reason we were here.

I said nothing as I clinked my glass against theirs.

My voice felt ... lost.

My throat was tight.

It didn't even help when I cleared it or when I tossed the tequila back or when the liquor burned all the way to my stomach.

That feeling, that nagging need, it was still there.

"I know that look," Cooper said.

A quick glance told me he was talking to me.

I set the small glass on the table and washed the shot down with some vodka before I turned toward my brother. "What look?"

I broke eye contact with him to gaze in her direction. She was still on the stage, bending as though her body were waves and her arms were surfacing through the water.

The only thing that had changed since the last time I'd looked in this direction was my desire to be standing beneath her, gazing up at what I assumed was the most beautiful pussy.

A pussy that, from the way I was already feeling, had the power to bring me to my fucking knees.

"The look of a guy who's so lost in his thoughts that it wouldn't matter if a tsunami burst through the glass wall and took out this entire club. You still wouldn't take your eyes off her."

I licked the vodka from my lips and faced my brother. "Take a look for yourself." I paused. "Do you blame me?"

17

"I don't want to talk about her. I want to talk about you."

I gripped the glass even harder and stood. "There is no me at this moment. Right now, all I can think about is us. Watch and see how it's done." I nodded toward the group, knowing Cooper was the only one who could hear me. "I'll be back."

Before anyone could ask where I was going, I rushed through the VIP area and descended the stairs. I didn't check to see if there was anyone in front of me. My eyes stayed on her.

Fixed on her movement.

Her expression.

Her beauty that was consuming me.

It took longer than I wanted to get to her; the dance floor was packed, and I had to weave my way around the crowd, heading toward the section of the club where she was suspended above. When I reached the ladder that she'd used to get on the stage, I did exactly what I'd planned.

I stood beneath her, and I glanced up.

Fuck me.

I drew in the deepest, most obsessive breath as I took in the sight.

A pair of dark panties covered her pussy, but I could still see the inside of her thighs.

Her muscle.

Skin.

She was addictive.

Provocative.

Consuming.

And now that I was this close, I could see the dimple that radiated from her left cheek—a trait that made her even sexier —the small freckle on the center of her thigh, and tiny toes that gripped the soles of her strappy sandals.

I searched the air, determined to get a whiff of her.

"Can I help you?" she asked.

It took a moment before I realized she had stopped dancing, spoken those words, and was looking down at me.

I had never been more grateful to be in a quieter pocket of the club, where the music wasn't as loud, so I could actually hear her perfectly.

I held one of the rungs and replied, "I saw you from over there"—with my drink, I pointed toward the VIP area—"and since we caught eyes, I thought I'd come over."

She shook her head, her long hair falling into her face. "I have no idea what you're talking about." Her voice was soft, gentle. Like a singer whispering through a song.

But as for her not knowing what I was talking about, I called bullshit. We'd had a moment.

I was positive of that.

"Do you need something? Or do you have a question? I'm ... confused." She sounded surprised that I was still here.

A response that had me chuckling.

"Need something? No." Even though that was a lie. "What I'd like is to buy you a drink."

"I'm not thirsty." She resumed her routine, eyes pointed everywhere but at me, her body finding the rhythm as though it had never paused.

What the fuck just happened?

Had she really just dismissed me? Like she couldn't care less that I was standing here? That my presence didn't matter?

Women didn't do that to me.

They begged for my attention.

My stare.

My cock.

Damn, this one had a fire inside her.

"If you're not thirsty, then what do you want?" I asked. "Something to eat? A towel to wipe away the sweat? Tell me ..."

A smile graced her lips, and her eyes closed.

God fucking help me.

I'd seen thousands of women smile—celebrities, models, even influencers.

Some directly at me, others online, in magazines, and on TV.

But none were as smooth, engrossing, stunning, or elated as hers.

"I want to dance," she said. "That's what I want ... and why I'm here."

Would her answer be the same if I offered her a key to my room? The Range Rover that had been loaned to me while I lived here? The black card in my wallet?

Something told me it would be.

I needed to offer her something she couldn't refuse.

"Can I join you?"

What came next was a laugh. A sound as light as her voice, as airy and fluid as the way she moved. "This stage is only built for one."

"So?"

She nipped her lip with her teeth, like she was trying to hide a smile. "So, there's not enough room for the both of us."

What the hell is going on?

I never had to work to get a woman interested—they already were by the time I spoke to them. It took no more than a few words, an easy exchange of a couple of sentences, and she was mine for the night.

But this one? This one didn't appear interested at all. She wanted to dance. She wanted ... nothing from me.

"You're telling me no?" I clarified.

"I'm just not saying yes."

Wasn't that the same thing? Or maybe she couldn't tell me no because it wasn't her stage and this wasn't her club.

I mashed my lips together, thinking of my next strategy. I

didn't care how much extra charisma I had to lay on; I was tasting her tonight. "How do I get you down?"

"You don't." Her arms lifted, her hips bucking as the bass thumped. "I'm right where I'm supposed to be."

I couldn't believe my ears.

Or that I was still standing here.

Or that everything she'd said only made me want her more.

I ran my knuckles across the rung, wishing the smoothness I was feeling were her skin. "What you're telling me is that I'm just going to have to enjoy you from down here, huh?"

"That's not any different from what you've been doing since you arrived at my stage or from the VIP lounge, according to what you said."

Maybe I was reading the situation all wrong. Maybe what she was really doing was playing hard to get.

That I could conquer.

"And you're okay with that?" I pushed.

"Hey"—her palms flattened against the air, like she was under arrest—"I can't tell you what to look at or what not to look at. If I'm the show you want to watch, then get your stare on, but"—her eyes dropped down my body as though she was taking me in for the first time—"just remember, you can look all you want, but you can't touch." Her finger rose and slid across the air, like a windshield wiper.

The thought of touching sent my hard-on straight to the waist of my fucking jeans.

"I wouldn't dare."

She gave me a quick smile. "We have an understanding, then."

That smile was life. It was fucking breath.

And now, I needed to play up the hard-to-get angle and see if that was what I was really facing here.

I took a drink of my vodka, holding it in my mouth,

swishing it around my tongue before I swallowed. "Unless you asked me to touch you." I focused on her eyes, seeing if they changed. "Kiss you."

She whipped her hair across her face, hiding her eyes and expression. "If I wanted those things, I'd ask for them." She waited a beat and said, "Do you hear me asking?"

She could have told me to fuck off. She could have called security.

Her response told me she wanted to play.

Normally, patience wasn't something I ever had, nor did it need to even enter the scene. But this scenario was nothing like the others in the past.

She was nothing like the others.

"You will." I crossed an arm over my chest. "And if I have to, I'll wait all night to hear it."

"Ah, you're the relentless type."

"And you are?"

She looked at me from over her shoulder. "The type who never gives in."

We'll see about that.

"I like that about you." She shook her ass, turning in a circle several times before I asked, "Are you on vacation?"

Her head tilted back, her profile showing me a grin. "You just can't help yourself, can you?"

She still wasn't telling me to leave. If anything, by staying on the stage, dancing even more seductively, it felt like she was goading me.

That could only mean one thing.

I traced the rim of the glass with my thumb. "You intrigue me."

"Why?" She took a seat on the stage, her legs dangling toward me, her body moving like she was still on her feet.

"What is it about me, dancing on this platform, that caused you to come over and want to interview me?"

My thumb paused. "You call this an interview?"

"Interrogation." She shrugged. "Maybe that's a better word."

I ignored her comment. "What caused me to come over is that whether I'm in the VIP lounge or standing beneath you, I can't seem to keep my eyes off you. You're the most beautiful woman in this club."

"And let me guess ... you assumed because I'm in this dress" —she ran her hands down her stomach, stopping at the hem that ended far above her knees—"and dancing alone, I'm looking for a man?" Her brows rose, causing those icy-blue eyes to pierce mine.

Was she schooling me?

Testing me?

I couldn't tell—and I could always fucking tell.

"That's where you're confused," I said. "Because I assumed nothing. Why I came over here—and why I'm still here—is because I can't get this thought out of my head."

She didn't nip this time; she dragged her teeth over her lip instead. "Which is?"

"I need to know what those lips taste like."

Her stare dipped again, but only to my chest. "The only thing in this bar that's going to know the flavor of my mouth is the edge of the water glass that I'm going to sip on my way out."

I could go round after round with this sexy stranger.

"That's what you think ..."

She tucked a chunk of hair behind her ear, showing lobes with small hoops. "That's what I know."

"And what if you're wrong?" I shifted my weight, taking another sip. "Has that ever happened?"

"About a decision that wouldn't amount to anything positive—"

A decision that would have her coming so hard that she wouldn't be able to stop herself from screaming.

But I didn't say that.

When I cut her off, I said instead, "How do you know spending a night with me wouldn't be positive?"

Her cheeks flushed.

"Don't assume my capabilities or my power ..." Something hit me as my voice drifted off, something I hadn't realized until now. I stepped forward and held out my hand, stopping inches from her legs to maintain the *no touching* request. "What's your name?"

She looked at my fingers, but didn't reach for them. "It doesn't matter."

"Why?"

"Because between us, names aren't needed."

Because she had no intention of letting me fuck her?

Or because it didn't matter what I screamed, as long as I screamed out an orgasm?

To confirm, I asked, "What should I call you?"

"*Hmm.*" She glanced around the club, her gaze slowly returning to mine. It was then that she finally dropped her fingers into my palm. Rather than a shake, it was more like a pat. "How about the girl who got away?"

Whatever the fuck it was, I could feel the sensation of her touch throughout my entire body.

My skin overheated.

My cock throbbed to be released.

What are you doing to me?

She quickly pulled her fingers away, like she'd felt the same thing, and I said, "But you're right in front of me. You're not *away.*"

24

"Now, I am, yes."

"You're saying you soon won't be?" When she didn't immediately respond, I added, "Do you want to know my name?"

She shook her head. "Like I said, names aren't needed."

And I was the relentless type?

This one wouldn't give an inch.

"What if I just ask one of your friends?" I searched the area around us, figuring that some of the women nearby were with her.

Chicks always came to clubs in groups of two or three or even four. But as I scanned their faces, none of them were looking at us. I knew how female friends worked; when their girls were approached by a man, they watched every move he made, and there wasn't a single set of hawk eyes glaring at me.

"What, you can't find my friends?" she asked as my stare returned to her. Her eyelids narrowed, giving me the sense that she was looking right through me. "I'm here alone."

Alone?

Women didn't do that. At least not the ones I'd met.

She leaned down as though she had something important to tell me. "Women are allowed to go to clubs alone, you know. There's no law that says we can't." When she straightened, her shoulders bounced to the new song vibrating through the speakers.

Intrigued was a fucking understatement.

I was haunted by her.

Captivated by every moment that had passed.

Cooper was right; a goddamn tsunami could come through, and I wouldn't take my eyes off her or leave her side.

I let out a small laugh, adding up each time she'd surprised me tonight. "You're unique."

And so were her icy-blue eyes—a color I was positive I'd

25

never seen before. The blue was so light that it was almost white.

"If you assumed I was like every other female in this club—you know, cut from the same cloth as her"—she nodded toward a blonde who was dancing not far from us—"or her"—this time, she chose a redhead—"I'd be extremely shocked." She gripped the edge of the stage, her knuckles never changing hue. "You knew I was different. That's what brought you over here. And that's why you're still here."

I wanted to be closer to her.

To accidentally brush my arm against hers.

To have a piece of her hair graze my nose, giving me those scents that I'd been sniffing the air for.

"Come down."

She inventoried the ladder, which I was still holding. "Even if I wanted to—and I'm not saying I do—you're blocking my escape."

"You don't need it." I set my drink on the floor and held out my arms. "I'll catch you."

"No—"

"You don't think I can?" I pulled at my button-down, and the shirt tightened across my arms and chest. I wasn't a scrawny man. It didn't take the adjustment of my clothes for her to see that. My build and definition spoke for itself. "Or are you afraid to jump?"

She was silent.

For the first time since we'd started speaking, I'd made her speechless.

"How about this? I promise on my life I won't let you fall."

She kicked her legs like she was on a swing. "Are you telling me you're Prince Charming? Because if I was looking for someone to sweep me off my feet, I would have asked you to dance with me. That would have done the trick, assuming you have rhythm." She bit the corner of her nail. "That's a weakness of mine."

And the first time she'd shown any weakness at all.

"I have all the rhythm." When I laughed this time, it was much louder than before. "But I'm no prince."

"Are you sure about that?" She pulled her hair to one side of her face, and it hung over her tit, hiding half of the most perfect view. "You've now offered to buy me a drink and catch me in your arms, and you've given me an answer that you're hoping will wake me from this cold, standoffish slumber." She winked. "Am I right?" She only let a second pass before she said, "That feels very prince-ish to me."

I wondered what kind of dudes she'd dated in the past. Certainly not ones who had spoiled her or, by the sound of it, even bothered to pick up her bill.

"All I want is to get you a glass of wine or a cosmopolitan or a water—if that's really what you prefer—and to see what you feel like in my arms." I felt the smile on my lips, the way it pulled so hard that I had to look away. "But I'd be lying if I said I wanted things to end there."

"You'd be breaking my *no touch* rule."

I locked eyes with her once more. "Trust me, it would be worth it."

"For you."

She reminded me of one of my favorite songs, so I said, "No, my Tiny Dancer. *For you.*" Could I be honest with her? She'd only bent a little, so would I be losing anything if I told her what I really wanted? "I've already sworn on my life tonight, but I'm going to do it again." I licked my bottom lip—the bigger of the two. "There's a reason you're in this club, dancing on a stage alone. Maybe you came to the island by yourself to get away from your life. Maybe you live here, and

27

you like to lose yourself in the music. Whatever the case is, this is your thing."

She said nothing, but the expression that passed through her eyes and lips told me that one of my guesses had been right.

"Sex is my thing."

Her pupils grew the moment I said my favorite word.

I fucking loved that it triggered something inside her.

But she responded, "Why should that matter to me?"

"Because if you let me touch you"—with my stare, I stroked from her feet to the length of her legs, slowly rising to her chest —"the experience will be something you'll never forget."

"Sex. With a total stranger." She rolled her eyes. "That already sounds forgettable."

"Hey, I offered to give you my name. You didn't want it." I was met with silence. "How about this? If you come down—and only if you let me catch you—I'll prove just how different I am."

"How?"

"With a kiss."

She laughed. "You're ridiculous. A kiss? That's not going to prove anything to me."

"You say that now, but I assure you, you've never felt lips like mine."

She crossed her ankles, her legs stilling. "What if I fall from your arms?"

"Something tells me that's not what you're afraid of ..."

The tides were changing.

The control shifting.

She was listening. Hearing.

Fantasizing—I could see it on her face.

I'd already told her I had rhythm. Now, she was filling in the blanks.

Emotion swept through her eyes before she said, "You

honestly think you can convince me to sleep with you just by pressing your mouth against mine?"

"I don't think. I *know*."

And my fucking body was already prepared. The hardness practically exploding in my pants. The desire raging through my fingers.

"I busted you looking up my dress the second you got over here. Do you think you've earned my trust?"

"I wanted to see what I'd soon be licking."

Her head gradually shook back and forth. "What are you ..."

What.

Not who.

Even her word choices were interesting.

"I'm a man who wants to rock your world."

"I must be nuts."

"Because you're considering it? No." I chuckled. "You just want to finally experience someone who's going to put you first."

"No, I must be nuts because I'm still talking to you. But, sidenote, you know nothing about my past."

In a sense, she was right. But I'd picked up on cues, and I'd listened.

"What I know is that you thought I was prince-ish, which tells me that you've never had a man lift you into his arms or buy you drinks or spoil the shit out of you. That gives me the assumption that when it came to fucking, they were just as selfish."

"You're going to change that?"

"Baby, if you were listening to the thoughts in my head right now, you'd be wetter than you already are." The term of endearment was needed. And just as she attempted to reply, I cut her off with, "Don't try to convince me you're not. I know you are."

"You must be a magician to be able to see through my panties."

"I have the nose of a dog, and I can smell you in the air." I drained the rest of my vodka and placed the empty back on the floor. "Don't make either of us wait any longer."

She moved to the edge of the stage. "I can't believe I'm doing this."

"I can." I lifted my arms and held them toward her. "I've got you. Jump when you're ready."

She looked around the club, and when her stare returned to me, she gave me no warning before she pushed herself off the platform.

Not that it mattered. I was more than prepared.

My arms immediately wrapped around her, and I held her against my body.

She was petite. I could tell that when she was dancing. But when I had her this close, bearing every inch of her, she felt weightless.

Even more perfect than I'd thought.

And, *damn*, she smelled good. A combination of the salty beach air and lemons.

I didn't want to put her down, so I held her high, focusing on her eyes, leading her legs around my waist while I steadied my arms on her back.

Her body aligned with mine.

Chest against chest.

Face to face.

A thought was already there, but the longer and tighter I kept her pressed to me, it deepened. A thought that was so foreign that I didn't know how to come to terms with it.

A thought that told me this woman was unlike anyone else.

"You broke my rule." She sighed.

There was mint and warmth on her breath, the same heat that was coming off her skin.

"I had no other choice ... unless you wanted me to drop you."

"You can put me down."

"I can. I don't want to."

"So, this is the way you're going to hold me for the rest of the night?" She clung to the tops of my shoulders.

I smiled. "You're already talking about spending all night with me, and I haven't even kissed you yet."

I had known my efforts with my Tiny Dancer would eventually pay off. I liked that I was right.

"That's not what I meant," she enforced.

I hadn't needed the warning when she jumped. My arms had been ready, waiting.

But she wasn't me.

And if I had to guess, this scenario wasn't her. She had come here for one of the two reasons I'd mentioned before.

What she ended up getting was me—an unexpected surprise.

That was why I felt the need to say, "I'm going to kiss you."

Her brows rose, eyelids lifting, like she was looking at a ghost. "Here?"

"Yes. Here."

"In front of all these people?"

We were in the middle of the club. I hadn't forgotten. I just didn't give a fuck.

"Yes," I replied. "In front of all these people."

"Now?"

Instead of answering, I moved forward, my mouth hovering in front of hers. "Tell me to stop."

I waited.

One second, two.

Three.

And when she said nothing, I closed the distance between us, breathing her in while my tongue parted her lips. The taste I'd wanted, the one I'd been craving since I'd first spotted her, was so fucking overwhelming that I moaned.

Jesus.

This was just a kiss ... but this was unlike any other kiss.

The flavor of her was consuming, the feel of her in my arms completely overpowering.

I pressed her even harder against my waist while I melded our mouths together, using my lips to give her everything I'd promised.

If I was going to score this woman for the night, I had to show her why I was different.

Why I was worth having a one-night stand with.

Why she should want me as badly as I wanted her.

With my lips, I knew I could make her pant.

I could cause the wetness to pool from her cunt.

So, that was what I did while I kissed her, my hips swaying, churning to the beat, showing her my rhythm, prepping her for my thrusts.

With each swing, the need inside of me built.

The want blasted up and down my body.

The desire to stroke my dick through her tightness—right here, right now—was enough to make me fucking scream.

After several dips of my tongue, circling around hers, as I memorized the scents that owned me, the feel and taste, the way this embrace had turned her so submissive, she pulled away.

Her eyes gradually opened, her fingers going to her lips as she gasped, "My God." She brushed those same fingers across her mouth, squeezing, releasing, and squeezing again.

Her head shook, the look in her eyes emphasizing, "Point proven."

She felt it too, just like I had known she would.

I gave her a small peck, teasing my hard-on. "And I'm not even close to being done."

"There's more?"

I laughed at the innocence in her voice. "If you want there to be."

I watched her swallow and process my statement. Her eyes changed as I shifted her weight to one arm so I could cup her cheek. My thumb grazed the mouth I'd just ravished.

"There's much more I want to do to you. Don't let this night be over." She still hadn't confirmed why she was here, but I was pretty positive I knew the answer. "You just lost yourself in the music. Now, lose yourself in me."

Her chest rose, her teeth giving her lip a quick bite. "Where?"

Fuck yes.

That answer earned her another kiss, this one longer.

More intense.

And while I locked her lips with mine, I thought about where this could go down. I couldn't take her to my suite. The guys could leave here at any time and barge in on us. I wasn't looking for an audience.

When I divided our mouths, I whispered, "Your place?"

"Not an option," she responded fast. "Both of my roommates are home."

She was a local—I'd guessed right. Which also made me believe I knew the reason why she was here.

But if we couldn't go to her house, that only left one other spot.

I set her feet on the ground and clasped our fingers. "Come with me."

33

As I walked us through the club, I took out my phone and shot off a quick text to Cooper.

> If you guys leave anytime soon, you need to take an Uber. The party bus is occupied.

I shoved the phone into my pocket and led her outside, locating the bus in the parking lot.

Once I reached the driver's window, I knocked, waiting for it to roll down before I said, "I need an hour. Alone." I pulled out a wad of cash from my wallet—an amount close to four hundred—and I handed it to the driver. "Don't come back even a minute early and make sure the door is locked."

"Understood," he replied.

I took my Tiny Dancer toward the side of the bus, the door opening automatically. After we stepped in, it closed, and I heard the click of the lock and the slam of the driver's door.

Finally, just the two of us. A thought that made me the happiest fucking man alive.

I brought her to the back, and while I took a seat in the center of the long row, I positioned her in front of me.

She took a quick glance around. "Why do you have this bus?"

I gripped her thighs, guiding her even closer. "We're celebrating a friend's bachelor party. I came with a bunch of buddies."

Her hands fell to my shoulders, her eyes on mine. "And this is where you plan to make me scream?" The flashing lights, rotating in colors, spread stripes of pink and blue and green and yellow across her face.

I smiled. Not from the pinwheel of hues, but from her question. "It sounds like you're challenging me."

"If I am, does that change anything?"

"Meaning will I make you come three times instead of two?" I growled.

The waiting was intolerable.

I wanted to sink into her wetness.

To get this flimsy dress off her body so I could drag my lips across her skin.

"Three?" She huffed. "That would be record-breaking."

I used just a solo finger to trace down to her knee, across the bone, and up her inner thigh, halting as soon as I felt the heat.

She inhaled, filling her lungs. Holding the air in and not releasing it.

"Then, maybe I should shoot for five."

"Impossible."

My smile grew. "Far from impossible."

I lifted the bottom of her dress only an inch, giving her notice of my intentions. When she said nothing, when she didn't attempt to stop me, I continued to hoist the material past her navel and over her strapless bra and collarbone, and once she pulled her arms through, I tossed it onto a nearby seat.

A lace thong and bra.

That was all that separated us.

"You know nothing about me," I told her. "Therefore, I don't expect you to know what I'm capable of, but if my kiss taught you anything, it's that you should never doubt me. Especially when it comes to sex."

Her hands went to her hips. "All right. Prove it."

A woman with spice. I fucking loved that.

I laced my fingers behind my head, arms bent and my legs spread wide. "Move to that pole." I nodded toward the one that was several feet behind her.

"You want me to swing around it?"

"No." I chuckled, although the idea of that was sexy as fuck. "I want you to show me what I've been dreaming about."

She stepped toward the shiny metal and placed her back against it. With about four feet between us, I had a better view.

"Take off your bra," I demanded. "Slowly."

Damn, that body.

The delicateness of her chest. The plane across her stomach. The soft dips of her waist. The arch of her ass. The curve of her thighs.

Her face a perfect ending, but also the most delicious beginning.

"*Mmm*," I hissed as she unclasped the bra, tugging at the cups until her tits bounced out of them, staying high and perky despite no longer being confined. They were the most gorgeous teardrops and a size that would fit right in my hands, nipples hard and in the lightest pink. "Now, that's a fucking sight to appreciate." My arms dropped, my palms pushing against my legs, running to my knees and back to a high point on my thighs.

I wanted my hands to be touching her.

I wanted my fingers settled in her pussy.

"It's going to be an honor to touch you."

She flung the bra toward her dress.

There was only one thing left.

"Now, your panties." I forced my fingers to stay put. "I want them off."

Her fingers tiptoed down her navel, my breath hitching the lower she got, my cock begging to be released. I needed to see what was under the lace. What was waiting for me. If the vision was as exceptional as I anticipated.

When her hand cupped her cunt, pushing against it, I couldn't stop the goddamn roar from erupting in my throat. "*Fuuuck.*"

This one ... whoever she was, she was for me.

I gripped my cock through my pants. "Does that feel good?"

I needed that answer.

I needed to know how much she wanted to come.

"Yes."

"Show me your pussy." I couldn't drag my stare away from it. "Show me what I'm about to fuck."

Her palm moved across her clit, and her head rested against the pole, grinding her hair over the metal the same way she was giving her pussy pressure.

As her expression filled with pleasure, my body ached.

It yearned for this beautiful stranger.

And when she finally pulled the sides of the lace down her hips and stepped out of the thong, I moaned, "Good fucking God."

I leaned forward to try to smell her in the air.

To get nearer.

And what met my eyes, what took ahold of me, was a view that was better than fucking heaven.

Tight oval lips concealed her clit, flesh that hadn't been touched by the sun, where tan lines showed the creamy difference. Hairless and, because of the revealing strobes of color, already slick.

"The woman who didn't get away," I referenced as my stare lifted unhurriedly. "Something tells me you're everything I need."

A need that was sexual. Fulfilling. Brimming with desire and beyond, reminding me that this wasn't similar to the others.

This was ... as unique as her.

"And something tells me you're my next big mistake." Her voice was a whisper, and it prompted the reason she was here, why she had allowed me to take her to the bus, and why she was naked right now. "You know what I need." She paused. "Give it to me."

I squeezed my tip. "Come here."

Still wearing her strappy sandals, she stepped closer until I said, "Stop."

With her about a foot and a half from me, I pushed myself to the end of the seat, and I got on my knees. I wrapped my hands around her ass, holding the bottom—the meatier section that could handle my grip—and while I kept our eyes locked, my mouth opened.

"I want to smell you." Holding her gaze, I moved my face until it hovered above her pussy. Inches away, I stilled. "The second I lick you, I won't be able to stop."

"Then, don't."

A smile stretched across me as my nose rested against her clit, where I took the longest, deepest breath. "Fuck," I roared. "You're sweet." I inhaled again. "So fucking sweet."

She had a scent I hadn't known I wanted until it suddenly became mine, making me realize just how much I'd been craving it.

How I needed more.

"I wonder if you taste just as good." My tongue slithered out, and I dragged it between her lips, running the whole length of her clit. "And you do ... *fuck.*"

Her fingers dived into my hair, holding the strands with so much strength. "*Ohhh.*"

"You like that?" I didn't wait for an answer before I swiped her again. "Do you want more?"

"*Yesss!*"

I wasn't just tasting.

Or just licking.

I was fucking eating.

Savoring.

And then bingeing.

I couldn't get enough.

I couldn't reach the point of satisfaction because her taste, her smell ... they fueled me.

They taunted me.

They made me into an addict, and I was feasting on my drug.

With my tongue, I took a third lap and a fourth, flicking the top, rotating back and forth, creating a heavy, sensual pattern.

The more I ate, the harder she arched her pussy into my face, her hips rocking after each of my swipes.

"That feels"—she let out a gasp—"unbelievable."

She didn't think she could have three orgasms.

I was about to knock one out and show her just how wrong she was.

My hand dropped between her legs, spreading the wetness my mouth was leaving and mixing it with her own, the tip of my finger probing her tightness.

"Fuck!"

Hearing her curse only goaded me more; it moved me in further, deeper. Besides, I couldn't fucking wait to feel how hot her pussy was.

I was in just a little past my nail when the heat enveloped me.

The narrowness.

Damn it.

She was going to fit so snugly over my cock. I could barely wait.

But there was something I needed to do first.

With my chin already positioned between her legs, I tilted it toward her ass so I had a better view of her face, and I watched her expression while I picked up speed. I wiggled my tongue across her, driving my finger as high as it would go. But I didn't just insert it tip to knuckle; I arched my wrist toward her stomach, finding that spot.

MARNI MANN

The one that made her buck.

The one that made her shout, "Oh my God!"

She was seconds away from coming. I could feel her tightening from the inside. Her wetness thickening. Her moans increasing, where she extended the end of each exhale into a song that got louder and louder.

But it was her face that I couldn't look away from.

The hunger in her eyes.

The satisfaction on her lips.

The gorgeousness that radiated.

And just when her head leaned back, her neck elongating, showing me that beautiful throat, she screamed, "Lick it!" When she drew in more air, she added, "Yes!"

Her stomach shuddered.

Her hips drove toward me and didn't move.

That was when I gave her all the speed and power my mouth was capable of, when I left my finger within her and circled her G-spot.

"*Ahhh!*" She clung to my hair. "*Fuuuck!*"

I didn't let up. I didn't even attempt to slow.

I just kept licking.

Circling.

Her yelling eventually died down, her stomach stilled, and she was staring at me with lips that looked feral.

I didn't wipe her off my mouth; I licked her off, shaking my head as I swallowed her. "I want to do that again."

"Now?"

I nodded.

"I mean, I wouldn't say no. That was—I don't know that I can even explain what that was, but can I tell you what I'd rather have."

Why was that statement so fucking hot?

"Tell me," rumbled through my lips.

She lifted her sandal, wedging it between my knees, and gently raised it until my sac was resting on the top of her foot. She rubbed my balls over the length of her, and then she set the bottom of her shoe on my shaft. She didn't push hard when she ran from crown to base. She was soft, enticing. "That's what I want."

Her neediness was causing a build that wanted to blow.

I reached into my pocket and grabbed my wallet, where I kept a few condoms in the inner flap. And while I stood, tearing off the corner of the foil, I demanded, "Show me how badly you want it."

She wasted no time, instantly unbuttoning my shirt and lowering my zipper, helping me get out of both, along with my shoes, before she brought down my boxer briefs. She was squatting toward the floor of the bus, looking up at me, when she said, "Nice body." Her gaze then focused on my dick. "And ... fuck."

"You wanted it. You asked for it." I pumped the long length. "You're getting every inch of it." I held the condom toward her. "Do the honors."

I wanted her hands on me.

I wanted to feel her grip.

I wanted her to see, up close and personal, exactly what she was getting tonight.

She aimed the tip at my crown and carefully rolled the rubber down my shaft. Once it was secure, she slowly gazed into my eyes. "Please don't break me."

"Trust me when I say, you're going to love every fucking second of this." I quickly reached under her arms, lifting her into the air, and placed her on the seat I'd previously sat on. I straddled her legs around my waist, and I moved closer until my tip was touching her pussy. "You're going to feel so fucking good."

I wouldn't just thrust in.

I was an asshole, but inflicting pain wasn't my thing.

So, while I crept through her wetness, going inch by inch, I listened to her sounds, I took in her expression, I went at a speed she could handle. And the entire time, I rubbed her clit, touching the very tip, rotating my thumb around it.

Her arms spread across the back of the seat, her teeth holding her bottom lip hostage until she sighed, "*Yesss*. You weren't kidding. I do love every bit of *that*."

I was fully buried.

Her pussy was so wet that it was dripping over me. The temperature a scorching level of heat.

A narrowness that I'd never felt before.

If there was a perfect sensation, it was this.

"You are"—a moan took over my words—"unimaginable."

Because no matter how many times I'd thought about this tonight, I couldn't have envisioned anything this incredible.

"You have two orgasms to go and probably only about fifty minutes left, and I think you're going to need every one of those minutes. Ticktock."

If I wasn't so turned on, I'd laugh.

This woman ... *damn it*, she was something else.

And I was going to show her just what I was.

I reared my hips back, pulling out of her pussy, and worked my way back in, my thumb staying on her clit, giving her friction from both angles.

"This is"—she stopped to pant—"amazing."

I was barely trying. This was just my way of having her get used to my size and power.

I swiveled my hips to show her what amazing really felt like, so I wasn't just penetrating her straight on; I was hitting her sides, brushing against her clit.

That was one hell of a combination.

"Fuck yeah," I hissed. "You're so wet right now."

Within a stroke, I could sense that she felt the difference. Her breathing turned louder; her nails found their way to the back of my thighs and stabbed the skin.

I liked the pain.

I liked everything she was giving me.

I wanted more.

So, I went faster.

"Yes!" she cried.

I pumped harder.

"Yes!" she yelled again.

And I watched the second orgasm begin to roll in, her body stiffening as she neared the peak, her eyes closing, her nails digging in even more.

"Give it to me." I tilted my hips upward, going faster than I had before. "I want to see it." I held her waist and bounced within her. "I want to fucking feel it."

It only took a few lunges before she was screaming, "*Shiiiit,* yes!" She gasped, "Fuck!"

A second later, ripples were moving across her stomach, her thighs closing in around mine, her back gradually lowering down the seat because she was losing control of her body.

What she lost, I took.

I dominated.

And I did everything I could to hold off my own orgasm, but, fuck, it wasn't easy. Not with the way her pussy was caging me in, getting wetter with each dive.

"Damn," I groaned as I watched her wriggle—certainly the hottest thing I'd ever seen.

"My fucking *Goood,*" she exhaled. "I don't know if I remember how to breathe."

I gave her several more pokes, using the same momentum,

before I lifted her into my arms and walked us to the pole, where I balanced her back against it. "Two down, one to go."

"I can't."

My lips, hovering in front of hers, let out a gritty laugh. "You will." I mashed our mouths together, needing a reminder of that rich taste that was still owning me, and when I pulled back, I said, "And when it happens, we're going to come together."

With both hands, she clasped the metal above her head, and while I held her waist, I stretched myself forward and resumed the same speed as before, twisting my hips every few plunges to ensure she felt me everywhere.

Rather than putting my thumb on her clit, I used the short, trimmed patch of hair above my dick, and every time I drove into her, that rough part of my body brushed against hers.

It didn't cause irritation; it induced stimulation.

And when she felt it, she rasped, "Oh!" A response that sounded half surprised, half quenched.

I couldn't stop the smile from spreading over my face. "You're starting to realize I'm always right."

"How do you know my body this well?"

When you desired sex as much as me, you wanted your partner to feel just as good. Just as turned on. Just as pleased.

The answer was simple.

I listened.

Not only to the noises she made with her mouth, but also the ones that came from her body.

I analyzed her movements.

I heard what was happening inside of her.

And when I determined what she needed, I fulfilled.

"Because I care. Because I want to know. Because nothing would make me more satisfied tonight than making you come again and again."

Her pussy responded.

It got wetter.

Tighter.

"I'm going to come—"

"I know," I growled. "I can feel it."

Her hands left the pole, and she wrapped her arms around my neck. Using my shoulders to hoist herself up, she began to move with me, meeting me in the middle, pouncing while I thrust.

"Oh fuck." I humped. I bucked. I felt the way she was bound around me, and I moaned, "You're milking me."

The second the final word left my mouth, my ears were filled with screams. Ones that not only pierced my eardrums, but also triggered my own orgasm.

The burst started in my balls and quickly spread to my shaft, the eruption building toward the most intense spike before it shot through my tip. "Fuck *yesss!*" I held her as hard as I could, sliding through her cum, filling the condom with a second load and a third.

I waited for her body to tell me she was done before I slowed.

Our faces, pressed so closely together, were breathing in each other's air.

Our grips were finally loosening.

Our bodies coming to a complete standstill.

"Three." I gave her a quick kiss. "I have another condom. We could go for four."

"Something tells me we're getting close to that hour mark and"—she looked at her wrist—"I have to go anyway."

I didn't want this to end.

I wanted a second round.

A third.

I wanted to wake up in the morning and taste her again.

"Where are you going?" I asked.

A grin spread across her face, and she wiggled—slowly at first and then a bit harder until I was willing to put her down.

She immediately went for her clothes, pulling up her thong and clasping her bra, tugging the dress down her torso until everything was back in place.

"I just ... have to go."

Leaving directly after.

That was different. Because that was always me.

I took out my phone, tapping the screen several times until I had a new Contact loaded. "Why don't you give me your number—"

"No numbers."

Her reply was like a slap. One that brought me back to reality.

When was the last time I'd asked for a woman's number?

Marley?

And that was how many years ago?

Why had I just asked for hers? Why had I made an attempt to get in touch with her when that was something I never did?

When that was something I never wanted?

Yet I found myself saying, "Why aren't we sharing numbers?"

"For the same reason we didn't share names." She placed her hand on my chest, like she was soothing a baby's back. "Because they don't matter. This was ... just this. One night, and"—she smiled—"it was a hell of a good night."

I laughed.

Was this a joke?

Was she really being serious?

How was she pulling a move from my playbook?

"You're right, I definitely lost myself in you." She leaned up on her tiptoes and brushed her lips against mine. "I did doubt you, and, man, did you prove me wrong."

She walked toward the door and hit a button along the side, which opened it.

"Hold on a second," I said, taking a step toward her, not caring that the condom was hanging halfway off my dick. "You're just leaving?"

She looked at me over her shoulder as she descended the first step. "And you're not going to follow me." Her fingers lifted into the air, and she gave me a slight wave.

And just as I got to the stairs to reach for her, she was gone.

TWO

Brooklyn

I *don't understand how our house gets this messy*, I thought as I stood in front of the kitchen sink, filling a glass of water and scanning the dishes that were overflowing.

Except I did understand.

This kitchen—no, our entire home—was the result of three women working different schedules, sharing a small villa that should technically be rented by only one.

But since the moment we'd signed the lease four years ago, the Bray women had been determined to make the seven hundred square feet work for us.

Besides, it was the only place on the South Shore of Kauai that we could afford, and we still struggled at the first of every month to get all our bills paid.

Why did Hawaii have to be so expensive?

As I took my first gulp of water, I heard movement in the living room. A stirring of sheets, followed by tiptoes. I stared at the doorway, preparing myself for which sister was about to

48

walk in, feeling guilty that I'd woken one up since I'd tried so hard to be quiet when I returned from the club. Because the kitchen and bathroom were the only two rooms that were closed off to our living room/shared bedroom, I had to wait until she rounded the corner to see who it was.

The moment the nest of dark brown curls came into view, I took another swig, waiting for the questions to start pouring from Jesse's mouth. My middle sister was the curious one. Clementine, the eldest, was the motherly type.

Jess eyed me down as I still stood by the sink, and she silently went over to the fridge, pulling out a to-go box. She lifted the lid and popped a cold French fry into her mouth. "How was the club?" Mid-chew, she held the box toward me.

I took two of the fries out of the Styrofoam, the ends already soaked from the blob of ketchup someone had squirted in earlier. "Fun."

"It was ... *fun*?"

The potato was extremely dry, hardened from the coldness, the center a gritty, gel-like texture, causing me to have to refill my water. "That's why I go twice a week—to have fun."

The club wasn't something we really ever talked about. Even though they both worked late, they were always asleep when I got home, and I left for work before they got up in the morning, so by the time I saw them again, we were discussing something more important.

"I still don't get why you go." She wiped a bead of ketchup off her lip. "It makes no sense to me."

I turned off the faucet and faced her. "What don't you get?"

"Why you go alone. If you picked a night we were off, we'd go with you. So, why not choose an evening when we could all go?"

I didn't expect my sisters to understand. They did nothing alone.

They even worked at the same restaurant.

And when I'd chosen to go rogue and gotten a job elsewhere, they had been upset with me.

Even though I was the baby of the family, I was the most independent. I never fit the stereotypical traits of a third child. I acted more like an only child.

And that often, like tonight, drove my sisters wild.

I reached inside the to-go box, this time pulling out a corner of a burger. I peeled the soggy bun off and devoured the meat. "We all have our things, Jess. You surf. Clementine runs. I dance."

"But the alone part is what bothers me." When she shook her head, the curls moved into her eyes, and she didn't bother to tuck them back. The breeze of motion sent me a whiff of salty air, a scent that clung to her, no matter how much she showered. "Clubs are places you go to with other girls. There's so much to navigate. Drinks—"

"I don't drink there."

She bit off the corner of a chicken nugget. "Dancing—"

"I wait for an available stage and don't get off it until I leave to go home."

Tonight had been an exception.

Tonight had ... broken every rule.

A thought that sent a wave of shivers through my body.

A wave that made it hard to breathe.

A wave that if Jesse looked closely, she would see the goose bumps all over my practically bare body.

"Okay," she groaned. "What about the parking lot? Do you know how many times a woman gets mugged—or worse—on the way to her car?"

"It's well lit." I grabbed her arm, trying to reassure her so we could move on from this topic. "I swear, it's fine."

Her black-rimmed eyes narrowed—she hadn't bothered to

wash off her makeup before bed. "Unless"—she tilted her head, analyzing my stare—"you're meeting someone there. And you're not really alone. And you just don't want to introduce us to him yet." She gasped. "That's it, isn't it?"

"Ha! No. Not even close." I stole the last nugget. "We both know I'm not looking, nor am I interested in any of *that*."

"But the dress." She grabbed my waist, smoothing out the fabric to show how it hugged me. "This is the sexiest thing you own."

It also happened to be the only dress I owned.

And the reason I wore it to the club was because it was so comfortable to dance in. The cotton shell didn't restrict me the way shorts and jeans would.

"I get why the outfit is misleading, but don't you think I'd try a little harder with my hair and makeup if I was attempting to impress a guy?"

I'd only given my locks a quick brush, my lashes a solo swipe of mascara, and my lips a thin coat of gloss before I left for the club.

Most, if not all, had probably worn off.

From the way I sweat while I danced.

And from *him*.

The tingles were back, strumming through my muscles even harder than before.

What the hell did I do tonight?

That deliciously handsome stranger—that was what I'd done.

I'd found him completely irresistible from the moment I'd spotted him in the VIP lounge. He had the most alluring green eyes, the color of a twinkling emerald, a stare that held me and wouldn't let go. With dark coffee-colored hair that he kept short besides the pieces in the front that he gelled to a point, an overly square jaw that was covered in a thick but well-manicured beard. Lips that were sexy and full, a mouth that had consumed me the second it landed on mine.

That had caused a spark through every muscle, bone—heck, even my blood.

And his body. Oh man, that was on an entirely different level. Corded muscles that bulged, each one so defined that it was like he'd been etched from rock.

His hands were so large that they covered me like a blanket, and when he'd held me, I'd felt like a feather.

I'd never felt like a feather before.

And that dick—*oh my God*.

The length. The girth.

The power and strength in which he'd fucked me.

I was wet all over again.

But I couldn't let that show on my face because Jess was taking inventory of the makeup I still had on, studying me while she chomped on fries, like she was trying to connect the pieces I was keeping from her.

"I suppose you'd put in just a little more effort, yes." She finally broke away, grabbing the bottle of ketchup from the fridge and squirting more into the box. When her eyes returned to me, she said, "But there's something I can't figure out that you're definitely not saying, and I'm going to get to the bottom of it."

She was right; I didn't tell them the other reason I went to the club alone.

Dancing was a major part of it. It was what I loved to do.

But there was more.

She expected it to be this epic surprise. There was really nothing epic about it.

The answer was stress. That feeling—that ball of tightness in my chest, the debilitating grip it had on me and wouldn't let go, no matter what—that was why I went.

Why I went alone.

Why I stood on that stage—I didn't have to answer questions or think about my responsibilities or focus on anything aside from movement and the way the music pulsed through my body.

"And whatever that reason is—the one you're keeping from us—it's making me really worried," Clementine said from the living room/bedroom.

I wasn't shocked that our voices had carried in there.

I rolled my eyes, swishing water around in my mouth.

And as my oldest sister joined us, she ran her hands through her do—currently a bleached-blonde pixie cut that was spiked in all directions, from either the way she was pulling on it now or from the pillow she'd been lying on. Clem treated her hair like wall paint, constantly changing the shade. It had been a rainbow of colors over the years. Recently, she'd started playing with the shape and length, doing it all herself.

Now that they were both about to interrogate me, I hauled myself up onto the only section of non-cluttered counter space and set my glass between my legs.

If I didn't put out this fire, it would spread.

Quickly.

I knew too well how my sisters operated.

"Listen to me," I began. "There's no reason for either of you to worry. I go, I dance for a couple of hours, I come home."

What little space their bodies didn't take up in the small room, their personalities did. Their presence filling every bit of open air.

"Really, there's nothing more to it."

I'd been going to the club for the last couple of months. I wasn't sure why they were suddenly making it a bigger deal than it was.

"One of the servers at our restaurant just got assaulted the other night. She was at that bar near the Lihue Airport—you know the place I'm talking about." She waited for me to nod. "Every time I've seen you since, I kept forgetting to tell you. And now, you went to the club again. Alone—*again*."

So, this was what Jess had been talking about when she mentioned getting mugged—or worse.

"It's the alone part that's really worrisome," Clem said.

"It's the alone part that I love the most," I whispered.

Clem moved directly in front of me after eating Jess's last fry and put her hands on my thighs. "What's going on, Little One?"

A nickname I'd had since birth because I had been born a preemie.

"Let's see," I sighed. "I have two months until I graduate." I attempted to fill my lungs again, but they already felt like they were at capacity. Tight. A swish of anxiety plowed through me as I mentally tallied everything I needed to accomplish from now until then. "I have a slew of projects, papers, and tests coming up. Everything needs to be wrapped up by the end of the semester, and then I have to study for finals, which are going to kick my ass. Mom and Dad will be flying in for my graduation, and this house needs to be cleaned and decluttered by then so they have room to sleep." I gave them a glare, letting them know they'd be helping with that part. "And the second that's all over, I have to start the job search."

Jess's dark brows rose high. "You're not going to stay working at—"

"No."

That was the part that not only ate at me, but also used fangs while it was biting.

Jess set the empty box on top of the trash—a bag that was already far too full and needed to be put in the can out front, so the to-go container balanced on a cereal box that was threatening to fall at any second. "I thought you were going to apply for a new role there? Or promotion?"

My job.

Thirty hours a week, and I hated every one of them. Not because the actual position was horrible, but because the company I worked for didn't take me seriously. I was twenty-two, a student. Someone who had no experience in any area of life, so what did I know, according to them?

"I've applied for other roles within the company—countless times. I'm always passed up. So, I'm moving on. Screw them."

"Why don't you just leave now?" Clem suggested. "Give yourself a little breathing room before school ends and wrap up everything you need to. This way, you're not so overwhelmed." She twirled a lock of my hair around her finger, doing the same to the other side, and pulled at the ends, like she was checking to see if both were the identical length. "That'll give you a lot more time to concentrate on school, and when you're free from that responsibility, you can start applying for jobs."

Aside from questions (Jess) and doting (Clem), they also strived to be professional problem solvers.

But I wasn't looking for anyone to solve my stress.

Besides, neither of them had ever been in my shoes. They'd gone straight to work after high school, taking jobs on The Big Island, and when I turned eighteen, the three of us left our parents' house and moved to Kauai because they thought we could make more money here. I'd immediately enrolled in an online bachelor's program through the University of Hawaii, packing each semester with a full load of courses. I took more classes over the summer so I could graduate in four years, majoring in business and double minoring in management and finance.

I had a goal.

I wasn't stopping until I accomplished it.

But for my sister to suggest that I quit now was absolutely ludicrous.

How would I live? Pay my bills?

It wasn't like I had a savings account to fall back on.

"Quitting is impossible," I told her. "I have a third of the rent to pay and a car payment and utilities, and I really love food—I can't exactly go two months without eating." I hadn't mentioned my credit card debt or the student loans that would kick in the second I graduated.

It was a lot.

Ugh.

I pushed myself off the counter, weaving around both sisters to dig into the fridge. I found the bottle of vodka we kept in there for the rare occasion that we were all home and Jess treated us to one of her famous vodka lemonades. I chugged the rest of my water and poured a few shots of booze into the glass, holding it to my lips, the liquor burning as it went down my throat.

I could feel my sisters' eyes on me.

Judging me.

Probably trying to come up with every alternate option for me.

"We could try and help you out over the next two months," Clementine started. "Maybe we could cover a little of your rent—"

"No." It didn't take more than a gulp's worth of time before they switched to full-on save-Brooklyn mode. "You're not doing that. I've never taken a handout, and I'm not starting now. I'll be fine."

I just needed to keep going to the club twice a week to clear my mind of everything. If I didn't have that pause, I'd be in a dark place.

But I also couldn't have a repeat of tonight.

Although that escape had been the best one I'd ever had—taking my brain to the calmest, most erotic place, with hands that had made me moan and a tongue that had licked me until I screamed and a body that had perfectly dominated mine—I couldn't afford the distraction.

Men were nothing but trouble.

They took up time, attention, money—and at the end, I was usually left with a broken heart.

I wasn't going down that road again, not when I was already drowning.

That meant no relationships, not even a steady hookup with no strings attached.

I didn't even want to be tempted, which was why I hadn't given him my number.

After tonight, the memory of that gorgeous man needed to disappear, just like the thought that I'd succumbed to a one-night stand—something I'd never done before.

But there was no chance I was telling these Nosy Nellies what had gone down in the party bus. I was sure they'd be proud that I'd let my walls down—it wasn't that they were anti-men—but they'd want to spank me for having sex with a guy whose name I didn't know and leaving the club with him when he could have so easily hurt me.

Maybe I am nuts?

Rather than letting those thoughts fester, I needed my sisters to go back to bed so I could finish the paper that was due at nine tomorrow morning. One I had to complete before I could get any rest because I had to be at work by six.

"What can we do, then?" Jess asked. "If you won't take money, let us clean the whole house, and maybe we can help with one of your school projects or something."

I traced my thumb across the top of the glass. "You're already doing so much. I'm lucky to have you both."

"I know we're fabulous," Clem joked. "But we want to help. Please let us."

"I'll think about it," I lied.

We all had plates that were overflowing; none of us needed more work or responsibility thrown at us.

Clem pulled me in for a hug, squeezing me with a strength she'd inherited from Mom. "Your butt needs to go to bed. You have to be at work in—"

"Less than four hours." I exhaled. "I'm just going to finish up my paper, and I'll be in to crash."

"*Ahhh*, fuck." Jess groaned. "There's a problem with your computer."

I pulled away from Clem, and Jess had an expression of guilt across her face.

"What kind of problem?"

"When I got home from work, I needed to pay some bills, so I used your computer." She reached for my glass and downed what was left in it.

My laptop was the only one we had. My sisters used it all the time, and I had no problem with that.

But as the guilt deepened in her eyes, something told me I now had a problem with it.

"The battery light was blinking," she continued, "and I didn't know where the plug was, so I pushed the chair back to get up from your desk and search for it, not realizing the cord was under the chair, and the wooden leg landed on the adapter, and it snapped off."

My heart sank, and my throat became so constricted that I almost wheezed when I took in a breath. "What are you saying, Jess?"

"You have a dead laptop and no way to plug it in. It was too late to go to the store when it happened, so I planned to get you a new one in the morning."

With no cord, I couldn't write my paper, especially adding in the references and special formatting—things my professor required, or I'd attempt to write it on my phone.

Aside from escaping, my computer was the one other thing I needed tonight.

My head fell back, my eyes squinting closed. "*Shiiit.*"

"I'm so sorry, Brooklyn." Jess's voice was filled with emotion. "I feel terrible. I didn't do it on purpose. I swear it was an accident."

"I know."

"I'll get up super early, and I'll get the cord first thing," she added.

I lowered my chin to look at her. "It won't matter. I'll be at work by then, and I can't write it there."

"Call in sick," Clem offered.

I couldn't do that either. My car payment was already overdue. I needed tomorrow's wages as much as I needed my laptop cord.

"It's fine." I swallowed, trying to push the knot down. "I'll get it done somehow." Another lie, but I didn't want Jess to feel worse than she did.

Jess squeezed my hand. "Please don't be upset. I'll make this right. Whatever I have to do."

I wrapped my arms around her and hugged her. "I'm not upset." When I pulled back, I said to both of them, "Now, I really need to get some studying done." I nodded toward our room. "Go."

Clem rubbed the top of my head. "Try not to stay up too late. As it is, four hours isn't nearly enough sleep."

I said nothing as they walked out, hearing the sounds of them getting into their individual beds.

I took out my phone that I'd left in the car while I was at the club, but it was now wedged into the top of my dress. I pulled up my email and wrote my professor a note, explaining the situation.

I just hoped he would forgive my tardiness because the worst case would be a failing grade.

A grade that was currently an A.

I finished my plea and hit Send.

I was just going through my emails when a reply came in.

From: Professor Lilo Akana
To: Brooklyn Bray
Subject: Out of office Re: Tomorrow's Paper Deadline

Hello!
I will be out of the office until next Wednesday. I won't be checking email during my absence, so don't expect a response until Thursday at the earliest. If this is an emergency, please reach out to the department secretary. Her information is below. If this is regarding an assignment, all exams and papers are due on their deadline. No exceptions unless it's a medical emergency. Anything turned in after the deadline will result in a failing grade.

Professor Lilo Akana
Business Department
University of Hawaii

I was screwed.

A failing grade would lower my A, which also meant it would affect my 3.8 GPA—something I'd worked so hard to maintain.

I set my phone on the counter and went back to the fridge, reaching inside for the vodka. I didn't know what Jess had done with my glass, so I sipped straight from the bottle.

This time, I didn't have anyone to judge me while I drank.

I was alone—again.

Anxious—again.

The dark place tugging at me.

Again.

The only difference was that I was sore from the moves and positions of tonight.

And I was left with the most satisfying ache between my legs.

Who was he?

I didn't care.

I couldn't care.

THREE

Macon

"Vodka tonic," the server said as she set my drink on a table next to my lounge chair. "And a strawberry daiquiri for you," she continued, placing the drink next to Camden.

I thanked her and said to my best friend, "I don't know how you drink that fruity, frozen shit." I glanced toward the ocean, where some of the guys were attempting to surf. "It's too much sweetness and not nearly enough booze."

Since we had been at the club so late last night, Jenner wanted to do a beach day today. Food. Drinks. Relaxation. And the ones who didn't mind getting blown across the waves, face-first, were on boards in the water, not a single one of them lasting through a whole crest before they wiped out.

"I got a rum floater."

I laughed. "Are you going to wear that paper umbrella behind your ear and dance the hula for us tonight?"

He shot me his middle finger and tossed the tiny umbrella

in my direction. "Are you going to finally tell me what went down in the party bus last night?"

A subject change.

That motherfucker thought he was slick.

I had known when I departed the VIP lounge that Cooper would tell the guys that I was off to get the girl. I also knew that after I sent him that text, he'd tell them I'd taken her into the bus. Once she'd left me naked, by the time I returned to the group, they had been so drunk that they forgot I had even been gone.

But from each of them, during breakfast and our short time at the beach, I'd gotten random mentions of it and questions.

Now, it was Camden's turn.

I returned the umbrella to the top of his drink and rested my arms behind my head, crossing my feet. "You know what went down. But the details about it? Nah, I'm keeping that to myself."

"Hold on a second." He sat up on his lounger and turned toward me, his toes sinking into the sand. "You're going to refrain from giving me details about this one? But all the others, you share every fucking detail the minute we're on the phone or when I see you." He pulled down his glasses, eyeing me from over the rims. "Why the secrecy?"

I didn't like that he'd picked up on that.

I didn't really like this conversation at all.

I faced the dudes in the water again. "No reason."

"I don't believe you."

"There's nothing to believe," I snapped. The patience from last night was long gone. "I saw a woman at the club. She was hot as fuck. We talked. We left. I returned to the VIP lounge, where we all partied like hell. End of story."

"Maybe that's the end, but you're leaving out a shit ton from the middle. Like ... are you going to see her again?"

That question had haunted me since she'd walked out.

Without getting her fucking phone number.

Without any way for me to reach her.

Without even knowing her damn name.

I ground my jaw. "No."

"For some reason, it doesn't sound like you're happy about that."

I wasn't.

I was fucking pissed.

Because from the second she'd taken off, I hadn't been able to stop thinking about her.

I couldn't stop wondering who she was, where she lived, what I would call her when I whispered in her ear.

How she'd tasted.

How she felt beneath my hands.

How her body was meant for my domination, how her pussy had been built for my cock.

"Why don't you just call her?" he pushed.

I finally looked at him again. "I would, asshole, if I had her number."

"You didn't get it from her?"

My brows shot up. "Why are you so interested in my sex life?"

"*Ohhh* shit. I know. She didn't give you her number, did she?" He laughed. "That's where all this attitude is coming from."

"I always have attitude."

"True, but you always talk about the women you fuck—except for this one." He reached forward, clasping my shoulder while he laughed. "You finally met a woman who's just like you." His laughter turned to a howl.

And as he got louder and as it lasted across a span of several seconds, my anger built.

"You can stop, you know. I get the point."

"I can't. This is just too funny." He took a sip of his bullshit drink. "How does karma feel? Is it stinging a little? Biting the cheek of your ass, and you're doing everything to swat it away and you can't?"

My friends gave me a lot of shit for my lifestyle, but before each of them had settled down, they had been no different. It seemed like the women they were chained to had given them amnesia, where they couldn't remember anything before dating them.

"Listen, when I hook up, I make it clear what my intentions are. Chicks don't wake up the next morning and expect a proposal and a guy who's going to fulfill every one of their dreams. Shit, most of the time, I'm not even there the next morning. I'm long gone before they wake up." I took a drink, chomping on an ice cube before I said, "If I lied to them, then I could accept this karma crap, but I never lie. They know going in, they know coming out."

"Would you have stayed the night with her?" His voice turned serious.

I didn't have to think. I already knew.

Because I'd wanted to go to her place, because I'd wanted to keep the night rolling.

And as those thoughts simmered and sank in, I didn't know who the fuck I was anymore.

What had happened to me.

What had she done to me.

Why this mentality was even a consideration when I'd normally be pleased with the results of last night.

"Yeah," I replied, "I would have."

"So, now what?"

I shrugged. I didn't know.

An island that had an area of over five hundred square

miles and more than seventy thousand people—that was a shit-load of ground to cover.

Did I attempt to look for her?

Ask around?

Have my assistant dig through social media to see if my Tiny Dancer had ever posted a photo from the club?

Fuck me.

"Now, I—" My voice cut off when a beep came from my phone—a special ringtone dedicated to Walter. I picked up my cell and checked the screen, reading a round of questions that were coming at me, one after the other, like rapid-fire. "Fuck. I need to run up to the room. I have to send my uncle some spreadsheets before he loses his shit."

He moved back into his chair, extending his legs across it. "Will you be a while?"

"I shouldn't be more than a few minutes." I got up and nodded toward the crew in the water. "You should join them. I promise not to videotape you from the room, where I'll have the perfect view of you fools."

"Dick."

I picked up my vodka, carrying it across the sand and over the pool deck until I reached the lobby, pressing the button for the elevator. Once I stepped inside, riding toward the top floor, I found the last text my assistant had sent and began to type.

ME

How difficult would it be to find someone who lives on Kauai when I don't have their name or address?

KATHLEEN

Your chances would be better if you bought a lottery ticket.

I sighed, shoving my phone into the pocket of my swim

trunks, and stepped out when I arrived at my floor. I walked down the short hallway and into my room.

The first thing I noticed was the smell. A scent far cleaner than the pigsty we'd left behind. That and the way everything now sparkled, unlike the clothes and pizza boxes and bottles these drunk bastards had left on every surface.

When I'd hurried us out for breakfast, I hadn't cleaned their mess.

It was their shit, not mine.

Aim, tidiness, and respect—three things that went out the window when a bunch of drunk dudes were crashing in a room together.

So, I left some cash by my computer, assuming the house-keeper would know it was for them.

As I walked toward that same spot to send Walter the files he needed, I saw the money was gone, and a note was in its place. Written on a small pad of paper with the hotel's emblem at the top—a pad that had been by my nightstand earlier.

Curious, I picked it up and read it.

Thank you for the tip you left me this morning. That was really nice of you.

You obviously felt bad for leaving the room in THAT condition.

You know what would have been even nicer? If you hadn't left the room in that condition.

It was disgusting and a total nightmare to clean.

And I think I even gagged a few times.

Please don't do it again. THAT would be appreciated.

I laughed as I carried the note into my bedroom and returned it to the nightstand.

If a housekeeper at a Spade Hotel had left a note like that for one of our guests, they'd be fired.

Immediately.

But it had happened at Spade's biggest competitor on the island, which was one of the reasons I laughed so hard.

The other reason ... they were right.

FOUR

Brooklyn

The beat of the music was pounding through my body. My chest vibrated from the bass. My heart thrummed from the constant movement. My brain focused on the lyrics, my limbs on the rhythm.

The stage I was on was in the center of the dance floor. It was the first one that had become available. I normally preferred a spot around the perimeter.

I didn't want the attention.

I didn't want to be seen.

I wanted to blend into the sides of the club.

And usually, besides the last time I had been here, I was able to make that happen.

But when this stage had become vacant, I wasn't going to miss out on the opportunity, so I'd climbed the ladder once the dancer got off, and I had taken my place on top of the narrow platform.

I needed to be here tonight.

In my head, I swore I said that every time, but this evening felt extra important because this week had sucked. The failing grade on my paper had only been the beginning, and that shook me to my core. When I returned home from work the next afternoon, a new power cord had been plugged into my laptop since Jess had gone to the store, and I sat down and wrote what I would have the previous night. After I read over each paragraph, deciding it was in the best possible shape it could be in, I emailed the final copy to my professor, reiterating what I'd said in my first email, along with pictures of the broken cord to prove I wasn't lying.

It wouldn't make a difference, but I couldn't go down without a fight.

I wished the bad vibes had ended there.

They hadn't.

An issue at work had also arisen.

Something that still made my hands tremor every time I thought about it. Something that made me question why I hadn't listened to Clem and quit so I could ride out the next two months in peace.

My coworker Malia and I split responsibilities. There were duties I preferred and duties she loved to do, so we swapped. We worked the same schedule—always. So, unless one of us texted the other to warn them that we weren't coming in, it was assumed that I would help her out and she would do the same.

I'd gone in yesterday, thinking it was going to be no different.

Except she'd called in sick and never told me.

And even though we never crossed paths during our shift, I thought nothing of it. I was too mentally consumed to pay attention to a detail that large.

When my manager called me about an hour after I got

home, asking why I hadn't finished all my tasks, I didn't know what she was talking about.

It didn't occur to me that Malia had bailed—she wouldn't do that to me.

But at the same time, where was my manager's accusation coming from?

My manager couldn't understand why I was asking about Malia's attendance, and when she finally answered me, telling me Malia was sick, I explained how we partnered up. My manager didn't think that was an efficient way to work. She actually wasn't impressed with our decision at all. I wasn't in a role where I was allowed to delegate. I was solely responsible for my duties, and they hadn't been completed, and my manager was pissed.

Which resulted in a write-up.

My first in the four years that I'd worked there.

And I had to drive back to my job so I could get the warning in person and sign the paperwork.

To make matters even worse, Malia wasn't sick. She'd come into Jess and Clem's restaurant that night with some friends and partied until close.

I couldn't understand why she'd do that to me.

I didn't even bother to ask her, but when we passed each other in the employee lounge during this morning's shift, I told her in the nicest voice I could muster up that she was on her own. I was taking care of my things, and she needed to accomplish hers.

The only people who had my back on this island were my sisters, and I couldn't ever forget that.

But, damn, it had been a hard lesson to learn.

And I really just wanted this week to dissolve into thin air, so that was why I'd been so excited about coming here tonight.

Why I'd been counting down the hours until I could stand on this stage and lose myself.

And why I was surprised that while I shimmied my body over the narrow platform, my arms waving over my head, my hips swaying, I felt something come over me.

Something that was incredibly strong.

Something that was achingly familiar.

Something that brought me back to the last time I had been here.

"Looking up my dress again, I see." I faced the direction in which I knew the devastatingly handsome stranger would be standing, his stare so overwhelming that I was positive of his location.

What shocked me was, first, how difficult it was to breathe and, second, the lack of distance between us.

He'd climbed the ladder, and he was on the top rung.

His gaze like a hunter.

His lips parted, as though he was ready to feast.

His body positioned in a way that he could easily sweep me off my feet.

Maybe he wanted to get close so he could hear me. This stage was most definitely in a louder location than the last one I'd been on.

Maybe he thought that because of what had happened between us, there were no longer any boundaries.

Whatever he assumed, he was wrong.

"Not looking up your dress," he growled, near enough that I could hear him over the beat. "I'm just admiring it."

A smile came across his sexy face. Scruff that had thickened in the days that had passed. Eyes that were a duller green with hints of blue that matched his shirt and speckles of gold, like the metal that was in his bracelets. There were several around his wrist—woven leather bands, some with clasps—that hadn't been on him last time.

I would have remembered.

There wasn't a detail I'd forgotten.

"Good evening, Tiny Dancer."

I felt him.

Everywhere.

In parts of my body that I hadn't even known existed.

An echo, a pulse that throbbed deep within me—that had nothing to do with the music.

"Tiny Dancer ..." I repeated.

He could never understand how ironic that nickname was. That "Tiny Dancer" was a song my parents would dance to on the night before my father was deployed and on the evening he returned. We'd moved often. Every couple of years, followed by a deployment. Each memory I had was in a different living room, the record player's location somewhere inside, but the dance was always the same.

With Elton John's record loaded, Dad would come up behind Mom and press both palms on her stomach. By the third verse, he would slowly turn her toward him.

Mom would be hiding tears, covering them in smiles.

Afraid he wouldn't come back ... relieved when he did.

"I've been to this club every night since we met, hoping you'd come back." His gaze dropped down my body, his face only about six inches from where I stood. "And here you are."

There was a reason I hadn't given him my name and number.

This feeling, this situation, his stare—those were the reasons. I didn't have time for this. I didn't have the mental capacity to take on any more. I was at my tipping point.

"You shouldn't be looking for me." I turned my back toward him while I danced.

"And why's that?"

He was so close that I could still hear him, but I still said over my shoulder to make sure he heard me, "Because I don't want to be found."

"That's a problem ..."

His tone made me turn.

Our eyes locked.

It was suddenly impossible to fill my lungs.

Why did he have to have the most delicious lips? Why did they have to be so thick and perfect and taunt me in ways that made me remember what he could do with them?

Why did that spot between my legs tingle, like he was blowing on it?

"Because I can't get you out of my mind," he hissed. "I've thought about you every single moment since you left me on the bus. And now, you're finally here again, and you know what?"

I didn't want to know.

I didn't want to hear any more of his voice—it was too hot, too alluring.

"Don't tell me—"

"I want you even more than I did when I saw you from the VIP lounge, which is nearly impossible because I would have done just about anything to taste you then." His gaze took another dive to my toes, gradually lifting up my body, stopping at each of the places that was throbbing for his touch. "Do you know how badly I want to break your rule right now?" He licked across his mouth, a steady swipe that had every thought in my head exploding. "Especially when I know how good your pussy tastes." He wiped his hand over his cheek, as if my wetness were there and he wanted to smell it. "How I want to hear your fucking screams again. You are"—his teeth rubbed over his lip while he moaned—"addictive, Tiny Dancer."

My body quivered in response.

Growing wet.

Tightening.

How did words—his words—have this kind of effect on me?

Why was I even letting him get in my head? When I had so many questions about him, starting with where he lived. Was he a local? Was he on vacation? He'd told me the bus was rented for a bachelor party, but that told me nothing. Four days had passed since I'd been with him, and that didn't help either because he could easily still be on a trip.

But I needed to understand something, so I asked, "You came all the way here just to sleep with me?"

He was the most attractive man I'd ever seen in person. His jeans, shoes, watch, button-down—they reeked of money. Moneybags, like him, attracted women. Surely, just based on his looks alone, he could get any girl in this club, and then you added in deep pockets, and the women would be lining up.

He didn't need to keep pursuing me.

Then, why was he?

"I came to see you. To be around you. Because if I didn't find you—and I wasn't going to let that be an option—I was going to fucking lose it." He reached forward, his fingers getting dangerously close to my ankle, but when he was a hair away from touching it, he stopped. "You're consuming my mind. I can't get you out of my thoughts." He paused, the intensity in his eyes multiplying. "I want you."

I wasn't going to let any of that sink in. I wasn't going to let a single syllable repeat in my head.

I couldn't.

So, I scanned the club, my finger tracing the air. "There are probably hundreds of women here—"

"I don't want them."

His words didn't need to be backed up. They were strong. I

believed him. And his stare emphasized everything he'd just said.

How could this man make me feel like I was the only woman in this club?

Why was he here?

Why did he want me?

Why was this happening now and not in two months, when I could think a little clearer?

Why? Why? Why?

I eyed a woman nearby. Her hair was almost as dark as my locks. Her body was similar. Her dance moves just as good as mine. "Why not her?"

"I don't even need to look at her to tell you." His eyelids narrowed. "The answer is easy. She's not you."

"But you don't know me." A feeling in my chest caused me to add, "You know absolutely nothing about me."

When he pulled his hand back, I swore I felt the tips of his fingers. Or maybe I was just remembering what they'd felt like, fantasizing about them.

Silently begging for him to touch me without my permission.

"You're right. I don't know your name. I don't know what you do, where you live. What you love and hate." He tucked that same hand under the opposite arm, like he was forcing himself not to reach for me again. "The things I know only involve your body. Your taste. Scents. The spots that you like to have licked a little harder than the rest of you. How you enjoy your clit rubbed as you come." He broadened his shoulders, reminding me of how muscular they were. "Those are the things I know for sure. The things that have brought me here every night, hoping like hell you'd show up."

Heat didn't just move across my face; it came through like a tsunami.

But it didn't stop at my scalp or the base of my neck; the warmth continued down my chest and over my back and into my stomach, where it increased in temperature before it plowed down my legs.

"I'm here because I want to know more."

I sucked in the tiniest amount of air—all that my lungs would allow.

He wanted to know more about me?

Or my body?

Did I even want the answer to that question? Because it had the potential to change everything.

Why was I even thinking about any of this?

My God.

"Since I'm already up here, I can't exactly catch you, so how about you let me carry you? Or I can walk you down the ladder, whichever you prefer."

"And go back to the party bus?" I shook my head. "No, thank you."

"It didn't seem like you had a problem with it before." He paused. "But there is no party bus this time. I'm here alone."

That reply made my thoughts run even faster.

Alone meant ... I'd go home with him?

But first, I'd be carried down the ladder, pressed against his hard, muscular frame. I would fit perfectly in his arms—I knew that. I'd been in that spot before. Even our hands were compatible—his huge and overpowering, making my fist feel like the size of a golf ball, palmed within a catcher's mitt.

My body was being tugged in only one direction while my head was all over the place.

I had come here to unplug, and I was completely plugged into him.

I had to ... stop this.

"You shouldn't be here." My hands went to my hips. "I'm

not what you want. Trust me ... I'm not." I waited for move-ment. For a change in his eyes. For a rebuttal. Anything. "Please accept that." When he still didn't move, his face unreadable, I turned around and began to dance.

But I could feel his eyes boring through my body.

His presence as it caused the air to thicken. To wrap around me. To coat my skin like lotion.

No matter what, I wasn't going to face him.

I wasn't going to allow myself to use him as an escape. That was what dancing was for. I didn't need to change that. I didn't need more. This club gave me everything I needed.

While I slowly lifted my arms, swaying my hips to match the calmer beat, there was movement behind me. Like a wall had been added to the stage—that was how hard it was. But it wasn't cold, like stone; it was scorching, as though the sun had been baking on it.

In my mind, I wished he would touch me without my permission.

And now, that was happening, as he'd taken the spot behind me, his hand flattening against my stomach.

"You're everything I want." He pressed our bodies together, his erection grinding into me. "I know you can feel that." His face went to my neck, each breath—both inhales and exhales—like a windstorm against my bare skin. "That's how hard you make me."

My eyes closed.

"And by the way you're breathing, how you're pushing your ass into my dick, I bet that if I reached under your dress, your pussy would be wet." His lips moved to the back of my ear. "Not just wet ... but soaked." He kissed that spot, a brief mashing of lips against cartilage, but it was enough to send the most blazing sensation through me. "Tell me I'm right." His fingers didn't stay flat against me. They swirled around my navel, like a choreographed routine. "Better yet, dance with me."

I hadn't realized I'd stilled.

Or maybe I was too afraid to move because the stage was barely large enough for the both of us.

Regardless, how did he know so much about my body? How could he make me feel this good?

They were just words. They were just fingers against my skin.

Yet it all felt like so much more.

I tilted my head back and instantly hit his chest.

My lips parted.

My eyes gradually opened.

I wanted him—

No.

I wasn't going to give in.

It didn't matter that I was wet. Needy. Wanting.

This was my stage. This was my moment to switch off.

I didn't need him to do it.

"The stage is too small."

"Then, you'll just have to stay close."

Before I could think, before I could even gather enough voice to reply, he was melding our bodies into a flow. Our speeds matched. We were like waves in the air, crashing together. Our limbs knowing just where to rise and fall, our hips locked.

My body didn't try to separate from his. It didn't want to. It was absorbed in a rhythm that was making me pant.

Yearn.

Forget.

He danced the same way he fucked.

With power.

Stamina.

Dominance.

And every second was foreplay.

It not only made me pull away from every painful thought that had driven me to the club, clouding them in layers of fog, but it also filled me with a desire that haunted my insides.

That grew with each of his thrusts.

"Come home with me."

My lungs gasped as I drew in air.

Home?

That meant he lived here.

Shit.

Had I wanted him to be a vacationer? So I knew he would be getting on a plane soon and I wouldn't have to worry about ever seeing him again?

Did I want to scream through multiple orgasms, knowing that, just like last time, this would be the best sex of my entire life?

"Let me do to your body what I've been dreaming about." His hand clasped around mine. "All you have to do is say yes."

FIVE

Macon

"Let me do to your body what I've been dreaming about. All you have to do is say yes."

I didn't wait for her to reply before I turned her around to face me, and the look of shock covering her gorgeousness only caused me to draw her in closer. She was probably worried because we were balancing on a stage so high up and I had been reckless with the way I quickly spun her.

But I needed her face.

I needed to see her mouth when it parted and responded.

Besides, she wasn't going to fall. I'd never let that happen.

"I—"

"Macon." I couldn't let a second go by without her knowing what to call me. "Whatever you're about to say, start that sentence with my name." My hands went to her cheeks, tilting them up toward mine.

"Macon." I watched it roll across her tongue. "Fitting."

I chuckled. "How so?"

"You're classic in an old-school sense, like your watch. It's not a shiny Rolex, it's a piece far more timeless than that. Something that appears to have been passed down through many generations and probably costs more than three Rolexes combined. And then there's the nickname you gave me. How many thirty-something-year-olds listen to Elton John to even make the connection to 'Tiny Dancer'? Not many, if I had to guess. But with that classic feel, there's something so rare about you. In your eyes, in your needs." She gave a half smile. "You don't look like a John or a David or an Andrew. That's why Macon works. It's uncommon—like so many things about you."

Now, that was a response I could appreciate.

She'd noticed. She was into detail. And she was right about the watch, except it hadn't been passed down in my family. There were only five of these pieces in the world. I'd flown to Dubai to get this one.

"So many things to comment on ... but I'm not quite thirty. I'm twenty-seven. Still, you were close, and you are"—I searched her face, where I couldn't find even a single fine line, eyes that had witnessed plenty of experiences, but not necessarily years—"twenty-three? Not more than twenty-five—I'm sure of that."

"You're so curious about me."

"That's because I can't get enough of you."

A feeling that had come completely out of nowhere not long after she left me in the bus, and it had only built as the days passed. It still shocked the fuck out of me.

I woke up thinking of her. I went to bed with her face behind my eyelids. I pumped my cock in the shower, visualizing her body—even though I couldn't get rid of the raging hard-on every time I thought of her.

And even the final night that the guys had been here, I'd insisted we stop by the club just in case she came in.

I didn't know why I was like this. Where this sudden change had come from. Why, after all these years of being single, of never sleeping with a woman more than once, of living the playboy lifestyle, this woman—whose name I still didn't know—was threatening to change me.

But I couldn't fight it.

I tried.

She was just what I wanted.

What I needed.

"I'm twenty-two."

A little younger than I'd thought, but that didn't bother me.

"And your name?"

She laughed. "I'm not a John or David or Andrew either."

"Jesus"—I shook my head—"you're fucking relentless— that's what you are."

"You like that about me."

I growled, "I like many things about you."

It blew my mind that she would barely give me an inch despite what had happened between us the other night. Or that I'd told her I'd been coming here to look for her, proving how interested I was and that I wasn't giving up.

The women I'd been with in the past would have killed for this. They would have done anything for me to show up some-where to look for them, for me to be consumed with them the same way this stunning stranger was owning me.

Yet she couldn't care less.

I didn't know if that infuriated me or gave me a constant erection.

"Your name ..." I echoed, letting her know I wasn't letting her avoid the question.

"Why does it matter?"

Her gaze intensified when I swiped my thumb over her lips. She didn't have on any gloss. Just some mascara, and that was about it. Her skin was a shade tanner than the last time I'd seen her, her freckles popping from the new glow. I wondered if I'd find tan lines under her black dress, one that looked identical to the previous outfit she'd worn.

"Because I want it."

"Do you know what I want?" She took a deep breath, like there was a war inside her and she was trying to settle it.

"Me."

She ran her tongue over her teeth, which bumped out her lip. "But didn't I tell you to leave? That I wasn't someone you should be interested in or pursuing? That I'm—"

"You're exactly what I want." I leaned my face down, our mouths so close. "I'm not asking you to marry me. I'm just asking you to spend the night with me. And while you're in my bed and my mouth is all over your body, I want to know what I should call you." I grazed my nose across her cheek, the only spot my palm wasn't covering. "What went down on the bus was hot as fuck, but if I'd been able to say your name while I was coming, that would have been so much fucking hotter."

Her chest rose.

Her body gave off more heat.

The tension gradually began to leave her posture, and she leaned in toward me, as though she wanted me to take her weight.

"Brooklyn."

Finally.

"*Mmm.* Almost as beautiful as you."

I pressed my lips against hers, waiting for her to pull away, and when she didn't, I deepened the kiss, parting her mouth for my tongue. And as I tasted, I breathed in that salty beach air that was mixed with lemon—scents that, I was learning, solely belonged to her. My tongue took several more dives before I separated us.

"Am I carrying you or holding your hand while you walk down the ladder ... Brooklyn?"

She smiled. "You're going to say that every chance you get, aren't you?"

I held out my hand. "No one gets tired of hearing their name moaned. You won't either. Trust me."

When she locked her fingers around mine, I took a step back until my foot hit the top rung, and I began the steep descent. As I reached the bottom, I glanced up her dress, seeing the darkness of her panties—a cave I wanted to bury my face in —and I held her waist, guiding her to the floor.

"My car is out back."

With our fingers locked, she silently followed me through the club and past the exit, the quiet, breezy sounds of Kauai meeting my ears the moment we got outside. We were just rounding the corner of the building when a thought struck me.

"How did you get here?"

"I drove."

I assumed it was all right to leave her vehicle here overnight. There had to be plenty of people who did that, too drunk to drive home, and they'd retrieve it the next morning.

"I'll bring you back to your car tomorrow."

"You'd better."

I laughed as I walked her over to the SUV, opening the passenger door for her.

As she climbed inside, she groaned, "Of course you drive a Range Rover."

"It's on loan. It's not mine."

She settled, wrapping the seat belt around her. "Are you going to tell me you normally drive a 2006 Corolla, like me?"

I raised my brows.

"Didn't think so."

I closed her door and rushed to the other side, and as soon

as I got in and turned on the engine, Lionel Richie began playing through the speakers.

"I'm beginning to think you were born in the wrong era."

Her voice was different now that we were in the vehicle. It had nowhere to travel to except my ears. It wasn't whiny or high-pitched. It was smooth, like the silkiness of her hair.

A tone I'd never grow tired of.

"I wouldn't appreciate the music or even the watch that I'm wearing if I'd been born in a different era." I pulled out of the lot and onto the road. "That's not to say I don't like current hits or Rolexes—I do. I just resonate with things that have a bit more character." As I glanced at her, she looked so tiny in the large seat. "Are you from Kauai?"

"No."

She had no accent that I'd picked up on, nothing that would lead me to believe she was from a specific area of the country.

"How long have you lived here?"

She moved her hair from one shoulder to the other. "Long enough to know the best place to get a tan on my days off. Which I'll be doing tomorrow for about an hour after you take me back to my car. *Mmm,* I can't wait."

Not that I didn't want to hear more about her in a bathing suit, but, shit, she had a hard time answering questions.

"That's all you're going to give me?" I stopped at the light, taking in her face, her features lit from the truck across from us and the beam of red that shone from above. Damn, my dick was already hard. "Fuck me, it's impossible to get any information out of you."

She turned her head, her cheek pressed against the back of the seat. "You're an escape, Macon. That's all this is. So, are answers, like where I'm from, really necessary?"

She didn't sound harsh. In fact, she was whispering.

Which was why I replied, "I like when you use my name." I dug my teeth into the bottom of my lip, pulling until it was free. "You do too ... I can tell."

"And you called me the relentless one."

"Come on, Brooklyn. You're intrigued. I know you are. You're just not willing to admit it." I traced a finger up her knee and thigh, stopping when I reached her hip. "What you don't know is that I can see right through you."

"Yeah? What am I thinking?"

I dived my hand over her vacant cheek and cupped it. "If I were only an escape, you wouldn't have gone on the party bus, nor would you have agreed to come home with me. Both are bold moves for someone who doesn't fuck around."

"How do you know that about me?"

"I can tell. I can feel it. I can see it all over you." I paused, but my gaze didn't. It stayed right on her—locked and deepening. "Something about me interests you. Admit it."

"You're not ... typical."

But before her, I had been. I had been everything she'd probably hate.

Careless.

Inconsiderate.

Selfish.

"And I can say that I haven't met many men like you," she continued.

"You're saying I'm rare ..."

"I wouldn't give you that much credit." She winked.

And, damn, it was sexy.

The light turned green, and I began to drive. "Give me something more. Something easy. Something like ... if Kauai isn't home, then where is?"

It took her several moments to respond. "I'm originally from Chicago. I only lived there for about a year or so because"

—from my peripheral vision, she pointed at her chest—"I'm an Army brat. We've lived all over. But about six years ago, Dad was stationed on The Big Island. That's what brought us to Hawaii."

That was why, when I'd looked into her eyes earlier this evening, I'd seen someone who had experiences under her belt, but not years.

I liked that.

A lot.

"Dad is still there?"

She nodded. "My parents are, yes."

"And you're here."

"I think I am." She pinched her arm. "Yes, I'm pretty sure I'm here." She giggled.

A laugh I hadn't heard from her yet, but her lighter side was extremely sexy.

"Smart-ass."

"Another thing you enjoy about me."

"You know what I find funny?" I turned at the next light. "That's not the first time you've pointed out a trait that you think I enjoy about you. But you're so quick to point out how I shouldn't be interested in you, how I shouldn't have come looking for you, and how you're not someone I should like. Is that your way of teasing me? Or you enjoy that you've been owning my mind and that turns you on?"

She didn't immediately respond. "It's flattering. I can't lie."

"Then, have dinner with me this week."

"Are you asking me out on a date?"

A date. A term I hadn't used in so many fucking years.

A week ago, if you'd told me I'd say that word to a woman, I would have laughed my ass off and bet every dollar to my name that I wouldn't.

But one look from across the club had changed everything.

There was no way she could know the kind of power she held.

"Yes," I replied.

She drew in a long inhale. "Let's take it one step at a time and get through tonight first."

Where she had sucked in the air, I was loudly letting it out. "You say that like it's a punishment to fuck me."

"That's not it at all. It's just that ..." She glanced out the window as I looked at her. "I've hit a period in my life where everything is so muddy and complicated. I don't even have time for me, never mind someone else. I go to the club to unplug from my life"—she connected eyes with me—"and what you gave me was total amnesia. And that's what I need tonight too." Her voice had gotten softer with each word.

"You want me to fuck you into forget mode."

She nodded. "Please."

"And that's all you want from me?"

When she didn't respond, I decided to give her a piece of me so she would understand the magnitude of what I'd been admitting to her. "I haven't dated a woman in seven years. Not because they haven't tried. Fuck, they constantly try. I just don't let it happen. And I don't believe in no strings attached— women can't seem to handle that. There are always strings. Therefore, I do my thing, and I'm out."

"So, you're telling me you're the king of one-night stands."

I laughed. "I've certainly earned that title."

"And here we are, on a soon-to-be night two."

"Which is why I just told you that about me." I looked at her before I switched lanes. "I've said things to you that I've never said to another woman. I know you're going to ask me why. That's your favorite reply—it keeps the attention off you." I smiled at her. "But the truth is, I don't know why. I just can't seem to be able to get enough of you. That's why I want to have dinner with you. Why I want your number. Why I want to be able to reach out to you in the interim."

"But dinner and texting—that's more than *this*."

Jesus, the roles had flipped.

"Would you rather me say *meet me in my room*? Is that less muddy?"

A second passed before she said, "Your room?"

I pulled into the hotel, parking by the front entrance, where two bellhops were waiting—one coming to my side and the other going to Brooklyn's.

"I thought we were going to your home?" she asked before I had the chance to explain why we were here.

"This is my home. This is where I'm living." I climbed out and met her on the curb, my hand going to her lower back.

She whispered, "I don't understand. How is a hotel home?" But as she spoke, she kept her head down, refusing to meet my eyes.

"I'm working on Kauai for the next couple of months, and this is where I'm staying. Home is LA."

As I led her through the glass doorway and into the lobby, she placed her hand over her eyes, like a visor.

There was only one reason she'd do that.

"Embarrassed to be seen with me?"

"No, it's not that at all," she replied without looking up. "I know a bunch of people who work here. If they see me going up to your room, rumors will run wild that I'm the girl who goes home with the vacationer, and that's not the kind of reputation I want ... nor am I that kinda girl."

"Ah. I get that."

She stayed quiet until we were in the elevator with her hair hiding both sides of her face, her fingers sealed to her forehead, and once the door closed, she turned toward me, but her hand stayed put. "So, question ... if you're in LA, how would dating even be possible? I'm here, and you're *alll* the way over there."

That had been on my mind for sure. But I hadn't given it too much weight. Locations were just details that could be worked out. I had access to a private plane. We were building a hotel here.

The possibilities, when it came to my work life, were endless.

I wasn't going to get into that now.

What was far more important was emphasizing, "I didn't think you wanted to date?" Even though her face was still hidden from me—assuming she was hiding from the cameras in the elevator and that she even had friends in the security department—both of my hands went to her sides, brushing up to her bra and down to her panty line. "Isn't that what you were feeding me when you complained about how little time you have?"

"Macon ... I see what you just did."

I brought her closer. "Let's take it one step at a time and get through tonight first."

She tapped my chest with her free hand. "Okay, Mr. Good with Words."

I laughed. "What, you don't like it when I use *your* words against you?" I leaned down to kiss her but had to maneuver my way under her eye shield.

As I got near her mouth, she stuck her finger over my lips. "Not even a little ... you *dick*."

"Is that like your *no touching* rule, which I've obviously broken?"

"*Ohhh.* Someone's on fire."

I chuckled again, my grip lowering to her ass. "Isn't that something you like about me?"

"I ... give up."

"Don't." I squeezed her cheeks. "Because I'm just getting started."

The elevator opened to my floor, and I walked her down the short hallway, waving my key card in front of the lock.

"PH 4," she said, reading the sign to the left of the door. "You must have a really nice boss if he's footing a bill like this."

"He's my uncle."

"That explains it."

I huffed air out of my lungs. "It explains nothing. I just hold an important role at his company, and with my title, I get certain perks. Staying in a suite is one."

I ushered her in first and heard the click of the lock as I joined her in the foyer, where her hand had finally fallen, revealing her whole face.

Since it was late, housekeeping had already stopped by, turning down the room for the night, which gave the interior a completely different vibe than in the daylight. The pendants were dimmed, making the white and mirrored finishes stand out, the mood as serene and sensual as the view—the one in front of me and the one outside the sliding glass door. There was soft, spa-like music playing from the speakers. Even a scent had been sprayed, a mist that was clean and beachy.

But it was nothing compared to the constant flavor that came from her body, a smell I inhaled every time I took a breath.

"I feel very ..." As her voice trailed off, she surveyed the room.

From the way she was glancing around, I couldn't tell if she had spent time in one of the suites and was refamiliarizing herself with the space or if she was shocked at how nice the room was. Whatever it was, at least the weirdness was gone, and she wasn't covering her face anymore, acting ashamed to be here.

"Dressed?" I played with the bottom of the black cotton, where it hit the upper portion of her legs, lifting it just a little to slide my fingers beneath. "Far too dressed."

While I stood in front of her, I leaned in toward her, pressing my lips against one of the most delicate places on her body—the spot where her neck met her collarbone, the small arch right before the bone jutted out. It was there that I kissed. There that I took the deepest inhale.

There that, as soon as my mouth left, turned into a patch of goose bumps.

Her hand dropped from my chest to my abs, inching lower until she hit my belt buckle. "We're both far too dressed."

How could just the sound of her voice, never mind what she'd said, make my dick throb even harder?

It hit me then that I hadn't been much of a gentleman since she'd entered my suite. I hadn't offered her a drink or anything to eat. I could have even suggested a dip in the jetted tub.

But by the look on her face, I didn't get the impression she wanted any of that.

Where I couldn't wait another second to have her, I was positive she felt the same way about me.

"I'm going to solve that right now." My hands trailed down her back, molding around her ass, giving her cheeks a quick squeeze before I began to peel the dress off her body. First past her hips, and then her tits, and finally over her head. While I held the tiny dress, my stare started at her feet and slowly rose up those perfect legs, the white lace of her panties, the flatness of her stomach, the matching bra, where those gorgeous tits were cupped, and eventually stopped at her face. "The fucking things I want to do to you right now ..."

"Tell me." She was unbuttoning my shirt, widening the collar around my shoulders, letting it fall from my back and arms. Once it hit the floor, she felt her way across me, like she was memorizing each plane of skin, the dents of muscle, every hair. "I want to hear, in detail, what you're going to do to me."

"Will it make you wet?"

"Wetter ... yes."

Fuck me.

As she pulled at my belt, loosening the hook, working her way through the button and zipper of my jeans, I said, "The second you're finished here, I'm going to lift you into my arms and carry you into the bedroom, where I'm going to set you on the bed. And from there, I'm going to wrap your legs around my face and lick your fucking cunt."

My jeans fell.

She lowered to the floor, unlacing my shoes, gazing up at me with her lips parted. "I get your mouth again?" She didn't stand; she stayed right there, gripping the waist of my boxer briefs as though the elastic were the side of a cliff.

"Yes. I've been dying to taste you."

"Why?"

My smile came with a low chuckle. "Because the first time wasn't enough. I haven't been able to stop thinking about your pussy."

"*Mmm.*" The moan came at the same time she tugged on my boxer briefs, making my cock spring out. "I've missed this." That was when I realized she was gazing at my dick and talking to it. "What are you going to do after you lick me?" She repositioned herself onto her knees, reaching up to wrap both hands around my shaft, aiming the tip toward her lips.

Fuck, she was naughty.

And this was a sight I would remember for the rest of my life.

She dragged her lips around my crown, gently kissing my head, using just enough pressure that it made me want more.

"I'm going to make you come."

She looked up at me as the point of her tongue touched me, and she circled it around my rim. She pulled it back into her mouth to say, "Only once?"

"When it comes to you, I don't do anything just once."

Her lashes fluttered, her stare still fixed on mine while she took her first bob.

My hand shot into her hair, gripping the long locks on the top of her head. "*Fuuuck.*"

It was the combination that was so explosive. The way she used her tongue, how her cheeks caved inward along my length, and the suction from her throat that made everything so tight.

My head tilted back. "Yes, suck it," I ordered.

She removed a hand, now using just one to cover the base and middle, her mouth going from the tip to the center, where she met her fingers.

"Yes. Like that ..."

What I'd learned over the years was that women didn't have to be experts at giving head. What made them good was their desire to want to do it. And Brooklyn sucked my dick like she lived for it.

Like this was the only thing she wanted in this world.

And watching her—*fuck.*

A vision so damn hot, especially when she pulled back and licked around the edge and across the center, lapping the small bead of pre-cum that had just leaked out for her.

She stared at me as she took it in her mouth.

And swallowed.

"My fucking queen," I roared. "Take it. Make it yours."

And she did.

She glided down without even gagging, swirling her hand and mouth along the stiff peak, closing in around me before she drew back to start over, establishing a pattern that grew in speed.

She didn't stop.

She didn't even pause to take a breath.

She gulped my dick down as if she was after my cum.

"Jesus Christ," I hissed. "Yes!"

There wasn't a part of me that wasn't screaming for her, and as much as I wanted her mouth forever and to draw this out all night, my tongue was getting restless.

"Come here." It was a demand that I wouldn't bend on.

As she rose, I placed an arm across the center of her back and another under her knees, and I lifted her against my chest, stepping out of the pile of clothes that she'd previously pulled down my legs.

"I would have kept going." Her lips were wet and sparkling under the faint light.

I nuzzled my nose into her cheek, where I growled, "I fucking love that about you, too, but it's my turn to feast."

She moaned, the same sound leaving her mouth again as I set her on the bed. As she balanced on the edge, I unclasped her strapless bra, tossing the lace to the floor, and yanked down her panties. I then laid her across the mattress, and while I held the inside of her thighs, I pushed her higher, toward the pillows, and I got on the bed between her legs, my face diving straight into her pussy.

"This"—I rubbed my mouth down the whole length of her, pausing at her entrance before returning to the top—"is what I've been dreaming about."

This scent.

Taste.

The feel of her as I licked.

The way her clit hardened from my tongue.

How I was going to make this pussy mine—and only mine.

But before I got too lost, I set my nose on the highest point, and I filled my lungs with her. Breath after breath of Brooklyn. "And this is what I can't get enough of."

A smell that was my perfect match.

A pussy that fucking consumed me.

Not just in a way that I wanted more, but in a way that I craved.

Yearned.

Required.

And what blew my mind was that this—every inch of this body—was enough to make me change my ways and change everything I'd thought to be true.

Why? I didn't know.

I just knew that Brooklyn was what I needed.

"Show me how much you've missed it." She clung to my hair, legs spread wide.

I pulled my nose away and began to lick, covering her with my spit, wiggling my tongue through each fold and dip.

"Oh God, yes!"

Her sounds were more foreplay.

And as my licks quickened, I heard, "Macon!"

"My goddamn name ..." Holy fuck, I was going to come without even being inside her. "Let me hear it again." I pressed harder, flicking directly across the top.

I earned myself a scream.

"Macon! Don't stop!"

I urged her orgasm to the surface, staying in just that spot while I slid a finger inside her to add to the build.

Her hand tightened on my hair, her nails digging in. "Fuck!"

From a vertical rhythm, I switched to horizontal, dropping to the bottom of her pussy, gathering the wetness that I spread back up. And when I reached the summit, her hand locked on my head. Her hips rocked forward. Her legs circled around me, her ankles crossing over the center of my back.

Her sounds told me everything I needed to know.

So did her wetness—thickening, sweetening. Her pussy holding my finger, narrowing around me each time I moved in and out.

She was climbing.

Every lick brought her closer.

And it was fucking beautiful to watch.

"Macon!" It hit me like it was the first time I was hearing her say it, and just as that one word left her mouth, the shudders took over, beating across her stomach, causing her muscles to go from taut to loose. "*Ahhh!*"

As she wriggled over the mattress, my mouth went faster. So did my wrist, turning, tilting, dipping that long finger toward her G-spot.

I didn't just want to bring her there. I wanted to send her over the edge.

And as she screamed, "Fuck," I knew I had.

That was when I slowed things down. When I decreased the momentum of my hand and tongue, waiting for her to turn silent before I stilled.

"If you promised to give me that every day, maybe I'd want you to ask me to marry you ..."

I chuckled, gently pulling my finger out, her eyes following me as it went straight into my mouth, sucking her off my skin.

"You don't waste any of me, do you?"

My finger left my mouth to say, "Not when you taste this good."

Instead of releasing my hair, she brushed through the top of it. "No one has ever made me come as hard as you."

"That's because I fucking live to get you off."

Since I was sure her clit was extremely sensitive, I carefully

98

kissed it, soothing the remaining tremors, and then I got up and went over to the nightstand. I took one of the condoms out of the box and tore off the foil corner with my teeth, pumping my cock a few times before I rolled the latex over it.

"My God, you're so ridiculously hot." Her voice was soft, but her words were full of emotion.

I set my knee on the bed. "Is that so?"

"Yes. Your body ..."

"What about it?"

"I can't get over it."

"You don't have to get over it." I grabbed her hand and placed it on my abs, rubbing her palm up and down my six-pack. "You can have it whenever you want it."

"And your mouth?"

I fucking loved how much she enjoyed my tongue.

I smiled. "I'll bring my mouth too." I set my other knee on the bed and tucked my arms under her thighs, returning to the place I'd just left to show her how much I meant what I'd just said.

But this time, I wasn't tame. I licked with the flatness of my tongue, spreading the wetness from the top of her pussy to the very bottom.

"Macon ..." she moaned.

I'd teased myself to the point of fucking losing it.

I needed her.

Now.

So, I kissed up her stomach, pausing my climb to suck her nipple, flicking it with my teeth, biting the hard peak.

"Fuck yes," she cried.

I did the same to the other side, gnawing across the surface before I continued up to her lips.

She wrapped her arms around my neck. "Unsatiated, much?"

"Because I can't keep my mouth off your pussy?" I positioned my tip right where it needed to be. "Yes. You could say that." I kissed under her neck and over that sweet spot by her collarbone, past her jaw, and hovered over her mouth. "I need a taste, Brooklyn." I put all my weight on my forearms, and I slowly sank into her tightness. "My fucking God. How is it possible that you feel this good?"

"Kiss me."

A demand I could certainly handle and one that made me thrust inside her even harder.

With her mouth busy on mine, her hands roamed my body, slinking down my sides, and around to my ass. She squeezed my cheeks, her palms pushing against them, like she wanted me to fuck her even harder.

There was a reason I'd only wanted a taste, and that was because I didn't like this position; it restricted me from touching her. So, I slid out and moved her onto her side and got in behind her, aligning her ass to my front before quickly burying myself back into her cunt.

"That's what I want right there." While I slammed back and forth, pounding through her wetness, I pinched her nipple. "You're so fucking tight."

"That's because you're so big."

"Keep complimenting my dick ... see what that earns you."

"I could talk about your dick all day." She laughed, the sound then turning to a moan when I grazed my thumb over her clit.

She circled an arm around my neck, holding us together, as if I were going to leave.

I was just getting started.

I lifted her leg and placed it across mine. By doing so, her thighs spread, allowing me to get in even deeper. I was sure she felt the shift—her breathing got louder, her pussy wetter.

"You're going to come again."

Her nails stabbed my skull. "*Yesss* ... don't stop."

I amped up my speed, strumming her clit at the same time, grinding my hips in a circle, the twist now giving her friction from every angle.

"Macon!"

Several things happened when Brooklyn came. The first was that her pussy closed in around me, her fingers puncturing whatever she was gripping. Her moans then filled my ears.

She needed me.

To finish her off, to bring her to that place where she couldn't return from.

All of it drove me fucking wild.

And right now was no exception.

I upped my strength, stroking her with even more power, giving her exactly what she needed to lose herself.

And she did.

"*Fuuuck*"—her nails were in so deep that it felt like she could draw blood—"*meee!*"

The neediness in her screams. The wanting. The building. It was enough to make me come.

But this moment was for Brooklyn, so I reared back to my tip and plunged in until my sac banged against her, giving her long, deep, hard strokes. Within a few seconds, she was shuddering, clenching my cock with her pussy, bucking against me.

"That's it, come on my dick." I hammered into her. "Let me feel it."

"*Ahhh,*" she gasped. "*Yesss!*"

As the orgasm hit her, I watched the waves slam into her body, I took in her screams, and I didn't slow until she finally calmed.

It took her several moments before she said, "I think I forgot how to breathe."

"You'd better learn because you're about to come again"—I hovered my lips above hers—"and don't tell me it's impossible, we both know what I'm capable of."

I earned myself a smile, and, fuck me, it was everything.

I took my time sliding out and moved into a seated position, leaning my back against the headboard, my legs extended in front of me.

Brooklyn looked at me from where she was lying. "What are you doing?"

I folded my hands behind my head, locking my fingers. "I'm waiting for you to ride me."

She slowly got up and straddled my legs, crawling her way up my body until she was over my lap.

This fucking view was exactly what I wanted. Her tits in my face, her pussy aimed at my cock. Her eyes in my direct line of sight. A quick reach around, and I would have access to her ass.

"Don't be easy on me, Brooklyn."

She was about an inch down when she stilled and said, "Can I admit something?"

The timing was a little strange for conversation—I would admit that—but I wasn't going to say it to her. "Of course."

"This is the first time I've ever done this position. I've never been in control before ..."

I swore my dick got even harder.

"A virgin at riding—is that what you're telling me?"

"Yes."

A thought instantly came to me. "What about your ass? Has that ever been touched?"

She shook her head.

I couldn't even imagine how fucking tight she would be. How she would pulse around me the second I entered.

We'd get there—I was positive we would.

But for now, "We'll start here." With my crown now fully buried, I gazed up her narrow waist, the hardness of her nipples, to the most gorgeous face I'd ever seen. "But what I want you to do right now is lose yourself." I brushed my thumb over her clit. Just a quick swish of skin against skin, and it caused her to draw in a deep breath. "If that's what you want tonight to be about, then show me how lost you can get."

She set her arms on my shoulders, and I took her nipple into my mouth, wetting it first and then breathing against it.

"Listen to your body. Then, go as fast or as slow as you need."

She began to rise toward my tip.

"You're going to know pretty quickly what you like and what feels the best."

Her chin tilted back, her spine arching. "*Thisss.*" She swallowed. "This is what I like."

She was squeezing me from the inside, throbbing around my cock.

A cave of warmth and perfection.

"I fucking agree," I moaned.

I kept my thumb on her pussy and switched my mouth to her other tit, biting the peak this time.

She whimpered from the pain, but it was a sound of pleasure. A noise that told me she wanted more. I swirled my tongue around the tight bead, soothing it before I used my teeth, scraping the length, tugging the end.

Her nails began to bear down into my skin. "What is this ..."

She was in her head, processing all these new sensations, questioning why she'd never done this before.

And I could tell she wasn't looking for an answer.

But I still gave her one. "This is what happens when you take what you want." I grabbed her ass. "When you take what you need." I wasn't leading her. I was just holding on. "Is this what you want?"

Her head moved forward until our eyes locked. "Yes."

"Do you want to come?"

Her head bobbed. "Yes."

"Then, fuck me, Brooklyn. Show me what it feels like when you get off on top of me."

The second I finished speaking, a switch went off. Her speed immediately increased. Her hands held me harder. She didn't continue to rise and dip. Instead, she kept me seated inside her and rocked her hips back and forth, circling me within her.

Now, this was what I was after.

This vision of pure beauty, this level of vulnerability.

And while she took what she wanted, using my dick to build toward her release, I watched. But she didn't just use my cock; she used my finger while it brushed her clit, used my mouth while it sucked her nipple. And as she swayed over me, she forced the tingles to move through my body. I neared the peak, close to bursting, her pussy trying to milk the cum out of me.

But I wouldn't let it go.

Not yet.

I waited.

I observed.

I fastened our mouths together.

And the second she began to shudder, I let go.

"Macon!" she shouted against my lips. "Oh my God!"

This was the best feeling in the whole world.

An intense, overpowering crest right before the cum shot through my head, filling the condom with the pure lust I had for this woman.

"Brooklyn," I roared back. "Fuck me."

But my orgasm wasn't the best part.

That was when I got to hear her screams. When I saw her body spasm. When she rode me with uninhibited thrusts, unhinging as she owned the control, in a way that she'd only done with me.

My ears fucking rang from the way she screamed my name.

Again and again.

But that shit was like music, and I could listen to it nonstop.

As she eventually lost her rhythm, too absorbed in pleasure, I took over, heaving my cock upward, emptying myself inside her. I didn't stop until the final quiver left her body, and I wrapped my arms around her.

Her skin was hot, slightly sweaty.

Sexy as hell.

"Baby, you are so good at that." I kissed up her neck and across her jaw, tasting the saltiness as it now mixed with the lemon that was already on her skin. "Damn, you can ride some fucking cock."

She was breathless.

Her hair untamed. Her eyes feral.

But on her lips was a smile. "Can we do that again?"

I chuckled.

Because in every possible way, I'd met my match.

"Yes. We can definitely do that again."

SIX

Brooklyn

The slightest movement on the mattress, a tug of the blanket, a tightening of his hand on my stomach—all signs that Macon was starting to wake up. The moment he finished stretching, I felt his eyes on me, obviously realizing I was already awake, and he said, "Good morning."

Since I normally left for work so early, it was hard for me to sleep past six. That was the time I'd gotten up today, according to the clock on his nightstand, and now, it was past seven. Rather than climbing out of this cozy bed, I'd spent the last hour in this exact position, frozen so I wouldn't wake him, recapping our whole evening together.

The images that flipped through my head began at the club, where he'd joined me on the stage, and continued all the way until now.

And they repeated.

Nonstop.

During each loop, my brain slowed for the intimate

moments, like the three times we'd had sex last night, dragging me through the details so I wouldn't just recall them, but I would also experience his touch all over again.

From there, I was reminded of the way I'd felt while his body was wrapped around mine. How, even hours later, I could still feel the soft kiss he'd placed on my cheek right before I fell asleep.

And as I turned toward him, I was hit again, this time with his appearance. His messy hair all seductive-looking, his beard thicker and even sexier than it had been yesterday. The temptation boiling within his eyes.

My God.

Macon wasn't just handsome. That word wasn't nearly strong enough for him.

He was a vibe.

A mood.

He could even be a religion.

And he was a man who, by just glancing at me, made everything inside me tingle.

But he was also a man who would distract me, who would take up an immense amount of my time, who was everything I didn't need right now.

I sighed, "Morning," and yawned as though I'd just risen myself.

His leg extended further across me, knotting us together. "Did you sleep well?"

I'd slept like I'd spent the night tucked inside a cloud. A real mattress with luxury bedding and fluffy down pillows—it was about a million and a half times more comfortable than my setup at home. The silence in the room was also quite different from hearing one of my sisters flush the toilet, waking me in the middle of the night, or the creak of the fridge when one of them grabbed some water.

But those weren't the only reasons I'd slept so perfectly. The feel of him next to me definitely added to it. So had the sense of protection when his arms stayed around me all night, the warmth of his skin against mine—things I could certainly get used to.

And things I needed to forget the second I left this hotel room.

"Soundlessly," I replied softly.

But once my eyes had flicked open, I'd remembered where I was and who I was with, and the thoughts had begun to drown me, tugging me in directions I hadn't been prepared for.

He traced the side of my face, his touch so gentle.

Sensual.

Inviting.

Consuming.

"You said you don't have to work today." He kissed my shoulder and then my collarbone. "And, just by chance, I don't either. How about we grab some breakfast?"

"Breakfast ... *hmm*."

A meal that would lead to conversation, allowing us to get to know each other better.

Even if I was tempted, why bother?

Because even if Macon was a good fit for me—which he wasn't—he was only on Kauai for a short time. His home was a place way too far from here. And I wasn't in a situation where I could start this—this being something so heavy and off-balance that it would never work.

What I needed to do instead was give my full attention to school and the few months I had left.

I needed to focus on my job.

And I needed to plan for the positions I was going to apply for the moment I graduated.

A career that could afford me an actual bedroom with a bed

I didn't have to blow up, inside an apartment that had rooms and doors rather than the efficiency we all shared.

But there was no way I was telling Macon any of this. He was quick with words, the smoothest talker I'd ever met. He'd have an immediate rebuttal to try to make me believe that our differences were positive.

Except they weren't.

Opposites were one thing, but Macon and I were on separate planets that didn't even revolve around the same sun.

Still, I had questions regarding some of the things I'd learned about him. Questions that really shouldn't matter, but my brain just wouldn't let them go.

So, before I answered him about breakfast, I said, "Why are you on the island? I know you said work, but what kind of work?"

His fingers slid into my hair, moving the strands off my face. "My family's in the hospitality industry. I'm here to manage the build-out of a new hotel."

A new hotel?

"You're not talking about the Spade Hotel, are you?"

If Macon was staying on the South Shore of the island, I had to assume the hotel he was building was in this area since that was the only one currently under construction.

It was rumored that it would be the most upscale resort on Kauai, and the brand alone and their loyal client base would bring in a slew of new tourists. That also meant it would be taking business away from the other hotels, especially the one we were in now.

Everyone had been talking about it.

"Yes, that's the one," he said.

My heart began to pound as I connected the other piece of information he'd dropped.

"You said you're related to the Spades?" I held my breath,

waiting for the confirmation that we weren't just planets, but universes apart.

"I am a Spade, Brooklyn." He smiled. "It's my last name."

Macon Spade.

Oh fuck.

"So, you're the owner's son?" I didn't know why I needed the clarification or why I was still digging, but the questions wouldn't stop swirling in my head.

"My father and his brother, Walter, started the brand. Dad retired, which leaves Walter—my uncle—his daughter, my two brothers, and me running the whole show."

The whole show was a company worth billions.

An amount that instantly made me sweat.

From our first meeting, I had known Macon had money. It wasn't just a sense I had based on his clothing and watch. It was a fact I'd felt in my gut.

But Spade money?

That was a league I couldn't even wrap my head around.

A level that made me extremely uncomfortable as I lay naked in bed with him.

I'd assumed he was wealthy—I'd even called him moneybags.

But a billionaire?

Hard no.

"And that's why you're leaving in a few months," I whispered, putting the last piece together. "It's when the build-out will be done."

"Yes." He pulled his hand down until it was cupping my cheek.

"You're Macon Spade." The second the words left my lips, a mouth he'd just stroked with his thumb, I wished I'd stayed silent.

I didn't need the validation; I believed him. But when he gave it to me by nodding, he sealed everything I'd suspected.

We weren't meant for each other.

Not even by a small percentage.

I pushed myself up, leaning my back into the headboard, bringing the blanket with me so it covered my whole chest. I wasn't going to act affected. I was going to let this morning play out, and then hopefully, I would never run into Macon again.

Despite how much I loved the escape he'd given me ... as much as I obsessed over his tongue ...

I couldn't have it again.

"I hear it's going to be a beautiful resort. At least from what I've seen so far it is." I paused, choosing my words carefully. "I drive by it on my way home almost every day."

He bent his elbow, resting his face on his palm. "Would you like a tour? Since I might know someone who could make that happen." His free hand slithered down my stomach.

Why did his caresses feel so good?

Why did he immediately make me wet?

Ugh.

"Maybe," I replied.

"We can stop there after breakfast."

"About breakfast—" I started, realizing I'd spoken without thinking and I had no idea what excuse I was going to give. Except all I had been doing was thinking. My mind was on fast-forward—a speed that was so jarring that I wanted to rewind to an hour ago when I hadn't known he was a Spade or how many bags of money he had. "I"—I cleared my throat—"unfortunately, have a paper due by noon." And just as my mouth closed, I remembered I'd told him I was going to the beach. *Shit.* "Which I plan to write at the beach." It wasn't a lie. I did have a paper and a project to finish. I was just going to do them after I spent a little time on the sand. "I need every

second I can get, you know? And if you come to the beach with me"
—something he hadn't suggested, but I needed to cover all the
bases—"we both know I won't get a single word written."

His finger rose over the blanket, sliding the covering down
so he could paint a thin line under my breast.

My nipple hardened.

He noticed ... he was watching.

His expression told me he'd expected this reaction, along
with the one that was happening between my legs. He had this
wild, uncanny ability to know what was going on inside my
body without even touching me.

Maybe that was because, like the first time we'd been
together, I wasn't able to hide how I was feeling.

My breathing had sped up, the same way it was doing now.

My chest rising as fast as it was falling.

My back arched, urging him down, down, down.

No.

This needed to stop. My thoughts, his actions—all of it.

I set my hand on top of his. "We need to get going." When
his eyes changed, I added, "To the club, I mean, so I can get my
car and a spot at the beach before it gets too crowded."

He didn't think I was talking about leaving. He thought I
was telling him we needed to speed things up, which was why
I'd added the clarification.

He laughed again, eyeing my entire body as he pulled the
blanket completely off me. "I'm going to get in the shower. Join
me." When I went to reply, he interrupted and said, "Then, I'll
take you to your car."

That laugh. I hated that I liked it so much.

That it was the sexiest sound.

That the only thing I could think about as it rang through
my ears was how it would feel if those same lips were pressed
against my pussy, vibrating as he chuckled.

What have I gotten myself into?

The last thing we'd be doing in that shower was washing ourselves in a way that we'd smell like soap when we got out.

Instead, I'd smell like Macon.

A scent I'd really grown to desire.

Just this once, and then I'm done.

Done, done, *dooone.*

"Okay." I nodded.

He kissed my neck—a spot he'd gone to before that was right at the bottom before my shoulder dipped. "I'll get the water warm."

He walked into the bathroom.

Naked.

A body that had muscles for days, their outlines so defined that it was like they were highlighted in neon yellow. Why did my brain instantly remind me of how those muscles had felt when my hands were squeezing them and how they had easily lifted me and dominated me for hours last night?

My stare dropped to his shoulders, a section that was so chiseled.

His back had edges that were as hard as his erection.

His ass ... *my God.* That man had one hell of a butt. I'd held it while he pumped me. I'd even clutched it. And the more I'd gripped it, the harder he had fucked me.

Without saying a word, he'd known that was what I wanted.

What I needed.

A knowledge of my body that no other man had ever had.

And it seemed that his only goal was to get me to scream.

Which I did.

Endlessly.

And that scream and that orgasm were the only things that had satisfied him.

Macon Spade was a dream.

But that was just it. None of this was reality. Not this suite, this man, this whole scenario.

It was short-lived and the two of us were an ocean apart.

It was a billionaire to a woman who made a little above minimum wage.

The only thing we had in common was sex.

That wasn't enough.

Even if I wanted more, I needed it to be with someone who was relatable. Who had just one bed, not an entire company of beds in locations I could only fantasize about visiting.

This had been fun. He'd given me the escape that I needed.

But after our shower, this was over, and it was never happening again.

I got off the bed and walked past the bottom of the mattress —the spot where he'd knelt as he lapped between my legs, where he'd wrapped those legs around his waist and slid inside me. Where he'd lifted me and held me against the wall and made me come.

Three times.

Every inch of this room triggered a memory.

I needed out.

I needed to forget.

I needed—

My thoughts came to a screeching halt as something on Macon's nightstand caught my attention.

Something I hadn't seen until now.

I checked the doorway to the bathroom, making sure I was still alone and he wasn't about to walk back into the bedroom, before I carefully made my way over to that side of the bed.

There was a small piece of paper on the nightstand. It was attached to a notepad, where the hotel logo was at the top, followed by a mix of curly and capital letters written in black ink.

My heart pounded as I lifted the small stack of paper and read the first line.

Thank you for the tip you left me this morning.

But the polite tone quickly shifted as the writer of the note began to reprimand Macon for the state in which he'd left his room.

THAT condition, I read. *Disgusting. A total nightmare ... gagged a few times.*

When I got to the end, I rescanned the words a second time.

A third.

And when I reached the last period, my eyes focused on that little dot, my hands shaking even harder.

My chest tightened.

Air was no longer filling my lungs like I needed it to.

"Brooklyn, are you coming?" Macon yelled from the bathroom. "The water's hot."

The water?

Shit, that was right; I was supposed to meet Macon in the shower. But I'd been in such a daze over the note that I forgot he was even in the room.

Or why I was here.

Or what I had told him I'd do.

"Be right there," I shouted back.

But despite what I'd just said, I couldn't move.

My feet were frozen.

My limbs so incredibly heavy.

Why couldn't I put this note down and join him in the bathroom?

Why didn't I want to let it go?

Why was everything burning inside my body?

I shook my head, drawing in the deepest breath I could hold, and I carefully set the paper on the nightstand, staring at it for several more seconds before I slowly made my way toward the en suite.

As soon as I walked in, I caught my reflection in the mirror above the double sinks.

What hit me the hardest about the woman gazing back was the expression on my face.

The emotion.

The shock and horror and fear and regret, the combination showing in my eyes and cheeks and lips.

I needed to replace it all with happiness, especially as I turned to Macon.

"Finally." Both of his hands pressed against the glass wall, his body slick, his dick already hard. "Get in."

Already naked, I released the air I'd been holding and replaced it with a new breath while I took the remaining steps toward the shower door and pulled it open, joining him under the stream.

He instantly took me into his arms, his face going to my neck, his lips pressed to my skin. "Do you know what I'm about to do to you?"

"Tell me." My voice was a whisper—that was all I had in me, and even those two words felt like a lot.

"I'm going to start by getting on my knees and putting my mouth right here." He grazed my clit. "Licking you so fucking hard and fast."

I should have been focused on his voice.

His presence.

His body that I couldn't get enough of.

I should have been so turned on that I was wrapping my hand around his dick and pumping it.

Needing it.

Begging for it.

But I wasn't.

I was lost.

Because I couldn't stop thinking about that note on his nightstand.

The letters that made up each word.

The words that had been constructed.

The handwriting that was so achingly familiar.

Because it was mine.

I was the housekeeper who had left that note.

That realization hadn't just eaten at me this morning, it ate at me when we'd arrived at his suite last night. While Macon had waved his key in front of the lock, I'd taken in the room number, connecting that number to the note I'd written.

A note I assumed had been thrown away.

But somehow, it had resurfaced, and when I saw it moments ago, the teeth that were already gnawing at me bit down even harder.

And I was doing everything in my power not to let it show on my face.

Oh God, what have I done?

SEVEN

Macon

The bar was off the hotel lobby, tucked in a corner by the windows, built in an oval shape with stools positioned around the entire circumference. Half of the seats were vacant, yet the stranger chose the one directly next to me. Without looking, the movement of them sitting sent me a wave of air, the scent telling me it was female. And the moment she was settled on her seat, I instantly felt her eyes on me. I heard her breath. I sensed the swish of her pants as she crossed her legs, the fabric brushing across the side of my thigh.

When I glanced in her direction, her expression confirmed exactly what I had suspected. She hadn't randomly chosen that stool, nor had her pants accidentally touched me.

This woman had a motive, the look in her eyes telling me it was sex.

She wanted it.

Now.

And she wanted it with me.

I'd been here many times before. It seemed wherever I was, regardless of what I was doing, women were drawn to me. I'd been told it was due to a combination of my good looks and that I was a man whose sex appeal dripped from every pore.

My friends called me a magnet.

Whatever it was, it happened nonstop.

And for the last seven years, it was a quality I had been blessed as fuck to have. I wanted as many women as possible around me. I wanted to pick my favorite and take her home.

I wanted to drown myself in pussy.

But last week, all of that had changed.

I wasn't that man anymore. Shit, I didn't even know who I was.

As I sat here with a tumbler of scotch, staring out onto the beach, for the first time in all these years, I wasn't looking for a woman to bring up to my bed.

I wasn't engaging in conversation.

I didn't even want her to glance in my direction or coat me in visual attention—something I always craved since eye-fucking was the first step of foreplay.

Because what I wanted was Brooklyn.

And only Brooklyn.

It was that thought, that realization, that caused me to lift the glass to my lips and take a sip of the amber liquor.

"Hi."

There it was—the initial start-up. Her way in. Her voice all soft and seductive, like she was hoping the small talk would lead to real talk.

This was what I'd been trying to avoid all along, which was why I'd chosen this particular spot since it wasn't around anyone else.

"Good afternoon," I replied.

I wouldn't ignore her. I was an asshole, but I wasn't fucking rude.

"I have to know ... what are you wearing? You smell positively delicious."

Another quick look showed she met my typical criteria. Fit body. Dark brown hair. Lips large enough to drag every thought to my cock—or would have prior to Brooklyn.

Sex in a bottle, was the answer I normally gave when I was asked that question. I had multiple bottles that I rotated constantly; I usually couldn't remember which one I'd squirted on. Whenever I described my cologne that way, if she wasn't already turned on, she would be.

Hearing *sex* come out of my mouth was an immediate aphrodisiac.

But that wasn't the answer waiting on my tongue tonight. "One of the designers. I don't recall which one."

"Well, don't ever wear anything else." Her eyes swept the whole length of me. "This one is *sooo* perfect for you."

"I appreciate that." I faced the bartender, shaking my glass in the air, letting him know it was time for a refill, and I downed what was left.

"Are you here on vacation?"

"Business," I replied. "All work, no pleasure for me."

"That's too bad."

A peek showed she was gazing at me with a stare I knew all too well. One that told me the only things separating us were clothes, and she was fucking dying to strip them off.

I grabbed the glass the bartender had just placed down and continued, "My last drink before I get on the plane in"—I checked my watch, but didn't pay attention to the time—"less than two hours."

A lie. But a necessary one.

Except I noticed it did no good. The look hadn't left her face.

It only intensified.

"I bet I can change the pleasure part." She reached across the space and set her hand on my arm. "You have about thirty minutes before you have to go to the airport. I know just how we should spend it."

We.

There was nothing hotter than a woman knowing what she wanted and going after it; therefore, I couldn't knock her for trying.

That target just wasn't going to be me.

I pulled my phone out of my pocket and checked the screen. It was full of notifications. What I wished for was that it were ringing so I could busy myself with a call. Since it wasn't, I'd have to make one happen on my own.

I hit the screen several times and held it against the side of my face. That was when I looked at her and said, "I'm going to spend it talking to my wife."

Wife.

Fuck.

A word I'd never thought I'd ever use, but when it came to Brooklyn, it'd so easily slipped from my mouth.

I stood from the stool, and when I got the bartender's attention, I let him know I wanted the bill charged to my room.

"Have yourself a good day," I said to her before I carried the scotch to the back of the hotel, where I took a seat on a plastic chaise lounge by the pool.

I wanted Brooklyn to be the one who picked up when the line connected. But that was impossible because it was Camden's number I'd called instead.

"What's going on?" my best friend asked.

"Jesus, I'm just dodging women left and right." I chuckled,

121

setting the glass on the small end table. "Are things good, my man?"

"Things are always good. Who are you dodging? I thought you had your sights set on ... Tiny Dancer—isn't that what you've been calling her?"

I took the drink off the table and sipped from the scotch. "Brooklyn. That's her name."

"Well, if you got her name, it sounds like she finally opened up to you a little."

I sighed, the memory from our last morning together burning a hole in my goddamn brain. "Barely." I balanced the phone on my shoulder and ran my hand over the top of my head. "I don't have her number ... still."

"But she has yours?"

"Yes," I hissed. "And she hasn't used it—no calls or texts."

A point that was driving me fucking wild.

Two days had passed since I'd seen her.

Two fucking days, and she hadn't bothered to reach out. I'd thought it was odd, when I pulled up to her car and parked in front of it, that she was willing to take my number and not give me hers. But because she'd told me she'd be in touch, I hadn't made a thing about it.

Now, I wished I had.

"Hold on. Let me get this straight," he said. "You've hooked up with her twice—"

"Allegedly."

"That's right, we're still in the *not admitting* phase because you don't want to talk about her that way. That's some bullshit, and we both know it." He exhaled into the phone. "So, let's just be real and say you've now fucked her twice. She got away a second time, like the first, and you have no way to reach her. Am I on track?"

I bent my knees, pushing on the straps beneath my feet.

"And I still don't have her last name, so I can't get my assistant to look her up."

"She could search by her first name."

I shook my head against the plastic chair. "Don't you think I've already asked her to try?"

"*Daaamn.*"

My eyes widened as I wondered if his response meant he was onto something that I'd missed. "What?"

"What?" He laughed. "Who the fuck are you?"

Except he wasn't onto anything. He was just repeating the same thought that had already been in my head.

Who the fuck am I?

"I don't know," I answered honestly.

"This doesn't sound like my best friend. In fact, it sounds like I'm talking to a total stranger. But I've got to admit, I like this side of you. The side that told that playboy pact to fuck right off."

Was that what I had done?

Fuck me.

I squeezed my fingers around the strands, pulling at them. "You want to know something else? I asked her out for dinner and breakfast. Two meals. And she didn't take me up on them. Instead, she gave me some bullshit response, something like she wanted to get through one step at a time and see how our night went first."

"And then you slept with her?"

I took a long, deep breath. "Camden ... come on."

"Buddy, I'm just trying to get to the bottom of this." He paused. "You know, maybe she's not digging the way you fucked her. Ever think of that?"

No.

Because I didn't believe that for a second.

I knew Brooklyn's body.

I had given her everything she wanted.

I'd made her scream so many times that she was hoarse in the morning.

There was no reason for me to think he was right, no signs that pointed in that direction.

Besides, if she hadn't liked the way I fucked, she wouldn't have joined me in the shower the morning after. She wouldn't have let me slip it in. She would have wiggled out of my arms while I held her against the glass wall, and she would have faked an orgasm, which I knew she hadn't because she couldn't fake the way her pussy pulsed around my dick.

I straightened my legs, the straps of the chair bouncing from the weight. "That's not it, trust me. But she did mention that she was in a muddy point in her life and ..." I'd recalled that morning many times in my head. Replayed it forward and backward. "Maybe I'm off, but when I explained why I was here, on Kauai, and that I worked for my family business, something inside her seemed to shift."

"She doesn't want to get attached if you're leaving in a few months."

"I can buy that."

"So, what the fuck are you going to do about it?"

My hand left my hair to raise the drink to my lips, and I held the liquid in my mouth for several seconds before I swallowed. "I'm going to go to the club to talk to her."

"And if she's not there?"

"That's her place, dancing is her thing. She's going to show up at some point, and I'll keep going until she does."

"From playboy to stalker. Jesus, I never thought I'd see the day."

"Relentless is more like it."

"For someone who said Kauai was a big island and you

were going to find out just how many women were on it, you've certainly taken quite the one-eighty, haven't you?"

He wasn't wrong.

I had flipped.

But she was worth it.

And even though I didn't know certain details about her, like the things she enjoyed doing outside of dancing and why she'd chosen to buy that black dress and what she was majoring in and the job she currently had, I was hooked.

And I wanted those answers.

And I wanted even more.

I crossed my legs, staring across the pool, ignoring the chicks dressed in bikinis, doing late afternoon swims, and I took in the view of the light-blue ocean. "Camden, I don't know what the fuck is happening to me."

There was noise in the background, and then he eventually replied, "Jenner just walked in. Do you want to hear it from the both of us or just me?"

Before I could respond, Jenner voiced, "Who are you talking to?"

I could tell Camden had placed the call on speakerphone.

"Macon," Camden said to him.

"*Ahhh*, my pussy-whipped friend. How's it going, man?" Jenner shot back.

"Fuck, you're an asshole."

I knew they'd all been talking about me behind my back. They couldn't help themselves. My brothers had been doing the same, sending me texts that gave me shit about being whipped, which I wasn't.

I just wanted her.

And I couldn't fucking have her.

"What are we telling him?" Jenner asked Camden. "That

he's ready to be tied down, like we suspected all along, or that he's pussy drunk—which he thinks he is, but we know better."

"Who's pussy drunk?" a new voice asked.

"Macon thinks he is, but he's really in love," Camden responded.

"Macon, my fucking man," the new voice said.

Dominick.

The eldest Dalton. Quite possibly the cockiest too.

"I'm going to tell you the same thing I said to the guys that night at the club," Dominick continued. "No pussy-drunk dude leaves a group of fellas, celebrating a bachelor party, to run across the dance floor, like a lovesick fool, just to get laid. Not when he gets laid five nights out of seven. And then proceeds to talk about her for the rest of the evening without giving a single detail about what happened. Only a dude who's whipped does that."

"And by whipped," Camden said, "he means in love."

"Jesus Christ," I groaned, thinking it was a bad idea that I'd called my best friend. "You guys really believe you're a bunch of relationship experts, don't you?"

"We're right," Jenner pressed. "And you know we're right."

I sat up, my feet falling to the pool deck while I drained the rest of my glass. "Right about what?"

"That you're in love with her."

That word hit me.

Hard.

Because I didn't know what it meant.

What it felt like.

What it even looked like.

All I knew was that I couldn't get that gorgeous woman out of my head.

And I didn't want to.

"I feel things for her, yeah," I admitted. "And I'm trying to hang out with her, but she's not giving me the opportunity."

"So, make the opportunity," Dominick said.

I didn't want to ask the question. I didn't want to inflate their egos any more since they already thought they knew everything. But these guys had more experience with relationships than I'd had, and maybe they'd thought of something I hadn't.

I squinted my eyes closed, hoping I wouldn't regret this. "And how do you suggest I do that?"

"You're Macon fucking Spade," Jenner said. "You find her. You lay the groundwork. And you make her yours."

EIGHT

Brooklyn

"Housekeeping," I called once I knocked on the door of Macon's suite, following the protocol even though I knew he wasn't inside. I waited a few seconds and knocked again. "Housekeeping."

Two attempts were required before we went into any room.

When I still got no response, I waved my key card in front of the lock and opened the door. I'd been stalking his suite since I'd arrived at work, secretly keeping tabs on him. Since he'd left about thirty minutes ago—dressed in business clothes, his beard trimmed, his neck shaved, a laptop bag hanging across his shoulder—I assumed that even if his meeting was short, I'd still have enough time to tidy things up in there.

I left my cart in the hallway, propping the door open with a wedge, and I grabbed the supplies I needed before I headed for his bedroom. I started with the bed, straightening the sheets and pulling up the comforter, positioning the pillows and decorative ones. I then wiped down both nightstands, my note still sitting in the center of the one on his—a side I only knew about because I'd spent the night in here.

As soon as the thought entered my head, I forced it out.

I tried to keep my brain busy with other things—the number of rooms I needed to get through before I could go home, the homework I had to finish before I went to bed, the dress I had to wash before I could go to the club again.

But zoning out toward those topics was almost impossible.

Because the entire room smelled of his cologne—a scent that was earthy and woodsy, like a spicy bergamot with a smoky nutmeg. And every time I inhaled, I recalled a memory of us.

One that featured his hands.

His lips.

His body.

Stop, Brooklyn.

I shook my head, hurrying into the en suite, immediately catching sight of the shower and the glass walls that encapsulated it.

The same walls he'd held me against while I was in his arms. The ones where, while I had been pressed against them, he'd thrust into me with all his power and speed, making me scream the loudest I ever had.

Good God.

I squirted some cleaner across the outside, running my squeegee from top to bottom, and I did the same to the inside. I didn't realize I'd been holding my breath until I reached the double sinks and my lungs felt like they were going to burst. I sucked in the air and scrubbed the counter and the hardware and across each bowl. And once everything was sparkling, I returned to the bedroom, and as I was passing through, on my way to the cart, the bed was what grabbed my attention this time.

Even though I'd already been in here, the memories were still swirling, hitting even harder.

It seemed like seconds ago when we were on this bed.

That we were tearing at the sheets and comforter—and at each other.

That he spread me across the giant king.

That he used his mouth and tongue to cover every inch of my body.

I wished Malia, my coworker, and I were still on good terms. I would do anything to switch floors with her so I could make a bed that I hadn't been fucked on.

I needed to get out of here; this room was too much.

The images, no matter what I tried to do, wouldn't leave my head.

And it was those details and each of the moments we'd spent together that were making me believe we were perfect for one another.

When I knew we weren't.

But they were strong enough to make me reach into my pocket and pull out my phone, bringing up my Contacts, where I clicked on his name.

Two days ago, he'd dropped me off at my car, and I almost deleted his number. I just didn't want to be tempted to reach out.

For some reason, I hadn't done either yet.

But my thumb was hovering over those ten digits right now

...

Why haven't I pressed down on the screen to call him?

But why would I? What would I even say?

Would he understand how badly I needed him for another escape?

But why would I want to strengthen our connection when nothing is ever going to happen between us?

Back and forth—that was my brain.

On repeat.

I was just grateful I hadn't given him my number so I could be the one to decide, the one who held all the power.

So I could remind myself that I had nothing in common with him, that he was leaving Kauai in a few months.

That he had more money than God and I was the maid who just cleaned his room—something that didn't upset me. I was proud of myself and the path I'd taken and all my accomplishments, but that didn't change the fact that we came from opposite sides of the track.

A track that needed to stay nestled in the middle of us.

And there was absolutely no reason to debate those wild thoughts.

My mind was made up.

Plus, I couldn't waste any more minutes, standing here, staring at his bed, fantasizing about nonsense. If this room took me too long to clean, it would set me behind and send me into overtime, which the hotel wouldn't pay, so I'd end up working for free.

And I couldn't afford that.

I exited out of my Contacts, darkened the screen, and shoved the phone back into my pocket. I emptied his trash and changed out his towels, keeping my head down the whole time. The final step was grabbing the vacuum from the cart and driving it over the bedroom floor and across the tiles in the living room, wiping down the surfaces as I made my way to the door.

Once I closed it behind me, I moved to the next suite.

But my mind wasn't any kinder in here.

My entire head was filled with Macon.

I didn't know how to purge him from my body. Maybe I could delete his number or schedule a time with him where the two of us could talk and I could ask him to stop coming to the club to look for me.

Would he even listen?

Would his charming ways convince me to go to the hotel with him?

Would a third session go down and I'd find myself in even deeper?

All I knew was that I couldn't have this man in my life. He was too dangerous—today certainly proved that. Still, something felt unsettled.

Unfinished.

And it was inside me.

A pulsing that throbbed in the spots where he had licked so expertly.

I wanted another escape.

No.

I was done—with him, with this mental angst.

Ignoring everything that was preventing me from being speedy and efficient, I focused on the rest of the rooms that had been assigned to me, and as soon as I finished, I hurried into the employee locker room. I changed into my regular clothes and draped my bag over my shoulder.

Normally, I would go out through the employee entrance and take the shuttle to the lot where we had to park a quarter of a mile off-site. But this morning, I had been running late, needing that extra twenty minutes of sleep, and I didn't have time to park where we were assigned, or I would have been dinged for being tardy. So, I'd left my car by the front of the hotel.

Something we weren't allowed to do.

Which also meant I had to exit through the lobby. If I was caught, I'd be written up.

Again.

Just to be on the safe side, I took the baseball hat out of my bag—the one I used whenever I was in my car since my air-conditioning was broken and I couldn't stand the open windows making my hair fly into my face. I secured the cap over my head, lowering the brim as far as it would go. And right before I left, I peeked at the full-length mirror by the restrooms, making sure the look was as inconspicuous as I needed it to be.

With my face this covered, even if I ran into someone I knew personally, they would have a hard time recognizing me.

Still, I needed to be quick and unseen, so I rushed down the long hallway, taking the stairs to the ground floor, and I checked in both directions to make sure there weren't any executive-level staff around. When I was sure there wasn't any, I walked past reception and through the lobby, the beautiful windows that showed the beach outside, and just as my stare dragged back toward the exit, something in the center caught my eye.

A man sitting at the bar.

With an unmistakable broadness and bulging muscles and dark hair and a thick beard that could only belong to one guy.

Macon Spade.

Shit.

But it wasn't my fear of him seeing me that made me stop. It was the woman who was sitting next to him and their close-ness that prevented my feet from taking another step.

My stomach began to bubble as I took in the way her hand was resting on his arm, how her thumb stroked the patch of hair that was there, how their faces were only six inches apart.

She was practically on top of him.

Petting him.

And he wasn't telling her not to or removing her hand.

That meant he was enjoying it.

Encouraging it.

Hell, maybe he'd even instigated it.

This was not the kind of guy who wanted to settle down. This was the kind of guy who would break me.

And if he saw my heart, if I ever dared to show it to him, he'd shred it.

Why was everything in me suddenly aching?

Why were my hands clenching?

Why did I want to rush over to them and call his ass out for the things he'd said to me just two days ago?

The dinner he'd wanted to spend together, the breakfast.

How I was different.

How he'd been a playboy for such a long time, his desire changing when he'd met me.

Yet I was looking at *this*.

At them.

At the possibility of him asking her out for dinner. Of him bringing her up to his room, where he'd fuck her on the bed I'd just made.

Of him saying the same words to her that he'd recently said to me.

Ugh.

I hated him for owning my thoughts today. For making me question my decision. For the war he'd created in my head.

And I hated myself for even thinking about calling him.

I took out my phone and pulled up my Contacts, giving one final glance toward Macon and his new girl toy, and on the way out to my car, I deleted his number.

NINE

Macon

"Impressive as hell," Walker Weston said as he stood within the restaurant wing of our hotel, wearing a hard hat, like his three other brothers and sister and me, but with a tablet tucked under his arm.

The Weston family had flown in today to check the progress on the latest build-out of their steak house, Charred, and the club, Musik, they were constructing next to it. They'd come during the very beginning stages when the entire building was still being framed. The progress so far wasn't just impressive; it was over the fucking top.

This hotel was going to be a damn masterpiece, and this wing would be no different.

Even though Walker and his siblings had become friends with my brothers and me—the result of many business deals and build-outs they'd done with our brand—they were still here for one reason, and it wasn't to go surfing. This conversation would be full of pressing questions, I suspected.

"Isn't it?" I replied. "Our nicest property, in my opinion."

"You wouldn't be biased at all?" Eden, the youngest and only woman in the family, asked. She was also the shortest, but where she lacked in height by at least a foot, she made up in personality.

She was one fierce chick.

"Nah," I responded. "Not even a little."

"Didn't think so." She laughed.

"You know, Hawaii has been a long time coming," Walker continued. "I was pushing your uncle for fucking years to make this happen. When he finally pulled the trigger on the land"—he released a mouthful of air, like a deflating balloon—"I became one happy man."

There was a haze of gray that ran along the sides of Walker's high fade. A dude who could rock any color, and the women would still flock to him.

He was as much of a playboy as me.

"That makes two of us," I told him.

"And because our expectations are so high for this location, we've gone all out with the interior design," Hart said. He glanced at the arch that was being placed above the entrance to the restaurant, his green gaze eventually shifting back to mine. "Wait until you see the custom three-dimensional ceiling we're having installed next week. It'll be unlike anything you've ever seen."

"I'll take photos and send them your way in case you don't want to fly in again so soon," I offered.

"As long as it's before preseason starts, we'll be back," Beck said.

He'd been playing in the NHL since he'd graduated from college. Because he was in the off-season, he was able to tag along. This was the time of the year when he was able to be much more active in the family business, but during the season, he was a silent partner and their financial backer.

"And if I can't make it, I'm sure my siblings wouldn't mind returning to paradise for a couple of days."

"I surely wouldn't," Colson said, pounding Beck's fist. He was the most laid-back; he'd rather spend his days on the golf course or the beach than dress in a suit and head into their corporate office.

If Colson was driven by anything, it was pussy.

Eden rolled her eyes. "Let's stop puttering around and get to the point here." She glared at her brothers before looking at me. "Realistically, how many weeks is the construction behind schedule?"

She'd never been one to lie back and take it, letting the company run itself or for her brothers to carry a heavier load. Arguably, she worked the hardest; she was the most innovative of them all, certainly the feistiest.

"It's not behind schedule," I replied, adjusting my hard hat so I could see her better. "We're going to make the deadline."

A part of me—a rather large part—wished that weren't the case. Although I'd get the wrath from my uncle, it would mean I would get to stay on Kauai a little longer.

And there was only one reason I would want that to happen.

A reason that was haunting me now, even as I stood here.

Goddamn it, I was in the middle of a business meeting, and I still couldn't stop thinking of Brooklyn.

Or why she hadn't gotten in touch with me yet.

"I don't believe you." Eden glanced up toward the roof, across each of the walls, and down the west end of the wing, where it led to the lobby.

But where her focus returned to was the dome above us. It had just been finished last week, the glass fully installed and cleaned. Given that it was now late afternoon, the sun wasn't directly above us, but that didn't deter us from seeing the beauty of the cloudless sky. We didn't want our guests to have to leave this area after dinner to take a stroll outside to see the stars, so we provided a way where they only had to glance up.

"Because the last two build-outs we've done," she continued, "the opening was delayed by over a month—let's not forget that."

"Were those build-outs with me?" I eyed her down, letting that fact set in. "I run things much differently than other project managers. When I give you a date, which I have, I stick to it."

A conversation I'd had with the Westons prior to them signing their contract. I'd promised a completion date because without the hotel open, the restaurant wasn't allowed to operate, and that meant they wouldn't be generating any revenue. That was a promise I wouldn't renege on.

"But just like your brothers, you're faced with the same issues where you can't force your crew to work harder than they already are, and that right there can change the completion date," Eden countered.

I chuckled. "You're right about that. A human can only work so many hours, and that caps production. So, what I've done is hire two crews, covering both shifts. When one leaves, the other comes in. I run my construction around the clock, and that's why my hotel will be finished on time. Possibly even a week or so early."

A smile peeked across her lips—but it was only a peek.

"I knew you'd like that answer," I said to her.

She crossed her arms over her chest. "Yes, it's true, I appreciate the importance of a deadline. In the construction industry, it's rare, and I have a hard time tolerating any delays. But oftentimes, like the work we've done with your brothers, I don't have a choice."

"We have that in common," I told her. "I have zero patience for anything or anyone who's late."

"Which is why we need to do more hotels with you, Macon." Walker clasped my shoulder after he moved in next to me. "Where's the next location?"

The question I was constantly asked. That bit of information was so under wraps that only our executive team knew the answer.

Of course, nothing had been purchased. Cooper was still looking for land, meeting with realtors, discussing our requirements, passing up on opportunities that just hadn't been right.

But that search was taking place in Banff—a spot my uncle had wanted to build in for years.

"Here's what I can tell you," I said to the group. "It's Cooper's project, not mine."

Hart smiled. "*Ahhh*, my man, Cooper. Looks like I have someone to take out to dinner when we return to LA."

I chuckled. "Court his ass. He likes that."

"And that's just what I'm good at," Hart replied.

"Why is it Cooper's and not yours?" Eden asked.

A detail I wasn't surprised she had inquired about. Whenever we worked together, I noticed she always wanted the full picture—not just the scenery that was inside the frame, but the weather that was above the photo and the kind of soil that was below it.

"I'll be tackling a whole new beast once I finish things here," I said to her. I shifted my weight, shoving my hands into my pants pockets.

"Anything we might be interested in?" Beck asked.

The money guy. I wasn't shocked at all that he'd want first dibs if my project could be lucrative for his company.

"Maybe," I replied. "We're revamping a handful of our

older properties. Streamlining processes, doing some needed remodeling. Possibly making additions to the existing structures. If space opens for more restaurants, you know I'll be in touch. But for now, that'll be my role for the next year."

"How can you make more money? Always the question on every owner's mind," Beck replied.

I nodded. "And in older facilities, where things are already working so well, it's a hard task to conquer, but I'm determined to find ways while saving us money at the same time."

"You know, I wouldn't hate it if you made room for us at the Beverly Hills location, which I believe is your oldest resort, so I'm assuming that'll be one of your projects." Walker's grip strengthened. "If you can make that happen, there could be a nice little bonus coming your way."

This wasn't the first time I'd been offered money. Other vendors in different avenues—from bedding to cutlery to beverage brands—had done the same.

I didn't need their money, nor did I want it.

I had plenty of my own.

And no amount would persuade me to do a business deal that wasn't right for the Spades—our company meant far too much to me for that.

I smiled at my friend. "If a spot becomes available—and that's a small *if*—you'll have the same shot as all the other restaurateurs we do business with. But what I can say is, if that happens, you'd better prepare one hell of a pitch. Everyone wants Beverly Hills. My team is going to want to see why we should pick you."

"Nicely done." Eden clapped. "That just made me respect you more."

I winked at her. "Now, if you had offered a 1962 Ferrari 250 GTO, my answer could have been different."

"The one that recently sold for over forty-eight mil?" Hart bellowed.

"That's the one," I confirmed.

"I call bullshit," Beck countered. "Like me, you're a man who enjoys buying his own toys." He paused. "I'm right, aren't I?"

I nodded again. "You are correct."

"So, you're saying a few mil on a check made out directly to you won't do the trick?" Hart pushed.

I smiled at the whole group. "Not even if you add another zero—or two."

The second I wrapped up dinner with the Westons, I drove to the club, parking the Range Rover in the last available slot, and headed for the entrance. I hadn't told them I was going out; I'd told them I was going to bed instead. The last thing I wanted, in case Brooklyn was here, was to entertain a group of five and not be able to speak to her.

It had been four long, fucking miserable nights since I'd seen her.

Since she'd been at the club.

Since my hands had touched her body.

I hated that Camden was right, that I was stalking this place, but I had no choice. I refused to give up, and coming here was the only place I knew to look for her.

Because I frequented so often, I'd gotten to know the bouncers who worked the door. Instead of waiting in the long line that wrapped around the entire building, I walked straight up to the front and shook the bouncer's hand with a hundred-dollar bill tucked into my palm, and after the money was in his possession, I went right inside.

Within a few seconds, my body began to pound, my hands were sweating, and my eyes darted around the interior like I was watching a fucking tennis match.

She was here.

I didn't know because I'd spotted her that quickly—there were too many people, and the entire dance floor was packed; I knew because the air was different when Brooklyn was present.

I studied each of the stages until my eyes fell upon her.

Fuck me.

She was along the edge of the room, near the section where I'd seen her from the VIP area the first night I was here, wearing the same skintight black dress. Her long, dark hair cascaded down her back like a goddamn waterfall. Her hips swayed as if she were in a boat in high chop. And even from all the way over here, with my zoomed-out view of her face and body and much too far away to get a whiff of her smell, my dick was already so fucking hard.

Not a single woman in this club could compare.

Not in the way they looked or danced.

She was perfection, and they couldn't compete.

I weaved through the dancers, around the stages, through the patrons until I was positioned beneath her platform. I gripped the highest rung I could reach and moved in as close as I could get without climbing the ladder. She was, once again, at a height that allowed the most sensual view, my eyes meeting a pair of dark panties that unfortunately covered her pussy. But the creaminess of her inner thighs and her lean, toned legs made up for it.

"How did I know that when I sensed someone looking up my dress, it would be you?" Her eyes finally met mine as she glared at me from her perch.

I couldn't help but smile. "You haven't called or texted."

"And you still dragged your ass here. I'd think you'd have

taken the hint by now." She turned her back to me and danced in the opposite direction.

"Or I assumed you liked the chase."

"You assumed wrong," she said over her shoulder.

The area we were in was almost like a corner pocket; the music was not as loud, so neither of us had to yell.

I gazed at her heart-shaped ass, imagining what it would feel like if I sank my cock into it. "Then, why was your skin flushed when you caught me looking up your dress?"

She whipped her head in my direction, her hands gripping her hips. "I'm hot."

"And that's the same reason why your pupils grew?"

"Macon ... you've got to be kidding me ..."

"And why you're breathing harder now than you were a few minutes ago. That's how long I've been watching you, Brooklyn, so I would know."

Her eyelids narrowed, but she still refused to turn the front of her body toward me. "I—"

"And if you knew I'd come, then why are you here? There are other clubs—"

"This is *my* club." She faced me. "I've been coming here long before you. The real question is, why are *you* here?"

"Because I can't stop thinking about you." I pulled at the collar of my shirt, the heat from her body making me fucking sweat. "Because I want you. Because the two times I've had you weren't nearly enough."

"Bullshit."

"Ah, she's sassier than normal tonight." I reached up to where she was standing to graze my fingers across her ankle, but she moved out of the way, not allowing me to. "You know, from the way you were screaming in the shower, I really thought you were going to reach out to me to give you another round."

Her lips bared her teeth, like she was about to hunt. "I don't need you to make me scream. I can do that on my own."

"I don't doubt that. But it's not as good as me." I licked across my bottom lip, reminding her of the strength and power of my tongue. "You remember just how good it is, and I know you want it again."

Seconds passed before she said, "What I don't want is a guy like you." Her throat bobbed as she swallowed. "I feel like I've already made myself clear. Please listen to me this time." She nodded toward the exit. "You can march your butt back to the hotel or LA, whichever you choose. I just don't want you here, and I don't want you around me."

There was something she'd said that hit me the hardest.

Something I needed her to answer.

"A guy like me?" I waited. "What the hell does that mean?" I paused again. "I told you who I was before and how I was with women—I didn't hide that, if that's what you're even referring to. But I also told you that since I met you, something inside me has changed, and I want more."

"I don't believe that."

So, I was right—this was about my old ways.

"Why? I've given you no reason to doubt me." When she said nothing, I added, "I've come here every night, Brooklyn, waiting for you to show up. If I just wanted to fuck you, do you think I'd bother doing that? I'd find a chick at the hotel to bang. I don't want that, and I don't want anyone else. I want you."

She moved to the edge of the stage. "You're going to try to convince me that you're not the biggest flirt? That women don't drop at your feet? That you don't fall for their advances? Because that's something I don't believe."

I rubbed my teeth over my lip. "They don't drop, that would be a little extreme."

"Asshole." She rolled her eyes. "You know what I mean."

"Women tend to be a little on the more forward side with me, yes."

Where the hell was all this coming from? These were accusations she hadn't thrown at me before. It hadn't seemed like she even cared enough to. But now, here, she was suddenly questioning whether I was the man I'd said I was. If she had these questions, why hadn't she called me? Why had she avoided me? Why had she let these feelings simmer to the point where they obviously reached a boil?

"Women have treated me that way my entire adult life. Sometimes, I bite. Sometimes, I don't. I can tell you that since we started hooking up, I haven't been with anyone else. I haven't wanted to." I waited for her to say something. "I'm not lying to you, Brooklyn. I wouldn't lie. And I realize those are just words, that I can't exactly prove it to you, but I hope you believe me." I looked toward the entrance of the club and chuckled. "The bouncers over there will confirm I've been coming here every evening for you. I've been lining their pockets in hundreds just so I didn't have to wait in that line. Tell me, what fucking idiot would do that if he felt nothing?"

She remained quiet, but continued to stare at me, almost like she was looking at me for the first time. "What do you want, Macon?"

I wanted to fly her to Napa for a long weekend. I wanted to buy her fifty new black dresses.

But I got the sense that I would be hit with no after no.

So, I started small and said, "I want to take you out for dinner."

Those gorgeous tits rose as she filled her lungs. "If I decline, will you keep coming here to look for me?"

"Even if you say yes, I'm going to keep coming here."

I earned myself a small grin, and she immediately shook her head as if she was trying to force it off her face.

"I've never met anyone like you."

"And I've never met anyone like you. That's why I want this. Why I want you." I grabbed the stage next to her feet. "When can I take you out?"

She shrugged.

I didn't want to let this moment go. It seemed that I was warming her up just a little, and if we spent any time apart, that could change.

"How about now?" I suggested.

"Like *now*, now?"

I nodded. "There's a twenty-four-hour diner not far from the hotel."

I was met with more silence until, "Would you take no as an answer?"

My smile grew. "Fuck no."

"Then, I guess ... let's go."

TEN

Brooklyn

What am I doing?

That was the question that had been repeating in my head since I'd followed Macon to the diner, taking a seat across from him in the booth. My thought was that if I had my car, I wouldn't be persuaded to go to the hotel with him afterward since I certainly couldn't pull up to the front and take the risk of my car and me being recognized by one of the bellhops.

It was one thing to hide my face and keep my eyes low, like I'd done the last time. It was a whole other thing to hand my keys to someone and give them my last name—a requirement of all guests and visitors.

That was why driving here was the safest option.

But I was learning, when it came to Macon Spade, there was no safe option.

How many times had I told myself tonight, while I was putting on my black dress and swiping gloss over my lips, that I wouldn't speak to him? That I wouldn't leave with him? That I was most definitely not going to allow him to touch me?

As I'd jumped off the stage and into his arms, I'd broken every one of those rules.

And as I gazed at him from across the table, I was breaking another.

I was thinking about what it would feel like if he leaned across the space between us and put his lips on me.

How they would make me forget.

How they would send tingles through my whole body that would be even stronger than the ones that were already fluttering.

"Are you hungry?"

His voice pulled me away from the piles of regret I had been sorting through.

As he stared at me from over his menu, the light in here so bright and morning-like, I could even see the pores in his skin. All it did was magnify how hot he was. The deepness of his emerald eyes. The thickness of his soft red lips. The darkness of his coarse, coffee-colored beard. The squareness of his jaw, the broadness of his neck, the way his shirt hugged his chest and shoulders, showing off the ripped muscles beneath.

Brooklyn, you need to stop.

You need to look away.

I swallowed, reminding myself that he'd asked a question, and quickly responded, "No. I'm not really hungry."

"Perfect. That means the best eating is about to go down."

While he licked across his lips, dragging my attention there, I forced myself to look at the menu. "What do you mean?"

I hadn't even bothered to scan the menu when the hostess placed it in front of me. I had no intention of ordering anything, and I still didn't as I took in the photos and descriptions, waiting for my stomach to react to something other than him.

"Haven't you noticed that when you go out to eat when you're not hungry, you order the most random things?"

Go out to eat when you're not hungry?

I didn't do that. What would even be the point? That sounded like a lot of wasted money.

"Who goes out to eat when they're not hungry?" I huffed.

"Come on. I know you've done it." He waited for me to respond, and when I didn't, he continued, "How about when you join a friend at a restaurant, but you accidentally ate an hour before? Or out of boredom? Or when you've got to fill yourself up after a long workout, but still have the shakes, and you're not necessarily ready to eat?"

I finally looked up, instantly wishing I hadn't because my eyes met his beautiful smile. "Sure, I've snacked out of boredom, but the others, I can't say I've experienced those."

"Then, you'll see what I mean in a few minutes." The grin on his face changed. He'd had it since we sat down. But now, it was larger, wider, deeper even.

All it did was make me mad.

Mad that I wasn't mentally ready to take this on.

Mad that I was so attracted to him.

It was that feeling that made me say, "Our differences are adding up so fast that I've lost count of all the check marks."

"That's a good thing."

"Why?"

His smile dimmed halfway, but the corner of his lip lifted, showing his perfectly straight white teeth. "I don't want to hang out with a woman who's just like me. What would I learn from her? What would we talk about? All we'd do was agree, and there's no fun in that. I don't want to spend hours upon hours trading yeses. That's a waste of my time."

I folded my hands together to stop them from fidgeting. "You'd rather argue?"

"I'd rather have a conversation that had meaningful points so I could see a side I hadn't thought of."

Macon didn't seem like he would be an easy person to argue with. Although he was sweet with me, I saw an extremely dominant side. Like when it came to work, I sensed it would be his way or no way.

"Are you telling me you're open-minded?" I asked.

He laughed. "No. There's one way to do things, and that's my way, but I'm still willing to listen, and if the opposing side is compelling enough, I might be persuaded." He pointed at the top of the menu. "Tell me ... what's your flavor?"

"Sushi." I laughed. "I guess that's not a flavor, is it?"

"When it comes to a milkshake, I would hope not." He cleared his throat. "Everyone has a go-to. What's yours?"

"Coffee."

"I can hang with that. But if you'd said vanilla, you'd have had to sell me on it—and that's probably an example of something that, regardless of your fight, I couldn't be persuaded on."

Even a simple conversation was full of weight when it came to him.

"Is vanilla too simple for you?"

He rolled up the sleeves of his button-down, the veins in his forearms popping, the muscle corded and defined. "It's like celery. It's just so bland."

I whispered, "I hate vanilla."

"Everyone should hate vanilla."

Before I could even think of a response, the waitress appeared with a small pad in her hand. "What can I get you?"

"Two vanilla milkshakes, please." I smiled.

And Macon laughed. "She's joking." He winked at me, appreciating my humor. "A coffee milkshake for the lady, and I'll take chocolate. We'll also go with the appetizer platter."

"Easy enough." She collected one menu. "I'll leave the other menu in case you want to order more."

Once she was gone, I voiced, "Who orders an entire platter of food when I just told you I wasn't hungry?"

"Once you see it, you'll be tempted. You'll take a bite, and you'll want more. And more." The smile was back, but just halfway, showing enough of his teeth that I watched him nip his bottom lip. "The same way you've been doing to me since the first time I saw you. I've smelled. I've tasted. And now, I want more." He let those words simmer through me, and as he turned quiet, the look in his eyes became more dominant than they had been all night.

There was something different about the way he was gazing at me now versus all the other times.

If I could see inside his head, which I wanted to, I was positive it would be so busy that I wouldn't be able to follow all the different streams of thought.

"I want to know something."

I'd suspected as much. I'd felt something coming.

I took a deep breath, trying to prepare myself for the unexpected. "Okay."

"And I want you to be honest with me."

An immense amount of pressure began to push against my chest, causing my legs to straighten and cross again. "Ask me."

"Why did it feel like something happened between us that I'm unaware of, and that's why you were so standoffish when I approached you at the club?"

"Unaware of?"

I knew exactly what he meant. I just needed to buy myself time to come up with an appropriate response.

If I told him why I was angry, then I'd have to admit that I'd seen him in the bar with that woman, that it'd looked like they were seconds away from hooking up. And then I'd have to explain why I had been there and all about my job—something I just didn't want to do. I wasn't trying to hide my employment; I wasn't embarrassed by it. I was proud of the fact that out of the forty-seven housekeepers, there were only three other women who had been there longer than I had. That I was about to celebrate my four-year work anniversary.

But something was stopping me from telling him. Like the fact that the dreamy suite he'd taken me to on our second night together was in actuality the room I cleaned for a living. It made the moment feel almost tainted.

Maybe I just wasn't ready to give him more.

Maybe I was worried he'd judge me.

Or maybe I was concerned that if I let him in further, it would be hard to maintain this edge. Because even as I looked at him now, knowing what he was capable of, it was impossibly difficult to force away what I really wanted.

And that was him.

"When I left you in the parking lot that morning after you spent the night with me, things were good. You took my number. You kissed me good-bye. I assumed, at least from the way you were acting, that you'd be in touch. That didn't happen, and on top of it all, you acted as if you didn't even want me to talk to you. To go from one extreme to the other, something had to have happened." His brows pushed together. "What was it?"

"It's just the timing of it all. It's wrong—I've told you that. My life is muddy and—"

"That could be a reason you don't want us together, but it's not the reason you were extra spicy this evening." He leaned over the table, moving closer to me. "But just for a second, let's talk about timing. Because you weren't bothered by the timing when I was stripping you naked, or bothered when we spent hours fucking in my hotel room, or bothered when you came in my shower—twice."

"You invited me into your shower. I didn't just come in."

"You misheard me, Brooklyn. I said you *came* in my shower twice. I wasn't talking about why or how you'd gotten into my bathroom."

My face instantly reddened.

"Let's go back to my question ... what happened?"

I glanced at my hands, my fingers moving like I was going to crack them, but I didn't pull hard enough to make the sound.

I couldn't tell him it was a gut feeling I had; that was stupid. *What can I say?*

What can I ...

"I came to the hotel the other day to talk to you." *Have I lost it? Am I really going to tell him that I made the effort to come see him? Shit, it's too late now.* "As I was walking through the lobby toward the elevators, I saw you in the bar with another woman."

"You saw me"—he paused, rubbing a hand through his hair—"and you assumed, and that's the reason you treated me that way?"

"I assumed nothing. You were in her face—"

"Let's get one thing straight. She was in *my* face."

"Her hand was on your arm—"

"Which fell from my arm once I declined her advances and stood to leave, but not before I told her I was going to spend the evening talking to my wife. A description I used for you, Brooklyn. Because since the second you came into my life, I've no longer wanted to touch any other woman." His head dropped, his eyes staying on me. "But I couldn't call you—you hadn't given me your number. So, I called my best friend, Camden, instead as I walked away from her and sat outside by the pool."

I didn't know what to say.

"I understand." He took a breath. "You saw us together, you didn't like it, and your brain filled in the missing pieces. But what you could have done was come into the bar. Or if that made you uncomfortable, you could have called and told me, and we could have spoken about it."

"We're talking about it now."

He turned quiet after my statement and then laughed. "I understand you're defending yourself, but there was no reason anything before this moment needed to take place. We could have come straight here—to this moment—so the both of us were satisfied and you understood exactly what you had seen." He paused, his stare now taking in my whole face. "What I find interesting is that you were even bothered. For someone who keeps preaching about time and muddiness, why would you be upset if I was talking to another woman?"

And there it was—the hole I now found myself in.

"You don't want me, but you don't want me with anyone else." His finger brushed across my hand. "You can't have it both ways, Brooklyn."

His smile was eating at me.

So was the tone of his voice.

The knowing look in his eyes.

I couldn't win this.

And he was right about everything he'd said. What I'd seen clearly bothered me. I should have just spoken to him about it. But in handling it the way I had, I'd not only proven that I was interested in him, but I'd also told him I'd come to the hotel to speak to him. Something I wouldn't have done unless I cared.

His lips pursed. "You've got nothing to say now?"

"Macon—" On the verge of saying something extremely sassy in response, my voice was cut off as the waitress appeared with our milkshakes, setting them down in front of us.

"Your appetizer should be out in a few minutes," she said and left us again.

I was grateful for the interruption and reached for mine, chugging a few sips' worth. I was just swallowing when I heard the beep of my phone.

I'd forgotten that I'd brought my bag inside the diner, and I slipped my hand inside and grabbed my cell—something I hadn't looked at since I had gone into the club much earlier this evening.

The beep was a text from Clem, asking if I wanted her to bring home any food from the bar since her shift was about to end.

My reply let her know I wasn't home, and as I was slipping the phone back into my bag, a notification on the screen caught my attention. This one was from my professor. The one who had been on vacation when I missed my deadline due to the broken laptop cord.

"Everything all right?" Macon asked.

I finished skimming the professor's email and put the phone away, sighing. "Yeah. Just a text from my sister and an email from my professor."

"How many siblings do you have?"

I held the straw, but didn't take a drink. "Two sisters."

"Are they on Kauai or The Big Island?"

"Here. I live with them."

"You live with them," he emphasized. "That must make things interesting."

"Always." I took a drink, groaning at how good it tasted, and I immediately took another gulp. "Not that I don't want to live with them, but once I graduate, I'm hoping to make enough where I can get my own place. I just need space and quietness."

"Are you the youngest?"

I nodded.

"I am too," he told me. "I have two older brothers, and as much as I love their asses, I couldn't live with them again."

"Most days, it's fine. It's just a tiny place, and we're *always* in each other's way. Someone is *always* in the bathroom. Someone is *always* using my computer—and even breaking it, like the other day." My heart ached from my professor's email. Enough so that I found myself saying, "I turned in a paper late, all due to a little mishap that had been an accident, but it still shouldn't have happened. My sister feels awful about it. Anyway, my professor just got back to me. Even though the tardiness earned me a failing grade, he still read it and told me it was the best written paper in the whole class."

"Fuck."

I nodded again. "I know."

"What did you write it on?"

I stirred the thick shake, lifting the straw out and licking across the bottom of it. "My job." I'd answered too quickly. I hadn't really thought about the consequences of my response when I should have considered that Macon would only ask more questions. "It was for one of my business classes, so I took a long, hard look at my department. In my opinion, they run it all wrong. There are so many things I would change that would save the company money, time. Far less labor. Six Sigma kind of stuff—which I plan to get certified in once I graduate."

Within a month of taking the job at the hotel, I could see the changes that needed to be made within the department. While I had researched ways to present this information to my boss, I had come across Six Sigma—a type of management practices and methodologies that were used within businesses to increase efficiency and lower the chance of waste. That was what sparked my interest and why I'd be pursuing a certification the moment I graduated.

"You don't say ..." At some point, he'd pushed back, but

now, he was leaning across the table again. "Tell me more. I want to hear everything."

I laughed nervously. "I feel like I'm on an interview."

"You might be. Keep going."

"Well, I'm a business major. I try to look at things from a business and owner perspective and what's best for everyone involved. Without happy employees, things aren't going to run the way you want them to or the way you need them to regardless of how much cost you're trying to cut."

"Give me an example of how you'd use Six Sigma at your job."

The example was the housekeeping department at my hotel. I'd done a complete analysis of how they operated, how many shifts and employees were on at all times. The amount of supplies used. How I could save them money by tweaking things.

But these were things I wouldn't know unless I worked for a hotel, and that wasn't going to be mentioned tonight.

I had to pick something else—something I knew just as well.

"Let's say we're talking about a restaurant-slash-bar." I glanced around the diner. "Not a place like this. I'm talking about somewhere that serves alcohol and is open until one or two in the morning."

"I like where this is going."

I laughed. "It sounds like you're turned on."

"I am."

"Because I'm talking business?"

"Because you're breathing."

My eyes widened, my skin starting to prickle with sweat.

"And because you're talking business. Go on."

I pulled the shake closer and took another long drink, stopping before I got an ice cream headache. "I'm not saying it happens at every restaurant, but I'd say, at most, there's an epic amount of alcohol that either gets wasted or given away for free."

"I agree."

"As a business owner, I wouldn't be all right with that. Not when liquor and wine are top money producers with massive profit margins." The more I said, the harder he looked at me. "On the flip side, there's nothing worse than those automatic pourers that control the amount of booze allowed in each drink. They're impersonal. When a patron sees one, they think the restaurant is cheap."

"Again, I agree." He was nodding.

"Therefore, it boils down to the bartenders. If you give them an incentive, they're far more likely to care about the amount that's dispensed."

His head now turned. "You mean, a bonus?"

"Yes." I traced my thumbs down the glass, feeling the cool condensation on my skin. "When you're talking about the fruit that's served, the straws that are used, mixers, garnishes, and then you factor in the alcohol, there're many layers to it. But if you make them conscious of certain numbers, keeping them in a reasonable perimeter, giving them a monthly bonus if they maintain, say, five hundred to a thousand, that would, in the long run, be losing the business only a little while saving them a whole lot."

His head now shook. "You're fascinating."

"I could keep going."

"I want you to." His eyes narrowed as he continued to gaze at me. "So, I'm going to put you on the spot—is that all right?"

"Try me."

"Toiletries have always been something we offer in our hotels, and it's a high expense. The lotion and soap are custom-made for our brand, incorporating our signature scent. The soap, for instance, comes in small bath bars that are placed by the sinks and within the shower. All unused bars get thrown away. If a guest runs low, a new one is given. Some guests pack the bars into their suitcases, so housekeeping will leave a new one the next day, and that continues until they check out. How would you eliminate the amount of waste that goes into this practice?"

"That's easy." I smiled. "I would provide body wash instead of bars. Will guests use more squirts than they need to? Sure. But if the bottles are bolted into the shower and the wall above the sink, the guests can't take them with them. The bottles won't have to be replaced in between stays, only refilled, which eliminates most of the waste you mentioned. And if I had to guess, it's cheaper to have liquid soap manufactured than a bar because there are less steps involved, so by trading one for the other, that's also going to save you money."

He was quiet, taking in my face like he was memorizing every freckle. "With bottles bolted into the shower and sink area, won't guests find that tacky?"

"Not if it's done right. You might have to splurge on a fixture that's on the fancier side or have a product engineer design something for you. That's certainly an investment, and I obviously don't have any numbers that I can run for you, but I bet, in the long run, it would be well worth it."

"You're good."

My lips moved back into a grin. "That's because I love it. It's a passion."

He reached across the table, placing his hand over mine. "I want to know something ... what are you doing after you graduate?"

I glanced at his fingers.

Stared at them.

Felt them in every part of me.

"Applying for jobs." My voice was softer than I wanted it to be.

"Where?"

"Anywhere I can find one."

"Would you move?"

I finally looked at him. "You mean, off the island?"

"Yes."

"I'd go anywhere if it was the right opportunity."

His thumb flicked across my knuckles. "You'd be okay with leaving your family?"

I really thought about his question.

"It wouldn't be easy, but, yes, I would."

He let go of my hand and reached into his pocket, taking out his phone. He pressed the screen several times and handed it to me. "I want you to put in your contact information, and in one week, I'm going to ask you the same question—if you'd be okay with leaving your family. When I know you're one hundred percent sure and on board, I'm going to give your résumé to my HR department. Spade Hotels could desperately use someone like you, especially someone with their Six Sigma certification."

"Macon—"

"I know what you're going to say. I'm doing this because I care about you, because I want you to change your mind about us. That's not why, Brooklyn." He stalled, staring at me, each word sounding so convincing. "I have plenty of friends who are entrepreneurs. The Daltons, who own the largest law firm in LA. The Westons, who own a massive restaurant and now bar conglomerate. All I would have to do is send your information to one of them, and they'd hire you in a second. I don't want to do that, not when the Spade brand needs someone like you." He set his phone down in front of me. "We're about to take on a massive overhaul with several of our properties, looking for ways to save money, cut labor, while not losing the prestige that makes us unique. You would be perfect for that team."

My entire body was numb.

Except for my heart.

That was pounding so hard that I was positive he could hear it. "You're offering me a job?"

"I'm offering you an interview. You have to earn the job." His expression turned serious. "You have to impress the executive-level staff the same way you just impressed the hell out of me."

His phone was now in my hand, my fingers on the screen, keeping it from turning dark.

Did I want to open this door?

Did I want to let Macon in this closely?

But this was an opportunity that I'd wanted for as long as I could remember. How could I possibly give it up just because the most gorgeous man in the world—a man who had licked every inch of my body a few days ago—was offering it to me?

"What would I even wear to an interview like that?" I was mostly talking to myself. I sucked in the deepest breath. "I'm pretty certain there's nothing good enough in my closet. But still ..." My gaze lowered from his face to the phone, where I typed the ten digits, hit Save, and handed it back to him.

"Excellent decision." He shoved his phone into his pocket. "Remember, my text will come in exactly one week. That gives you plenty of time to think about everything."

ELEVEN

Macon

"I honestly never thought I'd see the day when I'd be dipping my fries into my coffee milkshake"—Brooklyn laughed—"or my mozzarella cheese sticks into ranch."

I held the small of her back as we walked out the door of the diner. With our cars parked next to each other, we headed in the same direction, halting in front of our hoods.

I turned her toward me, gazing into her eyes. This gorgeous but stubborn woman had insisted on driving here. I could have driven her back to the club—something I'd mentioned before we left—or even better, she could have left her car there and spent the night at the hotel with me. But once we'd reached the parking lot, she'd told me she wanted to drive, and I hadn't pushed the topic.

I was just glad that she'd finally agreed to come out to eat with me after playing hard to get.

"But it was delicious, wasn't it?" I didn't wait for her to

respond before I continued, "Like I told you, random eating is the best."

"There might just be a new sweet and savory combination that's become my favorite."

My hands went to her sides.

She didn't push them away, although she noticed the placement because her expression immediately changed. Her breathing did as well, speeding up as her body stiffened.

When I took a step closer, she didn't move back.

She didn't move forward either.

She stayed right where she was, waiting for what I was about to do.

What I wanted was to convince her that we were perfect for one another. That I was everything she needed.

But I suspected she already knew this.

She was scared. Unprepared.

She used timing and muddiness as her excuses.

The truth was, there was never a perfect scenario for anything. Things happened. You learned to roll with each hill you faced. As you got older, you got busier. And you attempted to find a balance despite how hard that was.

Somehow, someway, she would learn this too.

Even if I was the one who had to show her.

I held her even tighter, exhaling as I took in those beautiful eyes. "You know ... I have your number now."

She looked at my smile and began to laugh again. "Why do I have a feeling you're going to use it for reasons other than texting me that question in a week?"

"You're right." I drew her in even closer. "I'm not going to give up, Brooklyn. I want this." I licked across my lips. "I know you do too."

She wasn't speaking her thoughts, but I could hear them.

There was too much happening in her life. She didn't know how to separate work from pleasure.

But this felt good—and was that okay?

I was going to show her just how all right it was.

My hands slowly slid up her ribs and shoulders and neck and stopped at her cheeks, where I tilted her face up at me. "I want to take you home."

Her eyes closed, and I felt her take the deepest breath. "Macon ..." When her eyelids opened, she studied my stare.

"Tell me what you're thinking." When she stayed silent, I added, "Spit it out. I don't care what it sounds like, just get it off your chest."

She filled her lungs, holding in the air until she finally voiced, "My head is all over the place. It can't even form a solid thought that makes any kind of sense. And then there's my body. A body that wants you. A body that is addicted to you."

Why were those words so fucking sexy?

Especially when they were spoken in such a needy tone like hers.

"Every time I'm with you," she continued, "I unplug. I forget. I'm not filled with any stress or that overwhelming feeling that causes my chest and lungs to tighten. And then there's the flip side to that. The side that surfaced tonight with the opportunity you presented. One I've dreamed about since I started college."

"And things suddenly just got muddier."

She nodded. "I can't want you and also want to work for your company. That feels ... wrong."

My cousin, Jo, had dated our corporate lawyer, Jenner, for a while before they aired their relationship, and now, they were on the verge of getting married. Declan, one of the Daltons' top lawyers, had dated his intern and a member of the Dalton family, and they couldn't be happier.

Shit like that happened in the real world.

Even if we had a nonfraternization policy at Spade Hotels —which we didn't—Brooklyn and I would be an exception because things had started between us prior to her employment.

An employment that still had several steps before she got the green light.

"I didn't ask you to interview for the job just because I care about you—even though I do, and you know that. I did it because you'd be perfect for the role." My thumbs rubbed across the sides of her mouth, reminding her of a similar conversation we'd had inside the diner. The last thing I wanted her to think was that I had done this out of pity or obligation or to advance things between us or for her to feel like she was indebted to me. "One thing has nothing to do with the other. They're separate entities."

"But it's your company."

"It's my family's company," I corrected her.

"But I'm going to be interviewing at your family's company, the same place you work."

I tightened my grip. "We employ thousands of people. You wouldn't be entering an office with only five employees, where you'd see me every time you took a breath." I chuckled. "Besides, you wouldn't be interviewing with me."

Because she couldn't technically interview with me if I was the one referring her. Even I knew how wrong and fucked up that would be.

But I didn't mention that part to her.

"You have an answer for everything, don't you?"

I calmed the buildup in my chest.

Where I had an answer, she had an excuse.

And I could go round for round, but I had to remind myself that this wasn't a fight. This wasn't even a negotiation.

Brooklyn wanted me. She was just confused, overstimulated, trying to sort what she couldn't control and make sense of it all.

I traced my thumb across the softness of her lips. "I'm just reminding you that there's us. And there's Spade Hotels. Don't categorize them together."

As she stared at me silently, I saw the battle in her eyes that seemed to intensify every time she blinked. "I don't know if I can separate them."

That was because this was new—me and the offer, one she'd just learned about tonight.

So, for now, she was using it as another excuse, fearing that things would get muddier.

Yet, less than an hour ago, she'd admitted that she'd come to the hotel to talk to me, and that was when she had seen me in the bar with that woman. She'd assumed the worst; she had been overflowing with jealousy, and that had been the cause of her attitude earlier tonight.

If she hadn't cared, she wouldn't have given me attitude. She wouldn't have listened to my side of the story. She wouldn't have jumped off the stage and into my arms. She wouldn't have let me take her to the diner. And if she didn't like the idea of being around me, she wouldn't accept the offer to interview at Spade Hotels.

Really, it was as simple as that.

So, all she was doing now was filling me with words—words she thought were right, but they didn't have any meaning behind them.

She wanted me.

She wanted us.

And over the next two months, while I was still on Kauai, I would make her realize that it was more than just her body that was addicted to me.

I leaned my face down until my lips were hovering just inches above hers. At first, her eyes closed, like she was anticipating my kiss. And when I didn't give her one, they slowly opened again.

"You're saying you don't want me to kiss you? Is that what I'm hearing, Brooklyn?" I tugged at her lip with my thumb. "Because that's not what your body or your face is telling me at all." I moved her neck back a bit more, giving me better access to her mouth. "What it looks like is that you'd do fucking anything to have my lips on you." I dipped into her neck, that spot I always went to. The one, when kissed, initiated goose bumps all over her skin. "I can hear your pussy purring right now." My lips pressed down. "I can almost feel how wet it is." I slid my lips up her neck and positioned them directly in front of hers. "Do you know how badly I want to taste that wetness?"

Her response came out as a moan.

Just the way I had known it would.

"Tell me to back away, Brooklyn." I waited. "Say the words. I need to hear them."

I was met with total silence.

But there was movement—her hands, they were on my waist, holding on like she was afraid someone was going to pull her away from me.

When I still got nothing, I said, "You don't want me to back away, so does that mean you want me to reach under your dress and play with your pussy right here?" I grazed my nose over hers. "Rub your clit until you come?"

I earned myself a deeper moan.

"Or maybe you'd rather have me spread you across my front seat so I can eat your cunt."

"*Mmm.*" A response that was even louder this time.

"I'll take your moans, Brooklyn, but I'd rather have your screams."

Her hands moved to the bottom of my shirt, and they pulled the fabric. She arched into me, her back concaving as she held our torsos together.

Oh, she fucking wanted it.

"There's only one problem ... you're not getting any of that tonight."

The longer I made her wait for it, the more she'd want me.

Because if she was having a hard time separating work from pleasure, then her waiting until she got home with a pussy that hadn't been satiated, combined with the text I was going to send her in about an hour, that would be a kind of want she'd never experienced before.

Now, this wasn't a game.

This was me proving a goddamn point.

"Macon, I—"

"But that doesn't mean I'm going to send you home without a taste." I didn't want to hear her response—that was why I'd cut her off. I was the one in control here. Not her. "You're going to get my lips," I hissed against her throat, "and when you're in bed, all alone tonight, you're going to remember how they felt, and you're going to wish you'd gotten more."

I connected our stares.

I let my words hit her as the silence between us grew.

I let her take a breath.

And then I slammed our mouths together, devouring the flavor that I remembered so well, inhaling her into me.

Fuck me.

How could she be so perfect, so sweet?

How could I want her this badly and, at the same time, force myself not to carry her into my SUV?

Because I couldn't.

If I'd learned anything over the last seven years, it was that women wanted what they couldn't have. Which had always been me. But this evening, I'd reversed the roles between us—she was used to getting my mouth and cock, so what would happen when I took them away from her?

She'd crave them.

Desire them.

Dream about them.

Before I knew it, she'd be blowing up my phone, the way I wanted her to.

I just had to show her more of who I was and what she'd be getting if she was with me and the life we'd be living.

Together.

As I mashed our lips, my tongue gradually slid in, circling hers, reminding her of what it would feel like if I was doing this between her legs.

She felt it because the second my tongue lifted and lowered, like a fin, her arms wrapped around me, and I knew I had her.

In this moment, I could do absolutely anything I wanted to her.

But instead of taking things further, I pulled back. I locked our eyes. And I said, "Get home safely."

She looked up and said nothing.

I'd surprised her.

And, fuck, I liked that.

"Now?" she gasped.

I reached down to her ass, squeezing it before I gently slapped it. "Yes. Go."

She unraveled her arms from my waist, and they dropped to her sides. "Okay." She swallowed. "Yeah, you're right. I should go." She was full of raging emotion. So much so that she was almost panting.

She took her time unpeeling her body from mine, taking a step back, and made her way over to her car. She stood outside the driver's door, fumbling in her bag until she found her keys. And even when she got into the seat, she didn't hurry off. She rolled down the windows and checked her phone before finally driving away.

I waited until she was out of sight before I got into my SUV, and as I began to head toward the hotel, I called Cooper.

"Dude, it's three in the fucking morning. This'd better be good," Cooper barked in a deep, raspy tone.

I'd woken him up.

Shit.

I always forgot about the time difference between Hawaii and LA.

"Sorry, buddy. Look at it this way, if you stay up for another hour, you can hit the gym early and get a solid head start on work today."

"Fuck that and fuck you for even suggesting it." He yawned. "Tell me why you're calling so I can go back to bed."

I turned at the light, seeing the glow from the hotel ahead. "She specializes in change management. She's even getting her Six Sigma certification after she graduates in a couple of months."

"Wait ..." There was rustling in the background, which told me he was probably sitting up in bed and turning on the light. "We're talking about the chick, right? The one you've been hooking up with?"

"Brooklyn."

"Yes, that one." His tone was getting a little higher and louder, and I could hear the excitement. "The one you're fucking head over heels for."

"Jesus, Cooper, this isn't why I called you."

"I'm just making sure we're on the same page." He laughed. "So, you're telling me this"—he paused—"because, I assume, you either offered her a job or you want to."

"You're correct and that job will be within my new department."

I slowed and pulled into the valet and disconnected the Bluetooth, holding my phone against my ear. When the valet opened my door, I handed him the fob, and I walked inside the lobby.

"And you think that's the best idea?" my brother asked.

My head turned even though I was looking at the bank of elevators.

Is he serious?

"Are you questioning my decision?"

"I know you wouldn't suggest this unless you really believed she was good for the Spade brand, brother. You wouldn't put our company in that situation—none of us would. What I'm questioning is whether you think it's a good decision to have her work beneath you since you'll be spearheading that division."

A detail I'd intentionally left out when I told Brooklyn about the job. I knew working beneath me would bother her and that the lack of separation between our personal and business lives would be even harder for her.

And now, Cooper was bringing it up because he saw a problem with it too.

Damn.

"I'm going to take your silence as either, one, the logistics of that arrangement haven't even entered your head or, two, you have no idea how to navigate those waters." He was silent as I walked into the elevator. "My guess is two."

"She doesn't know I'm leading that team. I told her the interview wouldn't be with me."

"Which isn't a lie. If she came as a personal referral, which she did, you wouldn't interview her. Brady, Jo, or I would. That's standard protocol."

"But I withheld that information because I knew it would bother her. Shit is already complicated. Being her boss—that would end things before they even really began." I pressed the button for my floor and leaned against the back wall. "Her favorite fucking word is *muddy*. Can you imagine how dirty it would be if she had to report to me? And take my orders?"

I couldn't let that happen.

"Listen, you'll figure this out, whether that means having her work for our brand or not. Just don't put yourself in a situation where it has to be one or the other. Both can happen, and you'll find a way."

"I know. I'll find it." I stepped out of the elevator and waved my key card in front of my door.

"You really like her, don't you." Cooper wasn't asking; he was telling me.

I filled my lungs with the scent that the housekeeper had sprayed in my room when they did the turndown service. "You know I do."

"That was one hell of a quick response." I could hear the asshole smiling. "And, fuck, that makes me happy."

TWELVE

Brooklyn

My body was on fire. Tingling from head to toe. There was a slickness between my legs that I felt every time I shifted in the driver's seat. A hardness in my nipples that ached as they pushed against my bra.

This was what Macon had done to me.

He lit me up.

And during every past occasion, he'd licked those flames until they were dying embers.

Except for tonight.

It was my fault. I'd told him I couldn't separate work and pleasure, which was true—the line between the two was too gray. He was giving me the most incredible opportunity to interview with his company—a company that shared the same last name as him. How awful would it look if I was sleeping with one of the executives? If after I got the job—and that was a big assumption, but still—I continued to sleep with him? If I was thinking about him instead of my responsibilities?

But the thing was, I wanted to sleep with him.

I wanted to think about him.

And this was exactly why I hadn't wanted to get involved with him. These thoughts were far too muddy. These questions were owning my mind in a way I couldn't handle. In a way that was overlapping the time I spent at work and doing schoolwork.

Because all I thought about was him.

When I needed to focus on what I had to accomplish before I graduated, rather than writing a few sentences of a paper and having an image of him fill my head.

When I needed to complete my shifts at the hotel, earning the money I needed to survive without being consumed by him.

When I needed to dance away my evenings at the club, unplugging from everything and everyone, without wondering if I was going to see him there.

And once I received my degree, I needed to concentrate on finding a position within a company where I could make a difference. Where they would listen to my suggestions rather than blow me off and tell me I knew nothing, like the hotel I worked for now.

I wanted to feel needed.

Valued.

Respected.

Something told me I would find that at Spade Hotels, especially because Macon had said that they needed someone like me. Someone with my skills and passion.

But really, it was the other way around. Spade Hotels was what *I* needed.

Those words hit me like a boulder, rippling across the surface of my brain, and as the whole picture came into view—my wants, my future, my dreams—I realized what was in front of me.

Our home.

I was parked in front of it, and I couldn't remember a second of my commute here.

Oh God.

My lungs, still so tight from all the bursts exploding through my body, had a hard time filling as I shut off my car and walked inside. My sisters were in the kitchen, standing at the counter, chowing on some chips and salsa.

"And she went to the club again," Clem said, her stare dipping down me. "Were you also alone this time?"

The dress was a dead giveaway, but I wasn't trying to hide where I'd been. "Sorta."

"Sorta?" Jesse repeated.

When I got close enough, Jesse wrapped her arm around my shoulders, and as soon as I was at her side, she leaned her face toward mine and kept it there for a second too long. "You smell like cologne ..."

I pulled back and looked at her.

"Like an expensive, yummy, super-sexy cologne," she added and moved around to my front and rested both hands on my shoulders. "All right, spill it, Brooklyn."

I glanced from her to Clem. "That's actually what I was going to talk to you about tonight." A bolt shot through my body, reminding me that the feeling of Macon wasn't even close to being gone. "I've sorta met someone."

"Again with the sorta," Clem joked.

I stepped back, the movement causing Jesse's hands to drop, and I went to the fridge. I took out the bottle of vodka we kept in there and found three glasses in the cupboard, pouring a couple of shots' worth in each. I added ice and a little Diet Coke from a random can I'd found by the ketchup.

"Does this make it easier to talk about?" Clem asked when I handed her my concoction. "Because for someone who isn't much of a drinker, it's interesting that the moment we start discussing cologne and the man you sorta met, you're handing us vodka."

"Yes." I nodded for backup. "And it's layered, so all the things"—I held up my glass—"will help."

"I'm lost," Jesse said.

Since we didn't have a kitchen table and I needed distance to think, I said, "Come on. I'll explain everything. Let's go in here," and I led them into the living room/shared bedroom. I sat on my bed and pointed at theirs, instructing them to do the same. I waited until they were settled before I continued, "I'm just going to lay it all out there." I paused. "I met a man."

"Tonight?" Jesse asked.

I crossed my legs, holding the drink on top of them and a pillow in my other hand, hugging it against my side. "A couple weeks ago, at the club. I'd never seen him there before—not that I pay much attention to the people who go there since I really do my own thing, but he didn't look familiar. We talked, connected, and"—I sighed, unable to hold in the air for a second longer—"he's everything, you guys. Extremely successful, devastatingly handsome, smart, charming." I was saying all the things I'd been thinking, but hadn't yet voiced out loud because, ironically, this was the first time I'd ever spoken about Macon. And really, I could go on and on, those descriptions not nearly strong enough to cover the depth of that man. But there was something else that needed to be mentioned, something vital. "He's into me. Like really, really into me."

"Of course he's obsessed with you," Clem said. "If he wasn't, there would be something grossly wrong with him."

"What she said." Jesse tucked a curl behind her ear. "But also, he sounds dreamy."

I nodded. "He is."

"Then, what's the problem?" Jesse took a sip. "You said it's layered, and so far, this sounds like a no-brainer. The only question I have is, why aren't you with him right now?"

I gazed at the top of my glass and slowly lifted it toward my lips. As the liquor hit my tongue, my mouth watered, and I forced the mixture down my throat. I needed this—this potential buzz, this relaxation, this liquid courage, whatever it was.

"There's two parts to this, you see. There's the part where this guy really likes me, but he doesn't live here. He's only here for two months while he finishes out a major build-out, and then he's going back home to LA. I know things would only be temporary, and these next two months need to be all about school and work—I can't afford to be tied down, diving head-first into something super deep and emotional and sticky, only to soon have an ocean between us by the time I graduate." That admission felt more exhausting than it needed to be, but what it did was make me cling to the glass and keep it near my mouth. "Then, there's the part where he offered to have me interview at his company—the company his family owns and is headquartered in LA." I halted, chewing the corner of my lip. "The position is everything I want, my dream job right out of the gate."

"Brooklyn ..." Clem's voice was a little above a whisper.

And as I heard her, as I processed her tone, as I thought about everything I'd just said, emotion began to fill my eyes. "They're looking for someone who specializes in Six Sigma. Who can come in and reorganize and restructure and is willing to relocate."

"Shut up," Jesse said. "I mean, keep going, but shut up."

I smiled. "And the best part is, it's a hotel brand."

Clem's back went straight, her eyes widening. "Hold on a second. The pieces are now fitting together." She wiggled toward the end of her bed. "You said a build-out and a hotel. The only hotel I know they're building on Kauai is the Spade

Hotel." Her eyes grew even larger. "Is that the one you're talking about?"

I tried to take a deep breath and couldn't. "Yes."

"Holy fuck," Jesse sang. "My sister is dating a Spade!"

"Not dating. We're—"

"Screwing around," Jesse finished for me. "We know exactly what you're doing, girl, and I'm so proud of you that I could scream."

"You are kind of screaming," Clem told her.

If I wasn't so twisted within all of this, I probably would have laughed, like the two of them were doing. Instead, I said, "Listen, there's more to the story. A lot more. Like the part where, if I went in to interview for the position, there's the fact that I've seen one of the executives naked, and that makes things—"

"Even better," Jesse said. "Does he have a problem with it?"

"Macon?" I asked. "No. He has no problem with it. He said they're separate entities—me and him and me and Spade Hotels and that I shouldn't see them as the same."

"Macon?" Jesse cooed. "*Ohhh*, that name is hot." She held her glass up, like she was giving me a cheers. "I like him. A lot. And I haven't even met him yet."

Just as I was about to respond, Clem said, "If Macon doesn't have a problem with it, then why do you? At least, I'm assuming you do by the way you're explaining things."

I released the pillow and drove my hand through the side of my hair, combing it with my fingers. "They're not going to take me seriously. Not when I've slept with an executive. That's no way to start your dream position."

"Who's they?" Clem asked.

I shrugged. "Whoever interviews me." And when that didn't feel like enough, I added, "They're going to take pity on me because I've slept with him."

"Not when they meet you, they won't." Clem's voice was now so dominant. "You're a badass. You need to know that and believe it. You're brilliant. You're a straight-A student. You've put yourself through college while working full-time. You'll go into that interview and blow them away. They won't even have a chance to feel pity because all they're going to see is a strong, mature, smart, skilled, and qualified woman."

But a woman with no experience.

Who was only twenty-two years old.

Reasons my current employer wouldn't listen to anything I suggested when it came to the housekeeping department. I was just a maid, so what the hell did I know? Those were things they'd told me on more than one occasion.

And then there was the issue of my résumé. That the only job I'd ever had, except for babysitting, was the position at the hotel.

Something I still hadn't told Macon.

Something I didn't want to tell him.

Not now. Not after all of this.

"It would be one thing if, all of a sudden, you started sleeping with your boss after you got the job, but that's not the case here at all," Jesse said. "You're going into the interview with an established connection to him. That's a totally different scenario."

I understood that point. I could almost accept it.

But there was just so much happening, and that was one of many, many points.

"The only downside that I can see is if you decide you don't want to be with him after you take the job," Clem said. "Things could get a little sticky."

"Yes, that." I exhaled.

"But if that did go down, you're both adults, and you'd handle it," Jesse offered. "Besides, from the way you're describing him, I highly doubt you're not going to want to be with him."

"It could happen though, Jess," I whispered.

"Plus," Jesse continued as though ignoring me, "while you're employed at Spade, you're going to be soaking in every second of the experience. If you did have to change employers, the time you spent there would open tons of doors, and you'd be walking into a new company in no time."

Another solid point.

But there was the distance, the relocation.

My voice turned quiet as I said, "You two haven't said anything about the LA part."

Clem looked at Jesse before she said, "Because we knew it was going to happen." She then directed her gaze at me. "We've talked about it many times between the two of us."

"What do you mean?" I asked.

"Jess and I had a feeling that once you graduated, you were going to find a job on either The Big Island or somewhere on the mainland. So, to us, this conversation isn't coming as a surprise." A smile grew across her face. "We're so proud of you, Brooklyn. You've worked extremely hard to get to where you are, and we've watched you become this outstanding woman. We knew you were going to go off and do amazing things, and now, our dreams of watching this happen are finally going to come true."

"We're going to miss you like hell," Jesse said softly. "And it does suck that you'll be leaving us—we hate the thought of it—but wherever you are, you'll only be a plane ride away. And we'll be coming to visit all the time."

"Are you sure you really want to go?" Clem asked with puppy-dog eyes. "Don't answer that. It's just my heart having a hard time with even the idea of you not being with us."

The emotion that had been rising was now filling my eyes, a knot wedging into my throat. "I love you guys. So much."

"Girl, we have nothing but love for you," Jesse said.

"And we love you more." Clem's voice lightened. "Don't stress about Macon. Just have fun with him. Enjoy him. Learn everything you can about him. And see what the future holds—with him and with the interview. Who knows what's going to happen when you see his company up close? But don't shut yourself off to the possibility of being with him and simultaneously accepting a job offer."

"Clem's right," Jesse voiced. "And Macon's right too—both he and the hotel stuff can happen at the same time. It doesn't have to be one or the other. And just imagine, you could end up falling in love with both. Girl, that's swoon central right there."

I was overwhelmed—with this conversation, with the possibilities, with the future.

With the way my body had felt and still did after his kiss in the parking lot.

I downed the rest of the vodka and set the empty glass on the floor beside my bed. "That's all I've got for you girls, and now, I have about an hour's worth of homework to do before I can go to sleep. The longer I put it off, the faster tomorrow morning is going to come."

Jesse nodded toward my desk, where my computer was sitting. "Go get your work done. We're going to bed anyway."

I gave them a small smile, and I brought my glass into the kitchen, seeing my purse on the counter, not even remembering I'd placed it there. I draped it over my shoulder and took a seat at my desk, removing my phone before I turned on my computer.

Within my notifications was a text from a number that wasn't saved in my Contacts.

I swiped the screen and began to read.

UNKNOWN

> I hope you're still wet … and I hope you're still thinking about me.

I'd deleted Macon's number when I saw him in the bar with that woman, but it had to be him—he was the only person who would write me something like that.

Something that made me tingle again.

Something that made me smile so hard.

I saved his number and typed out a reply.

ME

> Wouldn't you like to know?

MACON

> I do want to know.

ME

> I can't lie … I am.

MACON

> It's all right. I've been hard all night, and that hasn't gotten any better since I got back to the hotel.

ME

> At least you're able to take care of it, LOL. ;)

> I'll be doing homework for the next hour. Jealous?

MACON

> Yes, I am actually. Because the homework gets to spend time with you and I don't.

ME

> Aww. Sweet dreams.

MACON

> They will be … I'll be dreaming about you.

MACON

Good morning, gorgeous.

ME

Don't even tell me you're just waking up.
Because now, I'M jealous. I've been awake
for three hours already.

I stilled in the middle of the en suite—a room three doors down from Macon's that I'd been cleaning for the last couple of minutes—and I watched the dots appear under his message, telling me he was typing a reply.

I hadn't known he was still sleeping, but I knew he hadn't left his room. I'd been stalking it since the moment I'd gotten to work, determining when I should attempt to tidy it up.

Since I needed to quickly finish this room and move on to the next and figured he was still in bed, it was safe to run out and grab the glass cleaner I needed for the shower—something I'd forgotten on my way in.

I tucked my phone into the front pocket of my uniform and headed for the door that was already wedged open, a standard practice for our hotel—we never cleaned rooms with the door closed. Just as my hand was running over the numerous bottles, feeling around for the one that was shaped like the glass cleaner, I heard the sound of a door.

A door opening.

A door that was extremely close to the one I was standing by.

My hand froze.

My heart began to thump at a rate I couldn't control.

I scanned the hallway, trying to see which room the noise was coming from, and then I saw the movement.

The opening ... from the door that was three rooms down.

A room that belonged to Macon.

Fuuuck.

He was stepping through the entryway, and I watched him immediately notice my cart.

He only had to lift his eyes a few more inches, and he would see me.

That was seconds from happening.

I didn't know what to do.

If I dashed back into the room, I'd draw even more attention to myself.

But I couldn't let him see my face.

So, I turned my back toward him and pretended to clean the doorframe with a rag that I'd pulled out of my pocket.

"Good morning," he said from behind me.

Is he talking to me?

He has to be. There's no one else in this hallway.

I held in my breath, attempting to sound congested, and used the highest pitch I could muster, replying, "Good morning."

"Have a good day."

He wouldn't have to walk past me. The elevator was in the opposite direction.

But my heart still thumped away in my chest, my muscles screaming, my knees locking, as I feared he would recognize something about me—the color of my hair, the frame of my body in this uniform, the curve of my neck, anything—and he'd come closer to me.

I waited.

I pretended to scrub an invisible dot off the paint.

And suddenly, the sound of his door closing was filling my ears.

Followed by his footsteps.

I was so in tune to him and his location that I could hear his steps getting quieter.

And quieter.

Until I knew it was safe to turn around.

I pressed my back against the outside of the door, panting until I found my breath again.

My God, that had been far too close.

I couldn't let that happen again. I didn't want Macon to find out that way.

I needed to tell him the truth.

I needed to come clean.

Not now, but very soon.

With my chest still heaving, I took out my phone and read his reply.

> **MACON**
>
> I can do early, but three hours ago is a kind of early I don't want to fuck with.
>
> When can I see you?

> **ME**
>
> See me?

> **MACON**
>
> Yes. As in take you out, spend time with you.
> Kiss you again.

My thumbs hovered above the screen as I thought of just minutes ago, when he had been so close that he could have kissed me.

> **ME**
>
> Soon.

> **MACON**
>
> Not a good enough answer. Tonight?

I had so much homework. I wouldn't be able to get it all

done this afternoon. I needed this evening too. Tomorrow, I had to work, but I could wrap up my homework right after and be free before dinnertime.

But that meant I was agreeing to a date with a man I'd just hidden from.

I would be squeezing in more time to get to know him, allowing things to move in a deeper direction.

Could I keep the potential interview and Macon completely independent of one another?

Do I want to do that?

Am I really seeking more? Of him? Us?

When I just pretended to clean the door so he wouldn't see that I was the housekeeper who was going to tidy his room next?

I ran my tongue across my lips, gradually drawing in air, and as my thumbs touched the screen, I let my body and my heart type the reply.

ME

Tomorrow night.

MACON

Wear the black dress ...

ME

That's your only request?

MACON

Text me the address where I can pick you up.

THIRTEEN

Macon

My beautiful *Tiny Dancer*, I thought as the door opened to Brooklyn's home.

She walked out to meet me, my stare rising and falling down her body.

"My God, you're gorgeous."

She still wore black—a color I assumed, at this point, was her favorite—and she also had on a dress, but this one wasn't as sexy as what she always wore to the club. Rather than hugging every inch of her torso, it cut low on her chest, pinched her waist, and flared out as it made its way a few inches past her knees. On her feet were sandals, giving her petite frame an extra couple of inches of height.

She smiled. "You don't look so bad yourself."

When she reached me, I wrapped my arms around her and hauled her up against me. Before she could stop me, I pressed my lips against hers.

Fuck, this was everything I'd been wanting.

Her taste.

Feel.

The way her distinct scents and heat went from her body to mine.

She didn't pull away or arch in the opposite direction.

What she did was lean into me and part her lips so I could get even more of her lemon flavor.

After a few seconds, I had to force myself to separate our mouths, licking her off me, and I took several deep breaths to calm myself down, my dick relentlessly hard, not softening anytime soon. "Before you get in the car, I have something for you."

She swiped her fingers across her lips, back and forth, multiple times, like she was processing what had just gone down and the way it made her feel. Once a few seconds passed, her hand dropped, and her brows rose. "You do?"

I took the same hand that had just dropped and led her behind the SUV, waiting for the driver to hit the button that opened the trunk. As the latch lifted, I grabbed the four garment bags lying across the floor, holding them in the air by their metal hangers. "For you."

"Macon, what is all of that?"

There was too much to unzip and show her, so I answered, "I know I haven't asked that all-important question yet, but in case you want the interview to happen, I got some things for you to wear to it."

"What?"

"You said you were certain you had nothing good enough in your closet. I'm sure you do, but in case you don't, I took care of that problem."

Her head shook, as though she was trying to knock out the dizziness. "Hold on a second. You went shopping for me?"

I chuckled. "I had someone do that part. I just chose my

favorites from the collection she presented. Outfits I would fucking die to see you in."

"How did you know my size?" Her voice was so low, quiet.

"You're tiny. It was an easy guess." With my free hand, I rested those fingers on her cheek. Her skin was already turning red but was now flushing even harder. "Don't worry, I stuck with mostly black, although you'd look incredible in other colors."

She glanced from me to the bags, her lips staying open even though nothing was coming out of them. "I ... can't."

"Can't what?"

"Accept this. It's too much. You didn't have to—"

"I wanted to."

Her hand went on top of mine. "But you spent all this money on me and—"

"And I wanted to." I would repeat those words until she understood them, until she believed them. I tilted her face up, aligning our lips despite them being over a foot apart. "It's just a gift. That's all this is. Money that I happily spent on you."

And there would be so many more coming her way. I would spoil the shit out of this woman. This was only the very beginning. But I wasn't going to tell her that and overwhelm her even more when I knew she was still struggling with the muddiness of her life.

She squeezed the sides of the bags, assuming she was trying to feel how many outfits were inside. "This is a whole closet's worth of clothes." She took a breath. "Macon, I can't—"

"You can." I nodded toward her place. "Now, bring me to your room so I can put this stuff in there. I have a lot planned for us tonight, and we need to get going."

She didn't move. "Macon ..."

"Listen to me," I said softly, keeping my voice tame even though I wanted to bark orders that were even stronger than my last set. "I'm fucking obsessed with your body. Getting to dress you in what I've picked out ... there's nothing sexier. If you continue spending time with me, giving you gifts is one of the things I'm going to do. Not that I've ever done this before. I've told you about my past, but I have this desire to do it for you."

As I thought about the red dress that I'd thrown in at the very end, my thumb dragged across her lips, tugging the bottom one. The dress wasn't appropriate for the interview, not with the way the whole back was open, but when I had seen it on the rack the shopper had rolled into my suite, I had known Brooklyn had to have it, especially because she had one hell of a fucking back.

"Don't deny me something I want to do for you."

She stayed silent for several seconds. "I don't know what to say." Her hand left mine and went to my chest, gently stroking the center between my pecs. "Except for my family, no one has ever done anything like this for me. No clothes, gifts, nothing. I ..." Her stare shifted from me to the bags and back again. "I'm truly speechless. Thank you."

I gave her a quick kiss. "Take me inside."

Instead of words, she gave me a grin, and I followed her to the front door that she unlocked with her key. Once she stepped in, she stayed near the entrance until I joined her, and then she brought me through what I guessed was supposed to be the living room, except there were three blowup mattresses on the floor, a wooden table that had a laptop, and a closet in the back.

"I just have to make some room in here. One second."

As she stood in front of the closet, she began to slide things to either side. A closet that was smaller than the one in my current hotel suite. Once she created enough space, she took the bags from my arms and hung them.

"So, this is our tiny place." She turned toward me. "My bed

is there"—she pointed at the mattress a few feet away—"and that's my desk." Her finger traced the air around her laptop. "Jesse and Clementine sleep over there," she said, aiming at the other two beds. "Kitchen is through that archway." Her finger was back in the air, directing me to the room next to this one, her hand shifting a couple of inches as she continued, "And the bathroom is that way." She paused. "Now, you see why I'm ready to move out."

I was no longer visually taking the tour. I was focused solely on her. "There's nothing wrong with this place, Brooklyn."

Sure, it was minute. The women slept on air mattresses instead of real beds. The amount of stuff they had well exceeded the allotted space. But I knew the demographics of this island, something I'd thoroughly researched for months to prepare myself for the build-out and the staff we'd be hiring. Therefore, I knew what it cost to live here, and the rent, based on the average income, was outrageous.

These three women made it work. They pooled their resources, and they had a place of their own that was close to the water.

That was fucking admirable, not something to downgrade.

"There isn't anything wrong with it," she agreed. "But I dream of the day when I have my own bedroom and I can close the door and get a second of silence. Not to mention privacy. Unless my sisters are at work, like they are now, I barely even get a minute alone in the bathroom."

"You need to install a lock on that door." I laughed.

She rolled her eyes. "Knowing them, they'd pick the lock." Her hand went to my arm. She held it, rubbed her thumb across my bicep, and then squeezed. "For so many reasons, thank you."

"You already thanked me. You don't have to do it again."

"But I do."

Quietness passed between us. A period where I could say so much. Where I could lift her into my arms and set her on the bed. Where I could send the driver home and spend the whole evening here, doing the things I'd been fantasizing about. But that would mean missing the opportunity to see the look on Brooklyn's face when she saw what I had planned.

I wasn't going to pass that up.

"You're welcome." I wrapped an arm around her back. "Are you ready to go?"

She didn't immediately pull her hand away. She kept it on my chest, spreading her fingers, taking in my face and the way I was staring at her. "Yes, I'm ready."

My grip moved to her lower back as we walked through the door and toward the SUV.

"A driver tonight?" she asked as I opened the back door for her.

"It's needed." I shut the door and went over to the other side, climbing in beside her, where I placed my arm around her shoulders.

I couldn't take my hands off her. I wasn't even attempting to hold back. Whatever my fingers wanted, I let them touch. Whenever my lips ached for hers, I kissed her.

She gave me no indication that she wanted me to stop.

And until she told me to, I had no plans to back off.

She needed to feel how badly I wanted her. She needed to experience the emotion pulsing in my body for her.

She needed to see that, if we were eventually going to be together, this was how our future was going to look, and this evening would give her a solid taste of that.

We weren't even a few minutes into the drive when we began to approach the construction of the Spade Hotel. I hadn't realized how close she lived to it. "You know, I haven't gotten a chance to show the hotel to you."

"Is that what we're doing tonight?"

"No." I huffed. "But you're going to see it very soon."

Her fingers touched the glass. "I would love that. I know it's going to be so beautiful."

"I helped design it."

Her head whipped in my direction. "Are you normally part of that process?"

"No, but when I came here and looked at several pieces of land and chose that one specifically, I saw the hotel in my head. I told my uncle I wanted to be on the design team. I met with our in-house architect, and we worked on it together."

She glanced back out the window, following the property until it was past our line of sight. "It reminds me of the ocean."

I smiled. "That's what I intended."

The wavy shape of the high-rise, the texture across the exterior, the way the structures were connected by wings, representing strips of beach. So much symbolism had gone into this one.

"So, as far as your role," she said, "do you stick around until the hotel's fully operational?"

"I'll leave a few weeks after the grand opening. We'll have a management team in place who will oversee everything. By then, I'm just ensuring there's a smooth transition between the team and employees, that there aren't any issues with the building or grounds, and that the logistics of getting every department up to speed, where they're working efficiently, are all handled correctly." I sighed. "So much goes into operating a hotel."

"I know."

That comment made me pause. "You do?"

She looked from me to the window and back. "I just mean,

that hotel's a beast. Of course it'll take some time and lots of eyes and hands to get things running the way you want it to." She hesitated for a second. "I get how clients and guests can be."

"Are you in customer service?"

She nodded. "You could say that."

"So, yes, you do understand how that's a giant understatement." I laughed. "And the sole reason why we only book to about sixty or seventy percent capacity for the first month. There are too many kinks to work out. I don't want the guests to experience those hiccups, so working with a smaller occupancy gives us room to fuck up." I leaned into her neck, breathing her in. "You'll be learning all these things very soon—some of which, it sounds like, you already know."

It hit me that I couldn't recall what she did for work. Had I asked? Was it a detail I'd forgotten or something we hadn't discussed at all?

"What kind of customer service work do you do?"

"Macon ... there you go again, teasing me about the job at Spade Hotels. The way you word it, it sounds like I already have it."

I knew she'd impress the team during her interview, and after the two examples she'd given me at the diner, I believed she had the skills to analyze each department within our older locations and determine specific areas of improvement.

I kissed the side of her ear. "Should I not keep bringing it up?"

"No, please do. It's just that you're assuming I'm going to get it, and I don't even know what it really entails or if the manager of the department will even like me or want me to work for them."

The manager of the department.

Something I'd been thinking about endlessly since I'd

offered her the interview and had that conversation with Cooper on my way home.

At some point, she was going to find out it was me. Not necessarily during the interview—I could make sure that wasn't revealed. But if she got the job and I decided to stay in the position, it would be inevitable.

What would that do to us?

Would there even be an us by then?

Fuck, I hoped so.

"You know, if you decide to interview, HR is going to fly you out to LA fairly quickly." I pulled my mouth off her skin and straightened in my seat. "They want to fully staff the team within the next couple of months, which means they'll start recruiting now."

"That timing is perfect. I'll be graduated by then."

With my arm still wrapped around her, my hand sank into her hair. "Would going to LA in the next week or so be a problem? With school and work, could you swing it?"

"I'd make it happen, no matter what." She bit the center of her bottom lip. "What would a visit there look like exactly?"

"They'd give you a tour of our corporate headquarters. You'd have one interview, most likely two. They'd put you up in a hotel for the night and fly you home the next day."

Her head shook, and her eyes went wide. "Wow."

I chuckled at her amazement. "Is that a good wow or ..."

"I never thought I'd ever be flown somewhere to interview for a job. I had goals and dreams, of course—I've told you that. I just didn't think it would happen like this or so fast." She let out a deep breath. "This is all just wild to me." Her hand went to my leg, her eyes on her fingers until she finally lifted them. "And it's all because of you."

I pushed the hair out of her face. "You've earned it." My hand stilled on her cheek. "You fell into my arms at the right time, and since I met you, I don't even recognize myself. I've done a one-eighty. That's what's wild to me." I took a quick glance through the windshield, seeing that we were approaching the airport, and I leaned toward Brooklyn. "The things you've made me realize, the things you've made me want —I never thought it would ever happen ... until you."

I kissed her.

But this kiss wasn't like the others I'd given her tonight.

When my lips surrounded hers, they moved with urgency.

I was hungrier. Needier.

Demanding.

And she felt it.

I heard it in her breath; I sensed it in her fingers as they clung to my leg.

And when I finally pulled away, feeling the SUV come to a stop, I whispered, "We're here."

Her eyes slowly opened, staring into mine before they gradually searched the windows. "We're at ... the airport?"

"We're going to fly to dinner and fly back. Just a quick trip."

"What?" She swallowed. "Where?" She scanned my eyes. "And how is that even possible?"

I smiled at her innocence, even laughed a little. "When I asked your favorite flavor, *sushi* came flying out of your mouth. If I'm being honest, I was going to take you to Japan for a couple of days. That's the best in the world, in my opinion. But I assumed you either had school or work or both, and I didn't want to keep you from those, especially knowing how important they are to you." I kissed her again, just a quick peck to get more of her taste, to satisfy that deep need pulsing inside me. "I found the highest-rated sushi restaurant in Hawaii, so that's where we're going."

"Macon ..." She looked at the private plane, her stare

returning to me. "This is far too much. I mean, the clothes were *a lot*, a lot. This is—"

"Here's something else you need to know about me. When I'm craving croissants, I fly to Paris. I go to Siesta Key in Florida when I want to feel the softest sand under my feet. When I want to unplug from the world, I go to Puerto Natales in Chile. I don't hold back—ever. I follow what's calling to me, and I indulge." I spread my fingers across her cheek. "This is how I live my life, Brooklyn, and how I want to live it with you." I allowed those words to wrap around her the way my hand was doing.

"Those dreams and goals you've mentioned are important to you—I know that. And after you graduate, all of them are going to come true. That's important to me as well, but so is this. This is what you'll also have if you're with me—a balance between work and play—and I promise we'll maintain it."

"I ... don't even know what to say." Her lips hung open. "Have I already said that tonight? Because if I haven't, I meant to, and now, it needs to be voiced again." She took a breath. "And again."

I pulled her bottom lip with my teeth, needing the taste, the sensation, and eventually released it. "We're going to have so much fucking fun tonight."

FOURTEEN

Brooklyn

"This is ..." My voice faded away as I glanced toward the ceiling of the sushi restaurant in Honolulu that Macon had brought me to, at the wooden design that hung across it, shaped like waves to represent the sea. "So incredibly beautiful. I can't ..." I gazed toward the walls painted in these elaborate, colorful fish, at the dark blue floor with tiny hints of glitter speckled within, like the moonlight capturing just the tips of the waves. And finally, I met his face. "Believe I'm here ..." I finished. "That you took me to this restaurant. That we flew on a private plane. That you put this whole evening together because I'd mentioned sushi was my favorite flavor, which made no sense at the time, but it turned into this ..."

An act of kindness and generosity that I would never get over.

Macon found whatever it was that I liked or needed, and that was what he gave me each time we were together. Whether it was physical, like burying his face between my legs because he knew I was obsessed with his tongue. Or gifts, like the ones I'd hung in the closet tonight, which I needed for my upcoming interview—something I was positive he'd assumed since I wore the same outfit almost every time he saw me. Or professional, like allowing me the opportunity to fight for a job that I wanted more than anything.

He was a giver.

A man who thrived off the satisfaction he saw spreading across my face or he heard in my breath or he felt within my body.

I'd never met anyone like this before.

And aside from the complications of us working for the same company and how that would affect things if we broke up, could I really turn down the chance of being with someone as amazing as him?

Despite the muddiness around me.

The busyness.

The responsibilities I had until I graduated.

Because in less than two months, that would all clear up. I would have a job—that was it. Something I could surely manage after balancing all of this.

All I would have to do was say yes—a word he was ready to hear.

"All it took was a simple mention of sushi," he said, his gaze swallowing me whole. "And now, we're here, at the best place in Hawaii."

"All it took for someone like you," I corrected. I leaned across the small table that was decorated with so many tiny plates that I was nervous I was going to knock one onto the floor. "This isn't normal, Macon. This is ... completely bananas."

He laughed at my description.

An expression so carefree and honest and incredibly handsome on him that it made me ache. I took in the way his mouth parted and how his throat bobbed and how his lips were emphasized by the perfectness of his dark beard. He was more than just the most attractive man I'd ever seen. More than gracious and dominant and sexy.

He was everything.

But I couldn't get lost in that thought. I had to keep it together. I had to remember that there was nothing wrong with going slow. That I had a lot of major changes coming up, and I didn't want to be influenced by this gorgeous man, whose eyes were currently stripping me naked.

Whose presence was making me want those clothes to peel right off my body.

I cleared my throat and said, "I don't know a single person, except you, who has ever flown privately, let alone taken a plane to dinner." I lifted the small cup of sake and held it. "If I haven't already said it enough, I'm saying it again. Thank you."

"You've said it more than enough." He lifted his sake and clinked it against mine. "You realize this is our first official date."

My brows rose as I sipped the drink. "What about the diner?"

"That wasn't a date. That was me begging you to come out to eat with me and giving you almost no other choice until you caved. Hopefully, we're past the begging phase."

"Ha!"

His eyes narrowed. "Unless we're talking about me begging to lick your pussy—then it's all right."

A wave of tingles passed through me. "Is that what you're asking for now?"

"Not yet, but only because the night is so young."

I smiled, instantly wet from the thought, the feeling causing me to wiggle in my seat.

"I want to know everything about you, Brooklyn. Tell me, besides going to the beach and the club, what are some of the things you like to do when you're not working or doing shit for school?"

"*Hmm.*" My hand left the cup and went into my lap, where I linked all my fingers together. "That's hard because both have monopolized me for the last four years." I continued to think as I stared at him. "Music and dancing—those are things I obviously love. Whenever my sisters and I travel to The Big Island to see my parents, we try to catch a concert while we're there. And I really enjoy taking walks on the beach. Long ones. At least four or five miles, where I can lose myself."

"Just like you do at the club."

"Yes." My list of enjoyments was short. It was easier to tell him the things I wasn't into or I didn't have time or money to explore, so I added, "You know fashion isn't a priority. I'm not much of a foodie either. Don't get me wrong, I love food, but I'm a bargain eater." I moved in closer to the edge of the table so no one could hear me. "The sushi I typically get is at a place super close to where we live. On Tuesdays, they have a half-off menu. When my sisters are free, we go and eat our weight in rolls."

"Which means you eat about one."

I laughed. "Come on. Give me a little more credit. I can put down four on a good day." I winked. "As for traveling, I haven't done any—not on my own or with my sisters. I've told you, I'm an Army brat, and we've lived all over, so I've seen other places from all our moves, but we've never vacationed as a family unless it was somewhere nearby, like an amusement park or a beach. In the last four years, besides here, the only place I've flown to was The Big Island to see Mom and Dad."

He rubbed his thumb against the side of his mouth, the

whiskers beneath making an enticing sound. "Do you want to travel?"

"Desperately." The answer was there—I hadn't even needed to think about it. "I feel like I've seen nothing, and I want to see everything."

"Where would you start?"

I laughed. "Japan sounds nice. Their sushi is calling to me."

"You're cute."

"But I'm serious. I follow tons of travel accounts on social media, and I'm so envious of their adventures. I want to experience everything that they see. Dubai and Africa. Thailand and Nepal. Venezuela and Alaska. I could keep going." I leaned back in my seat since there was no longer a need to whisper. "I want to learn the history and absorb the sights and landscapes and fill my phone storage with pictures that aren't just of the South Shore of Kauai. Our beach is beautiful, I'm not dissing it, but there's so much more to explore. I feel confined."

His brows rose. "*Confined* is an interesting way to put it."

I tucked all my hair onto my left shoulder, freeing up the bareness of my right collarbone. Macon immediately noticed, instantly looking there. It was a spot that was his favorite, and his posture softened before his eyes rose to mine.

"I've been in school for four years," I told him. "I've taken classes throughout each summer and even during Christmas break. Even if I had the cash to go somewhere magical, which I don't, I'd be too consumed with my assignments and studying to be able to focus on what was in front of me. That's confinement at its best."

"I can appreciate that." He crossed his arms over his chest. "School is consuming. It owned me for four years as well."

"Where did you go?"

"University of Colorado."

"The one in Boulder, right?"

He nodded.

"Is it as pretty as it looks there?"

"Prettier." He took a sip of water. "They wanted me to play soccer, like I had in high school, but I didn't want to be a student athlete chained to practices and games—and feel confined." He grinned. "I wanted to have fun, so that was what I did."

The thought of him in soccer shorts and his tight, defined calves wasn't an image I hated.

Neither was the high school version of Macon—I envisioned hair that was too long and patchy scruff on his face and that straight-out-of-the-shower look that every male senior had.

God, I was positive he was delicious at all ages.

I raised my hands as though a beat began to play through the dining room. "I'm almost at the finish line, and I can't wait." The relief that came with that statement was enough to make me dance a little, for my shoulders to relax and my hands to stay in the air.

"What about you, Macon?" I slowly lowered my arms. "I know travel and food and buying gifts are things you love." The heat that entered my face from saying that four-letter word caused me to smile. "What are some other things you love?"

"My family. Friends. Work." He sighed. "Sounds so basic, but it's the truth. They own my life. Playing is just a bonus that my job has afforded me, and with that comes travel and tasting different cuisines and doing outdoorsy things wherever I go—whether that's skiing or kayaking or hiking. I just like being in nature."

"I've done the other two, but I've always wanted to try skiing."

"We'll go to the Alps. That's the best in the world."

I took a deep breath. "How did I know you were going to say that?"

He smirked. "Are you telling me you hate the idea?"

I shook my head, unable to form a response just yet. "I'm saying I can't even comprehend that idea—it's that dreamy." I needed to shift things, to focus on him, where the conversation was easier to process. "Has working for your family business been the goal all along?"

"For as long as I can remember." One of his arms dropped, and he picked up his sake. "Until my father retired, all I'd ever seen him do was work. My mother was the same. She wasn't employed at the company. She's an artist, and she's sold her paintings to galleries around the country. She has a studio next to their house, and that's where she spends most of her time, which instilled quite the work ethic in me. My brothers too. We all work our asses off, and as soon as my uncle retires, we have this burning desire to take the company to a level neither my father nor Walter has reached."

"Do you think a higher level is even possible?" When I didn't receive a response, I continued, "I mean, Spade Hotels has locations all over the world with a massive following and loyal guests. What would that level even look like?"

He nipped his lip, setting his arms over the plate in front of him, staring at me like I was meat. "When you've signed the NDA, I'll tell you my aspirations for this business."

"But not before?"

"No."

"Because you don't trust me?"

"It has nothing to do with trust, Brooklyn."

Although I was just teasing, I was curious about his reply. "What does it have to do with, then?"

He was quiet for a moment. "It's funny, you've talked about separation and how you weren't sure if you would be able to do it. How, in your mind, Spade Hotels and I were the same beast. But here's a great example of how we're not." He pointed at his chest. "This side of me—the personal side, the one who's been gawking at you because you're so painfully stunning—wants to tell you everything. But the work side of me—the professional side, who has obligations and responsibilities to my family—can't."

"That makes perfect sense to me." And it did. "I swear to you, I get it."

He folded his hands together. "Work is a heavy part of me, but it's not all of me, Brooklyn. You got a glimpse of that part tonight, and if you accept the job, you'll see a lot more, but work Macon needs to stay put. He can't enter this conversation. Not yet at least."

There were two versions of me as well, and he didn't know the other.

I hid it from him.

I even lied about it.

The guilt was suddenly eating at me, even stronger than it had before.

I reached across the table, placing my hand on his arm. "I respect that," I said softly. "More than you could ever know."

As I went to pull my hand back, he stopped me by placing his fingers on mine. "Stay."

"I think our first round of sushi is going to be here at any second."

"Then, I'll feed it to you." He licked across his lips.

A command that came through smooth and silky, like feeding me rolls and nigiri was a typical Tuesday for him.

"How do you make everything sound so easy?" I inhaled, my lungs so tight that I kept in the air and didn't release it.

He shrugged. "When it comes to you ... it is."

FIFTEEN

Macon

Brooklyn didn't need to tell me that the sushi blew her away. I could hear it and see it every time she took a bite —the quiet moans as she chewed, the way she closed her eyes right before she swallowed, the smile she gave me every time she dipped a piece in her soy sauce.

The food was exceptional.

But what made me the happiest was watching her enjoy it, knowing that the effort I'd put into tonight was well worth it.

And it seemed that, in some way, the meal was bringing us closer. Whether it allowed us to get to know each other better, or she was dropping her shield a little further to let me in, or her mind was finally starting to shift and she was coming to terms with wanting more.

She didn't say.

But I could tell—by the way she looked at me through the rest of the dinner; how she held my hand as we walked out of the restaurant; how she sat, pressed against my side, in the backseat of the SUV without my having to pull her closer—that we weren't the same people who had come in for sushi a few hours before.

She didn't admit that something had clicked inside her. She didn't tell me that she wanted to date me.

This was purely just speculation based on a feeling.

But it was one I was holding on to.

Shit, I'd never thought I'd be the man who fell first. I'd never thought I'd be the guy waiting for the woman to express her feelings after I'd already voiced mine.

But here I was.

I had no shame or regret.

I didn't give a fuck how much shit my friends and brothers gave me about stalking the club or being obsessed with her or pointing out that I was pussy-whipped.

They were right.

I was.

Because Brooklyn was worth it.

She was everything I'd never known I wanted.

And the more I learned about her, the harder I wanted to draw her in.

With my arm around her, I placed my lips against her cheek, breathing her in, inhaling those salty beach and lemon scents. "Oahu tastes delicious on you."

As she smiled, I kissed the soft lines by her mouth.

When she tilted her neck, I kissed down to her collarbone.

While we had been in the restaurant, she'd teased me with this spot, moving her hair to either side, revealing the bone that jutted out below her neck and the delicate skin that surrounded it.

She knew exactly what she was doing each time she showed it to me.

And each time, my dick throbbed inside my pants, dying to

be released, to sink into her wetness, while my lips were right here, kissing this.

Licking across it ... like I was doing now.

"Different than Kauai tastes on me?" Her voice changed now that her head was back, the top of it pushing against the seat cushion behind her.

"Yes." My voice turned to a growl from a need that was making everything inside me pulse.

As my mouth lowered to the tip of her chest, she straightened her head and turned toward me. The headlights from the cars opposite us were shining stripes of light across her face, showing the intensity in her eyes and her parted lips.

"You have no idea what you're doing to me right now," she whispered in a low tone so the driver wouldn't hear.

"Tell me."

With our stares locked, she took my hand and placed it on her knee, just under the bottom hem of her dress, and using her strength, she slid that hand toward her pussy.

Slowly.

Inch by fucking inch.

"You're making me crave you in ways I didn't even think was possible."

My dick, already so hard, now ached as her words penetrated through me.

"Fuck me," I hissed.

I put no momentum behind the movement of my fingers. I just let her guide me. And by the time I reached her inner thigh, I could already feel the heat, her skin scorching.

As I got deeper, I began to feel the wetness.

She was desiring me in a way she could no longer control.

Needing me.

Yearning for me.

A want that was as strong as mine.

And once I made it all the way in, where her cunt was covered in lace, her hand left mine, and it reached across the small space between us to cup my dick.

That right there was the only thing that could make this moment any hotter—and it was happening.

Damn it.

"I don't know how I'm going to wait to have this," she moaned, stroking my cock through my pants.

She didn't know what she was starting.

She didn't know what the fuck she was doing to me.

The fire that was roaring within me.

The restraint I was using to not tear this dress off her.

"Brooklyn ..."

There was something incredibly sexy about a woman taking charge, voicing what she wanted and going after it, when she was the one who instigated what was already on my mind. I brushed my fingers up and down the fabric that separated us, feeling the wetness through her panties. I slipped the material aside, just enough to graze the outside of her lip.

"What if I told you, you didn't have to wait?"

Her head tapped against the cushion as she circled her thumb over my crown, like it was her tongue and she wanted nothing more than to lick me. "Don't tease me, Macon."

Her choice of words was as taunting as her hand.

I swiped her clit.

Just once.

But a movement that was strong enough to make her gasp.

"I'm not teasing you."

"Then, what are you telling me?"

"I'm telling you that if you want to come, in about fifteen minutes, I can make that happen."

I lowered my finger through her wetness, feeling how

turned on she was, and when I reached the bottom of her pussy, I dipped inside.

Just to my first knuckle.

That small amount made her legs spread, and she rocked her hips forward, probably figuring that would score her my whole finger.

But it didn't. I stayed there, about two inches in, and I didn't move.

Her grip tightened around my dick. "I don't know if I can wait fifteen minutes."

I chuckled, a laugh that was deep and gritty, dripping with fucking need. "You'll wait. I'm giving you no other choice."

The SUV came to a stop on the tarmac, feet from where the red carpet had been laid out, the staircase from the plane meeting the center of the rug.

Brooklyn glanced out the windshield before looking back at me. "But we have a forty-minute flight ahead of us. The math doesn't add up."

If the trip were just a little longer, I would take her into the bedroom in the rear of the plane, and once we reached cruising altitude, I would spend the remainder of the flight with my face between her legs. But once we got in the air and the seat belts came off, the ten or so minutes wouldn't be enough before we'd have to buckle up again for landing.

My finger went all the way in, twisting as it reached the end of her, aiming toward her stomach, where it hit that famous spot. "You're going to get touched. Don't worry about that."

"*Fuuuck.*"

She felt just what I wanted her to, and her moan made everything all right.

I pulled out to the tip of my finger and dived back in as she said, "What about you?"

"What about me?"

"When do I get to touch you?"

I fucking love that she wanted to.

But I also loved working her up to the point where she was ready to explode, where she was on the verge of begging, where she knew, without any doubt, how much power I had over her body. So, after our flight, she would go home and climb into her bed—a plan I'd had all along—and desperately want to be under my covers.

"When I allow it to happen," I told her. "That's when."

The backseat door opened, the lights from the plane illuminating the short walkway from us to the plane.

My body was blocking the doorway, so the driver, while he stood outside the SUV, couldn't see in. Reluctantly, I removed my hand from her pussy, holding my finger to my lips, where I sucked off the wetness, not letting any of it go to waste.

"Come with me, Tiny Dancer."

I climbed out, waiting for her, and nodded at the driver and flight attendant as my hand went to the small of Brooklyn's back to guide her up the stairs.

Within a few steps down the plane's center aisle, she faced me.

Before she could ask where I wanted to sit—a question I knew was coming—I pointed at a row with two seats. "Right there."

The placement didn't matter. The plane was small, open. Wherever we sat, we'd be in the flight attendant's direct line of sight.

Without a word, she followed my instruction, crossing her legs, wrapping the seat belt over her lap. And I took the spot on the other side of her. The flight attendant began making her way over to us.

"As requested, I didn't have any hors d'oeuvres prepared for this leg of the trip," the flight attendant said. The same crew had flown us here, and she had confirmed my request before we departed the plane. "I have champagne on ice and lemon water prepared. Is there anything else I can get either of you to drink?"

"Champagne sounds perfect," Brooklyn replied.

I had known we were going to have dessert at the sushi restaurant since I'd already taken a long look at the menu before I booked the reservation. That was why I didn't think food on this flight was necessary, but I'd asked for champagne. One that was dry and crisp, that would pair well with a full stomach.

But now that I had the taste of Brooklyn in my mouth—a taste I needed much more of—I wanted something a bit stronger.

"Scotch," I told her. "Several fingers' worth."

"Of course. I'll be right back."

Once she was gone, I glanced at Brooklyn. The seat was far too big for her, her tiny frame getting lost in the leather.

"Fifteen minutes," she groaned.

"Or less."

"Less?" As she arched her back, her chest became my focal point, those perfect fucking tits dying to be freed from her bra, nipples needing to be licked and bitten. "You're teasing me again."

If this were the private Spade jet, there would be more room in between our two seats and a set across from us. But this plane was much smaller, so our seats were directly beside each other with an unmovable armrest in between.

Even with the hard armrest, I would have no problem reaching her.

I grazed the outside of her thigh. "Yes. Less."

Her eyes widened. "I'm onto you, Mr. Spade."

"Then, you know I'm looking forward to finishing what I

started." As she slowly licked across her lips, I added, "You know, for someone who's only looking to unplug, you're certainly good at goading me into what you want."

"Who says I'm goading you?" She tilted her head just a little. "Or that this is even about unplugging?"

The change that I'd seen on her face throughout dinner needed to be confirmed.

And it just was.

But I said, "That's been your goal all along."

Another shift happened, this time in the seriousness of her expression. "What makes you think that's the case now?"

"If it isn't, then why don't you tell me?"

I wondered if she realized I was goading her to answer a question I hadn't yet asked.

And if she did realize, I was curious if she cared.

She clasped her fingers around my wrist, holding it, staring at me. "I don't want to be anywhere except right here."

"You want to be present ..."

"Yes, Macon." She linked her fingers with mine. "Unlike the previous times, I'm not looking to forget. I want to remember every single detail."

"Of tonight," I clarified.

"Of all of it." Her tone was just a little above a whisper. "If you're looking for more words than that ... I don't have them. Yet."

So, she did understand where I was going with this, and she knew what I wanted to hear.

And even though she had given me as much as she could, I liked what she'd said.

There was plenty of time for more.

Because what Brooklyn didn't realize was that she was almost giving me everything I wanted. As long as she nailed the interview, she'd be starting the job right around the time I'd be heading home to LA. Her relocation package would include six months of housing in a room at the Beverly Hills Spade Hotel until she found a place of her own. Not only would she be working for our company, but she'd also be living ten minutes from my house.

But Brooklyn could be feeling some trepidation about becoming a Spade Hotel employee and how that would affect things between us. If that was the case, she'd want to move at a speed that was slow as fuck.

The same speed she was moving at now.

All that did was give me more motivation to make her mine before she found out I was going to be her boss.

A situation I still hadn't handled, but I would.

I pulled my fingers out of her hold and touched her cheek. "It's enough."

I was just lowering my hand toward her leg when the flight attendant returned.

"Your champagne." She positioned the glass in the cupholder next to Brooklyn's window seat. "And your scotch," she said, handing me my tumbler. "Is there anything else I can get you?"

"A blanket." I nodded toward Brooklyn. "She's cold."

"I have some heated ones in the back. Let me grab one for you."

The second she was gone, Brooklyn laughed. "A blanket? Really?"

"You'll be impressed with what I'm able to do under there."

She glanced behind her, checking on the flight attendant. "Wait ... you're really going to—"

"Yes."

Her mouth stayed open, almost hanging. "While the flight attendant sits directly behind us?"

"She won't be directly behind us. She'll be by the restroom, which isn't in the main cabin."

"But it's close enough."

I lowered my voice as I said, "You didn't seem to have a problem with me playing with your pussy in the backseat of the SUV. Why is this any different?"

"I don't know." She filled her lungs. "I guess because there was music playing, so the driver couldn't hear me."

I tapped the screen of the tablet that was built into the back of the seat in front of me, selecting music out of all the entertainment options, and picked the first station I came across. Country rock instantly came through the speakers.

"That's solved. What other excuse do you have for me?"

While Brooklyn seemed to be contemplating my question, the flight attendant returned with a thick black fleece blanket that she spread over the front of Brooklyn. "The captain just notified me that takeoff is in about four minutes. Is there anything else I can get you in the meantime?"

"We're good," I told her. I even added a smile, which I shifted toward Brooklyn. "Aren't we?"

She nodded, her skin flushing. "Yes."

"I'll be back after takeoff to check on you."

Once we were alone again, I said, "Four minutes until take-off. We'll have another five, maybe six until she's back."

Her brows rose. "What are you saying?"

I chuckled. "There's something you want ... am I right?"

"Yes."

"Then, you'd better start begging me, Brooklyn, because from my calculations, you have no more than ten minutes to convince me to finger-fuck you and make you come."

"I thought—"

"You thought wrong." I leaned back in my seat, folding my hands behind my head, arms bent at my elbows.

She turned toward me, holding the armrest that was between us with both of her hands. "You want *me* to beg *you* to finger me?"

I chewed my bottom lip. "You're wasting time by asking questions."

"But weren't you supposed to be begging to lick me?"

"That was then." Instead of biting, I dragged my teeth over the same lip. "This is now." I glanced at the tablet, seeing that a minute had passed. "Nine minutes."

"You're unbelievable."

"No." I shook my head, feeling the grin deepen the lines by my eyes. "I'm relentless. That's something we both know, and up until now, you've appreciated that about me. You'll appreciate this, too, once I cave and give you what I want."

"What *I* want, you mean."

"No, Brooklyn." My brows furrowed as I studied the outline of her body through the heavy blanket. "What I want is to please you. To hear you scream. To taste your cum on my tongue. To feel your cunt tighten around my dick. To watch you lose control of your body, allowing me to take the power and bring you to places you've never reached. That's what I thrive on. What I desire. What I want more than fucking anything." I brought my finger up to my nose, the one that had been inside her. The one I'd licked clean. "Maybe the men in your past were focused on themselves, but that's not me. I think you know that by now."

Her throat moved as she swallowed. "I can't breathe ..."

"Good. Now, make it hard for me to breathe."

She sank a little lower in her seat, her arms going beneath the blanket so I couldn't see what she was doing, and when they surfaced, there was black lace in her hand. She tossed the lace onto my lap. "Smell them."

Now, she was giving me orders.

But, fuck, it was a hot one.

I lifted her panties to my face, rubbing the thickest part under my nose and across my lips. "They're wet."

"That's from you."

The scent was everything I remembered about her pussy. Sweet with a hint of softness, like baby powder even though the rest of her was citrus and beachy.

As I continued to watch her, she pushed the blanket to the far side of the seat and lifted her dress to her waist, showing me the bareness beneath. "This is where I want you, Macon." She ran two fingers down the front of her, pausing at her clit to give it a quick swipe before continuing lower until she was at the base of her pussy.

The spot where I wanted my cock.

Where I would kill to take a whiff.

"And this is where I need you." Those same two fingers jabbed inside her. But they didn't go far. They went in only an inch or so, and when she pulled them out, her skin glistened from the wetness.

Wetness I wanted to feel on my cock.

My hand.

My tongue.

"I want to taste them," I demanded.

Her stare narrowed. "What would you do to make that happen?"

I chuckled. "You're smooth."

"Let's negotiate." She held up her hand. "I'll give you a taste, if you give me a finger."

"Just one?"

She smiled. "I'll start with one. Who knows? I might beg for two."

Sounds were coming from the cockpit, telling me we were almost four minutes into the ten I'd allotted.

"I'll make that deal."

As she lifted her fingers into the air, my mouth met them, my lips surrounding the two until I reached her knuckles.

"*Mmm,*" I moaned.

The flavor was different on her skin. Richer. Tastier. Even more fucking delicious.

"Damn it." I shook my head as I pulled back. "I want more."

She pulled her hand back and removed her seat belt, turning her body toward me. She then lifted the leg closest to me, bending it at the knee and setting her foot on the edge of the seat to give my eyes even more access. "Here's more."

That view.

The vulnerability.

The wetness I could see on her skin.

The folds of fucking pleasure I wanted to bury myself in.

For the moment, it was mine.

Every inch.

Every drop.

God, that was one gorgeous cunt.

"It's almost too pretty to touch."

"But—"

"I said, almost," I voiced, cutting her off. "I want to touch it too badly to renege. Besides, my word is bond, and I never back out of a deal." My hand crossed over the armrest and stopped the second I felt her heat. "Has a man ever made you come by fingering you?" She said nothing. "Answer me, Brooklyn."

"No."

"Has one tried?"

She nodded.

"And why didn't you come?"

She shrugged. "I just couldn't. It wasn't enough."

I didn't know why I found it so sexy when she gave me one

of her firsts. Licking her to an orgasm and now this. Next would be her ass. But I fucking loved the thought of her experiencing something with me that she never had before.

"Do you think I'll be enough?"

"Yes."

My lips pulled wide. "And why do you think that?"

"Because you seem to know my body better than I do."

I gave her no warning. No sign that I was going to touch her.

I wanted to catch her off guard.

So, when I thrust a finger into her pussy—my middle one, which was the longest—she drew in a deep breath, her eyes closed, and her head tilted back, exposing her whole throat.

"*Yesss.*"

I was going to make her come. There was zero question about that.

"This is Captain Ron," the captain said through the intercom. "We've been cleared for takeoff."

The moment he finished speaking, the plane began to move across the tarmac.

Brooklyn was now focused solely on my eyes, her gaze feral, almost rabid.

Her mouth was open.

And my finger, unlike the jet, hadn't moved. It was all the way inside her, my thumb hovering above her clit, but not touching it yet.

"Have you ever had an orgasm during takeoff?"

Air came through her lips, as though she wanted to laugh but was too turned on to make the sound. "No."

"You're about to."

"But that's in—"

"Probably about two minutes," I roared. "I know." I slid

back to my tip and repeated that pattern several more times, proving the words, "That's how fast you're going to come."

Her stare couldn't challenge me.

Because she knew I was right.

Because even as I arched my finger toward her navel, circling her G-spot before I dipped out and stroked back in, she could feel the build.

And I knew that from the way she was tightening.

How she was breathing.

How the second I skimmed my thumb over her clit, it was already hard.

"Macon ..."

She was gripping my hand. Almost clawing it.

"Does that feel good, baby?"

She was moving with me.

Her pussy was letting me in, holding my finger so tightly, like it didn't want to let my hand go.

"Fuck yes," she cried.

The plane had driven toward the runway and was stopped. Every time I flew, there was always a brief pause before the captain stepped on the gas and the plane sped down the tarmac and lifted into the air.

As soon as I felt the pause, I flicked my thumb over her clit.

"Macon!"

Once my name left her lips, I felt the acceleration as we shot across the ground, the captain quickly picking up speed.

Just like my hand was.

I wasn't just slamming my finger into her pussy. I was turning my wrist. I was aiming the tip toward her G-spot. I was giving her clit the pressure she needed to get off.

And she was close.

I heard it in each breath.

Every moan.

I felt it from the buck of her hips as she met my finger, rocking against it, sliding back and shoving back in.

The whole time, her eyes were locked with mine.

Her lips stayed parted.

Her nose flaring as she inhaled.

And the jet was going faster, the landscape of Honolulu passing by the windows—if I were looking through them.

But I wouldn't dare.

Because I wouldn't miss this moment.

Not when I was fucking dying to watch her come.

And from what I could tell, she was seconds away from that happening.

I pressed down on her clit, pushing it from side to side, while I added a second finger. She didn't have to beg for it. Her reactions were doing that for her.

The panting.

The gasping.

The way she was moaning, "Macon," every time she released the air in her lungs.

As she began to close in around me, her wetness thickening, I kept my finger all the way in and twisted it upward, brushing the tip against that spot.

It took only two grazes before the plane was rising in the air and Brooklyn's stomach was shuddering.

"Fuck!" Ripples pounded across her. "Yes!"

I kept up the grind, rotating around that sensitive place, milling across it.

And as we got higher, the wheels pulling back, the rush of sensations floating past us as we climbed toward the clouds, waves of pleasure spread across her.

They hit her lips as they curled. Her eyes as they closed. Her skin as it reddened.

And my dick fucking chaffed across my boxer briefs,

yearning for the pressure of her hand, mouth, pussy—anything that would alleviate the cum inside me.

"Macon!" she hissed for the last time, her body slowing, her stomach stilling.

Until she was looking at me, trying to catch her breath.

I gently pulled out, my thumb leaving her clit, and I held those same fingers in front of her. "Taste yourself."

She hesitated as she gazed at my fingers and then carefully took the wet tip into her mouth, flicking her tongue across it before her lips left my skin.

"Do you taste that sweetness?"

"Yes."

"I'd give you more, but I want it for myself." I quickly devoured it all, swirling my tongue around it.

As I swallowed, she pierced her lip with her teeth, releasing it to say, "I don't know how you just did that." She glanced at the window. "We probably still even have a few minutes left."

I checked the time on the tablet. "Four, based on my estimate." I reached across the armrest again. "I like that challenge. What else can we negotiate?"

"Whether I get to touch you or not."

Now, this was going to be fun.

"How about this? If I can make you come before the flight attendant returns to check on us—so, about four minutes—then you don't get to touch me."

Something I didn't fucking want, but I was determined to make her crave me.

"And if I don't?"

"You'll spend the night in my hotel room."

She winked. "Good luck."

I laughed. "Game on."

BROOKLYN

Thank you for the most incredible evening of
my life. Even though I should be in your suite
right now, it was a night I'll never forget.

ME

My pleasure.

And, yes, you're right, having you in my arms
would be the perfect ending, but a bet is
a bet.

BROOKLYN

One I can't believe you made.

ME

Sweet dreams, Brooklyn.

BROOKLYN

You too. <3

P.S. I don't need the full week. My answer
is yes.

SIXTEEN

Brooklyn

"One last scan of your résumé, and I think we'll be done here," Cooper, Macon's middle brother, said from the other side of the conference room table.

With his face pointed down, reading the copy of my résumé that he'd brought in with him, I stared at his forehead while having the most intense out-of-body experience.

For one, since Macon's brother had walked into the room, I hadn't been able to stop comparing his face to Macon's, dissecting the similarities, noticing each of the differences.

Two, I was in LA. The HR department of Spade Hotels had flown me over on the red-eye. Once I landed this morning, they checked me into the Beverly Hills Spade Hotel, where I had five hours to nap and get ready before I was picked up and brought to their corporate office. HR had then met me at the entrance, giving me a full tour of the building before I was brought to the executive-level floor and into the private conference room, where the next steps were explained to me, along with who I'd be speaking with today.

And three, I was at, what I assumed, to be the tail end of my first interview, and with one more to go, as long as I did as well on that one as I'd done with this one, there was a good chance this job would be mine.

With those three points swirling through my head at a speed that was making it hard to breathe, there wasn't a single inch of my body that wasn't covered in a thin layer of sweat.

"Yeah, we're good." Cooper finally looked up. "Do you have any questions for me?"

I had tons.

What has Macon told you about me?

Do you know that we've had sex?

That he wants to date me?

If you do, is that affecting the way you're looking at me? Considering whether I'll be good for this position?

And in addition to questions, there was relief. I'd gotten past the part where I had to discuss my job history, and I'd survived all the lies I'd fed him.

Even though I felt like shit about it.

Even though it made me feel like the worst person in the world.

I blinked several times, focusing on his golden-brown hair— a color much lighter than Macon's and a length slightly longer —and his dark blue eyes, compared to Macon's deep emerald, and said, "I think you've answered everything."

"Great." He folded my résumé, holding it in his large palm. "I'm going to let Jo know that you're ready for her."

Jo was Macon's first cousin, Walter's daughter. From what I'd read online, Jo was a boss lady.

I didn't know why, but I had more anxiety about meeting her than talking with Cooper.

About looking her in the face and giving her the same job history speech that I'd just given to him.

That I didn't have the nerve to tell Macon about being a maid at the hotel, and now, I was in this horrible situation, and it was my fault.

He stood and reached across the table, clasping my hand, giving it a shake that wasn't weak, but wasn't crushing either. "It's been nice to meet you, Brooklyn."

"And you." I smiled. "Thank you for the opportunity to talk to you. It would be an honor to work for your company."

His lips spread into a grin, and he released my hand and turned his back, leaving me alone in the room.

My purse was at my side, and I quickly grabbed my phone from the inside pocket and checked the screen, where there were texts from Clem and Jess in our sister group chat.

CLEMENTINE

How's it going? Have you taken any pictures? We want to see the building and the offices. Show us everything.

JESSE

You're still in the interview???

CLEMENTINE

If she was finished, she would have replied. She must still be meeting with them.

JESSE

I can't take all this waiting. My anxiety is through the roof.

ME

I'm here! One down, one to go. Next one is starting any second.

CLEMENTINE

How do you feel? Have you eaten anything?
Are you doing these interviews on an empty
stomach?

JESSE

Mother hen is worried sick, obviously, and I'm
an anxious ball of nerves. Text us the second
you're done.

"Brooklyn, hi."

The sound of my name caused me to look up. I was relieved when I saw Jo was a woman not too much older than I was, and, oh man, was she strikingly beautiful. She had long black hair and the most brilliant blue eyes with cute little freckles underneath them. She had on a light-pink suit that I could never pull off with heavy gold jewelry that balanced the feminine touches of the outfit.

"Hi," I replied and stood to greet her.

"No, no, please sit." She came over to my side of the table and reached for my hand. "I really prefer to keep things as informal as possible. I'm Jo, by the way."

As we shook hands, her smile was attempting to send a wave of calm through me. But it didn't work. If anything, all it did was claw at the guilt.

"I've been talking to Macon over the last couple of days, and he's told me lots about you, so I've really been looking forward to this meeting."

Our sushi date had been three days ago. We hadn't gotten together since because I'd been working doubles and juggling school to make up for the time I'd be here, but we'd texted and even talked on the phone. During all those conversations, never once had Macon mentioned anything about Jo or that he'd spoken to her.

I wasn't surprised. I was just curious about what he'd told her.

"I've really been looking forward to it too," I said.

Which was the truth, aside from the emotions eating at me.

"Great dress."

I glanced down the front of me, forgetting which one I'd put on. I'd brought three in my suitcase and tried them on multiple times, taking pictures to send to my sisters, unable to choose on my own. But a quick peek reminded me that I'd gone with the tighter of the three. It was cinched at my waist with a built-in belt and hit at my knees.

"Thank you so much." When I looked at her again, I knew my face was red. "It's new."

"Well, it was a wonderful purchase. It looks fabulous on you."

Sweet, complimentary.

From our little interaction so far, she felt too nice to be fed lies.

"I really appreciate that," I said softly.

"Of course." She was holding a piece of paper, and as she moved to the other side of the table and took a seat, she placed it in front of her. "I've had a chance to look over your résumé. I see you've only had one job, which is awesome. Longevity and loyalty are definitely things I look for in a candidate."

My stomach started to ache.

Because the one position listed was fake.

I'd put down that I was a server and did the inventory at Clem and Jesse's bar. Since Jess filled in as assistant manager one day a week, I used her as my reference and changed her last name so it wouldn't look suspicious.

Clem wouldn't have been happy that I'd lied, so I'd made Jess promise not to tell her.

And I felt sick over it.

Sick that I wasn't telling the truth, sick that I hadn't yet told Macon that I worked at the hotel. I just didn't want him to find out this way; therefore, this'd felt like my only option.

But I hated that—and I hated that I wasn't being honest to the people who were giving me a chance to interview at their company.

They deserved the truth.

"So, it looks like you've been working at the bar full-time throughout college?" Jo confirmed.

"My sisters and I left The Big Island once I graduated from high school and moved to Kauai, and I got the job within the first few days of being there. I just gave myself enough time to unpack and get settled before I went straight to work."

"You're a go-getter. I love that. You remind me a lot of myself." She tucked a chunk of hair behind her ear. "You'll be graduating in what, about five to six weeks?"

I nodded, smiling. "I honestly can't believe it."

"It's wild how fast it goes by, isn't it? In some ways, it feels like the longest four years of your life, and in other ways, it feels like you just got started."

"Perfectly described." I wiped my sweaty hands over the bottom of the dress, hoping it wouldn't leave a mark. "But I'm excited for the next step, and I've already enrolled in the Six Sigma certification class. That starts the day after I graduate."

"Fantastic." She grabbed a pen off the table and jotted down a note on my résumé. "And you'll be able to balance work while taking the class, I'm guessing?"

"It won't be a problem."

She grinned. "I had a feeling you were going to say that. We're going to get along just great." She winked and folded her hands over the paper, no longer looking at it. "I want to shift gears a little and chat about your current job. It's mentioned that you do inventory at the bar. If we can, let's go over a couple of instances when you possibly saved the bar money or, even better, where you came up with a process to make things more efficient." She held up her finger, like she had more to add. "They don't have to be things you've actually implemented. If they're just ideas, I would love to hear those too."

I had an example ready to go. One that had zero truth to it.

And when I started to tell her what it was, for some reason, I didn't know why, but the words just weren't there.

Not in my head.

Not on my tongue.

I took a deep breath, my lungs feeling so tight that the air burned as I sucked it in. "The bar ..." I was able to get out until my voice faded, my chest pounding. I tried clearing my throat. "The bar ..." The words came out scratchy, and I coughed.

"Do you need more water?" Jo was looking at the bottle in front of me that HR had given me when I came in.

"No." I swallowed. "I'm fine. I'm just ..."

A mess.

And a total fucking disaster.

My thoughts, my head, the regret that was stabbing me—all of it.

Why was this suddenly so difficult?

Why had I answered all of Cooper's questions, and now, when it came to Jo, I was locked up, unable to spit out even a full sentence?

I knew the example of how I'd saved time and money at the bar. I'd rehearsed it on the plane and when I woke up in the hotel room after my nap and in the car ride on the way over here and during the tour of the building.

It wasn't that.

It was that I was staring at the face of a woman who was only a year or two older than I was, who had worked and fought for the position she had at this company, who had led one of the brand's most successful launches—a hotel in Utah, according to everything I'd read.

Who I wanted to give so much respect to.

"Jo ..."

She leaned her arms on the wooden table. "We can start somewhere else. Let's move on to the description of the position and—" She cut herself off as I shook my head.

"It's not that." I wrung my hands together, locking my fingers. "I need to be honest with you."

I knew how hard that was going to be.

How I could lose this opportunity.

How she could ask me to leave.

How she could walk out of this meeting and call Macon and tell him the truth.

Am I stupid for taking this risk? For potentially blowing this shot?

It didn't matter. I couldn't go on until I came clean.

"Something's been eating me up, and I have to be honest with you." I exhaled loud enough that she could hear. "I don't work at the bar."

Her eyelids narrowed. "Okay ... then where do you work?"

"I work at a hotel on the beach on Kauai." My body was jittering so badly that I swore she could see the vibrations. "In the housekeeping department." The pulsing in my heart was rocketing through my chest. "And I've worked as a housekeeper for the last four years."

I separated my hands and gripped the armrests. "In fact, it's at the hotel Macon's currently living in. Before I even met him, I was cleaning his room from the day he checked in." I wrapped my arms around my stomach, the armrest not giving me enough support. "I know that's something I shouldn't be ashamed of. I know I should have been truthful on my résumé. But Macon doesn't know about my job. I've kept him in the dark, and if I listed it, I was afraid one of you would discuss it with him before I had the chance to tell him the truth."

I mashed my lips together, fighting the emotion. The urge to cry became so strong, but I wouldn't. I needed to get through this. I needed to show her who I was, not the person I'd created on my résumé.

She pushed my résumé aside. "Let's stop the interview part and talk as friends, okay? I want you to feel comfortable enough to say everything you need to tell me."

"Please." I nodded extra hard. "I need that." I waited several seconds before I continued, "I'm sure you're wondering why I haven't told Macon any of this."

"I am, yes." Her voice was delicate, even-toned. "And I say that because you should have heard the way he spoke about you, so I'm not sure why you've even hesitated to tell him."

I'd been looking at the table, her stare too much, but her response made me gaze up.

"He's enamored with you, Brooklyn."

Words that only made me feel worse.

Because despite my unwillingness to commit to the next level, I cared about him deeply.

I wanted him.

His feelings, his opinions—they mattered.

And to hear that he had spoken so highly about me was a feeling I just couldn't get over.

My head hung low. "I didn't think it was ever going to lead to this. He and I, I mean. There was a time when I wouldn't even give him my name." I was giving her backstory and probably more information than she needed, but I just wanted her to see my side. "My life is muddy. I'm too full, between work and school and juggling things, and then Macon came in out of nowhere, and suddenly"—I looked at her again after glancing away—"he was bringing me up to the room that I'd just cleaned the day before, and I learned that he was the one staying in it, and I just couldn't tell him." I swallowed, the angst so thick that I could barely get the spit down.

"I clean guest rooms for a living, and his family owns a hotel brand. It's an intimidating feeling."

"But nothing you should be embarrassed of."

"I wasn't"—I drew in more air, holding it inside—"and then I was when it came to him. It just didn't feel like enough, and that was a hard thought to navigate." When I inhaled again, my eyes briefly closed. "I've always been this confident person. Independent. And when he came into my life, I locked up. I couldn't tell him the truth—not quite the same way that just happened with you, but the feeling was similar."

She leaned forward, her dark hair falling from behind her ear, and she didn't push it away. "We all come from somewhere, Brooklyn, and we all have a starting point. You're a full-time student. You're enrolled in a Six Sigma certification course. You have a skill that's not extremely common, which means you're going to be in high demand the moment you graduate.

"So, you've cleaned hotel rooms"—she gave me a soft smile —"and in your mind, that's not the ideal way to begin. That doesn't change who you are or make you less of a woman or inadequate or on a level that isn't equal to him. What I think it shows is that you're willing to do whatever it takes to support yourself through college, and that's honorable, Brooklyn."

"And if I had to guess, I bet you've reorganized the entire structure of housekeeping to save them time and money." She paused. "Am I right?"

"You're right, except they won't listen to my ideas." I sighed.

"I'll listen." She licked her lips, the gloss that covered them not even budging. "Tell me."

I huffed, my body frozen, as though I were standing on a tightrope. "You want to hear my ideas?"

"I want nothing more."

My face turned, looking at her from almost my profile. "You're not kicking me out of this interview because I lied on my résumé?"

"We both know you would have gotten this interview whether you lied on your résumé or not." She glanced toward the door and then the window before her eyes returned to me. "The foundation of my relationship has some similarities to yours. One day, over a very large glass of wine, I'll tell you the whole story."

The knot was still in my chest, another in my throat, but her statement was easing out the tension, like she was massaging them away.

"I hope, more than anything, that we get to have that wine together."

She gave me a half smile. "I can understand your feelings and why you didn't tell him and how that carried forward to now." She reached across the table even though she wasn't anywhere close to my hand. "At least to me, you came clean almost immediately, so I can't really say you lied to me. Your résumé, well, that's a different story." She quieted for a moment. "It took a lot of courage to come clean in the middle of an interview when you just met me. I know it wasn't easy. I give you a lot of credit for that."

I nodded. "I really didn't expect you to react this way. I was thinking just the opposite."

She moved her hand back and held her engagement ring,

circling the massive diamond around her finger. "You know, it takes someone who's been in familiar shoes to understand. Sympathize even." She halted the twisting of her ring. "Our scenarios aren't identical by any means, but I knew who my fiancé was long before he knew who I was—and at the time, my last name would have mattered to him."

"*Ahhh.* Got it."

"Yes." She nodded. "So, I happen to know a little something about revealing who you are and what you want the other person to know."

"I have to tell Macon ..."

"You do," she agreed. "And that's coming from someone who knows the repercussions of lying."

This conversation had turned so personal, diverting in a direction that wasn't even close to the original question that had been asked. I was afraid Jo wasn't seeing why I wanted this job and why, in my mind, I was perfect for it.

"Thank you for being so kind and patient with me."

She crossed her arms over the table. "As soon as he told me about you, I had a feeling I was going to like you. I don't know why, it was just something in my gut. I still feel that way, Brooklyn. And if anything, that feeling has grown."

Now, more than ever, I needed to show her why she should want to hire me. Why I wouldn't let her down in this role. That despite a rocky start, I was someone she could trust.

I set my hands on the table and focused on her eyes. "I want to tell you about me. Is that okay?"

"Please, I'm dying to hear everything." She pulled my résumé back in front of her, a pen now ready in her hand.

I let out a small laugh, which was needed. "When I moved to Kauai, I wanted a job that was mindless. Where I could complete my tasks without someone looking over my shoulder and where I didn't have to constantly wear a smile on my face.

I'm not saying I have resting bitch face"—I winced, making sure it was all right to go there, and when she grinned, I knew it was fine—"but most of the time, I'm deep in thought, thinking about school and homework and bills, and none of that makes me smile."

"Those wouldn't make anyone smile, girl."

"Right? Anyway, within a week, I realized it wasn't a mindless job at all. I was in a position where I could make a guest smile. Where I could go the extra mile to get them things that they didn't know they wanted or needed. That became important to me, and eventually, it was recognized by my manager, and I was promoted to the suite level, where I've been ever since. But it was around that time when things within our department stopped making sense to me."

I crossed my legs, relaxing my arms. "From what I've calculated, the average stay is five nights. Our policy is to change bedsheets after a guest has been with us for four nights. Why flip the sheets after four and then flip them again a day later? Then, there's the towels. If they've been used and are hanging on a rack, we're required to replace them. But if they're still clean, why can't we swap them out after a second use? All of this takes extra time, unnecessary labor, and it's money wasted."

"I like where you're going. Tell me more."

"Our hotel provides sewing kits. Guests almost always take them home with them, and if I had to place a wager, they go unused. Now, someone in the marketing department could argue that when the guest has a button pop off their pants in three months, it's brand recognition when they pull out the sewing kit, and that can trigger a rebooking, a referral to a friend or neighbor since the vacation will be refreshed in their mind. But based on our demographic of guests—and Spade Hotel guests—are they really sewing their own buttons, or are they taking their pants to a tailor?"

She wrote another note on my résumé and said, "We provide sewing kits."

"Move them to suite level only as a bonus bathroom amenity, offering a larger collection of toiletries to those spending top dollar, or eliminate them completely. The savings by keeping them in just your suites would be tremendous."

"I'll bring it up in our executive-level meeting tomorrow."

"Really?" My hand went to my chest. "That makes me so happy." I moved closer to the table, the energy now pulsing through me. "Here's another item you can mention. I assume your housekeepers have a checklist of things they must clean in each room, and they're trained on how to clean them properly, but there's no control over the supplies. Window spray and polish, room scent spray—so much gets wasted. And on our carts, the squeegees don't have a holder, so they often fall off and get rolled over and ruined."

"What's your solution?"

"It should be ingrained in each trainee that it takes three pumps to clean the shower walls, a two-second spray on the rag for nightstands and dressers. There's a process for cleaning and a process for the supplies. How can there be one without the other?"

"*Yesss.* I agree."

"And staffing, that's a never-ending issue." I rolled my eyes. "Our manager is constantly trying to accommodate so many different people that it's an inefficient process. There should be three shifts—no more, no less, and no half shifts." I held out my fingers and used them to count as I said, "By the time the housekeeper changes into their uniform, loads their cart, wheels it to their floor, they've wasted almost thirty minutes. That means the hotel is only getting three and a half hours of cleaning time from them. When you times that by a year, it's a scary number."

"Brooklyn ..." Jo was shaking her head. "I'm extremely impressed."

"Thank you, but it's not just housekeeping. I see changes that need to be made in many other departments. The bar in the lobby, the front desk. The maintenance department and the grounds staff. I don't know what it is or why this happens, but the problems just stand out to me, probably more so than the positives do."

I lifted the bottle of water off the table. "I haven't even opened this yet, and I probably won't. If HR had just given me a washable cup filled with purified water that was installed in your tap with a few ice cubes, that would have been more than fine. Not to mention an astronomical cost savings over the long run."

I turned the water bottle. The Spade logo was printed on the label that was wrapped around the middle of the plastic. "Brand recognition, personalization—all things that have value and add lots of class. But at the same time, a washable cup with your logo on it wouldn't make me or any visitor to your corporate office feel any differently."

She let out a small laugh. "Wait until Walter hears some of this. You're going to make my dad's entire world, and he's going to eat this up." She paused. "He couldn't join us—he's out of the office today—but I know he'll go wild when you analyze our processes and individual hotels and provide this kind of feedback."

The way she was speaking, I already had the job. But I wasn't going to point that out.

"I can't wait to meet him," I said instead.

"Your brain is going to do wonders for this company, Brooklyn."

I stared at her in amazement. "I don't even know what to say."

"Because you're humble, and I love that about you." She checked her watch. "Do you have any questions for me?"

I thought about it.

I really dug.

"Not yet, but I might in the future."

She stood from her chair. "Then, come on. I'll walk you out."

I joined her at the door, and she pulled a card out of her pocket and gave it to me.

"This has my cell number on it. Feel free to reach out anytime."

I took a deep breath. "I appreciate you, Jo. Know that, please."

Her hand briefly went to my arm before she opened the door, and I walked with her down the hallway and into the elevator, taking it to the lobby. There was never a moment of silence between us; she filled the seconds with questions about Hawaii and how excited she was to come to the grand opening of their Kauai hotel. And when we reached the sidewalk outside the building, she turned toward me.

"HR will be in touch tomorrow. I'm assuming there will be something in your inbox before you land."

"I can't even begin to process what you're saying."

Her laugh was so carefree. "It'll sink in when you see it in writing." She nodded toward the curb, where an SUV was parked. "That's your ride back to the hotel. Have a safe flight, Brooklyn. I'll be seeing you in Hawaii very soon."

I found myself hugging her. I wasn't sure if that was appropriate or professional, but it was something I had to do for myself. And as she squeezed back, I was hit with the realization that this could very well be the start of a friendship.

One that would mean so much to me.

"Bye, Jo," I whispered as our arms dropped.

We gave final smiles, and I opened the door of the SUV, jumping when I saw who was in the backseat.

"Macon ..."

"Did you really think I was going to let you tour LA all by yourself?" His grin dripped with charisma and sex. "Get in."

SEVENTEEN

Macon

"What do you think?" I asked Brooklyn while we sat in the backseat of the SUV, tucking her hair behind her ear so I could get a better look at her profile.

We'd spent the last hour riding around LA, the driver taking us on a route that I'd mapped out, making sure we went through some of my favorite parts of the city—sections that were popular, where I hung out, and where I assumed she'd spend most of her time.

"About LA?" She turned toward me. "Or you?" She smiled.

"Both."

"LA looks beautiful." She shrugged. "But let's face it. I'd move here even if it wasn't."

"For the job?"

She nipped one of her lips. "That's one of the reasons."

I wasn't going to push—she didn't seem ready—so I returned to the original question and voiced, "And what do you think about me?"

She scanned my right eye and then my left. "I can't believe you came all the way here to see me after my interview. That's a long flight, Macon." She found the hand that was on my lap and held it. "Especially because I know things are winding down at the hotel and they need you more than ever."

"I wouldn't have missed this."

But it went beyond that.

The idea of her sitting alone in a hotel room tonight after an interview with my company hadn't felt right. And as far as I knew, she had no family or friends here. I couldn't have sent her out with Jo even though Jo would have taken her out.

I wanted to be the one she celebrated with.

"That means everything to me." Her voice was quiet, but the emotion behind those words wasn't.

I kept my fingers on her face, holding the side of her cheek. "I wasn't going to let you be in a place where you've never been, in a hotel room all by yourself. Nah"—I shook my head—"it wasn't happening."

"Good, because this is so much better."

I found myself moving in closer. I needed her scents and less distance separating us.

"Aside from the tour, what do you have planned for us?"

Her question hit my ears and bounced right off. I was too focused on her face. Her eyes. The way her lips curved. How the dress that I'd picked out was covering her body, hugging her tits, waist, riding up a few inches above her knees.

"I want to kiss you."

She licked the corner of her mouth. "Are you asking for permission?"

"I'm just vocalizing what's on my mind." My hand moved to the back of her head. "It's been three days since I've seen you. God, that feels like a fucking eternity."

Her skin flushed. Her lips pulled into a grin. "I've missed

you too." Her stare then deepened. "This surprise ... it's one of my favorites."

That admission was so damn sexy.

Enticing.

I needed to taste those words on her tongue, so I leaned forward and pressed my lips to hers. I didn't smash our mouths together, like I'd done in the past. I took my time. I was gentle. But my grip, the way I was holding her hair, wasn't. I squeezed her locks into my palm and directed her face toward mine, holding it there while I parted her lips, sinking my tongue into her mouth.

I already had an erection, but the feel of her, the flavor, the way her exhales were ending in moans just loud enough for me to hear, made me even harder.

When I pulled away—something I was reluctant to do, but I'd felt the SUV stop, and I knew what that meant—I held our faces together. "We're here."

"Where's here?"

"My house ... where you'll be staying tonight."

"Are you asking? Or telling?"

"You know how badly I want to tell you," I growled. "But instead, I'm going to ask." I paused to take a breath. "Brooklyn, would you like to sleep over tonight? I'll even bring my tongue ..."

"*Mmm*. That tongue." She smiled. "But what about my things? They're at the hotel."

"I had a hunch that you weren't going to fight me on sleeping at my place, so I went and picked them up while you were at your interview." I nodded toward the trunk. "Your suitcase and carry-on are back there."

I hadn't been sure how she'd feel about me going into her room while she wasn't there. I took the chance anyway. I hadn't wanted to waste time driving back to the hotel for her to pack up her things. The timing would have messed with everything I had planned.

"And if I did fight you on it?"

"I'd drop you off at the hotel. Your room is still available. I didn't check you out."

She reached inside the bag that was on the other side of her and placed something on my lap. "You can check me out."

I looked down to see what it was, and the key card sat on my thigh.

"I won't need that room anymore."

When I glanced back up, I kissed her, harder this time, and I heard the driver get out of the front seat. He came around to my side and opened the door.

As I pulled back, I whispered, "Let's get you inside."

I climbed out of the SUV and held my hand in her direction, waiting for her to clasp her fingers around it so I could help her onto the ground. Once we reached the front door, I entered my code and brought her into the house.

"Wow." She was only in the foyer, staring past the long, wide hallway that led to the living room and the wall of glass that showed the Hills—a view that had sold me on this property. "Macon ..." She gazed up at the thirty-foot ceiling and toward the open kitchen and my office—a floor plan that allowed her to see it all from here—until she eventually locked eyes with me. "This is ... stunning."

The driver set her things by my front door, where my housekeeper met him and wheeled the bags toward the primary wing.

"I'm glad you like it."

She stayed frozen in the same spot, appearing to take it all in. "And you have a chef too?" Her eyes widened. "Is that normal for you?"

Klark had been in there for hours, working his ass off on the menu I'd created when I knew Brooklyn was flying to LA and I was joining her.

I laughed. "Pretty normal." I walked her into the kitchen. "Klark, meet Brooklyn."

He wiped his hands on his apron before shaking hers. "It's a pleasure to meet you."

"And you," she replied.

"Klark works for my brothers and me. But Jo and Jenner have their own chef, who has worked for the Daltons for years. During holidays, which we take turns hosting, it becomes chef wars over who's the better cook."

"And I always win," Klark shot back.

I nodded. "By a landslide." I clasped my hand on Klark's shoulder. "You'll see his talents soon. He's preparing us dinner."

"Seriously?"

The amazement was so obvious on her face that Klark and I both laughed.

"And I was given firm instructions that I needed to come up with a dessert that was coffee-flavored."

Brooklyn looked at me. "You remembered ..."

Of course I had.

There wasn't a detail I'd forgotten about her.

"And forget the kind of milkshake you ordered at the diner? Come on."

She squeezed my hand and said to Klark, "I can't wait to try it. All of it, not just the dessert. And whatever it is that you're making, it smells delicious."

"Trout and halibut piccata with sautéed broccoli rabe and crispy rosemary potatoes," he responded. "That's for the main course. I'm working on something new and extra special for the appetizer."

"I'm drooling," Brooklyn replied to him.

Klark looked at me and said, "I'll cook for her anytime."

I chuckled. "The champagne has been iced?"

"On the patio, with two flutes, waiting for you, buddy."

"Appreciate it," I said, and my hand went to the base of Brooklyn's back. "Let me know when you're ready for us."

I led her through the rest of the kitchen and into the living room out the sliding glass door. "Drinks first, then dinner and dessert. Followed by a dip in that"—I pointed at the hot tub that was on the edge of my infinity pool—"once the sun sets. Seeing LA at night is an entirely different feel and experience than it is during the day. Out here, under the black sky, you'll have one hell of a view."

"I can't wait. But I didn't bring a bathing suit."

I smiled as we took a seat on one of the couches, and I held her against my side. "I wouldn't let you wear one even if you did."

"If we're going to be naked, does that mean you're going to let me touch you tonight?" She drew her bottom lip into her mouth, her teeth holding it tightly.

I could feel the change between us. I could see things starting to move forward.

But today had been a big day for her, and I didn't want her to feel muddy with the connection between me and Spade Hotels. What we had was one thing. The employment she was going to be offered tomorrow was something entirely different. I didn't want her to feel pressure from either entity.

So, if that meant we needed to continue taking things slow until she figured that out and all I got to taste was her lips, I was fine with that.

"Is that what you want?"

She nodded. "Yes. More than anything."

The bottle of champagne was on the table in front of us, the cork already out. I poured some into the two glasses and gave one to her, clinking mine against hers.

"Then, it's going to be one hell of a memorable night."

JO

Things went great with Brooklyn. I ADORE her. Never thought I'd see my big cousin settle down, but she's a good one and the right one. Perfect pick.

ME

Did you mention anything about who's managing the new team?

JO

Not a word, and she didn't ask.

ME

The offer letter is going out tomorrow, yeah?

JO

I've submitted the paperwork to HR. By the time she lands, it'll be in her email.

ME

The salary we discussed and the relocation package we offer to all new hires?

JO

Yes, and yes.

I've asked HR to leave off any management information since I'm assuming you want to be the one to tell her it's you.

ME

I do ... and I will.

EIGHTEEN

Brooklyn

"Do you have any idea how beautiful you are?"

Macon's words almost felt like a dream. Actually, the last twenty-four-ish hours had felt that way, starting with the flight to LA and the meeting with Cooper and Jo and then finding out Macon had flown in from Kauai just to spend the evening with me.

Which was one of the sexiest, most thoughtful things anyone had ever done for me.

And now, we were in his hot tub after the most incredible dinner and coffee cheesecake, and just as he had described, the dark night sky was hanging over us with the view of the Hollywood Hills in front of us. Mountains were covered in the most extravagant homes, their lights twinkling while the stars shone over us. And on Macon's patio, where we'd eaten dinner and relaxed for hours after, there were pots of fire aligning the pool as we soaked in the steamy, bubbly tub that was attached.

How is this my life?

If I moved here, which seemed like a strong possibility, would nights like this one become normal? Where our evenings would end in this hot tub and I'd crave Macon's mouth, like I was doing now? Where I'd spend the night in his bed and wake up in his arms?

I was sure he wanted that.

But if that was ever going to happen, I had to tell him the truth.

The thing was, as I stared at him just to the side of me, the words weren't there.

I wanted them to be.

I wanted to speak them, get them out of the way and off my chest, so the guilt would ease up, the weight less heavy in my gut. But the unknown of how he'd react was just as heavy. So was the fact that I'd lied on my résumé and what he'd say about that too.

God, this is so much.

Especially as Macon moved closer, draping my legs across his lap, surrounding my shoulders with his arms. "Answer me, Brooklyn."

I'd been so lost in my thoughts that I almost didn't remember his question.

Beautiful.

Yes. That's it.

I gazed in his eyes. The glimmering lights around us, along with the fire, were just enough of a glow to show his face. The thickness of his beard. The heartiness of his lips.

"I can't say I look at myself in the mirror and think that about the person staring back."

"What do you see, then?"

"Just ... me." I tried to think of the exact feeling that had been in my body when I took the last glance at myself before I was picked up for the interview. "Like this afternoon, when I was in the hotel, I was looking at the dress my sisters had helped me choose. I was so grateful that I had options, and they were all amazing, and worrying about my outfit was one less thing I had to think about." I wrapped my arms around his neck. "Your level of kindness is something I've never felt or experienced before."

His smile made everything inside me tingle. "That's what you were thinking when you were looking in the mirror earlier?"

"Yes."

His chuckle was a smooth sound that seemed to vibrate through the water, sending waves across my legs. "You're something else."

He was right about that.

And what he was, was perfect.

His nakedness allowed me to take in the dips in his chest and the cords of muscle across his arms and shoulders and his etched abs, the fiery reflection allowing me to see them at certain angles under the water. His skin was silky as he held me, and as I adjusted my position, circling both legs around him, I could feel the tip of his hard-on.

And because I was naked, too, I felt it on a spot where it would take one small push and he would be inside me.

"I can feel how badly you want me."

He brushed his beard over my cheek. "I'm hard every single time I'm around you. This is what you always do to me."

"Yet the last two times we were together, you only kissed me and fingered me." Those tingles turned to flames as they licked through my body when I recalled how I'd felt during each of those occasions. "We'd already slept together by then, Macon, so why didn't you take things further?"

A question that had haunted me both times after I returned home.

He hesitated before he said, "I wanted you to know I was in this for more than my gratification. You're not just someone I want to sleep with. And since sex can make things complicated, I didn't want to add to what you were already feeling."

I knew he cared. I felt it. But to hear his reasoning, I felt it even more.

I slowly exhaled. "Because I keep telling you how muddy my life is ..." My famous line that, every time I spoke it, seemed to drive an even bigger wedge between us.

He traced the hair around my ear. "Yes, that."

"And you think if you sleep with me, my brain will intertwine you and Spade Hotels."

His hand stilled. "You told me you couldn't separate us, and since the interview was going to happen soon—and just did —that was going to make things even more realistic." He paused. "Break this down with me, Brooklyn. I fingered you a couple of days ago. You interviewed at my family's company today. You're with me now, naked. That's quite a few layers to work through."

It made perfect sense. I'd told him I was using the times we'd slept together as an escape, to completely unplug. Maybe that had been the case at the time, maybe I just hadn't realized what it actually was, but it wasn't like that now.

He needed to understand that.

"When you're with me"—my hand went on top of his—"that's when I feel the closest to you."

His words, when talking about the way he felt about me, were always so naughty. I wanted to give him a piece of that, to let him hear what it sounded like in my voice.

"When you're inside me, when your moans are in my ears, when I get to feel you come, there's this bond that happens between us. It makes us closer. It makes me want so much more." I took a breath, attempting to calm the flutters that were on the verge of exploding.

"Yes, I've used those physical times to unplug, but not in the way you think." I pushed my fingers into his skin, wanting him to feel the meaning behind these words, not just hear them. "I was unplugging from my life and plugging straight into yours." I took a breath. "It was my life that I wanted to forget, not my time with you." I pressed my nose against his. "I want this. I just want to take things slow."

A speed I couldn't move beyond until I came clean. I wasn't about to do that tonight, not while I was in his arms, unclothed, with his dick rubbing against me.

During the silence, I ran my thumb across his lips, and after I backed up a few inches, I deepened our stares. "When I say I'm the happiest, now, with you, I mean that with everything I have, Macon."

"You just need time ..."

"Yes." I swallowed, filling my cheeks with air and gradually releasing it. "Time to figure this all out in my head—graduating from college, finishing up my job, wrapping up my life on Kauai, saying good-bye to my family, and moving to LA if I get the position at Spade Hotels." And if I didn't, the start of a very daunting job search. "There's a ton of change on the horizon. Things I've worked so hard for. That's why I've been scared to add you into my life, for fear that I'll lose my focus and the only thing I'll concentrate on is you."

The list that I'd rattled off didn't include telling him the truth, which was one of the first things I had to do before considering any of the others.

Oh God.

"I understand, and I'm not rushing you."

I nodded. "I know." I dragged my fingers across his cheek,

sinking them into his dark hair. "But don't put distance between us. That's the last thing I want."

"What do you want, Brooklyn?" His voice was now gritty and powerful.

"You know ..."

"I want to hear you say it."

When I shifted my hips up, I brushed over his tip again, and as I drew our chests together, my breasts flattened against his muscular pecs.

"I want you. I want your touch." My lips went to his ear as I hugged him into me. "I want your dick in my mouth so I can suck it." I kissed his earlobe and around the shell of his ear. "And then I want you inside me until you come. But I want to feel you bare, Macon."

"You don't want me to wear a condom?"

"No."

He studied my eyes. "You're on the pill."

It was a confirmation, and I gave it to him by saying, "Yes."

"Brooklyn ..."

"What I know is that I want you." I just didn't know if, after all of this, he would still want the same. "Nothing is going to change that—for me. If we're both safe, protected, then there's no reason we need to use one again."

"Something I never ever do."

"I remember you saying that you never dated either, and now, we're here."

He laughed. "You're right about that." As he quieted, he didn't stop scanning my eyes. "You're sure about this?"

I nodded.

And when I leaned back, he gripped both my cheeks. "Say it, Brooklyn, so I can lick the words off your tongue. I want to feel them in my mouth, and then I want to lick your cunt."

His presence and feel were so powerful that it felt like he was already doing that to me.

My nails found the back of his shoulders, and I let them dig in. "No condom. I want to feel you, and I want to feel you fill me."

"So fucking dirty," was the last thing he uttered before his mouth was on mine, his tongue moving between my lips.

As my lips parted to let him in, I was overcome with Macon's flavor. That woodsy scent, mixed with spicy bergamot and smoky nutmeg.

I couldn't get enough.

Of him.

Since there weren't any clothes covering us, there was nothing to take off, so the touching came immediately. A graze across my nipple, a grab of my ass. A tug of my hair. A brush against my clit.

His hands were everywhere.

His mouth now on my neck, moving until it touched my collarbone, pressing sweet but hungry pecks across it before it began to lower to my chest.

"Macon," I moaned as he took one of my nipples into his mouth.

My hand slid into his hair as he sucked that hard peak.

As he bit it.

As he flicked it with just the point of his tongue.

He wasn't gentle. That part of him was gone. And in its place was the feral side, the dominant side, the side that wasn't satiated until I was screaming.

I didn't know how that was going to happen while my lower half was submerged under the water. But as that question began to really settle in my head, he lifted me out of the water and placed me on the edge of the tub, spreading my legs across the rim.

I looked down at him as he knelt in the water in front of me, the look in his eyes making me even wetter.

"Do you know how long I've wanted to do this?"

"Tell me," I whispered, using his favorite words.

"Too fucking long." He moved in between my legs and swiped his tongue down the entire length of me. "Fuck me, you taste good."

Maybe it was the fact that I was naked on his patio on a mountain, surrounded by homes and lights.

Or that I could feel the fire on my skin, warming parts of me that his mouth wasn't.

Or that his tongue was something I'd been dreaming about, fantasizing over, and I was finally getting it.

I didn't know.

I just knew that I was already so close, moaning, "You're going to make me come." An admission that was easy to make as he added more pressure to my clit, his finger slowly inserting inside me.

The build I'd felt on the plane was back, but this was so much more intense.

Because it came with the wetness of his mouth.

The twisting of his hand.

The friction from both.

And the combination was mind-blowing.

"Macon!" I gasped.

He knew just where to lick. Where to focus. Where to add extra strength. When to increase the speed in both his finger and mouth.

I rocked my hips toward him, urging him on even though I didn't need to. He was determined and after one thing, and he wasn't going to stop until I lost it.

That was about to happen at any second.

I was too sensitive. Too needy to hold it off any longer.

And his tongue was far too good at what it was doing.

Within a few more licks, the build was there. At the base of my pussy, rising through my stomach and into my chest, forcing me to scream, "*Yesss*! Oh God!"

The orgasm came in waves.

Each one causing me to yell, "*Fuuuck!*"

They weren't soft, like the lap of water across sand. They came in hard, they came in rough, they came in demanding.

Shudders moved through my stomach, sending my balance way off, my hands attempting to hold on to anything even though I was grasping at nothing.

"Macon!" The only thing I could control was my voice, and there shouldn't be any question in his mind how he was making me feel.

His neighbors wouldn't question that either.

I was louder than I'd ever been.

My voice only calmed as the peak rushed through me, and I was left with small, shallow quivers.

I gripped his hair, pulling until I moved his tongue off me. "My God. You are ..."

"Fucking hungry for more. That's what I am."

I didn't even have a chance to take a break, to catch my breath, before I was back in the water, sitting on the shelf that surrounded the inside of the hot tub, my legs straddling him while he positioned himself at my entrance.

"You're going to feel so fucking good," he groaned.

He wasn't all the way in, just tapping, plunging in an inch or so.

But he was so big, his crown so wide, it felt like much more.

"I need you." My claws found his skin again, digging, stabbing, begging. "Please." I drew in air despite everything being so tight, even my lungs. "Macon, I need—"

I didn't even have the full word out, and I was already getting what I'd asked for.

"Goddamn it," he roared. "I've never felt anything so tight. So wet."

And I'd never felt anything so smooth.

Because I'd never had sex without a condom before now, the feeling different than anything I'd ever experienced. He moved in and out with no effort, the texture of his skin so soft compared to the latex.

"You have no idea how this feels."

But I did.

And the speed in which he moved and the way he twisted his hips and how he was rubbing my clit with his thumb were burying every thought, preventing me from speaking.

Because it was too much.

Too many feelings.

Too many sensations swirling through me.

All I knew was that I had no control over what was happening in my body, but I was returning to that familiar place, and there was nothing I could do to stop it.

But he could.

And he did the moment he pulled out.

"Macon!"

The change of position caused the orgasm to fade. Before I could even realize what was happening, I was suddenly on top of him while he sat on the shelf I'd previously been on.

He wasted no time reminding my body how much control he had over me and my pleasure. Especially as his teeth found my nipple, as he placed a finger on my clit. As he pumped his hips upward, meeting me every time I lowered down his shaft.

The fullness caused my orgasm to return.

It caused his moans to get louder.

It caused his free hand to hold my hip, guiding me even though I held the control.

"Ride me, Brooklyn," he ordered.

I knew what it would take, and there was nothing more I wanted than to feel Macon's cum squirting within me while we both screamed out in pleasure.

But to make that happen, I had to move faster.

I had to buck harder.

When I reached the base of his cock, I twisted my hips in a circle, absorbing the full length of him before I rose back to his tip.

"That's it," he hissed. "Fuck me, Brooklyn. Make me fucking come."

I was so focused on how good this felt that I could barely respond. The only things that came out of me were moans.

And they were constant.

Loud.

They showed him exactly what was happening within me.

Because the second I felt the sparks start to rise through me, Macon took over.

His strokes were deep.

Relentless.

Consuming.

"You'd better come with me," he warned.

He knew what he was doing as he pounded into me, my body reacting just the way he wanted it to and I was positive he could feel it.

"Oh God." I tried to draw in air. "I'm going to come right now."

There was nothing I could do to hold it off.

It was there, wrapping around me.

And what helped move it along was his thumb grazing my clit, his mouth on mine.

His body owning me.

Within a few drives of his hardness, I was shuddering.

"Fuck!" I wrapped my arms around his shoulders, using his muscles to keep me from falling back in the water. "*Ahhh!*"

"Jesus fucking Christ." His strokes changed. They were deeper. Sharper. "You're milking me, Brooklyn." He bit my lip, releasing it to say, "Your pussy is telling me how badly you want me to blow my load inside you."

My moan was my reply.

Because that was what I wanted from him.

What I wanted to feel.

Watch.

Hear.

Experience.

A fullness that only his cum could give me.

And within a few more plunges, holding on with all my strength as he plowed into me, giving me harsh, rocket-like thrusts, I felt the first shot as his thickness mixed with my wetness.

"Yes!" His voice was a deep growl. "Fucking yes, Brooklyn."

I moved with him.

I arched my back to give him a new angle.

"Fuck! Me!" His sounds were so deep and erotic that another shudder spread across me.

I took in the swipes he gave my clit, the bite on my nipple, the slamming of his lips eventually on mine, and I got to taste the orgasm on his mouth.

The breathlessness.

And finally, the way he filled his lungs as both our bodies stilled.

"*Mmm.* You're fucking amazing," he exhaled.

I was surprised there was any water left in the tub when

the waves calmed. I stayed straddled around him, my arms crossed over his shoulders, my eyes closed while I gave him soft, patient, loving kisses, the bolts of electricity just starting to die down.

"We need a shower."

"And then bed," I told him. "I have to get up early for my flight. It's at eight, so I have to be at the airport around six, I think." I pulled back to look into his eyes. "I don't want you to feel like you have to take me that early. I'll catch an Uber. I really don't mind."

He kissed me, slowly at first and then a little harder. "Your flight isn't at eight, Brooklyn."

I analyzed his face, trying to understand what he was getting at. "I don't know what you mean. I have the email HR sent. I'm pretty sure the time hasn't changed, or the airline would have messaged me."

He kissed my collarbone. My neck. My cheek. "Do you really think I'm going to send you on a commercial flight when I'm flying private back to Kauai?"

I hadn't even thought about the logistics of Macon returning to Kauai or when his flight would be or how he would get there. This world of private flying and thinking about a man and his actions and wants—it was still so unfathomable to me.

"Before you attempt to answer that, no, I wouldn't." His hands cupped my cheeks. "You're flying back with me. We'll leave here at ten, which gives us some time to sleep in." He nuzzled into my neck as he lifted us out of the hot tub, carrying us across the patio and into his living room, where he walked us toward his bedroom. As we reached his en suite, he brought us into his shower, the water suddenly pouring over us. "Although, if I wake up with a hard-on, I don't know how much sleeping in I'm going to let you do."

The warm spray rained over our heads, and I sucked his bottom lip into my mouth before I said, "I need you to promise me something."

"Okay ..."

"Don't let me sleep in."

NINETEEN

Macon

"I know black is your favorite color to wear, but red"—I shook my head—"is fucking gorgeous on you."

The dress was one I'd bought her and slipped into the garment bag at the very last minute because I was dying to see the style on her body. But the image I'd had in my head didn't compare to how she actually looked.

The shade warmed her skin, intensified her stare and the sexiness of her face. The fit hugged each of her curves, the material just thin enough to show her lack of a bra and the hardness of her nipples. And whenever she turned around—like an hour ago, when she'd walked into the restaurant with me —her whole back showed, revealing the tan lines from her bikini and the softness of her skin.

"I've never worn red." Although her cheeks were turning that exact color. "I wasn't sure how I'd feel about it, especially given how revealing this dress is, but seeing the way you've been looking at me all night and the fact that you can't keep your hands off me, I think it might be my new favorite."

I wasn't the only man in this steak house who appreciated the gorgeousness of Brooklyn. The moment we had arrived and were brought to our table, every male in this restaurant had caught a glimpse of her.

I fucking loved that they were admiring something that was mine.

That they couldn't touch.

That, if they tried, I'd kill them, but they were more than welcome to gaze at her beauty.

Because my girl was breathtaking.

And since the highest-rated steak house was on the opposite side of the island, I'd booked us a night at a hotel nearby so I wouldn't have to wait the two-hour drive back home to peel this dress off her.

"Then, it looks like I need to fill your closet with more red."

"Macon ..."

I was holding my vodka on the rocks, no mixer or twist—it had just been that kind of workday, where every one of my employees pissed me off. But there was no way my foul mood was going to prevent me from celebrating Brooklyn.

"Don't *Macon* me." I smiled. "You got the job. You signed the paperwork yesterday. We're here, celebrating you." I licked across my lips as my stare lowered to her chest, her nipples taunting me in the candlelight. "I don't see anything wrong with giving you a congratulations present of some red dresses that will look amazing on you."

She hadn't stopped smiling since she'd gotten in the car this evening. Actually, since I'd shown up in LA for her interview. A grin that had grown when I took her back to my house and filled her with the best food and dessert. A night where she'd given me so much hope about our relationship when she suggested I didn't need to wear a condom and I didn't fight her on it.

We were in a good place. We were just going slow.

And now that we'd been back on Kauai for two days, the smile was at its largest.

Brooklyn had gotten everything she wanted, and even though I'd helped move things along, she'd earned the job on her own. Jo and Cooper had been impressed as hell, and HR had signed off.

She finally took a drink and set her glass down. "With the salary I've been given, I'll be able to buy my own dresses."

She'd been offered a fair and extremely competitive wage, along with bonus incentives based on how much she saved our company.

But I still didn't expect Brooklyn to buy designer clothes with the money she earned. I suspected she was the type who didn't give a fuck about designers or even know that the collection of dresses she now had were Dior.

"You certainly will," I agreed, "but I'm going to add a few pieces I want to see you in. Consider it a gift to me." I reached into the pocket of my sports coat, pulling out the box. "And this is a gift for you." I set it on the empty plate in front of her.

"Macon ..." This time, her voice was full of emotion and only slightly above a whisper. "You didn't have to get me anything."

"Before you open that, I want to tell you a little story." I took a sip of my vodka and continued to hold the tumbler in my hand.

"When I graduated from college and joined Spade Hotels, my father pulled me aside. He said there are two things anyone can control when they're starting a new job. The first is your reputation. How you treat others, how you demand respect. How dedicated you are to the job. Maybe a coworker doesn't end up liking you, maybe your personalities clash, but don't give them a chance to call you lazy or for them to question your work ethic. In a work environment, your reputation is all you have."

I paused as the waitress dropped off another round of drinks, and I downed the rest of mine before I handed her the empty.

"The second is punctuality. Neither my father nor Walter tolerates anyone being late. Ever. And when my brothers and I joined the company, he gifted each of us a watch."

Under the table, I rubbed my leg against hers. "I'm telling you this because it's your first post-college position, and watching you succeed will mean a great deal to me. Now, I'm not saying this because you're lazy—you're far from that. You work full-time, and you're one hundred percent dedicated to your dreams."

I swished a breath out of my lips. "But as for your punctuality, I've taken care of that." I winked and nodded toward the box. "Open it."

"I want you to know something." Her hands stayed in her lap. "That story you just told me—getting to hear a piece of your past and something so personal to your family—that means more to me than anything."

"I know, and, fuck, I love that about you." I held my arm out, lifting the sleeves of my shirt and sports jacket to show her my watch. "I have many at this point—I collect them—but the one Dad gave me will always be the most special."

"It's beautiful."

"I know you don't wear a watch—at least, I've never seen one on you." I lowered my arm. "I want mine to be the first and only one you wear." Another first to add to the growing list. "When you check the time, I want you to think of me and smile. When you show up to a meeting early, I want that grin to grow even wider. Because, Brooklyn, I'm fucking addicted to your smile."

Her hands went over her nose and mouth. "You're the sweetest man ever."

But I wasn't. This was just what she brought out in me.

"Open it," I repeated, "so I can see the expression I've been waiting for."

Her hands slowly dropped, and she lifted the lid of the box, her eyes widening as she took in the white gold Rolex with a bright black diamond-set dial.

"I don't even know what to say." There were tears in her eyes as she looked at me.

Whenever I did something nice for her, I got a similar reaction. I made her speechless. But seeing her eyes filled with moisture was new.

I got up from my chair and went to her side of the table, sliding the watch out of the box and wrapping it around her delicate wrist, where I clasped the band on the underside of her arm. "Stunning."

"It really is."

"I was talking about you, Brooklyn." I leaned down and pressed my lips to hers, a salty tear reaching my mouth right before I pulled away. I swiped under her eyes and licked across my lips. "But the watch does look great on you."

She laughed. "I love it. So much. And I'm going to cherish it—I promise." As I went to return to my seat, she grabbed my hand. "You are the most amazing man, Macon. I'm so lucky that you picked me." The emotion had thickened in her eyes.

I cupped her chin as she looked up at me. "Nah, I'm the lucky one, baby." I gave her another kiss, and when I sat in my chair, holding my new drink, I said, "You only have a handful of weeks left until you start your job. Are you excited?"

She dabbed her eyes with her napkin and placed the empty

box in her purse, taking several glimpses at the watch, her smile as big as ever. "Excited is an understatement. I've called my parents at least five times because I can't stop talking about it. That's all my sisters have heard about since the second I got the email. I even grabbed a few boxes from work so I can start packing."

She filled her lungs, holding in the air because her chest never lowered. "But I'm nervous too. *Sooo* nervous." She lifted her glass of white wine and took a few drinks. "It's going to be a massive transition, going from living with my family to living on my own in a hotel. And then there's my manager, who I don't know, but I hope they learn to love me, along with my coworkers. It's just a lot to think about."

I didn't think she'd be spending many nights in that hotel room. She'd be at my place, and eventually, once we were both ready, I wanted her to move in.

Something I'd never thought would ever happen with a woman.

But the nights we spent apart on Kauai, I missed her like hell. I wanted her in my hotel room, and I didn't see that changing once we were in LA.

As for her concern about her manager, I wasn't surprised to hear it. Brooklyn wanted every aspect of her job to be perfect, and the person overseeing her position and her coworkers would have a lot to do with that. There was nothing I could say to make her feel better since it was a piece of information I was still withholding from her. I just wasn't sold on the fact that she'd follow through with the job if she knew I was going to be her direct supervisor.

I wanted that to change.

I wanted that worry gone.

But there was something I could give her in the meantime, so I rested my arms on the table and said, "Would it ease your mind a little if you knew some of the plans for the Beverly Hills location, the hotel you'll be starting with?" I picked up my fork and ran my thumb across the tines.

"Yesss."

"You know, I couldn't discuss it before, but you've accepted the job, and you've signed the NDA. There's no reason now to hold those plans back from you."

She bit her lip and nodded. "Tell me everything."

I huffed all the air I had. "God, the work side of you is so fucking sexy."

"I'm laughing because I was literally just thinking the same thing about you. You've always been the hottest man ever, but I'm seriously digging the side of you that talks about Spade Hotels." Her stare dropped to my chest and slowly lifted to my eyes again. "Business Macon poked his head out not too long ago, but disappeared when you weren't able to discuss the hotels with me. But right now"—her voice lowered—"all I can see is that delicious beard and hear your gritty alpha voice and take in the way you're staring at me, like you want to eat me, and I'm feeling it hard, Macon."

I set down the fork and reached for her hand. "Hard enough to let me take you in the restroom and fuck you in one of the stalls?" I looked at my own Rolex, its face showing now that my arm was stretched across the table. "We probably have another ten minutes before dinner arrives."

"You think you can come that fast?" She smiled. "You're not really a ten-minute man."

"I know we can *both* come that fast."

She gazed toward the entrance, where the restroom was located off a hallway.

I knew the location. I'd already been in there.

And when her eyes returned to me, her lips gradually

parted and whispered, "It's a shame I'd have to hold in my screams."

"I'll bring my napkin and tie it around your mouth just in case one decides to slip out."

She got up from her chair and said over her shoulder, "I'll be in the last stall."

TWENTY

Brooklyn

MACON

How'd the test go?

ME

I got 95%.

Insert the biggest smile ever because there isn't an emoji that can capture how wide my grin is right now.

MACON

What I wouldn't do to lick that smile across your face.

But, fuck yes, I told you you'd kill it. And the paper? How'd you do on that?

ME

Pretty sure I'll end up with an A.

MACON

Proud of you, baby.

ME

Tell me about your meeting with the Westons. Are they happy with how everything is coming along with Charred and Musik? When we talked last night, you didn't say you were worried, but I heard it in your voice.

And I've been thinking about you all day and wanting to ask. I just didn't want to bug you while you were with them. I know you're slammed.

MACON

You could never bug me. Text or call me all you want.

They're happy—for now. But the whole time we walked through the space, they were harping on the 2-week completion date. They don't believe the hotel is going to open on time, so they feel like they're keeping their employees in limbo since they can't open without us.

ME

Will it???

MACON

It's me. Of course it will. Even if that means I have to work 24/7 for the next 2 weeks to make it happen.

ME

God, I can't believe the grand opening is THAT soon.

MACON

So is your graduation ... are you forgetting that?

ME

Macon, I just had a panic attack as I read your text.

271

I haven't forgotten. I just can't wrap my head around it.

Aaaaand the amount of work I need to get done before I graduate is WILD.

MACON

I guess it's a good thing I'm tied up with the Westons then.

But don't get me wrong, I'd much rather be with you.

ME

And I'd rather be tied up with you.

ME

My parents just sent me their flight information. This is suddenly becoming very real.

MACON

And it wasn't before? Babe, you've been studying for finals for the past couple of weeks.

ME

I know, but seeing their arrival time in my email and watching my sisters clean up our place to get it ready for their visit hit home in all the ways.

MACON

The next couple of weeks are going to fly by. Hold on tight and try to soak in every second.

ME

Perfect advice.

> Did the mess with the front-desk staff get worked out? Or is Cooper still flying in to give you an extra hand?

MACON

The head of customer relations started today. She laid down the law with the whole front-desk team and got everything sorted, so I told him not to come.

ME

> One less thing on your massive to-do list.

> But I know you must be so tired. You didn't get home until three this morning—and, no, your text didn't wake me. Tell me tomorrow won't be a repeat and you'll be able to get some sleep?

MACON

I hope so.

ME

> I should show up at the Spade Hotel and drag you home with me. I could give you a little of my homework to keep you busy, LOL.

MACON

Yes, you should. In fact, I'll be fucking pissed if you don't.

ME

> Ha ha.

> And have you sleep in the same room as my sisters? Oh ... the fun.

MACON

They need to meet me anyway, don't they? Why not make our first introduction while I'm naked in your bed?

ME

Ummm, NO. That nakedness belongs to only ME.

MACON

That was hot.

God, I miss you like hell. The last three days without you have felt like a fucking year.

ME

Tomorrow.

MACON

The best thing you've said to me all day. I'll see you tomorrow night, baby.

ME

Don't forget to sleep. XO

MACON

Don't be upset, but I can't make tonight work. I have the inspectors in the morning. Plus, I have three different vendors in town and six teams that we're currently training. We're going to be here all night, and I can't leave my staff—not now.

ME

I would never be upset about that. I completely understand—always. Just promise me that you're taking care of yourself. You know, eating, drinking (vodka), all those kinds of things?!

MACON

I need all the fucking vodka right now.

Thank you for getting it—I love that about you. You seem to just know and understand.

But I'd rather have you in my arms tonight …

ME

I miss those arms.

MACON

Tomorrow, during the day, do you have to
work?

ME

Yes. But since we're not hanging this evening,
I can get a lot of my schoolwork done and
see you tomorrow night instead.

MACON

We'll be past the inspection, so I'll be a little
more flexible. Tomorrow night it is.

ME

I can't wait.

MACON

Tell me the first thing you're going to do
to me.

ME

I'm going to wrap my arms around you and
hug you. Maybe that sounds stupid, but I
could use one of your hugs.

MACON

Not stupid at all. I want one right now.

———

MACON

I just got back to the hotel and climbed in
bed. Not my plan, but, man, I'm cozy.

How about instead of going out for dinner,
you come over here? We'll stay in and order
room service. This way, I can keep you naked
from the second you walk through my door.

ME

Even when we're eating?

MACON

Especially when we're eating.

ME

You like to keep things interesting, don't you?

MACON

I like to look at you without any clothes on.
Nothing wrong with that. I fucking dream
about your body.

You good with that plan?

ME

Yep.

MACON

You don't sound too excited, LOL.

ME

No, I am. Really.

I get to be with you, so of course I am.

But I have to work super early in the morning,
so I'm going to have to leave around 6 a.m.

MACON

As long as I get to spend the night with you, I
don't care what time you leave.

See you in an hour?

ME

Can't wait. <3

"I've never seen you look so tired." I ran both hands across Macon's face once we pulled out of our hug. "I'm making you sleep tonight. Phone off. Eye mask on." I giggled, knowing he was never going to wear one. "But eight hours of rest, no exception."

He laughed as well.

But I hated that he had bags under his eyes and dark circles surrounding them, that his beard was messy because he hadn't had the time to trim it—although it still looked sexy as fuck.

"I'm good." He rubbed his nose over mine. "Don't you worry."

Before I could say a word, he lifted me into his arms and carried me toward his bed, where he spread me across the mattress, immediately climbing over me.

I could smell the shower he'd recently taken on his skin and the minty toothpaste on his breath.

And as his lips found mine, he kissed me with a raging hunger.

The type of passion he always had with me, but it was amped up due to our time apart.

Even though it technically hadn't been that long since we'd seen each other.

From the moment we'd returned from LA, our schedules had been packed. We still made things work with dinner dates and a few overnights. We even chatted on the phone. But I knew both of us wanted more time together, and we had been bummed that we couldn't make that happen.

Now, if I was willing to come here more often, I was sure that would make things easier, but every time I walked through the door of the hotel, I had to risk the staff recognizing me and asking why I was here. And then I had to worry about them reporting my presence to someone in management.

Fraternizing with guests was against the rules.

Soon, it wouldn't matter because once I graduated, I would

be giving my two-week notice, but I just wasn't there yet. I had a little more time to go, and I counted on these paychecks.

And then there was the issue of Macon, how he still didn't know, how badly I needed to tell him.

As I pulled away from our kiss, scanning his eyes, wiping my gloss off his lips, the words were there.

The courage.

My mouth parted and—

"Fuck, I have to see who this is," he groaned, reaching into his pocket to pull out his ringing phone. "Shit, it's my project manager. I have to take his call." He gave me a quick peck. "Be right back." He got up from the bed and went into the living room area.

I peeled myself up from the fluffy comforter, kicked off my shoes, and moved higher up the bed until my back was resting against the headboard. Since I didn't have my phone—it was in my purse, which I'd dropped, along with my bag, somewhere near the entrance when he met me at the door—I busied myself with the notes Macon had kept from the housekeeper.

Unbeknownst to him, that was me.

He'd lined each one up in a pile on his nightstand.

There were three.

The first welcomed him to the hotel, which had been written on the day of his arrival—standard for all new check-ins. The second reprimanded him for the mess he'd left in the room. The third was an apology. It told him how sorry I was for leaving him the previous note, that I had no right to speak to him that way, and that I appreciated his tip—once again—and I didn't believe I deserved it. That I was willing to get him whatever he wanted—he just needed to ask.

I never should have spoken to a guest that way, and I'd needed to acknowledge that and make it right, which I had.

But it went so much further than that.

Because the moment Macon had led me to his room and I saw the PH 4 outside his door, I'd realized he was the guest I'd left the note for.

And the guilt came on fast and thick, my heart completely sinking.

So, the next time I'd cleaned his room, while being eaten with regret the entire time, I had done the only thing I could at that moment. I'd attempted to use my words to smooth over my mistake.

And as I looked at the notes now, flipping through each one, I couldn't believe he'd kept them.

But that wasn't the only thought in my head.

What I also wanted was to rewind time. I wanted to be honest and up-front with him.

Why had I been such a coward?

Why had I kept this secret for so long?

"You're probably wondering why I've kept those."

I hadn't heard him get off the phone or move into the doorway, nor did I realize he'd been watching me.

My face flushed, and I couldn't stop the color from deepening, not even when I returned the notes to his nightstand.

"They're from the housekeeping staff. I'm sure you figured that out."

"I'm curious why you've kept them"—I took a deep breath—"yes."

"I keep forgetting to bring them to the hotel, but when I remember and I have a meeting with the housekeeping staff, I'm going to show them those notes. I want our team to welcome each guest this way—with a friendly note left near the bed that shows our staff is willing to make the extra effort when it comes to our guests and their happiness." He reached to the top of the doorway, gripping the molding, looking so incredibly handsome as he held it.

I gasped in some air. Holding it. Releasing it. And sucked in more. "And the note that chewed your ass out? Why did you keep that one?"

He chuckled. "Because I deserved it. The room had been in bad shape after the bachelor party. I was embarrassed as hell that someone had to clean up after us. But was it right for the housekeeper to call me out on it? Fuck no. But they followed up with an apology, and I give them a lot of credit for that. And because they did the right thing, it's an apology I accept."

My chest felt like it was going to explode. "Macon—"

"I have bad news." He paused for only a second. "I don't know how to tell you this, but I've got to go back to the hotel. There's nothing but issues going on there, and I have to go fix them."

"Go." I swallowed. I felt the burn in my throat, the acid swishing in my stomach. "They need your help—I get it."

He came over to his side of the bed, where I was lying, and sat on the very edge. "I don't know how long it's going to take, so I want you to order food." He pointed toward the door. "Menu is on the table in the living room. Get whatever you want and lots of it. I'll try to keep you updated and let you know when I'll be back."

"No, no. I'll go home—"

"Please don't." His hand went to my cheek. "Whatever time I get back, I want to be able to sink into this bed and wrap my arms around you."

A request I couldn't deny.

Because even though I was filled with guilt, even though we should have been talking about the notes and why I'd left them, I wanted to wake up to him too.

"Okay." I nodded. "I'll stay."

TWENTY-ONE

Macon

BROOKLYN

I'm going to head to work. I hope you're doing okay. Last night wasn't the same without you.

ME

I'm so sorry. I thought I'd be back long before you had to leave. I didn't plan on staying here all night, but I'm still putting out fires. I fucking hate that I missed our whole evening together.

I hope you ordered room service and slept well.

I'll make it up to you.

BROOKLYN

Nooo, you don't have to. You're down to the wire, fires are bound to happen. You know I understand.

ME

Another reason why I'm wild about you.

I'm hesitant to make plans with you tonight. I don't want to do the same thing I did to you last night.

I'll call when I get back. Even if it's only for a few hours, I hope to hell we'll be able to meet up.

BROOKLYN

I would love that.

Get some sleep—that's an order. <3

The only thing I wanted was a shower.

So, the second I got back to my suite, I stripped my clothes off in the bathroom and turned on the water to a temperature I knew would scald my skin. I didn't give a shit if it burned me. I needed all the heat and massage and relaxation to work its fucking magic by shutting my brain off, enabling me to get at least a few hours of sleep once I got out and crawled into bed.

While I waited for it to warm, I stood at the sink and brushed my teeth, wondering how Brooklyn had looked in this exact spot earlier this morning.

I'd smelled her in the air when I got back to my room.

Those salty beach and lemon scents that I'd been craving all damn night. Ones I thought about every time I wanted to put my fist through a fucking wall.

The hotel was going to open on time, but that didn't mean it wasn't going to try to kill me in the process.

I finished brushing and spit out the toothpaste, left my beard trimming and shaving for another morning when I had more patience than I did now, and I got into the shower.

The steam was already starting to build as I stood under the spray, the warmth pounding against my body and raining over my head.

It felt good as hell.

But my mind was still so busy, filled with everything I needed to do. And as I stood under the stream, soaping my body, the more I washed, the more it all circled—employees, vendors, the grand opening—and then the cycle would begin again.

God, it was so fucking much.

I was willing to do anything to shut off these thoughts.

I needed just a second where they weren't churning.

Where I wasn't stressed over the outcome.

Where there was freedom in my head.

And pleasure.

Fuck, I wanted all the pleasure.

My hand, washing my neck, lowered, and my dick hardened as soon as I reached it. I wrapped my fingers around my shaft, and as I stroked to my tip and as far back as my sac, I thought of Brooklyn.

The way her naked body had looked when she took a long, hot shower this morning. How her nipples had become tight little buds from the water pressure. How the drips from the shower had run down her bare pussy, pooling on the tiles beneath her feet.

I wanted to be on my knees, looking up at her, with my mouth on her cunt.

I wanted the taste of her sliding down my throat.

I wanted the screams from her orgasm to be filling my ears.

My fist wasn't anything like the hot narrowness of Brooklyn's pussy, but it was enough to make me come.

I pumped toward my crown, circling the bulge over my palm, urging the tingles to work their way through me.

The build was there.

Sparking hard at first, but it took its time increasing, slowly growing, gathering enough speed to shoot its way out of me.

It was almost there.

Fucking boiling inside me.

My hand held the wall while the other used my soapy skin to rock my dick, back and forth, urging that feeling forward.

Demanding it.

And just as the peak came near, I heard, "Macon!"

Macon?

My eyes shot open, which I hadn't realized were even closed, widening like hell as I saw Brooklyn in the doorway of my bathroom. She was holding the doorknob, after just opening the door, with her cell phone up to her ear.

She'd returned to the suite to see me. *Ohhh*, I fucking loved that.

That woman could be the sweetest when she wanted to be.

The only downside to this perfect surprise was that my orgasm had faded the second I heard my name.

But my hard-on hadn't.

"I was just thinking about you ..." I pumped my cock a few times. "Get in and join me."

I gave zero fucks that she'd busted me beating off. Actually, I thought it was sexy. I wanted her to see that as she owned my thoughts, she gave me such a raging erection, and I had to touch myself.

But something was off in the way she looked at me.

In the expression that was growing across her face, one that was turning into a look that was over-the-top alarming.

"What's wrong?"

Why wasn't she responding?

"Brooklyn ..."

Why wasn't she moving from the doorway? Or giving me anything other than the shock that was thickening in her eyes and lips, even her cheeks?

But why would there be shock if she'd come back to my suite? Hadn't she expected to see me? Wasn't that what she wanted?

There was no other reason she'd return to my room—at least not one that I could think of.

Unless the jerking off bothered her.

But, shit, that didn't make any sense.

All dudes jerked off—that shouldn't be a shock.

"Brooklyn, talk to me."

When several seconds passed and her face still didn't change and her mouth didn't open to speak and her body didn't move, I turned off the water and opened the shower door, where I stepped out onto the rug.

"Are you all right?"

"Yeah." She swallowed. "I ..." Her voice faded out.

And she stayed frozen, staring into my eyes.

She didn't even blink.

I grabbed a towel and wrapped it around my waist. "You're too far away, baby. Come here while I'm drying off."

"I have to go," she said to whoever she was speaking to, and she dropped the phone into the front pocket of her shirt.

She didn't move.

She didn't even bother taking a step forward.

So, when I did, her hand rose into the air to stop me.

"Macon ... don't. Stay right there."

Stay right there?

I tightened the towel and halted halfway between her and the shower. "What's going on?"

"We need to talk."

I heard her words, but for some reason, I was drawn to what she was wearing, my gaze dipping down her body. It was an outfit I'd never seen on her before. A black V-neck top with two deep pockets at the bottom, pants in the same color that, like the shirt, hid her incredible body.

It was the kind of uniform that reminded me of the ones we ordered for some of our Spade Hotel employees.

But Brooklyn was employed by a restaurant, and since her text had told me she'd gone to work, I wondered what kind of boss would require her to wear something like this. Rather than having her hide her figure, a better marketing move would be to have her in something that showed it off.

I glanced back up, meeting her eyes. The way she stared back made my heart thump in a way I didn't like.

I pointed at the glass shower behind me. "Is this about what you just saw me doing?"

"No." She shook her head. "Not even close."

"Then, what the hell is wrong?"

"Everything." Her voice was a whisper, her eyes now filled with tears. "I wanted to tell you last night, and you left and ..."

"Baby, come here." I held out my arms.

Was she ending things? Was she trying to tell me this wasn't working? That she wasn't taking the job? That she wanted nothing to do with me?

"I have to get this out." She leaned her back against the doorframe. "It's been eating at me, Macon." Her hand was on her throat. "I didn't know how to tell you, and I just kept putting it off, and that was so wrong of me. Especially when I told Jo and—"

"What?" I didn't understand any of what she was saying. "What did you tell Jo? And what does she have to do with this?"

"I talked to her during my interview. I came clean to her. I told her everything I haven't had the courage to tell you." Her hand dropped to her chest. "Oh God, I didn't want you to find out this way." Her fingers were on the move again, this time wrapping around her stomach, her other arm doing the same. "Macon ... I have something to tell you."

What the hell had she told Jo during her interview?

How had she come clean?

What did this all mean?

Despite my questions, I couldn't just stand here or allow this much distance between us.

Nor could I let an important conversation, like the one I assumed we were about to have, take place in the fucking bathroom.

So, I moved closer and clasped her waist. "Let's go sit."

"No. I have to tell you—"

"Whatever it is that you need to tell me, you can do it while we're sitting on the bed." When I tried to lead her toward the bedroom, she didn't move. "Come with me, Brooklyn."

She was scanning my eyes, right to left and back.

"Please," I demanded.

She finally pulled herself off the frame, and as we were walking toward the bedroom, I noticed the door to my room was open. No one was standing in the doorframe, and the housekeeper or hotel employee—whoever had opened it— wasn't in my room.

"What the fuck?" I roared.

I was pissed that someone would have the audacity to open my suite and keep the door ajar when I was in the shower or in a towel or whenever the fuck it had happened.

The protocol was to knock. That was standard for any hotel.

Where the hell was the knock?

Brooklyn would have heard it; she would have told them not to come in.

I left her side to go close it, but within a step, she was next to me, following me, and within a few paces, she'd gained the lead. She pulled out the wooden block from under the bottom of the door—the wedge that had kept it open—and she set it on something in the hallway.

As I neared the area, I saw what she'd placed it on.

The housekeeping cart.

And when she turned toward me, a feeling hit me.

That there was something really off about this situation.

That the door being open hadn't been a coincidence.

My brain gradually began connecting the pieces that were lying directly in front of me.

The shock on her face when she had seen me in the shower.

Not because she'd found me beating off ... but because she hadn't expected me to be in the bathroom.

Or the room at all.

Then, there was the outfit she had on.

The way she had set the wooden wedge on the cart and let the door close behind her.

And the way she was looking at me right now.

She nodded as though she were seeing inside my head. "Yes, I'm your housekeeper. The one who's been leaving you notes. Who wrote you the nasty one for the way the room looked after Jenner's bachelor weekend. Who makes your bed in the mornings and wipes down your shower and puts your toothbrush in that pretty glass container that I wash every few days." Her voice had been getting quieter, even more so when she added, "That's been me. This whole time."

I didn't anticipate this—not until moments ago.

I'd never suspected a thing. She'd given no hints, no signs at all that she worked here, but ...

Fuck me.

That was why she hid her face whenever we came to the hotel. Why she always looked down until we got to my room. She'd told me it was because she knew a lot of people who worked here, which was the truth because she was a goddamn employee, but she'd spun it so I wouldn't figure anything out.

An employee who couldn't be seen with a guest.

An employee who would probably get fired if her manager found out she was spending the night in my room.

"What the fuck, Brooklyn? Why didn't you tell me?"

"Why?" She licked her lips, like she was trying to pull them apart. "I've been asking myself that question nonstop, but the only thing I could come up with was that every time I wanted to, I didn't dare." She shoved her hands into her pockets. "Once I found out who you were, telling you I was a housekeeper just didn't feel right. You own hotels, and I clean them." Her face pointed toward the floor. "Macon, we're on levels that couldn't be further apart, and the more we hung out, the more you gifted me, the more you wanted to be with me"—she finally looked up—"it became harder to tell you ... and harder to stay away."

"Did you want to stay away?"

Her shoulders lifted. "I was lying to you. Keeping a huge part of myself from you. I was afraid of how you'd see me. Of what you'd think of me. But I was drawn to you in ways I can't even explain." Her head leaned back, her eyes moving to the ceiling. "I know how fucked up this is. Trust me ... I know."

So many thoughts were hitting me at once, layers and layers unfolding.

The bits she'd revealed during this conversation.

The things I'd picked up on during our previous chats and not processed until now.

I shifted, holding the towel so it wouldn't drop. "But you told Jo?"

And Jo hadn't told me, which was a bunch of fucking bullshit.

She pulled her hands out, and once they hit the air, she didn't seem to know what to do with them, so she circled her arms over her stomach. "I felt like I was in a position where I had to. She was asking me questions about the restaurant that I'd put on my résumé, and I couldn't lie. Not again. Not anymore."

Fuck, I hadn't even thought of that.

The interview. The inquiries Cooper and Jo had made about her job history while she was in the conference room with them.

And all of it ... was fake?

Except for the conversation she'd had with Jo.

When she was honest with my cousin before she was truthful with me.

That made me boil.

And that fucking steam was about to whistle like a teapot.

It didn't matter that I was keeping a secret from her too. This was different.

This went beyond because, now, it trickled into Spade Hotels and the résumé HR had on file and ...

Jesus fucking Christ.

Why had she done this?

Why had she let it go this far?

"So, you felt the need to purge your truth to Jo, but when it came to me, I wasn't important enough to tell—is that right?"

"No, that's not what I meant."

"Except, from the way it looks to me, you gave zero shits that you were lying to me. You didn't even attempt to tell me, aside from last night, which could be another lie—I'll never know."

She shook her head. "No, I was going to tell you, I swear. I wouldn't lie about that—"

"You mean, lie again."

"Macon ..." Her eyes were pleading with me, and so was her voice. "I'm not lying when I say that—"

"Now, let's talk about your other lie." My fingers clenched into a fist. "The one on your résumé. Look me in the face and tell me that position wasn't real."

She took a deep breath. "The restaurant that's listed is the one my sisters work at. I used Jesse as a reference and changed her last name so if she was called by HR—and she was—it wouldn't look suspicious." She held her hand out toward me, but this time, it wasn't to make me stop; her fingers were outstretched instead. "I couldn't risk having you find out that way. When you heard the truth about my employment, you needed to hear it from me."

Except I hadn't heard it from her.

I'd uncovered it because she came in to clean my room and I was accidentally home.

She had been forced to tell me because she was in a goddamn housekeeping uniform and wedged my door open while her cart sat outside.

And now ... I'd heard enough.

I let the towel fall as I went into the closet, grabbing a pair of sweats and a sweatshirt and pulling both onto my body before I walked through the bedroom.

I was just passing her when she said, "Where are you going?"

I heard her behind me, following me to the living room.

291

With my back to her, I picked up my phone and key card from the table.

"To the bar."

"Right now? In the middle of this?"

I turned toward her, wishing I hadn't seen her expression. The one that was filled with so much remorse. The one that appeared like she would do anything to make this better.

"I'll be back after I clear my fucking head."

I let the door slam on my way and stared at the screen of my cell as I got into the elevator, scrolling through my Contacts, deciding what the fuck I should do.

Did I throw my phone on the ground, letting it shatter to pieces?

Did I call someone?

Did I try to work this out on my own?

The door opened to the lobby, and I saw the bar and how packed it was.

I had no interest in going there, downing booze that wouldn't solve any of these problems, having to people when I'd rather be alone.

I headed outside instead, the pool deck almost empty, and I took a seat in one of the lounge chairs.

Fucking Brooklyn.

I couldn't believe she'd done this. I couldn't believe she'd put us in this situation.

That she hadn't cared enough to be honest with me.

That, for some reason, she hadn't thought I could handle it.

That I wouldn't approve, that I wouldn't want to be with her—I didn't even know whatever her goddamn reasoning was at this point.

While my head was swarming with questions, my thumb was swiping the screen as I looked for the name I wanted, and when I finally found it, I hit Call.

"Macon, my man, what the fuck is up?" Jenner said after the second ring.

"A lot. That's why I'm calling."

I could have phoned Jo, his fiancée, but I wasn't ready to have that conversation yet. I also could have reached out to Camden, but I knew what he would say.

Jenner would have a different point of view.

Because Jenner had been through something similar.

"What can I do to help you?"

I released all the air I'd been holding in my lungs, brushing my fingers through my wet hair. "She lied to me about her job, and then to make matters even worse, she went into Spade Hotels with a fake résumé. She felt like shit about it, so she came clean to Jo during the interview, but she didn't say a word to me. I had to wait to learn the truth, which just happened a couple of minutes ago. Turns out, she's the housekeeper here, and she came in to clean my bathroom while I was in the fucking shower. That's how I found out the truth."

I didn't have to tell him who I was talking about. Jenner would know.

And I'd be shocked if he didn't know Jo's take on the story since I was sure she had told him after her interview with Brooklyn.

"And you want to know what I would do? Because the situations aren't the same, but they're not all that different either, am I right?"

I flattened my hand on top of my head. "Yes."

"Let's break this down. Yes, she lied to you, and you can be angry with her for that. Yes, she was dishonest about her résumé—another shitty check mark against her, which you can also be angry about. Since I can't ask Brooklyn what her motive was, I have to put myself in her shoes and ask myself what I would do if I was faced with that scenario." He turned quiet.

"I'll tell you what, buddy. If I was banging a Spade brother, heir to the Spade fortune, and I was a housekeeper at the hotel he was staying at, that wouldn't be an easy conversation for me to have."

"But would you lie?"

"Fuck." He became silent again. "Maybe ... and that's an honest answer."

"Even if I was bound to find out the truth?"

"I don't know if that would stop me."

I sat up, my feet falling to either side of the lounge chair. "You know how fucked up that is, don't you?"

"Listen, have you ever driven a car like hers? Ever lived in an apartment that didn't have a doorman and a rooftop pool? I know you haven't because our families are the same. But is Brooklyn's upbringing the same as ours? No. So, for just one second, see things through her eyes."

"This isn't about money, Jenner."

"But in a roundabout way, it is, brother. She sees who you are and what you have, and she compares that to herself, and something about that locked her up where she didn't want to tell you."

I understood what he was saying.

But that didn't ease the lie.

The way it was settling in my chest.

The way it was embedding in my heart because she'd felt like she couldn't tell me.

"I hear you," I growled.

"Do you?"

I did.

I just didn't want to.

Because I wished none of this had happened.

"Yes," I finally replied. "I do."

"Where is she right now?"

"I left her in my room. Told her I needed a drink. I'm assuming she's still in there."

"Jo tells me she's one hell of a woman, and for my wifey to say that"—he huffed—"that means a lot." He paused. "Don't lose her over this. Hear her side. Say your piece. And then get that shit worked out."

"You make it sound easy."

"It is."

"I'm not so sure about that." I moved my feet to one side of the chair. "I appreciate your help."

"Shit, I'm honored that of all the people you could have called, you chose me." He chuckled. "See you soon, my friend."

He hung up, and I stood from the chair, shoving the phone into my pocket while I made my way inside. At the elevator, I pressed the button to my floor and leaned against the wall, waiting for the door to open. When I reached my suite, I waved the key card in front of the reader and walked in.

Brooklyn was on the couch in the living room, her knees bent, arms wrapped around them, her tiny body rocking over the cushion. "You're back." Relief immediately filled her eyes.

I sat on the opposite side as her, silence simmering between us.

I couldn't allow the anger to erupt within me. Nothing would ever get solved. So, I tried to keep my tone even when I said, "I don't understand why you would keep this from me." As I stared at her, I attempted to see the reason, comparing it to the things Jenner had just said. "Did you think I wouldn't like you anymore? That I'd stop chasing you? That your job would turn me off? That—"

"Yes. No. I don't know." Her hand went to her hair, and the other joined, and she tugged on her strands. "I was just embarrassed, and then I was embarrassed that I hadn't admitted the truth to you, and then it became this vicious circle of lies." Her eyes filled with tears. "It's nothing you did, nothing you said. None of this is on you, it's all on me. I fucked up."

"But it is on me because something made you hold back, and that's because I hadn't given you enough confidence to believe that no matter what you did or what you said or the decisions you made, my feelings for you wouldn't change."

I didn't know where this emotion was coming from, but it was thrumming in my chest. In my hands. In my fucking legs.

"You know, I didn't care that you wore the same dress to the club every time I saw you. I couldn't stop complimenting you. Wanting you. Begging you to leave with me." I paused as the examples were flooding my head. "I didn't care that you wouldn't give me your name or your phone number. I still came looking for you. I didn't care that you told me to go slow, that your life was muddy, that you couldn't separate Spade Hotels from me. I never gave up, Brooklyn."

"I know." Her voice was barely a whisper.

"I did everything I could to show you the type of person I am, that the only thing that matters to me is you." I exhaled, the pain in my chest deepening. "And you still didn't trust me."

She got up and stood directly in front of me. "It was never about trust. That didn't enter my thought process at all. It was fear that you wouldn't want to be with me. That I was so far beneath you—"

"Don't even say that." My eyes narrowed. "I offered you a job because I was so enamored and blown away by your brilliance. That's not putting you beneath me, that's putting you far above me."

"I agree, and I'm not fighting that point. I'm not fighting anything. I'm in the wrong." Her hand went to my arm. "But if I had told you I was the woman who had cleaned your toilet that morning, I—my insecurities—would have had a hard time making you believe that I was really qualified to do Six Sigma work at your hotel." She squeezed my skin. "I'm not saying you would have treated me differently or that you wouldn't have believed in me. I'm saying I couldn't separate the two—the housekeeper and the Spade Hotel applicant. In that moment, I wouldn't have believed I was good enough."

When it came to insecurities, it didn't matter what I said; nothing would change her opinion.

If it were physical, I could preach about beauty, and the words would bounce right off her ears. If it were financial and I promised security was in the future, she wouldn't hear me.

In this case, it was professional.

She had an executive of a hotel brand sitting in her hand like fucking putty, and knowing my familiarity with her role, she didn't want to paint that picture.

Could I understand that?

Could I accept it?

Goddamn it, this wasn't easy.

And it only became harder as more quietness passed between us, tears now streaming down her cheeks.

"What did I do to make you think I would have cared what your job was?"

She shook her head. "Nothing."

"I wouldn't have cared, Brooklyn." I stopped myself from reaching for her. "My feelings wouldn't have lightened—they couldn't. I want you far too much to let anything affect that."

I wouldn't let myself wipe her face or catch the tears as they neared her chin.

Not yet.

"I'm so sorry." Her hand shook me. "I'm so, so sorry. Believe me. Please."

"Jesus ..." I sighed. "I just hate that you lied to me and that it went on for this long."

She nodded harder than she needed to. "I do too. I'm disgusted with myself. I know I lied, but this isn't who I am or what I stand for. And I know you don't believe that—I wouldn't either, not after this—but I'm not usually a liar, Macon. I hate liars."

My chest fucking ached.

Brooklyn didn't have the confidence to tell me and that became the foundation of her lies and that was what stung the most.

Even though it made sense in the way she'd explained it. I just couldn't relate, but I also wasn't in her shoes, and when Jenner had broken that all down, I could sympathize.

It just fucking hurt. It hurt that my cousin had known before me. It hurt that Brooklyn had had to go to such extremes, like lying on her résumé, to prevent me from finding out.

That if I had just stayed last night instead of rushing to the hotel, I would have heard this all from her lips.

"I don't expect you to forgive me." Her hand dropped from my arm and landed in her lap. "I don't honestly know what to even expect. I just want you to know how sorry I am. How the last thing I wanted to do was hurt you."

She glanced toward the door and then back at me. "If you want me to go, if you want me to resign or renege on the position—however that works—I will. If you never want to see me again—"

"That's the last thing I want." My hands rubbed over the soft sweatpants, an aching need to hold her. To put this behind us. To not let this ruin us. I reached across the distance between us and cupped her chin. "You deserve that job. I want nothing more than for you to take it."

"And us?"

When I released the air from my lungs, it came out in waves.

"Is there an us?"

She nodded. "I see it. I feel it." She put her hand on mine. "Believe me when I say, I want it."

I watched as she breathed, as she took in my face, as the emotion continued to pass through hers. "You know all I've wanted is you."

She mashed her lips together. "But?"

I thought about that question.

I really fucking dug through my head, my chest, eventually saying, "There is no but, Brooklyn."

Her arms flew into the air and circled my neck, and she moved her body until it was against mine.

"Don't ever lie to me again," I warned.

"I won't."

I pressed my lips to her neck. "We're in this together. As partners. Friends. That means, whatever it is, no matter how big or little, I want you to tell me. Do you understand?"

She squeezed me with all her strength. "I want you to do the same."

My eyes closed as I breathed her in.

And as I buried myself in her lemon scent, I remembered once again that there was someone else in this room who hadn't been honest.

Who had withheld the truth.

Fuck.

Me.

Once I separated us, which I didn't plan on doing for a while, I needed to get to my phone and reach out to Walter and pull the plug on my new position.

I wasn't going to be Brooklyn's new boss, so there was nothing to tell her at this point.

That didn't settle the guilt in my chest, but it would over time.

Especially when she came to me after her first day of work at the Beverly Hills Spade Hotel and told me all about her new manager. That was when I'd confess that it was supposed to be me.

"I'm sorry," she whispered. "I care about you so much, Macon. I never want to lose you."

My eyes closed. "You're never going to lose me."

ME

We need to talk.

WALTER

About what?

ME

The position I'm taking over when I return to LA.

WALTER

This wouldn't have anything to do with the new hire we just added to your team ... would it?

ME

It has everything to do with her.

WALTER

What's the problem?

ME

I can't do it. You're going to have to find someone to replace me.

WALTER

That's your final decision?

300

ME

Yes.

WALTER

Fine. But I'm calling you in fifteen minutes. I don't care where you are or who you're with. Pick up your goddamn phone.

TWENTY-TWO

Brooklyn

I can't stop thinking about this morning. I know when I left your room, things were okay. But I can't shake the feeling that they're not. I don't expect you to get over this immediately —that's not what I mean. I know what I did, and I know the heaviness of it.

I just want you to know how sorry I am.

And now, I worry that you'll never believe anything I say ever again.

MACON

I'm not the kind of dude who holds grudges. I accepted your apology, Brooklyn. I can't fix the past. Neither of us can. All we can do is move on.

ME

That's all I want, but with your trust.

MACON

Do I believe you'll lie to me again? No, I don't.

ME

I should feel relieved to hear that ... but ...

My cell suddenly started ringing, Macon's name filling the screen.

I took a deep breath and connected the call, holding my phone against my face. "Hello?"

"Would hearing my voice help you believe it?"

As I sat in front of my laptop, trying to finish the paper I'd started an hour ago, I leaned back in my chair. I'd only written a few paragraphs. I'd just been staring at the blinking cursor, thinking nonstop about my morning run-in with him. How, like an idiot, I'd been on the phone with my mom, talking about their upcoming flight and my graduation plans, so focused on our conversation that I didn't hear the water running in Macon's bathroom or even notice the light coming from under the door. I had just assumed he wasn't back yet.

When I'd walked in on him in the shower, I hadn't known how my face looked, but panic had run through me, and so had a wave of anxiety and fear and regret, slamming into me so hard that I couldn't move. I couldn't talk. I could just stare at him and think, over and over, *Oh God, what have I done.*

"Yes, hearing your voice definitely helps," I whispered. "I know I'm coming across as extremely needy. I just ..."

"Feel like shit about everything."

I set my hand on my chest while I attempted to fill it again, the tightness so overwhelming that I had to push my palm against it. "Yep, that."

"Listen to me. You explained yourself. You took responsibility. You told me how sorry you were. Just because I wish you had handled things differently—and I hate that it went as far as you having to lie on your résumé—it doesn't mean I'm going to dwell on the past."

There was movement in the background, the sound of construction, which told me he'd returned to the Spade Hotel. I wondered if he'd even taken a nap in the hours since I'd spoken to him.

"I had a long conversation with Jo this afternoon. She told me about your interview and how you came clean and how badly you felt about the whole thing. Hearing another person's perspective and talking it through helped a lot, especially since she could relate after going through something similar with Jenner."

I loved that she had been there for him, and even though he hadn't confirmed this, it sounded like Jo had had my back. That she'd used her situation with Jenner to make Macon see where I was coming from—not accepting my motive, but understanding why I had one.

I really owed her that glass of wine.

Shit, I owed her a case.

"I'm really happy you spoke to her," I said. "I still wish I hadn't told her before you—that was so wrong of me—but hearing her take on things certainly helped me too."

A few seconds of silence passed before he said, "When I think about my future, Brooklyn, it's you. That's what I want to focus on."

The emotion was already there—in my chest, in my eyes. But as his words sank into my body, those feelings came on even harder.

Our journey hadn't been overly long, but it felt like a battle. From where we'd started, back when I was dancing on a stage at the club, to now, where I was melting from his last statement.

"That's all I want." I knew he was busy. I could hear it from the way he was breathing, as though he was sprinting around the hotel, and the talking in the background that I assumed was directed at him, so I said, "I'll text you in the morning."

"You'd better."

My eyes closed. "Have a good night, Macon."

I waited for him to say good-bye, and I hung up.

ME

So ... weird comment, but hear me out. I just finished a deep clean on your room, and the more I scrubbed, the less it smelled like you. Now, I'm looking around your suite, and all your stuff is gone. It's like you've vanished. And I know this is going to make no sense, but seeing you gone makes me sad.

Aaaand I know it's fucked up to say this, and I don't want you to take it the wrong way, given everything that's recently happened, but it was kinda nice to go into your room during my shifts to tidy up. I don't know ... it made me feel closer to you. To know you were there even though you weren't there, just your things were, and I could smell you every time I took a breath. I loved that.

MACON

Sounds like you miss me.

ME

I do.

MACON

And I love that—but I'm not gone, Brooklyn. I'm just down the street in our new hotel, and you're going to spend the night with me tomorrow. Believe me, baby, I'm counting down the hours.

ME

Me too. I can't wait.

MACON

BTW, I didn't take it the wrong way. I know exactly what you mean. Maybe in some strange way, it allowed you to get to know me more and brought us closer.

ME

I think it did.

I'm off to take my first final.

MACON

Kill it. Text me when you're done.

ME

Done.

One down, two to go. I can't believe in just a few more days, I'll be completely finished with school, and in one week, I'll be graduating, and the Spade Hotel will be open.

We have a lot to celebrate.

MACON

We will tonight.

ME

I was so worried about what I was going to do post-graduation, and now, I have the best thing waiting for me.

MACON

LA is going to look so fucking gorgeous on you.

ME

Macon ... I was talking about you.

MACON

Even better—fuck yes.

ME

I'll see you at the front entrance of the hotel at seven. Don't worry, I won't be late. ;)

MACON

To quote you, I'm going to make a weird comment, but hear me out, LOL. I'm really looking forward to seeing you walk through the lobby without your hand shielding your eyes and your face pointed down. I don't ever want you to hide again, Brooklyn.

ME

<3 every word of this.

There was something extremely special about driving to the Spade Hotel for the very first time, parking by the front since valet wasn't yet operational, and taking a few moments to admire the grand entrance, the buildings, the symbolism behind the structure.

I'd come a few minutes early just so I could do this.

Because long before I'd met Macon, I'd watched his crew clear out this whole piece of land, witnessing each phase of construction. Now that I knew who was behind the build-out and the blood, sweat, tears, and love he'd poured into it, this project meant everything to me.

Macon wasn't the type of executive who sat in his suite and barked orders. He worked tirelessly, barely stopping to eat, hardly sleeping.

I admired that.

I respected that.

And I hoped whoever managed me in my new role took the

same approach, leading me with just as much enthusiasm, dedication, and passion as Macon directed his team. That when they spoke about the Six Sigma practices that we were going to implement in some of the older hotels, starting with Beverly Hills, they did it with a smile, just like Macon did whenever he talked about this hotel.

I could see that smile now as I began to walk toward the overpass, where valet would eventually be located, Macon standing directly beneath it. As his eyes connected with mine, a feeling began to fill my body.

An emotion.

A tingle.

A surge of electricity that started at my feet and rose to my face.

God, that man was beautiful.

But it wasn't his handsomeness that caused my heart to hammer away or my limbs to feel numb or my lips to spread so wide that my cheeks hurt.

It was caused by the way he looked at me.

The way he made me feel—that no other woman could ever compare. That everything he wanted, everything he needed, was me.

Before Macon, I hadn't known that existed. That someone could actually feel that way. Now that I had it, I couldn't imagine losing it.

Because he had become everything I wanted and everything I needed.

As I approached the underpass, he gazed at me like he hadn't seen me in months. And when I reached him, the hunger in his arms was equally as intense as they wrapped around me, hauling me up against his body.

His mouth instantly found mine, not giving me a chance to speak; it just parted my lips, his tongue sliding through, causing my body to turn weak. A weakness that then forced my balance to go off-kilter, which made him hold me even tighter, making sure I didn't fall.

"Macon," I exhaled after we finally pulled away, getting the chance to really take in his eyes, "this is the most gorgeous hotel I've ever seen." Heat was moving across my face, my expression beaming with pride. "Congratulations. I'm completely in awe of you, and I'm so, so proud of you."

"Thank you." He held my face with both hands, his lips hovering above mine. "You look fucking breathtaking tonight."

I was in a dress that he'd bought me, one that I knew he hadn't gotten for the interview because there was no way something this sexy could be worn to work. And when I'd stepped into it and had Jesse zip me up and peeked at my reflection in our mirror, I'd had a feeling he was going to go wild.

As his hands left my face, traveling down my back to squeeze my ass, I knew my feeling was right.

"Before you get any other ideas in your head"—I laughed— "I want a tour. I want to see every inch of this hotel, and don't leave anything out." I leaned back a few inches and lifted my hand, showing him the bag I was holding. "But first, this is for you."

He eyed the present. "You got me a gift?"

"Admittedly, it's impossible to get something for someone who has everything—and I can say that. I've been to your house, you literally have *everything*. So, I went a different route." I set the bag on his fingers as he held them toward me.

His other hand left my butt to stroke my face. "You didn't have to do this."

"This is a huge moment for you, which makes it a huge moment for me, and sometimes, words just aren't enough." I wrapped my arm around his waist. "Open it."

He reached inside the bag and pulled out the picture

frame. Within the two rectangles of acrylic, where I'd removed the magnets that held them together and glued them instead, I'd inserted four photos of us. One from inside the sushi restaurant in Honolulu, another from his bed at the hotel I worked at, the third from the steak house at the other end of the island, and the final from his house in LA.

"Let me explain this," I said, staring at his profile while he looked at the photos. "My sister Clementine is the oldest, and a project that she and my mom started when Clem was just a kid was saving things from each place we ever lived. We moved so much, so we couldn't have a ton of things, but the box where she keeps it all is something Clem has always held on to. Anyway, the thing she kept from Honolulu was sand from a beach in Waikiki, so that's what I put here." I traced above our sushi picture, where I'd glued sand around the photo. "And this sand here"—my finger moved to the two pics of us on Kauai— "is from the beach right by my place, and here"—I slipped down to the LA one—"is sand I ordered off the internet, directly from Santa Monica Beach, which Google says is the closest beach to LA."

His eyes slowly met mine.

"Hawaii is always going to be a special place for you because you built your dream hotel here, but knowing you're leaving soon, I wanted you to have something to take with you. Something you'll be able to have forever. And our sand, well"— I smiled—"in my opinion, there's nothing quite like it." I placed my hand on his chest. "But at the same time, I want this to serve as our beginning with hopes that we'll add many more photos and much more sand in our future."

He scanned my eyes, his stare reaching right through me, going straight past my skin and into my heart. "Brooklyn, I love it." He kissed me. "By far, this is the best gift anyone has ever given me and certainly the most thoughtful."

I blushed. "Stop."

"No, I'm serious." He placed the frame back in the bag and slipped the handles up his arm to free his hand so he could hold my face. "No one has ever made me anything before. It means a lot that the first handmade gift is from you." He rubbed his nose over mine. "It's going in my office."

"Perfect spot for it." I nuzzled my cheek into his hand. "I'll see it every time I walk through your front door since I pass it on the way to the living room."

"Not that office. The one at Spade Hotel headquarters."

"You're kidding?"

"Since I'll be back in LA soon, I'm about to be spending much more time there. When I'm home, I'll be with you. And when I'm at work, I can look at the pictures whenever I need you."

"Or you can go down several floors, where I'll probably be glued to some cubicle."

He swiped his thumb over my lips. "That too." He grinned. "We're going to have the best life together."

My eyes closed. "I don't deserve you."

Just as I began to open my eyelids, he kissed me. And as he pulled away, I placed my hand on his.

"Show me your baby. I'm absolutely dying to see it."

"Come on." He linked our fingers together and led me into the lobby.

The moment I stepped inside, I was overcome. This was a sensory overload that wasn't just sight, but also smell and feel and sound. There was something to gaze at in every direction— the floor that resembled the seabed, the ceiling that was cut in the shape of waves, the lighting that looked like coral and fish. Every surface—even the walls, the texture, and the furniture— only added to the theme.

Every time I took a breath, I smelled the beach. My ears

were filled with the lightness of crashing crests, and the sparkling reflections in the tiles and accents made me feel like the sun was touching my skin.

"Oh my God, Macon." My voice came out like an exhale. "I don't even have words to describe this." I couldn't stop taking it all in, noticing something new each time I scanned the area. "This is the most spectacular room I've ever been in."

"You think so?"

I turned toward him. "Are you for real?" I laughed. "This is paradise—and I live here. I work at the best hotel on Kauai—well, the best one before this one opens—so I know nothing like this exists on the island. Your guests are going to die when they see this."

I needed to touch him. I needed him to feel how serious I was. I rested my hand on his beard.

"When people on the mainland fantasize about the Hawaiian Islands, this is what they think of. This dream you designed. And you've done it. You've created a true-to-life fantasy." I released his hand but kept the other on his face. "Now, show me the rest—the pool and spa and restaurants, all of it—and then I have one final request."

He licked across his lips, as though he was already reading my mind. "What would that be?"

"I want you to take me to your room."

TWENTY-THREE

Macon

BROOKLYN

I just finished my last final. Macon, I'm officially done with college. I don't know whether to cry or scream.

ME

Save the screaming for when you're with me. ;)

I'm so fucking happy for you. You've busted your ass these last few weeks. You'd better have the biggest smile on your face right now because I have one for you.

BROOKLYN

I do, and it's huge.

My parents will be here in a few hours. My sisters are decorating the whole place. I'm overwhelmed with all the things.

ME

I can't wait to meet them.

BROOKLYN

I know we planned a dinner for tomorrow night to officially celebrate my graduation, but if you're free this evening, I'd love for you to come over. Mom insists on cooking, so the whole fam will just be hanging here.

ME

What time?

BROOKLYN

7-ish

ME

See you then.

BROOKLYN

Really??? You can make it?

ME

Brooklyn ... stop. (I'm using your words.) I wouldn't miss it.

BROOKLYN

<3

The last time I'd met the parents of a woman I was dating was more than seven years ago when my high school girlfriend invited me over for the first of many dinners. So, I felt a little rusty when I walked through the door of Brooklyn's home and everyone inside immediately turned toward me. Brooklyn, who had greeted me at the door and given me a kiss as soon as I walked in, took the bag out of my hands that I'd filled with bottles of champagne, along with red and white wine. Since I didn't know anyone's preference, I'd brought it all. And as she set the bag in the kitchen and poured everyone a glass, I had time to make all the introductions and connect the faces to the names that I'd been hearing a lot.

Like my siblings and me, the three sisters shared many similar physical characteristics, but when it came to their personalities, they were nothing alike. Clementine appeared to be the fill-in mom. I sensed that right away by the way she looked at her youngest sister and spoke about her, how she touched her in a protective way. Jesse was the wild one, outspoken with no filter, but the kind of woman who would be your alibi with no questions asked.

And then there were her parents. A father whose eyes were never far from me, as though he was assessing every move I made and whether I was right for his daughter. A mother who couldn't stop talking and hugging her girls, soaking up every second she was around them.

From the minute I'd arrived, there hadn't been a quiet moment.

Nor was there ever a vacant spot next to me, one side constantly occupied by her father and the other side rotated between her sisters, questions thrown at me from every direction.

I understood the need to know who I was.

I wasn't just a boyfriend who Brooklyn was introducing to her family for the first time. I was also the man who had gotten her an interview and the reason she was moving away to the mainland. And there was a heavy focus on that, on the job and her role within our company, and her living situation from everyone in this room.

Something I'd expected and something I didn't balk at.

Because despite things still being new and fresh, and we weren't even in LA yet, I saw the future, and even though I'd told Brooklyn that I wanted her in it, I didn't think she realized the strength and meaning behind that statement.

The gorgeous woman standing across the living room, having a one-on-one with her mom, was going to be my wife. And this family, the rest who surrounded me, would, at some point, be my family too.

Some would say it was too soon to know, but I knew.

There would never be a woman who captured my heart like Brooklyn.

"I've got to tell you," Jesse started, adding more wine to my glass before setting the bottle on a small table behind me, "you weren't on her bingo card."

I turned toward her, holding the heavy pour tightly in my hand. "She wasn't on mine either. To be honest, I wasn't even playing the game—that was how uninterested I was in finding someone."

Her hair was like springs, and she tucked some behind her ear. "What makes her so different? I mean, I know the answer to that, but I'd love to hear it from you."

I was positive her dad was listening. Not that it mattered. I wasn't formulating an answer for him. I was speaking straight from me.

"The thing about your sister is that the person she is on the outside doesn't even come close to matching how beautiful she is on the inside, and that's hard to believe, given how drop-dead gorgeous she is."

I shifted my gaze in her direction, seeing the smile covering her face, hearing the laughter from her lips, feeling the excitement as she spoke to her mom. "When you learn who Brooklyn really is and what she stands for and the things that matter to her, you realize how incredibly unique she is. Women like her don't exist." I connected eyes with Clementine, who nodded in agreement, and then Jesse before slowly moving my stare to her father.

"Most women care about status, money, and the importance of my family's last name—not her." I ran my hand down my arm, meeting the leather bracelets wrapped around my wrists. "She wants to do it all on her own."

And that was so fucking sexy to me, but I wasn't going to tell them that.

I let a moment pass before I added, "The biggest thing was that I wasn't looking. I wasn't planning. I was content with my life and the way things were, and then I spotted her in a crowd of people. This feeling came over me, and I knew I couldn't leave unless I spoke to her. When I did, something became painfully obvious." I remembered the feeling well because it was happening again as I looked at her. I took a breath, waiting for it to ease up, and when it didn't, I continued, "I didn't want another day to pass by without her in my life." I made eye contact with both sisters. "I care about her. A lot."

"I literally just melted into a puddle," Jesse cooed.

"My daughter is much more sentimental than I am," her dad said. "Feelings matter, sure. But her safety is my concern. LA is a big city. She's never been on her own. I'm worried."

"She's not alone," I told him. "She'll never be alone."

I hadn't won him over.

I could tell by his eyes.

"I was brought up by very old-school parents who struck business deals with no more than a handshake." I adjusted my grip, holding the glass in my left hand. "I wouldn't bring Brooklyn to a new city, not knowing a soul, unless I could ensure her safety and unless I fully intended to take care of her." I paused. "I do." I took one final look at my Tiny Dancer before I locked eyes with her dad. "Nothing is going to happen to your daughter, not under my watch. And when I tell you my word is bond, I mean that, sir." I held out my right hand in his direction.

I waited.

I observed the change in his expression as he took in mine.

And when his hand finally clasped my fingers, he said, "Don't let me down, Macon."

TWENTY-FOUR

Brooklyn

C elebrations, for me, usually only lasted a day. At least, my high school graduation and birthdays over the years had been that way. But my college graduation was a little different. I was sure that had to do with my parents flying in and staying with us. That Mom insisted on constantly feeding us girls so that we were always sharing a meal. That my sisters refused to take down the decorations, our place full of balloons and streamers and poster board that, in marker and big bubbly letters, told me how proud they were of me.

We'd rearranged our work schedules so we could be together for their entire visit, and it was the most amazing four days.

I didn't think it was a coincidence that most of my family's conversations revolved around Macon or my new job in LA. Aside from earning my degree, those were the biggest things happening in all our lives. This gave my parents a chance to have a second dinner with him and an opportunity to learn even more about him. That meal took place at Charred, the steak house in Macon's hotel—a suggestion from Macon when we had been in the planning stages of where to take my family out to eat. The owners of the restaurant, the Westons, had opened a few days early, and we were their first private party.

By going there, my parents were able to see how Macon used his contacts to make every moment so incredibly special and one that we would never forget, like the five-course meal we didn't know we were getting and the massive coffee-flavored cake that had been made just for me. They got to see his power the second they walked into his hotel, his influence, the way his employees respected him, how the Westons personally came to check on us to make sure we were pleased with the food and service.

But most of all, they got to see how much he cared about me.

By the time I dropped them off at the airport, they weren't nearly as worried about me going all the way to California without any family. They'd believed Macon when he told them he would do everything in his power to keep me safe and that I was in the best possible hands. He'd completely charmed all the women in my family, and even my father had softened up a bit.

And on the day they flew back to The Big Island, two things happened.

I gave my two-week notice at the hotel. That would give me exactly three work-free days to wrap things up and finish packing before I moved to LA.

The second was the grand opening of the Spade Hotel. A night that Macon had worked so extremely hard to prepare for. Even when he had hung out with my family, he had taken calls and put out more fires, directing his teams and answering endless questions.

For him, it never stopped.

His brothers and cousin had flown in to celebrate this monumental night, and so had his uncle Walter and his friends, the Daltons.

My sisters had also been invited, but since they both had to work and couldn't come, I opted to get ready in Macon's hotel room. Macon was somewhere downstairs, working out last-minute details, so I was alone in his massive suite. A room almost as gorgeous as his home in LA.

After finishing my hair and makeup, I sat around in a bathrobe, waiting until it was time to get dressed, taking in the views of the beach, checking social media to see what posts had been made about the event, giving love to each one.

It was the calm before tonight's storm, and I was soaking in every second.

When it was time to get dressed, I went to the walk-in closet, where I'd hung the outfit I'd brought—a dress that Macon had gifted me when he filled my wardrobe with interview clothes. But when I went to grab it off the rack, there was another dress hanging beside it with a note attached.

I KNOW BLACK IS YOUR FAVORITE, BUT RED, ON YOU, IS MINE.
WHEN I SAW THIS DRESS, THE ONLY THING I COULD THINK OF
WAS HOW SEXY IT WOULD LOOK ON YOUR BODY.
WEAR IT ... FOR ME.
SINCE I PROBABLY WON'T BE ABLE TO ESCAPE, JO WILL BE BY
TO ZIP YOU UP.
SEE YOU SOON, GORGEOUS.
—MACON

My body was already on fire as I started reading the note. By the time I finished the last word, the tingles were blazing through every single part of me.

My God, this man.

Not only had he gotten me another gift and gone to the extra effort to give it to me, but he'd also seen the dress and fantasized about how it would look on me. And now he was somewhere in this hotel, thinking about me wearing red, anticipating the moment when he'd finally see me.

There was nothing hotter—I was positive about that.

And the dress, despite being the loudest color, was absolutely beautiful. A strapless design with a sweetheart neckline, the fabric ending above the knee. But the bottom wasn't straight across; it was shaped in a V, so it would cut higher toward the center and inner part of my thighs.

I knew by the material that it would be tight and the shape would be overly sexy on me.

I didn't want any attention this evening. I wanted to blend into the background, like the nights when I went to the club, but this dress was certainly going to earn me some notice.

Just as I was taking it off the hanger, there was a knock at the door.

I set the dress on the bed and tightened the tie of my bathrobe, leaving the bedroom to walk through the living room and kitchen, and I checked the peephole when I arrived at the door.

Jo was standing on the other side of it.

I quickly opened it and smiled. "Hi! It's so nice to see you." As I leaned forward to give her a hug, I continued, "Girl, wow, you look beautiful in that dress."

Jo was in a black dress that had layers of lace and sky-high red heels with a clutch in the same color.

"You're sweet, thank you, and it's so great to see you too." She squeezed back. "You weren't kidding, Kauai is stunning. I never want to leave." She froze in my arms. "How dumb of me to say that when we're dragging you to LA. Oh man, ignore me, please."

I laughed as I pulled away and held open the door. "Please come in." Once she stepped inside, I let the door close. "Thank you for coming to help me get dressed. The outfit I'd planned to wear didn't have a zipper, so I was good on my own, and then Macon surprised me with a new one."

"That guy"—Jo shook her head—"he's done such a one-eighty since he met you."

"I heard he was a bit of a playboy before."

She laughed. "A bit? Yes. That's an understatement." She put her hand on my arm as we headed for the bedroom. "But he's not even close to the same man anymore. Even during our video calls, I can see the change. He has a permanent smile on his face—something he never wore, he's always been on the semi-grumpy side—and I know that smile is all because of you. And given everything that's going on here with the hotel, he should be stressed to the max. I'm positive he is. But he looks like nothing can bother him. He's just beaming with happiness." She turned toward me when we reached the bedroom. "I've obviously known Macon my whole life, and I've never seen him like this."

I didn't know that version of Macon. I only knew the sweet, kind, thoughtful, and giving side of him. But to hear how much he'd changed and that most of that was because of me, it made my heart melt.

"You know, I didn't think I could ever feel this way. I was just so focused on how much I had on my plate and what the future would look like that he completely caught me off guard."

"Oh, yes, the king of charm. I know—I'm engaged to one just like him." She grinned.

"And since I didn't plan for it or wasn't even looking for it, I

didn't think a relationship like this was even possible. And now
..." I swallowed as the emotion came on.

"You can't imagine your life without him."

I nodded. "Yes."

"Girl"—she tightened her grip on my arm—"from my experience, I can tell you, it only gets better."

"But this already feels like such a dream."

"So far, your lives have been monopolized by the opening of the hotel and your work and school. Just think about what will happen when you guys have more time, like when you move to LA. That's why I have a suspicion that things are going to get even better."

"I can't wait." I took a deep breath, my eyes briefly closing. "For moving to California, working for Spade Hotels, spending more time with him—all of it." I glanced down at the dress, knowing this was the perfect introduction to the conversation I'd planned on having with her at some point tonight. "Before I put this dress on, I want to thank you for not telling him about my housekeeping job."

"Brooklyn, I would never. It wasn't my story to tell, and you assured me you were going to confess to him. Now, if you hadn't, I would have said something to him."

"I just want you to know that I recognize that I put you in the most difficult position. And even though I'm a firm believer in girl code, you didn't know me, you had zero loyalty to me, Macon is your family, and you still kept the secret from him." My eyes took in hers. "That means more to me than you'll ever know."

Her head tilted while the softest expression moved across her face. "I told you I've been in your shoes, so I wouldn't do that to anyone, especially not someone who's about to be part of my family." Her hand moved down my arm and gripped my fingers. "Macon and I are very close—the whole family is.

You're going to be seeing a whole lot of me, and that's no way to start a friendship."

The first time I'd met her, I had been overwhelmed by the respect I felt for her.

I didn't think it was possible, but that feeling doubled.

Since I wasn't sure my words could even dent the way I felt, I wrapped my arms around her again and hugged her. "Just know that I'm so grateful for you." My voice was only a little above a whisper.

When I pulled away, she said, "You have no idea how relieved I am for you now that you don't have that conversation weighing you down."

"Honestly, it's the best feeling."

She laughed. "Trust me, I get that in every way."

Besides the way I felt, I was thankful Macon had forgiven me, that he wasn't constantly reminding me of the lie and holding it against me. That it hadn't become a daily thorn in our relationship.

That didn't mean he'd forgotten. I was sure the thought still crossed his mind often, but the important part was that we were able to move on and he wasn't dwelling on the past.

And now, I could focus on proving to him that I would never lie again.

"I don't want us to be late, so I'm going to put the dress on in the bathroom." I draped it across my arm. "Be right back."

She took a seat on the bed. "I can't wait to see it on you. That shade is going to pop on your skin."

"I'd say it is." I laughed. "I only ever wear black, but red is Macon's favorite color on me."

She lifted the bottom of the dress and held it near my face. "Oh, yes, I can definitely see why. Red is absolutely your color." She adjusted her position. "I'll be right here, waiting for you."

I hurried into the bathroom and took off the robe, hanging it on a towel hook. Since I already had on a strapless bra that I'd planned to wear with the other outfit, along with a thong, all I had to do was unzip the dress and step into it, lifting it up my body and positioning it across my chest. While I held it in place, I fixed the pieces of hair I'd curled earlier and checked my makeup. I normally didn't wear eye shadow or eyeliner or even such a thick coat of mascara. But with tonight being so fancy, I'd added all three, and I made sure none of it had smudged.

Pleased with the final look, I rejoined Jo in the bedroom.

Her eyes instantly widened, dipping down the whole length of me to take me in. "Holy shit. You look so freaking hot, my *gaaawd*." She moved behind me to zip me up. "This was literally made for you."

When she finished, I turned toward her, my stomach tightening from the sexiness of this tiny dress. "It's not too much?"

"Too much? Heck no! Macon is going to die when he sees you." She looked at my bare feet. "What shoes are you wearing with it?"

I'd only brought one pair, and that was a strappy wedge that I'd thought would look great with the other dress, but now that I was in this one, I wasn't so sure.

I returned to the closet to grab the shoes from where I'd placed them on the floor, and that was when I saw the box, positioned directly next to the wedges, with another note taped to the top.

I couldn't get you a dress without the perfect pair of heels to go with it.
I can't wait to see your legs in these.
And I can't wait to see you later tonight wearing only these.

"He thinks of everything," I said as I turned toward the doorway where Jo was standing.

"Christian Louboutins." Jo nodded toward the box, where the designer's name was on the top. "Macon has excellent taste."

"I have a feeling these are ungodly expensive—and if they are, don't tell me. If I know how much they cost, I'll make him return them."

"Let him spoil you. He can afford it." She winked.

I took a seat on the bed and opened the box. The black heels were at least four inches tall and the most beautiful I'd ever seen. A strap went across the base of my toes with a satin ribbon that tied around my ankle, the bottoms the same color as the dress. Once I had them on, I stood on the carpet, balancing on the thin stilettos.

Jo groaned, "Your feet are going to be screaming within an hour. Somehow, just deal with the pain because those shoes with that dress are everything." She took a few steps back to get a better view. "Poor Macon. He has no idea what he's in for tonight. The sight of you is going to torture him."

I laughed. "He's not so good at keeping his hands off me, so I think you're right."

She held out her fingers for me to clasp, grinning. "Come on. Let's go ruin his life."

We linked hands and took the short walk to the elevator, taking it down to the first floor and into the lobby, where the party was already happening.

Macon had debated on whether to have the event in one of the ballrooms or the lobby and opted for the latter, wanting his guests to experience the heart of the hotel.

I was so glad he'd gone this route.

After touring the entire property, which was undoubtedly the prettiest hotel I'd ever seen, there was something so warm and extravagant about this room. Something that, the first time I'd stepped inside it, had taken my breath away.

As I looked at the faces of his guests, their expressions and reactions, I could tell they were all feeling the same way.

"I'm sure Macon is slammed with schmoozing," Jo said as she led me toward the center of the space, "so I'm going to introduce you to some of his friends and, of course, my soon-to-be hubby. Unless you've already met the crew?"

"Just Cooper—that's it."

"Well then, it's time to meet the Daltons."

We approached a group of men, wearing suits in navy and black and dark gray. Their hair was gelled, their facial hair on point, their presence even louder than their voices as they spoke to one another. And even while I wore four-inch heels, they towered over me, just like Macon, their stature as built and intimidating as his.

Jo moved in between two of them, making sure there was space for the both of us before she said, "Gentlemen, I'd like to introduce you to Brooklyn."

The first thing I noticed was that, aside from my name, she didn't inform them of who I was. That meant everyone in this circle already knew. Either Macon had told them or someone else had, but they didn't seem to question who I was or need any further explanation.

Jo put her arm around me and laughed. "You're never going to remember all of these names, but don't worry, we won't quiz you later. We're definitely not that mean."

"She isn't, but I am," one of the guys said.

"We'll get to that smart-ass in a second," Jo said, "but we're going to start right here." She placed her hand on the chest of the guy next to her. "Arguably the most important man here because I'm about to marry his sexy ass. This is Jenner."

"Great to meet you," I said to Jenner as we shook hands.

Jenner nodded. "I've heard a lot about you, Brooklyn."

"That's because my brother can't stop talking about her," the same smart-ass said, who happened to be standing on the other side of Jenner.

Jo pointed at him and said, "That's Brady, Macon's oldest brother."

"It's a pleasure, Brooklyn." Brady clasped his fingers around mine. "At this point, I feel like I already know you, which gives me automatic permission to dig you all I want."

"Don't worry, I can take it." I winked at him.

She then pointed at Cooper. "You already know that goofball."

"I do." I smiled, my hand moving to his. "It's nice to see you again, Cooper."

"I haven't had a chance to officially welcome you to the company," he said, "but we're very excited to have you on board. Congratulations."

"Thank you," I responded.

The moment our hands released, Jo said, "We've somewhat bounced between the Daltons and the Spades, but we're back to the Daltons now." She was pointing at the man next to Cooper. "And that right there is Camden. He went to high school with Macon, where they played soccer together."

"*Ahhh*, yes, I've heard your name a bunch." I reached forward to greet him.

"Great to finally meet you, Brooklyn," Camden said. "I've heard your name more than a bunch."

I laughed.

"And that's Dominick"—her finger aimed toward the next guy in line—"and Declan—who isn't a Dalton, but will be marrying one—and last, but certainly not least, that's Ford."

I continued shaking each hand, attempting to memorize a

particular trait that would help me recall their name and keep the two families straight.

But my thoughts were interrupted when I heard, "You forgot someone, sweetheart."

The voice had come from behind me.

Jo and I turned to see who it was. The man was standing about a foot away, and I guessed he was at least in his late fifties with gray around his temples and a light dusting of silver across the rest of his dark hair. Deep lines were etched into his forehead and the sides of his mouth. And as he looked at me, I sensed he was someone with authority and great wisdom who had experienced more life than I could ever dream of.

I held out my hand, and before Jo uttered a word, I said, "You must be Walter."

He gripped my fingers, holding them for several seconds before he replied, "Brooklyn Bray, it's a real honor to meet you. I apologize for not getting a chance to speak with you while you were visiting our corporate headquarters, but my daughter has spoken so highly of you, Cooper as well, and my nephew is quite fond of you, as I'm sure you know. I anticipate you being a perfect addition to our team."

"Thank you." He released my hand, and it dropped to my side. "I'm so excited to start. The ideas are already brewing, and granted, I haven't seen the first property, nor do I know what I'm even walking into, but I've begun to outline a plan to assess your current strategies and procedures, and I can't wait for it all to come together."

Walter looked at Jo. "Yes, I see what you were talking about." His eyes returned to mine. "My daughter has never compared her work ethic to anyone at our company, and when she told me she thought the two of you were alike, I had to see it with my own eyes." His stare deepened within mine. "Hell, I think she might be right."

"Well, you haven't seen me in action, but I can promise that I won't let either of you down."

"I don't doubt that," Walter said.

"Neither do I," Jo added.

There was movement at my side, an arm that surrounded my waist that I'd been craving all night. A breeze of cologne that I knew all too well, that I'd missed since he'd gone downstairs.

"Do you need to be saved?" Macon whispered in my ear, just loud enough that I suspected Jo and Walter could hear.

And when Walter laughed, I knew he had.

"She's a Spade Hotel employee now," Walter said to Macon. "This is only the first of many talks I'll be having with her." He nodded toward us. "There are several more people I need to speak with, so I'll catch you all later." His eyes shifted across our small group, pausing on mine. "Brooklyn, I'm happy we got the chance to meet. I look forward to seeing you in a couple of weeks." He patted Macon on the shoulder and left.

"Don't get used to that side of Dad," Jo said, laughing. "It's reserved for events like this and family functions. At work, he's all business."

"A roaring fucking lion is a much better description," Macon said.

Jo smiled. "That too." She rubbed the top of my arm. "I'll leave you guys alone."

As she stepped toward the group of Daltons and Spades, I faced Macon. "This is—"

"No"—he put his hand on my cheek, immediately silencing me—"we're not going to talk about what this is. We can do that in the morning. I estimate we have about thirty seconds before we're interrupted, and I want to spend each of those telling you how fucking breathtaking you look."

"This dress—"

"And those heels ..." He shook his head, licking across his lips. "*Mmm*, I would do anything to toss you over my shoulder and take you to my room right now." He leaned toward my face, but didn't kiss me. "It's taking every ounce of self-control I have not to do it."

"You can't. This is your party, what you've worked so hard for."

"I'm a boss, Brooklyn. Technically, I can do anything I want. And what I want right now is you."

I couldn't stop the smile from filling my face. "You wouldn't dare ..."

"I would."

Even though he had one hand on my waist and another on my cheek, I didn't want to show too much affection. I didn't know if it was appropriate or if this was the place, so I set my hands on his stomach, feeling his abs beneath his tie and button-down. "Just think of how amazing I'm going to feel when you can finally touch me."

"You're teasing me ..."

"And how wet I'm going to be all night as I wait for you."

"Brooklyn ..."

"And how badly I want you to pick me up in your arms the second we reach your room and fuck me against the door of your suite."

A small chuckle came from his lips as he moved our faces even closer together. "You know what?"

"What?"

"I've met my fucking match."

TWENTY-FIVE

Macon

"Home," Brooklyn whispered, glancing through the windshield as I pulled up to the Beverly Hills Spade Hotel. "And, God, is she beautiful."

"After spending time in the one on Kauai, I didn't think you'd love the Beverly Hills one as much."

I felt her eyes on me as she replied, "It's a different kind of love. A love that comes with new beginnings."

My hand traced up the side of her thigh as I navigated around the cars waiting to be parked. "You mean, a kind of love that's temporary." This was the first time I'd said that to her, but I wanted to lay the foundation since the six months would be up before we knew it. "That is, until I convince you to move in with me."

What I had convinced her of so far was to stay on Kauai an extra week, allowing me to finish up with the opening of the hotel. I didn't want her to move by herself and do it all alone. But the additional seven days gave her more time with her sisters and to sell her car—something she'd decided since it wasn't cost-effective to ship hers from the island.

Yesterday was officially moving day.

Once we flew in, I checked her into the hotel, and the boxes she'd mailed from Hawaii were already in her room. I helped unpack her things, and we spent the first night at the hotel.

This morning, after a late breakfast, I showed her more of the city, and she bought a car.

I pushed for an X5—she'd looked gorgeous behind the wheel during the test drive.

When she saw the price, she wouldn't fucking hear of it.

She'd gone with a Jeep Wrangler with around thirty thousand miles. A vehicle more used than I'd wanted her to get, but one of my more dominant requests had been that she buy an SUV for safety. The Jeep was her compromise, and it was a car payment she could more than afford with her new salary.

"If I moved in, you'd get sick of me." Her voice was soft, her eyes still fixed on me. "That's why I should get my own place when the relocation package expires."

As I came to a stop, two valet attendants headed toward the car to open our doors.

"If you moved into my place, I don't think that would even give us enough time together." I shifted into park, my hand then returning to her leg. "I want you around me all the time, Brooklyn."

She sank back into the seat despite her door now being ajar. "Even when you wake up?"

"Especially when I wake up."

Her head shook. "Are you trying to make me melt onto the floor?"

I held the bottom of her chin. "Melt? No. Show you how fucking wild I am for you? Yes."

"That's something you've never stopped showing me." Her

voice was a little above a whisper. "I don't just see it and hear it, Macon. I feel it—everywhere."

She chewed her bottom lip, and I pulled it away from her teeth, running my thumb across it.

"When those six months are up, I can see that move happening." She grabbed my hand, holding it against her cheek, leaning her face into it. "As long as you'll have me."

The valet attendants were standing by both open doors.

I gave zero fucks.

"Kiss me, Brooklyn."

She leaned forward, gently pressing her lips against mine. But as she held them there, parting them just slightly, there was an intensity in the way she moved her mouth.

An intensity I'd felt every time she kissed me during the last couple of weeks on Kauai.

Brooklyn wasn't just giving me her lips. She wasn't just going through the motions.

She was showing me how much she cared, how much she wanted me.

How much she wanted us.

"Let's get you upstairs," I roared when we finally separated.

Her eyes told me she knew exactly how I was feeling and what that fucking mouth had stirred up inside me.

With a smile, she climbed out of the car.

I did as well, instantly greeted with, "Mr. Spade, welcome," by the valet attendant the second I stepped onto the pavement. "Would you like me to keep your car out front?"

Our dinner reservations were in an hour. We had only come back to shower and quickly swap out our clothes.

But what that kiss had just done was solidify that those plans were now getting changed.

"You can put it away for the evening," I told him.

"No problem, Mr. Spade."

I joined Brooklyn, my hand going to her lower back as we walked inside the lobby.

"I know I've only been here one night, and I don't start my job for a couple more days, but I already see things I want to implement."

"You're going to make Walter one happy man."

She laughed. "I thought I already did that at the grand opening?"

I lowered my hand to the top of her ass, leaving it there for only a second since there were employees everywhere. "Oh, you did, and you know that." Walter had had plenty of positive things to say after he met her at the hotel, and I'd shared some of that with Brooklyn. "But when he hears this, he's going to be even happier."

"Except my ideas aren't for him. They're for the whole brand, assuming some of these procedures are company-wide. And because I see them every time I walk into this hotel, knowing money is being wasted, I'm having a hard time keeping my mouth shut."

She was two weeks into her Six Sigma certification, and I could already see the difference. She'd had incredible ideas before she began the courses, things she'd expressed during our time together. As she got deeper into the program, her views were getting stronger, sharper, and she was looking at things differently than she had in the past.

All I knew was that she was going to be one hell of an asset to our company.

And the more she saved our brand, the more she was going to earn.

Something told me by year-end, Brooklyn was going to have quite an impressive income, possibly double her current salary.

"Do me a favor?" I pressed the button for the elevator.

She glanced up at me while we waited for it to open. "Okay ..."

"Don't ever keep your mouth shut."

Her smile made me ache. "Because you want to slide something in it?"

"That, fuck yeah." With one hand on her cheek, I stretched my thumb across her chin to hold both sides of her face. "But also because everything that comes out of it matters to me."

"Deal."

I nodded toward the open door. "Get in." I followed behind her, pressing the button for the top floor, and moved to the back of the elevator, where she was standing, wrapping my arms around her stomach. "God, I'm fucking hungry." My face was in her neck, and I kissed down to her collarbone.

As I stood behind her, she pressed her palms against my thighs. "Dinner's soon, right?"

"It was."

"Was?" She paused. "We're not going?"

Knowing we were on camera, that our security team often reviewed these tapes for extra measures and training purposes, I kept my hands on her navel. "I'll have food delivered when I'm done."

"Done?" She looked at me from over her shoulder.

I held the other side of her face, the one that wasn't pointed toward me, and I growled in her ear, "Done with your fucking pussy."

"Macon ..."

My name didn't come out as a sigh.

It came out as a breath.

Like the anticipation of having me inside her wasn't allowing her to get in enough air.

The elevator chimed, and the doors opened.

"Your room. Now."

Because I couldn't wait another fucking second to feel her.

And to get her moving even faster, I gave her ass a small spank.

"*Mmm*," she moaned as my hand pulled away. "So, you are going to feed me."

The longer we were together, the dirtier she got. It was the hottest thing ever.

I held the base of her neck. "With every part of my body."

"I think you need to promise me something."

"Yeah?" My thumb went into her mouth, scraping the sides between her teeth. "What's that?"

I pulled it out so she could say, "You need to make me scream louder than I ever have."

Her request made my dick throb even harder, my hard-on grinding against my boxer briefs, which then forced my crown to rub against the back side of the zipper.

"Get your ass in that room before I carry you."

She gave me a long grin before she walked out of the elevator, getting her key card ready so that by the time we reached the door, she only had to wave it in front of the reader.

Once it was open and I moved in behind her, I surrounded her waist and turned her toward me. "I can't wait to fucking taste you."

There was no reason we needed to wait until we got to the bed. Not when I could easily strip her in the doorway, so that was what I started doing, dropping her pants down her legs and helping her out of her shoes, lifting her shirt over her head. When she had only her bra and panties left, I backed her up against the door. While I took her mouth, ravishing those perfect lips, I unclasped the hook, tossing her bra, and I pushed the lace past her hips, hearing the soft fall of her panties.

"Are you wet?" I asked as soon as I separated us.

She used the door as support and arched her back, forcing her chest to stick out. "Why don't you tell me?"

"No, Brooklyn, I asked you a question." I put a few feet of distance between us. "Now, tell me, are you wet?"

"I'm dripping."

"Fuck yes." I got to work on my clothes, unbuttoning each of the small holes that ran down the front of my shirt, followed by my jeans, boxer briefs, and shoes. As I stood naked in front of her, I pumped my cock. "I want you to show me."

"How?"

"With your fingers—that's how."

Still in the same position, she ran her hand down the front of her, her palm pressed to her clit while her fingers dived deeper. Her eyes briefly closed as at least one slid in, gathering enough wetness before she raised her hand in the air.

"Brooklyn, do you want me to lick that off your finger?"

She nodded. "Yes."

"Then, feed it to me."

She held her hand toward me, and I leaned in closer, swirling my tongue around the tips of each finger, swallowing the sweetness off her skin.

"Goddamn it, you taste good." I lowered until her whole pointer finger was in my mouth, and when I finally pulled back, I ordered, "Now, rub that wetness over my dick."

I moved in closer so she could reach me, and she gently grazed the length of my shaft.

But the whole time she touched me, her eyes didn't leave mine.

They stayed locked.

Silently begging.

Needing.

Demanding more.

My arms reached above her head, caging her against my

body. With her hand still stroking me, I asked, "Do you want me to fuck you?"

"Yes. Now."

"What are you going to do for it?"

She licked each lip. "Get on my knees."

I chuckled. "As much as I want your mouth, I don't think I can wait that long to have your pussy."

"What am I going to do for it?" she repeated. She circled my width with her palm, bobbing to my sac before rising to my tip. "I can come. I guarantee that's something you want. And I know it's something you love to hear." She tightened her fingers. "And feel."

"*Yesss.* I want that." I kissed across her neck, settling against my favorite spot—right at the base where the bone jutted out. "I want that right fucking now."

Without warning, I lifted her, but I kept her back against the door and circled her legs around my waist. The moment I had her in place, I sank into her tightness, slowly at first until I got a few inches in, and then I fully buried myself.

"Fuck, you're so wet."

"Oh God." Her nails found my shoulders, like they'd never left. "You feel so good."

She was breathing against my face, our noses close, our lips teasing each other.

"You want more, baby?"

"Always." She rocked forward, as if she was trying to rub her clit against me. "Until I come. Don't stop. Please."

Hearing her command made everything inside me fucking pound.

It made me churn.

It made me rear my hips back and plunge into her.

"Fuck." I took a breath and increased my speed. "I can't get over how tight you are."

A kind of narrowness that, within a few pumps, I could easily come.

But that wasn't happening yet.

First, I needed her screams to fill my ears.

"How do you constantly know just what I want?" Her nails left me, and she hitched herself up higher, crossing her arms over my shoulders as she began to move with me.

"Because I can feel it." The short hairs above my dick were grazing her clit each time I slid in and out. "Because I know your body." I bit her lip. "Because nothing makes me feel better than making you come."

As I went faster, her hand shot into my hair, pulling the strands. "I don't deserve you."

"You do."

"But no one deserves to feel this good."

I exhaled across her mouth. "Then, we're both fucked because that's what your cunt does to me every time I'm inside it."

"I make you feel good?"

"Yes," I roared.

"Show me."

I had a feeling she was using my words to increase the build happening within her.

I could feel it by the way she was tightening, her wetness getting thicker.

But I also knew that words could be a sexy part of foreplay, and since I hadn't given her my mouth tonight, I was verbally licking her instead. Each one of those word-licks was getting her closer to the fucking edge.

An edge she couldn't come back from.

But there was something else that would send her there even faster, which was the twisting of my hips and a sharper power in my thrusts.

"*Ohhh!*" she gasped when she felt it.

The combination was what did it for her.

Was what made her narrow, to the point where she was milking my fucking dick.

Where she was screaming, "Macon," directly next to my ear.

Where she was shuddering against my body, her stomach full of waves, fingers full of tension, throat full of moans, riding out the orgasm.

"*Ahhh!*" She drew in air. "Yes!"

"Fuck me," I growled as soon as she stilled. "Knowing I can make you come like that—and that quickly—is the best feeling in the world."

She panted in my neck. "I don't remember how to breathe."

"I'll breathe for you."

I pulled her off the wall and walked her toward the bed, where I laid her across the mattress, adjusting her position until her head was on a pillow.

"You're going to have to trust me."

Her eyes had closed the second her head hit the fluff, but then they burst open.

"Yes, Brooklyn. I said trust. Do I have all of yours?"

She leaned up onto her elbows to get a better look at me. "Of course ... but why?"

"Because I'm about to take another one of your firsts."

As she processed what I'd said, her brows rose high. "My ass ..."

"Yes."

Her throat bobbed as she swallowed. "Now?"

"Fuck yes."

I dipped my face between her legs and spread her thighs even farther apart, my tongue starting at her clit and lowering to her pussy.

342

She was already so fucking wet.

But assuming she didn't have lube, I needed her wetter.

I needed her sopping.

And as I added spit to her pussy, I dragged it toward her ass. Each time I neared it, she tensed up, even when I was only running my finger around it.

"I'm not going to surprise you, don't worry." I glanced up, and she was gazing down at me. "I'll talk you through everything that I'm about to do."

"But the pain, Macon. You're huge." She sucked in some air. "It's going to kill me."

"I know you don't believe this, but it's also going to feel good." I licked her more, urging the spit down to her ass, rimming around that entrance. "Remember, you have to trust me." While the saliva was leaving my mouth and traveling down in small streams, I soaked my finger, making sure it was covered, and I aimed it at her ass. "This is all I'm giving you right now." I added a little pressure, surprised at how easily it slipped in. "You're so wet, you took that with no problem."

Her neck leaned back as tiny moans began to fill the air. "Wow." Her legs were straining, eventually falling to either side. "This isn't anything like what I expected."

"I told you it was going to feel good."

I was only in as far as my first knuckle, and she was so tight that I wondered if I was going to have a hard time fitting, but that was why I was doing this first. To prepare her, to ready her for what was coming next.

"It's only going to get better," I warned, continuing to slide until I was all the way in.

Her ass was pulsing around my skin.

I allowed her a few seconds to get used to it before I picked up speed, gradually getting her to where she could handle another finger.

"I'm adding more," I said, only because I'd promised I wouldn't surprise her.

Her chest didn't move while I wedged in my middle finger, her eyes not leaving mine, her body stiff again, like she was hanging on to a fucking rope.

Within a couple of dips, her muscles relaxed, her breathing became more labored. Each of her exhales ended in a moan. "I don't know how ... but I feel like I'm about to come."

It was time.

"Now, you're going to get me." I pulled out and knelt on the bed in front of her, straddling her legs around me. "I'm going to go slow, and I won't give you more than you can handle." She attempted to respond, and I reminded her, "Trust me."

She sat higher on her elbows, staring down between her thighs, watching as I spit a few mouthfuls of saliva into my palm and rubbed it across my tip and past the bulge of my crown, adding more until my shaft was fully lubed. That was when I positioned it at her ass.

"Just relax."

I eased through her rim, the inside hugging around me, spreading to take in the end of me. And she really had to take it in because—*my fucking God*—she was tight.

"You just have to get through this part, and it'll get better." I paused once I got past my crown. "Are you okay?"

"Keep going."

She was fighting through the pain—I could see it on her face.

But what I was feeling was the opposite.

Her ass was even snugger than her fucking cunt.

And the way it was feeling, I knew it wasn't going to take much to make me come.

"Hang in there. I'm halfway." I stilled again, allowing her to get used to the intrusion, for her to widen around me. And then

I moved a bit more, the final few inches until I couldn't go any farther. "You have all of me."

Her head hung back, her neck exposed, but this time, I didn't hear any moans.

"Brooklyn, I need to know you're okay."

Her head gradually straightened, and when our eyes met, she nodded.

"Give it a few more seconds." I rubbed my thumb over her clit and instantly saw the change in her face. The way her lips opened. The way her eyes were no longer as wide and filled with an ache. "You like that?"

She didn't respond; she just stared.

She breathed.

And I could feel the moment when her body let out the pressure and she was no longer choking my shaft.

As I strummed her clit, I tilted my hips back and began to pull out toward my tip. "Talk to me. Tell me how this feels."

Her lips were parted, her chest rising much faster than before. "I ... don't know what's happening."

I touched her pussy, my finger meeting a whole new wave of wetness, and my question was suddenly answered. "That's because you've never had this, so you don't know what it can do to you." I waited for a few more dives and said, "It doesn't hurt like it did, does it?"

She shook her head.

"And it's even starting to feel fucking good."

"Yes." Her teeth scraped her lip. "Macon ..."

Oh, yes, it was definitely starting to feel good.

But for her first time, I wasn't going to make this last longer than it needed to. I wanted her to experience the pleasure of anal and not be afraid of it. I wanted to hear her, one day, beg for my cock in her ass.

And for that to happen, I needed to end this sooner than later.

So, my hand focused solely on her clit, grazing it horizontally, keeping it wet and stimulated, rotating the top in a circle. With my dick, I gave her long, deep strokes, letting her take in the whole length of me, goading her body toward an orgasm.

But it didn't take more than a few pumps before mine began to brew.

I couldn't hold it off.

I couldn't even attempt to fight it.

Not with her this tight.

"You're going to make me come," I roared.

The look on her face told me the same thing was happening inside her, and so did the way her clit had tightened into a hard bud.

"*Yesss*," I hissed. "You feel so fucking perfect." I bucked my hips forward, the orgasm moving into my balls. "Do you want my cum, Brooklyn?"

"Yes."

"I need to hear something first. I need to see it. I need to feel it."

"Then, listen and feel," she whispered. Her legs widened the farthest they had been so far, her body sliding with me, her ass contracting around me. "Oh God ... Macon!" Once the words left her, the moans took over.

So did mine.

My movements turned harder, more intense, even needier as my body filled with tingles, and the cum shot through my tip and straight into her.

"Brooklyn!" I arched back and blasted forward. "Fuck yes!"

Her nails were stabbing the skin around my knees, her nipples hard as her tits bounced from the motion, her lips not closing until the last groan left her mouth.

I slowed down to the speed of a crawl and eventually pulled out. As I did, my cum began to drip out of her. I circled my tip around that puckered hole, coating myself in the thick white seed that continued to fall from her and glided right back inside her. "Brooklyn, you're mine." As I watched her ass swallow the cum I was feeding back into it, I barked, "All fucking mine." I gave her a final pump, separating our bodies, and glanced up at her face. "And you're coming with me." I gathered her in my arms and carried her into the bathroom, holding her as I turned on the shower. As the water warmed, I moved us under the stream, staying silent while I held our bodies together.

When she lifted her face out of my neck and placed her hands against my cheeks, I could no longer hold back the words I was feeling.

The ones I'd been wanting to say.

"Brooklyn ..." I took a deep breath as I scanned her eyes, back and forth. "I love you." I gently kissed her. "I fucking love you so much."

"You do?" She wasn't testing me; she wasn't questioning me. It was as though she knew the answer and was confirming the statement out loud.

I still said, "Yes, I do."

"Macon ..." Instead of only holding my face, she buried her fingers in my beard. She then placed her thumbs at the edge of my mouth and set her nose on mine, breathing in my air. "I love you too."

TWENTY-SIX

Brooklyn

"How do I look?" I asked Macon as I walked into his kitchen.

He was leaning over the counter, drinking coffee and reading the newspaper.

If I had to guess, he was the only twenty-seven-year-old in this city who got the actual paper delivered every morning.

That man had the oldest soul, and I loved him for it.

He turned toward me, holding his mug, a smile instantly warming his face. "Jesus …" His stare dipped down to my heels and crawled back up. "You're sexy as fuck."

"Am I too sexy?" I glanced down the front of me, making sure I was as covered as the mirror in his walk-in closet had shown once I finished getting ready.

My dress went as high as my chin, where it wrapped around my neck. The material was light and transparent along the top until it met my chest, where it then thickened to an opaque material. From there, it hugged my waist and ended a little above my knees.

All black.

Even the heels.

A purchase I'd made during my last week on Kauai while I was out with my sisters, knowing I wanted to get something extra special for my first day.

"Not too sexy, just business sexy," he replied. "That doesn't mean I won't want to spread you over my desk and fuck you on top of it." He left the coffee and paper on the counter and came over to me. "But if you're worried it's inappropriate, it's not. It's perfect." He surrounded my waist with his hands, but he didn't hold me with the strength that he normally did. He was gentle —gentler than he'd ever been. "How are you feeling?"

As he stood in front of me, I inhaled the woodsy and smoky scent of his cologne and processed the feel of his warm skin against mine.

Macon dressed to go into Spade Hotel corporate headquarters was one delicious sight. He had on a charcoal-colored suit and a crisp white shirt and a silver tie that had thin lines of the same dark gray across it.

Casual was a look I'd gotten used to on him, one that had fit in well with Hawaii.

But this version that was starched, polished, and professionally spicy was the pure definition of business sexy.

And if it were any other morning, I was positive I'd be begging him to lift me onto the counter and dominate my body while still keeping that suit on.

But that was for a different day.

Today, I was a bundle of anxiousness.

"Nervous." I took a deep breath. "I don't know anything about any of the people I'll be working with, and getting to meet them and learning their work styles, it's always a big adjustment." The thought of that alone made my nerves double. "All I have from HR is the location of my desk and a breakdown of my schedule and that my first meeting is with my manager at eight o'clock." I glanced at the gorgeous Rolex on my wrist. "Which is in forty minutes." I felt my face drain of all its color. "Shit, I have to go."

"Don't worry. It'll only take us ten minutes to drive there. That'll give you plenty of time to get settled before your meeting."

The anxiety in my chest made everything feel so tight and achy and jittery. "About that." I set my hand over his heart, the edge of his tie tickling my skin. "Would you be upset if we drove there separately?"

"No." He paused. "But I'm curious why you don't want to go to work with me."

"It's not that I don't want to. I just ..."

I lifted my hand to his face. He'd trimmed his beard in the bathroom this morning—him at one of the double sinks, me curling my hair at the other. His quietness the entire time showed me that, on workdays, he just wasn't a morning person. At least that was what I assumed. But what the situation had also made me realize was that this getting-ready-for-work-together life was going to become our new normal.

"I don't feel super comfortable showing up with one of the bosses on the first day. If anyone sees us walk in together, word will spread, just like any other workplace, and there's a chance my team could treat me differently." That didn't sound the same as it had in my head, so I felt the need to add, "I don't want to hide our relationship—that's not the case at all. I just want their respect, Macon. I want everyone's respect. Especially on day one." I combed my fingers through his thick whiskers. "Please don't be mad or upset—that's the last thing I want."

His thumb stroked my side, causing my back to arch. "One of the things I love about you is your independence. You want to do it on your own, and I find that not only so fucking hot, but also admirable." He leaned down, his lips now close to mine. "I understand, Brooklyn, and I would never be mad or upset about this." He gently kissed me. "I'm so proud of you and what I know you're going to accomplish for our company."

I felt the relief instantly, not enough to take the flutters away, but enough that I knew I didn't have to worry about the ramifications of this conversation. "Thank you." I set both arms on his shoulders. "I hope I get to see you at some point today."

He tugged at my lip as though he was trying to tease himself. "You'll see me today, Brooklyn."

"Perfect." I stood taller on my toes and gave him a kiss. "I'm going to get going."

He stole a few more kisses, like this was the last time he'd ever lay his lips on me and he just didn't want to let me go. When I pulled back, I adjusted the bag on my shoulder, and I gave him a squeeze before I made my way toward the door.

"Kill it today, baby."

I glanced behind me, smiling. "I will."

And then I walked outside and climbed into the front seat of my new Jeep.

A vehicle so nice that I couldn't believe it was mine.

That I could afford the payments.

That living in LA, rotating between my home at the hotel and Macon's mansion in the Hills, had become my life, how amazingly perfect it all felt and how lucky I was.

That I was working my way through the certification course, and within a couple of months, I would be the only Six Sigma–certified employee at Spade Hotels.

Right before I turned out of Macon's driveway, still getting used to the feel and drive of an SUV, I dug through my bag until I found my purse, located Jesse in my Contacts, and hit Call.

I knew my sisters were still sleeping. Kauai was three hours behind LA, but I'd promised I'd call them on my way to work regardless of the time.

"Good morning," Jesse rasped as she answered. "Hold on a sec. I need to put you on speaker." I heard her in the background, telling Clem to wake up. "Okay, we're both here. Hi!"

"Morning, guys. I'm officially on my way to work and *ahhh!*"

"How do you feel?" Clem asked, her voice as raspy as Jesse's, making me feel awful that I'd woken them. "Did you eat any breakfast before you left Macon's?"

"No breakfast. I'm too nervous to eat," I told them. "But I had coffee while I was getting ready, and I'll grab something at work if I get hungry. I saw the kitchen during my tour, and there's tons of food always available—they employ a full-time chef to feed everyone."

"Isn't that fancy?" Jesse said. "Are you excited?"

"I'm all the things." I reached the first light, knowing I had to turn at the next one. From there, I'd be about a mile from the office. "Excited, nervous, anxious, overwhelmed, humbled." I tried to take a breath, the anxiety increasing so much that I could no longer fill my lungs all the way. "Once I get my first meeting behind me, I'm sure I'll be a little calmer."

"Who's that one with?" Clem asked.

"My boss."

"*Ooh,*" Jesse sang. "And then what does the rest of your day look like?"

"More meetings," I replied. "For the first week, I'm going to be analyzing all the numbers for each department at the

Beverly Hills hotel. Week two, I'll be working inside the hotel to evaluate their processes."

"And that's where you're living, right?" Jesse asked.

"Right." I turned at the second light. "I'll be at that hotel for probably a couple of months. Then, assuming I do a good enough job, I'll be moving to another property."

"My sister is such a fucking badass," Jesse said, "with a big corporate job and an awesome new Jeep—"

"It's not *new*, new," I said, laughing, "but the Jeep is new to me."

"It's new to us," Clem added. "And once Jesse and I arrive for our visit, we're going to be driving that baby everywhere."

"I can't wait." My voice quieted. "I miss you guys *sooo* much, it hurts."

"Us too, babe," Jesse replied.

"In ways you can't even imagine," Clem voiced.

I could see the building up ahead, so I said to the girls, "I'm going to pull in at any second. I'll try to text during the day, if I can. If not, you'll hear from me when I head home."

Home.

For tonight, that was Macon's house, where, last night, he'd told me he had something special planned for this evening to celebrate my first day.

I didn't know what I had done to deserve that man, but my love for him was growing by the minute.

"We love you to the moon and back," Jesse said, Clem almost instantly mirroring her words.

"I love you both too."

We said good-bye and hung up, and I drove around the back of the high-rise to the employee lot, going down several rows before I found an open spot to park. I grabbed my bag from the passenger seat and hurried to the entrance. Since I didn't yet have my ID badge, I showed my credentials to the security guard, and once I was cleared, I took the elevator to my floor.

HR had sent a map of the layout, an arrow pointing over the spot where they'd assigned me, so I knew which direction to head in as soon as I got out of the elevator. It was a busy area. Employees were everywhere—at their desks, walking through the sections of cubicles, inside the private offices that ran along both sides of the floor.

Born with no sense of direction, I took a couple of wrong turns before I found where the arrow was pointing.

And when I did, I stopped in front of the door and checked the map and the number that was printed on a plaque right outside to confirm that what I was seeing was correct.

Because what I was seeing couldn't be right.

There was no way they had assigned me an office.

Of my own.

It wasn't even possible ...

"Welcome, Brooklyn," I heard from behind me.

I quickly turned around. The woman from HR—who had given me a tour the last time I had been here—was standing there, smiling.

"Hi," I said, holding my hand out to her. "It's nice to see you again."

"And you." She released my fingers after shaking them. "Security notified me that you'd arrived. I just wanted to pop over and see if you needed anything."

I pointed to the open doorway. "Is this really my office?" I moved my hand, aiming it in the other direction toward the rows of cubicles. "And I'm not supposed to be somewhere over there?"

She smiled bigger than before, laughing a little. "No, this is correct." She stepped inside the office with me. "Cubicles are mostly reserved for entry-level positions. As you know, that's not what we hired you for. With your qualifications and knowledge, you're a huge asset to Spade Hotels."

I couldn't believe what I was hearing.

My mind was going completely wild because of it.

But I didn't want her to know that I was going nuts, so I grinned and said, "The office is perfect. I love it."

"You're free to decorate it any way you'd like." She moved toward the doorway. "I'm just one floor down. If you need anything at all, don't hesitate to ask."

"Thank you so much."

"Have a wonderful first day, Brooklyn." She gave me a small wave before she left.

My very own office.

I couldn't even wrap my head around this.

I set my bag on top of the desk, right next to my computer, and took a seat in the chair, opening the drawers to see if there was anything inside. The top one had been stocked with supplies—pens and paper clips and sticky notes, a stapler, and a pair of scissors. The rest of the drawers were empty, so I stuck my bag in the largest one and then shook my mouse to wake the monitor.

There was a sheet of paper next to the computer that had the username and password information, so once that was entered, I was able to access the system, my email immediately popping up.

There were several already waiting in my inbox. The one that stood out the most was from Jo.

From: Jo Spade
To: Brooklyn Bray
Subject: Your first day! Whoop, whoop!

*I just wanted to wish you allll the congrats and all the love going
into your first day. I know you're going to do amazing.
Drinks soon, okay?*

XO,
Jo

*Jo Spade
Chief Marketing Officer
Spade Hotels*

I couldn't stop the smile from growing across my face. Jo's
email was everything I needed this morning, along with the
quick chat with my sisters and the kiss from Macon before I'd
left his house.

As I set my hands on the keyboard to type a reply, I noticed
the time in the upper corner of the screen.

My meeting with my new boss was scheduled to start in ten
minutes.

I didn't want to be on time.

I wanted to be early.

I pushed my chair back, double-checking the office number
I needed to go to—which was office number four—and I closed
my door on the way out. As the elevator opened, I smiled at the
people I joined inside and hit the button for the executive-level
floor.

There was a receptionist at a desk as soon as I stepped out,
her eyes greeting mine as I walked up to her.

"I have an eight o'clock meeting," I told her. "My name's
Brooklyn Bray."

She glanced at her computer. "Ah, yes, I have you right
here." She lifted a phone off her desk. "Give me one sec." She
held it against her ear, staring at me as she said into the receiver,

"Ms. Brooklyn Bray is here to see you." She smiled. "Perfect. I'll bring her right down." She hung up and stood from her desk. "I'm Kathleen, by the way."

I shook her hand. "Brooklyn, but you already know that." I laughed.

She made the same sound and said, "Yes, please follow me."

She waited for me at the side of her desk and waved a key card against the wall, which opened a set of double doors. I followed her through them, and we went down a long, wide hallway decorated in large, framed photos of what appeared to be all the different Spade Hotels located around the world.

Somehow, someway, I would be affiliated with all of them. *Breathe, Brooklyn. Breathe.*

"How's your day going?" she asked.

I didn't want to tell her how much of a mess I felt, so I replied, "I've only been here for a few minutes. It's my first day. But those few minutes have been great."

She laughed. "Well, welcome. I just had my eighth anniversary of working here, and this is the best job I've ever had. I think you're going to love it."

I grinned. "I think you're right."

She began to slow as we neared the corner of the building, and she came to a stop directly outside a door labeled number four.

"We're here. Have a good meeting, Brooklyn."

"Thank you. It was so nice to meet you, Kathleen."

As soon as she was gone, I took a deep breath and raised my hand, holding it inches away from the door, attempting to calm my nerves before I gave it a solid knock.

Which I did a few seconds later.

"Come in," I heard a male's voice say from the other side.

Whenever I brought up my boss or team to Macon, he

rarely commented. He also never told me who my manager was going to be, and I never pushed him for a response. I figured, if he wanted to talk about it, he would.

But that made me wonder why he hadn't.

Was he trying to let me form my own opinion of the person and not persuade me with his?

I wasn't sure, but I planned on asking him tonight.

I carefully wrapped my fingers around the doorknob, twisted it, and pushed the door. As it slowly opened, tiny bits of the office were revealed. The rich carpet and wallpaper, the sections of shelves, the wooden desk, the edge of a dark suit and—

I froze as I connected eyes with the face staring back at me.

The face that was all too familiar.

The face that I had kissed this morning.

The face that was devouring me as I stood here, shocked and paralyzed.

"Macon"—I caught my breath—"I don't know why Kathleen brought me here. There must be some kind of mix-up. I'll just go back and tell her to take me to my manager's office."

He stood from his desk and walked over to me, extending his hand the second he reached me. "Macon Spade. It's nice to meet you."

What?

I didn't understand.

Why was he speaking to me this way?

Acting so professional?

Introducing himself when he was my boyfriend and I clearly knew who he was.

And then, suddenly, out of nowhere, the pieces began to fit together in my head.

Why he'd been so quiet while we were getting ready in the

bathroom when I knew he was a morning person and usually full of chatter.

Why he'd kissed me and held me before I left his house, like he didn't want to let me go.

Why he hadn't discussed with me who my manager was.

Why HR had told me my meeting would take place in office number four, the same number that was outside Macon's door.

Oh my God.

"I'm the director of business development and project management," he continued, "and the leader of the all-new Six Sigma Team."

This was business Macon.

The man I had kissed this morning was the other side of him.

He wanted me to keep the two separate.

"And you are?" he asked.

I shifted my weight, taking in his face, his stature, his presence, and how it filled the entire room. "Someone who's extremely angry right now."

He nodded. "I deserve that."

"That's all you're going to say?" I crossed my arms over my chest. "I think you're forgetting the part where you admit that you're a fucking liar. That what you did to me is so messed up on every single level." I glared at him. "Was it even hard for you to keep this from me? Or am I the only one who struggled with my lies while you just carried on, all easy-breezy?"

He ran his hand over the top of his hair. "Don't think I've had an easy time with this because I haven't. It weighed on me every goddamn day."

"You're unbelievable."

He exhaled slowly, as though whatever he was about to say was going to eat him alive. "What I did was wrong—there's no question about that. But I knew you wouldn't take the job if I told you the truth. That's why I did it, and that's why we're in this situation."

The anger was throbbing inside my chest. "I don't care what you thought you knew, it wasn't right. None of this is right." My voice was rising, and I didn't attempt to stop it. "You were upset that I'd confided in Jo, but what about all the people who knew you were going to be my manager? Jo? Cooper? Brady? Walter? HR? The entire company? How do you think that makes me feel? That I was left in the dark, just like you had been about my job. And now, I walk in here on what's supposed to be one of the biggest days of my life, and it's you who greets me. The man I love, the man who was so willing to lie to me, and the man who's also a giant hypocrite." My jaw clenched. "You had some nerve to come down on me when you were doing the same thing. How dare you!"

"I fucked up."

I huffed out a breath. "You more than fucked up."

"Brooklyn, I need you to hear me out." He glanced toward the ground, appearing to gather his thoughts, and when he raised his head, he continued, "Spade Hotels needs you. I need you. And even though you don't need this job, I know how great you would be and the kind of experience you would gain from it. I didn't want to get in the way of that. I wanted you to have everything you'd ever dreamed of, and if that meant getting the wrath from you and sacrificing the truth, then it was worth it." He shoved his hands into his pockets, like he was trying to stop himself from touching me.

"I could have handed this position to one of my brothers or a high-level manager. I even tried to. I reached out to Walter right after I found out the truth about your job and told him I couldn't do it. And you know what he told me?"

I rolled my eyes. "I can't wait to hear."

He shook his head at my sarcasm. "He told me there was no better person to guide you because I eat, sleep, and breathe this company. Did I want Cooper or Brady to be spending all that one-on-one time with you when it could be me? Fuck no. Spade Hotels is part of my soul. It's all I've ever wanted to do, and I want nothing more than to share that love with you and for you to love it as much as I do." He pulled his hand out and wiped it over his beard.

"Macon ..."

"I'm sorry. I'm sorry for lying. I'm sorry for not telling you. I'm sorry that you had to find out this way. I'm sorry my family and HR knew and you didn't. But, Brooklyn, you have to know that I was scared as hell to tell you. Because in my gut, I knew what would happen, just like, in your gut, you thought you knew what would happen and you were scared to tell me."

Silence ticked between us.

Seconds turning to what felt like minutes.

"I hope you'll find it in yourself to forgive me," he said.

"Because you forgave me, so it's only right."

"No, Brooklyn." I could hear his emotion building with each breath. "Because deep down, you understand why I did this, and even though you don't agree with it and you wish I had handled it differently—and I take full accountability for that—you get it. You know you belong here. And you know that the truth would have spoiled this opportunity and you wouldn't have wanted that either."

Of course he was right.

But I was still devastated by what he'd done.

I was pissed that everyone at this company had known before me.

I felt, in some way, manipulated.

But I knew what I could offer them. I knew what I could do

for them. I knew that, in this position, I was going to shine in ways they couldn't even dream of.

Having Macon as my manager was something I could handle.

Had I known this before, I wouldn't have taken the job.

Because, back then, I couldn't separate the two sides of him.

Now, I most definitely could.

That realization, that truth, even that conclusion didn't make me feel any better.

Maybe, in the future, it would.

But now, not enough blood had been shed.

"Macon ... you have a lot more groveling to do."

He cracked a smile. "You're probably right about that."

"This conversation isn't over. When we get home, we're going to talk lots more about it. And just when you think we're moving on to a different topic, we're going to talk about it some more. And more. Until I can look at you and not feel as murderous as I do right now."

"I figured." He scanned my eyes back and forth. "But for now, please tell me you're willing to stay." He took a step closer. "And, fuck, please tell me you're willing to sit down at that desk with me and let me go over every duty and responsibility of your job—a job that no one else but you could handle."

I could forgive him.

I felt that in my heart.

We'd both messed up.

We'd both wronged each other.

But I wasn't going to let that prevent me from moving forward.

I couldn't.

I wanted this—Macon and the position—far too much for that.

I filled my lungs with as much air as I could hold, and I held out my hand. When he gripped it, I shook his fingers with all the power I had and said, "Brooklyn Bray. It's a pleasure to meet you, Macon." I paused as I stared into his smoldering green eyes. Despite how furious I was, I loved this man more than anything in this world. "For the record, I'm going to more than handle this job. I'm going to fucking rock it."

"All right, baby." He winked. "Let's take over the world."

EPILOGUE

Eight Months Later

Macon

"I was going to ask you how the sushi is," I said to Brooklyn as she sat across from me, "but your moans are answering that question for me."

"Macon, what am I eating? And how is it possible that anything can taste this good?" She popped another piece into her mouth. "I mean, I don't even have to chew, it just *melllts*," she sang behind her hand. "There's nothing normal about sushi that melts."

The table was tiny. A small two-seater against the window in a restaurant I'd eaten at once before during my last trip to Japan. But there was something extremely special about the location of this table and the view we were able to see out the window.

I reached across the plate in the center and over both of our bowls of soy sauce to place my hand on her face. "I told you, there's nothing like the sushi here."

She finished chewing and swallowed, nuzzling her face into my palm. "I can't believe I'm here." Her voice was so quiet, emotional.

"You earned this trip, my Tiny Dancer."

From the moment we'd started dating, she never once took anything for granted. And the deeper we got into our relationship, the more we traveled, the additional Spade Hotel properties she saw, that humbleness only grew.

Sure, there had been hiccups, like when she'd walked into my office and realized I was her new boss. In that room, she really gave it to me. When we got home, she chewed my ass out even harder.

I deserved it—every word, every accusation, she was dead-on.

But after I'd explained my reasoning again, she'd understood, the same way I had when I learned about her job.

Nothing was ever going to break us.

And even though she'd had concerns about living and working together, the combination hadn't been an issue. After six months at the hotel, she'd moved her things straight into my place. And because she was running her own show with a small team of employees beneath her, all I did was oversee the end results, giving her my okay to move forward with the strategies and cost-saving measures she wanted to implement.

Aside from that, Brooklyn was her own boss.

The balance was fucking perfect.

And she'd already saved Spade Hotels over four million, awarding herself a two-hundred-thousand-dollar bonus. There were even more bonuses on the way since her most recent proposal for our Manhattan hotel was about to save us another five million.

She finished her nigiri and set her chopsticks down, lifting her sake and holding it while she leaned back in her chair. "How exactly did I earn this trip?"

I could lick that expression off her face—it was so damn sexy.

Man, I was one lucky motherfucker.

"Two reasons." Still holding her face, I pulled my hand back and set my elbows on either side of my small plate. "Eight months into the job, and you're fucking killing it, Brooklyn. Walter has been blown the hell away since your first proposal, his reaction even greater for the second one you just presented."

"*Mmhmm.*" Her eyes told me she knew I was up to something.

"So, one, I wanted to bring you here to celebrate a job well done." I clinked my glass against hers.

"And two?" She took a sip.

I glanced out the window, placing my finger on the thick pane. "Do you see that building right there?" I watched her eyes follow to where I was pointing. "The one with the dark gray windows that's about forty stories high?"

"Yes."

"We're buying it."

She looked at me.

"It's the next Spade Hotel."

Her face filled with a smile. "Stop it. Are you serious?"

"And I'll be managing the conversion as we completely wipe out the hotel's current branding and decor, gut almost half the building, and replace it with Spade branding and high-end finishes. We're essentially transforming a three-star hotel into a five-star resort."

"Macon ..." Her voice was soft and endearing as she

reached across the table and put her hand on my arm. "I'm beyond excited for you."

"Except there's more."

Her neck jutted back as my words hit her. "More?"

I nodded. "We've decided that all new conversions need not only a project manager, like me, who focuses on construction and appeal, but also someone who can come in and develop the most effective processes and procedures for each department within the hotel."

Her jaw dropped.

"And Spade Hotels would like that person to be you, Brooklyn."

Her head shook in disbelief.

"The role is considered high-level management, so the salary is quite an extensive bump, and if you accept the job, we'll be moving to Japan in less than a month and staying until the build-out is finished."

"Are you kidding?" Her lips closed and then parted again. "Yes. Yes. And hell yes."

I laughed, placing my hand on hers. "I had a feeling you were going to say that." I rubbed my thumb across the back of her palm. "A promotion like this deserves a celebration."

"All we do is celebrate." She grinned.

"We're going to do a little more. In fact, I took the liberty of setting something up."

"What?" She waited for my response, and when I didn't give her one, she added, "Macon, Japan is more than enough. I don't need anything else. This is a celebration."

I leaned across the table, avoiding the plates, to whisper, "Brooklyn, I love you so much."

"I love you." Her eyes weren't filling with tears, but they beamed with emotion. "Endlessly."

"Baby, do me a favor ..."

"Of course. Whatever you need."

I held her face one last time and removed my hand. "Turn around."

I watched my statement hit her, and slowly, she looked over her shoulder. Her hand covered her mouth as she realized her parents, Clementine, and Jesse were sitting directly behind her.

"You did this," she said softly, her eyes returning to mine. "For me."

She made it easy to want to do things for her. To want to spend time with her. To want to be around her as much as possible.

To want to propose when the time was right.

That sweet, naughty woman wasn't going to be my girlfriend forever.

I had plans.

Of a ring, of a wedding.

Of little girls who inherited Mom's icy blue eyes and boys who inherited my green ones.

But for now, I was just going to drown her in love.

"Brooklyn," I said as I gazed into her stare, "there isn't anything I wouldn't do for you."

Check out the other books in the Spade Hotel Series
Cooper's book: The Rebel
Brady's book: The Sinner

Interested in reading the Dalton Family Series, best friends to the Spades?
Dominick's book: The Lawyer
Jo and Jenner's book: The Billionaire
Ford's book: The Single Dad
Declan Shaw's book: The Intern
Camden's book: The Bachelor

ACKNOWLEDGMENTS

Nina Grinstead, when I think back to *then* and I look around and actually process *now*, I can't believe it. Where we started, where we are, and where we're going. It hasn't just been a journey; it's been a lifetime worth of goals and dreams, and you've helped me achieve each one. I know this is just the beginning, and that makes me cry even harder. Love you so much. Team B forever.

Jovana Shirley, your acknowledgment is always the hardest to write because I never feel as though my words accurately describe my love and appreciation for you. The relationship between an author and her editor is a special one; like handing over your newborn to its first sitter, it comes with a level of trust that most people don't understand. The amount of trust I have in you is endless. Please be my word-sitter—ha-ha—for life. I can never do this without you. Love you so, so hard.

Ratula Roy, a million years later, and we're here. Partners. Walking hand in hand through this wild, turbulent ride. You get me in ways I never could have imagined. You're there day and night. You're never afraid to tell me the good, the bad, or the very ugly. Because you believe in me. Because you want this—for us. What you are to me and what I've found in you goes beyond words. I love you more than love—and I'll never stop saying that to you.

Hang Le, my unicorn, you are just incredible in every way.

Judy Zweifel, as always, thank you for being so wonderful to work with and for taking such good care of my words. <3

Karen Lawson, I'm so excited to have met you, to be working with you, and I hope this is the first of many projects together.

Vicki Valente, you jumped right in, and I appreciate that so much. Thank you for all your help.

Nikki Terrill, my soul sister. Every tear, vent, virtual hug, life chaos, workout—you've been there through it all. I could never do this without you, and I would never want to. Love you hard.

Pang and Jan, you both mean the absolute world to me, and I love you so much. Thank you for everything, always.

Sarah Symonds, we've been on this journey together for such a long time. You've witnessed every stage, and you've endlessly cheered me on. Having that, having you, having us—it's everything. LY.

Kimmi Street, my sister from another mister. Thank you from the bottom of my heart. You saved me. You inspired me. You kept me standing in so many different ways. I love you more than love.

Brittney Sahin, this book, just like the last one, wouldn't have happened if it wasn't for you. You have been there for me in ways I can't even describe—not just when it comes to writing, but all the life things too. Our chats, our texts, our visits—they mean everything to me. Love you, B.

Extra-special love goes to Valentine PR, my ARC team, my Bookstagram team, Rachel Baldwin, Valentine Grinstead, Kelley Beckham, Sarah Norris, Kim Cermak, and Christine Miller.

Mom and Dad, thanks for your unwavering belief in me and your constant encouragement. It means more than you'll ever know.

Brian, my words could never dent the love I feel for you. Trust me when I say, I love you more.

My Midnighters, you are such a supportive, loving, motivating group. Thanks for being such an inspiration, for holding my hand when I need it, and for always begging for more words. I love you all.

To all the influencers who read, review, share, post, TikTok —Thank you, thank you, thank you will never be enough. You do so much for our writing community, and we're so appreciative.

To my readers—I cherish each and every one of you. I'm so grateful for all the love you show my books, for taking the time to reach out to me, and for your passion and enthusiasm. I love, love, love you.

MARNI'S MIDNIGHTERS

Getting to know my readers is one of my favorite parts about being an author. In Marni's Midnighters, my private Facebook group, I post covers before they're revealed to the public and excerpts of the projects I'm currently working on, and team members qualify for exclusive giveaways.

To join Marni's Midnighters, click HERE.

ABOUT THE AUTHOR

USA Today best-selling author Marni Mann knew she was going to be a writer since middle school. While other girls her age were daydreaming about teenage pop stars, Marni was fantasizing about penning her first novel. She crafts unique stories that weave together her love of darkness, mystery, passion, and human emotions. A New Englander at heart, she now lives with her husband in Sarasota, Florida. When she's not nose deep in her laptop, she's scouring for chocolate, sipping wine, traveling, boating, or devouring fabulous books.

Want to get in touch? Visit Marni at ...
www.marnismann.com
MarniMannBooks@gmail.com

ALSO BY MARNI MANN

SPADE HOTEL SERIES—EROTIC ROMANCE

The Playboy

The Rebel

The Sinner

HOOKED SERIES—CONTEMPORARY ROMANCE

Mr. Hook-up

Mr. Wicked

THE DALTON FAMILY SERIES—EROTIC ROMANCE

The Lawyer

The Billionaire

The Single Dad

The Intern

The Bachelor

THE AGENCY SERIES—EROTIC ROMANCE

Signed

Endorsed

Contracted

Negotiated

Dominated

STAND-ALONE NOVELS

Even If It Hurts (Contemporary Romance)

Before You (Contemporary Romance)

The Better Version of Me (Psychological Thriller)

Lover (Erotic Romance)

THE BEARDED SAVAGES SERIES—EROTIC ROMANCE

The Unblocked Collection

Wild Aces

MOMENTS IN BOSTON SERIES—CONTEMPORARY ROMANCE

When Ashes Fall

When We Met

When Darkness Ends

THE PRISONED SERIES—DARK EROTIC THRILLER

Prisoned

Animal

Monster

THE SHADOWS DUET—EROTIC ROMANCE

Seductive Shadows

Seductive Secrecy

THE BAR HARBOR DUET—NEW ADULT

Pulled Beneath

Pulled Within

THE MEMOIR SERIES—DARK MAINSTREAM FICTION

SNEAK PEEK OF THE REBEL

The Rebel, book two in the Spade Hotel Series, features Cooper Spade and it's a scorching hot, billionaire, alpha romance that's releasing February 29, 2024.
Here's a sneak peek ...

"Don't fuck this up," my uncle, Walter Spade, roared from the head of the conference room table, his salt-and-pepper hair glistening from the fluorescent lights above.

As he looked at me, squinting, the lines around his eyes deepened. His hands gripped the back of his chair as he stood behind it, refusing to sit.

When Walter was disconnected from work, he was the nicest guy in the world.

When it came to anything related to Spade Hotels, the company he had founded and my brothers and I worked for, he was one nasty motherfucker.

Today was certainly no exception.

"You have nothing to worry about," I replied. "The land

will be ours as soon as I see it, assuming I deem it worthy enough to add to our collection."

"You'd better act fast," Macon, my youngest brother, said from the seat next to mine. His dark brown beard was coming in thick, longer than I'd ever seen him grow it. Since spending all those months in Hawaii to build one of our latest properties, he'd developed a more relaxed, surfer-like appearance. "You know we're not the only ones looking at it, right?"

The land he was referring to was supposedly a slice of paradise along the shoreline of Lake Louise—a lake within Banff National Park, nestled in the Canadian Rockies.

Until I saw it in person, I wouldn't be able to confirm just how perfect it was.

"I bet all the big names are eyeing it," Brady, my oldest brother, said from the other side of me. His hair was freshly spiked, like he'd just stepped out of the shower. If I had to guess, while his driver had brought him to work this morning, he'd probably fucked a woman in the backseat and showered in his en suite once he arrived in his office. That man wasn't just a player. When it came to women, he was a goddamn sinner. "If the realtor reached out to us, then she reached out to everyone. That means all our competitors will be viewing that property tomorrow."

"I fully expect a bidding war," Jo, my cousin, said with a smile, clasping her hands and aligning each finger before she tapped them together. Her white nail polish caught the light above, reflecting the illumination and shining like a mirror. "This is going to be fun."

Walter's daughter thrived on the anticipation of the fight and the win.

Even though she was a Dalton now—married to Jenner, my best friend, who happened to be sitting beside her—she was full of Spade blood.

And the Spades always won.

"Let's not get ahead of ourselves, honey," Walter said to Jo. "Cooper will arrive before any of the others, and the offer that Jenner's going to submit will be more than fair."

"And contingent on an immediate decision," Jenner added, completely relaxed in his seat, unfazed by Walter's orders. "We're not giving the others time to counter."

Jenner's family owned one of the largest, most successful law firms in the country. The Daltons—Jenner and his two brothers, Dominick and Ford, along with their twin cousins, Hannah and Camden—represented all different fields of law.

Jenner had been working with the Spades long before he became part of our family and was a wild bachelor prior to him settling down with my cousin.

Confident. Cocky. And a hell of a good time.

That was Jenner Dalton.

He also happened to be one of the richest, most successful people I knew.

"Which means, again, Cooper, you can't fuck this up." Walter wiped his mouth, like he'd just spit. "Timing is the only thing we have on our side."

I'd been working for my uncle since I'd graduated from the University of Southern California, following in my father's footsteps. He was Walter's business partner before retiring about ten years ago, preferring a life on the beach with my mom rather than reporting to his office every day. Walter had bought him out, and part of the deal was that when the three of us had enough years under our belt and put in our time, we would be equal owners, along with our cousin, Jo. The transition hadn't happened yet. Walter wasn't ready to retire. But in the seven years I'd been employed with Spade Hotels, I'd done some remarkable things for his brand. I'd established levels of luxury that our competitors hadn't even thought of launching.

I'd hired some of the most competent, efficient general managers.

But this—this property, this acquisition, if it went through the way I hoped it would—would be my biggest accomplishment to date.

"Don't stress. I've got this," I said to Walter. "I fly out in the morning. Since the following day is Christmas Eve, I'm not staying the night. I'll call Jenner from the property and have him process the offer so it hits right before the holiday. We'll have things signed and sealed before the new year."

Walter's knuckles turned white before he released the chair and crossed his arms over his chest.

I knew the gesture well.

We were about to get another earful.

"One day, I'll hand over the reins to the four of you—Jenner, I'm not leaving you out. I just know I'll never be able to drag you over to our side." Walter offered a rare smile. "And when you all run this business, you'll know exactly the kind of pressure that's involved on a daily basis. Don't tell me not to stress—stressing is my fucking job." He cleared his throat, not out of nervousness, but out of necessity. "If I want the company to stay on top, I have to continue growing it, but it has to be the right kind of advancement, for the right dollar amount, and I need the right people running the operation." He nodded toward the monitor in the back of the room, which showed aerial footage of the land in Alberta. "You all know Canada has been on my radar for a long time, but the land and price were never right."

His stare returned to me. "I'm counting on you, Cooper. Don't fucking let me down."

I nodded.

Walter then glanced around the room. "Anyone else have anything to contribute?"

There was silence.

Until Jo said, "There's something I need to discuss with you. I'll walk you to your office." As she got up from her chair, she clasped Jenner's shoulder, waving at me and my brothers before she followed her father out of the room.

The moment the door shut, Jenner said, "Don't fuck this up," in a voice that was meant to sound like Walter's. He placed his hands behind his head, his elbows bent, leaning back in his chair like he was in a goddamn recliner.

"Come on, my man. Everyone in this room knows I've got this. This is what I'm good at." I circled the air, pointing at my brothers. "What we're all good at."

Macon had done the same thing in Hawaii, and Brady, in Florida.

My brothers and I weren't meant to sit behind a desk and push paperwork. The three of us needed to be out in the field, overseeing the design, build, and changeover of our properties, making sure things ran according to our standards.

The Spade standards.

We didn't do it for higher titles—we were already part of the executive team. We did it because we loved it, because this was what we had been born to do.

And when situations like this occurred, it came with a rush.

A surge of adrenaline.

A level of control that we all strived for.

Like laying a woman on her back and thrusting into her cunt.

Fuck, there was nothing better.

"You know I'm just giving you shit," Jenner said. "You're going to crush this, and then I'll take care of things on my end."

"And then we're all going to celebrate on Christmas," Brady said.

Jenner chuckled. "Another Dalton and Spade celebration."

His arms dropped, and he shook his head. "You should see the amount of wine and booze Jo had delivered to the house last night in preparation for the party. Do you know the mayhem that's about to ensue?"

Since our families had melded, the Spades now spent the holidays with the Daltons. Birthdays were celebrated together. This year, the newlyweds had requested to host Christmas, and no one had put up a fight.

"All I know is that I won't be the first one to pass out," Macon said.

We all laughed.

Macon had fallen asleep at the last get-together after drinking way too much, and Ford's daughter, Everly, had drawn all over his face with a marker.

Of course, she hadn't come up with the idea on her own. Camden and I'd had a little something to do with it.

Still, he'd never live it down.

"I ordered three bottles of tequila just for you, brother," Jenner joked.

"Tequila and I broke up after that night." Macon shoved his hands through the sides of his hair. "Never again, do you hear me?"

"No one told you to have that many shots on an empty stomach, asshole," Brady said.

"Listen, I was dealing with some shit, all right?" He paused while we all remembered the ordeal. "Besides, I can hold my liquor, and I guarantee I can outdrink all you fools."

Jenner smiled at him. "I don't know about that, but what you *can* guarantee is that you are an expert at getting Sharpie off your skin."

Macon flipped him off. "Fucker."

Jenner chuckled as he stood. "I need to get back to the

office." He looked at me. "Have a safe trip to Canada tomorrow. Call me the second you're ready to submit that offer."

"I will," I replied.

Click HERE to purchase The Rebel.